MURDERS AT THE ROOKERY GRANGE RETREAT

A PRUNELLA PEARCE MYSTERY

BOOK THREE

GINA KIRKHAM

For Drew
Grief is just love with nowhere to go...

Drew Peter George Cockton
1986-2022

OWEN DREW
England

'The weather outside is frightful,
But revenge is so delightful...'

PROLOGUE

CHRISTMAS EVE 1989

*V*iolet melodically hummed to herself as she propped Tattlington Ted up on the small nursery chair. He instantly disobeyed her by tilting to one side, then teetered momentarily before falling to the floor with a gentle thud, his one good eye glaring at her, glassy and accusing.

'You're very, very naughty...' Violet spat in exasperation. She picked him up and roughly pushed him back down onto the pink chair that had seen better days, not dissimilar to the rest of Rookery Grange which was clinging on to life with ravaged shingles, woodworm-infested beams and fractured windows. She rearranged the little ceramic cup and saucer in front of him and waited. 'You're supposed to drink it up – ALL of it, or they will be very, very cross!'

Tattlington Ted didn't move. He didn't touch the cup and he most certainly didn't drink it up. If teddy bears, particularly ones as old as he was, could have been capable of independent thought, he would have rightly trusted his instincts. His bad eye, dangling by a single frayed thread, saw only beneath him. Its sightline rolled across the battered green box of Eureka Weed Killer where the contents had been scattered over the small round table. The white powder resembled a flurry of snow, stark against the deep blue painted surface.

'Drink it up – NOW!' Violet set her lips into a thin line and clenched her teeth. Tattlington Ted continued to blatantly disobey her. Feeling the fury rise, she yanked him up from his safe sanctuary and held him aloft in front of her. 'You know what happens to naughty boys, don't you, Ted?' Her fingers plucked at the good eye. She hooked her nails under the amber glass and pulled, the skin on her fingertips burning with the effort. Feeling more resistance than she had expected, she changed tack. Taking the eye between her teeth, she bit down and drew the bear away from her. The eye relinquished its grip on the soft fabric as it tore from its moorings of brown cotton.

Violet's satisfaction was short lived. She spat the glass eye onto the wooden floorboards. It skittered across the room, rolling several times before it came to a halt by the skirting board. Within seconds the poor bear followed, hurtling across the room.

Tattlington Ted landed awkwardly, his head bent at an unnatural angle against the nursery wall that was papered with pink rosebuds, his little mouth still open in a surprised 'O' as the voice box inside him expelled his last breath.

'Grrr...'

Violet turned her attention to the rest of her toys that sat regimented in the remaining chairs. Poppy ragdoll, her wide eyes topped with deft strokes of black for eyelashes, Rumminy Rabbit, with one ear up and one ear down, and Molly Jane, Violet's inherited Bisque doll – all exhibited an air of fear which served to strengthen Violet's need to obey the instructions that had been given to her. She cocked her head and listened intently.

'Inky, pinky, ponky...' She touched the head of each toy, tormenting them. '...daddy bought a donkey...'

The door to the nursery suddenly burst open, throwing her obnoxious brother Vincent through its threshold. He stopped in his tracks, taking in the scene before him: the upturned box of weed killer, the sightless Tattlington Ted and the potential victims next on the list of his younger sister's pique.

'Nanny! Nanny, quick... Come and see what Vile Violet's done...' he *gloated loudly, relishing the look of terror on Violet's face as she tripped and fell over a discarded toy, whilst begging him not to tell on her. He shook his head. 'Naughty girls need to be punished, and you're a very naughty girl, aren't you, Violet?'*

'I'll say you told me to...' she whimpered, before drawing into herself, into her auditorium of make believe. She picked along the rows in her mind, finding the best seat.

The show was about to begin...

Rookery Grange groaned as a sudden gust of wind hit the gables, sending a flurry of leaves swirling into a maelstrom outside the nursery window, drowning out Vincent's sly taunts to his sister. If truth be known, even if there had been calm weather and peace at Rookery Grange, it would not have helped Vincent's voice to flow along the corridors and stairs to be heard by anyone, least of all the family nanny. She lay in a deep slumber in her quarters, one that had been facilitated by too many sweet sherries at supper, content that the parents of the terrible twosome would, for once, take charge of their offspring.

She could not have been more wrong.

If anyone on that fateful night had cared to peek through the leaded glass of the mullioned bay window into the drawing room of Rookery Grange, their eyes would have fallen upon a festive scene. One that was gently lit by the twinkling lights of the Christmas tree, a tableau paused and silent, as though time had ceased to be. An orange glow from the dying embers of the log fire had produced a warm, if slightly eerie, shadow to the waxen features of Violet and Vincent's parents, each slumped in their respective high-backed leather chesterfield chairs. Penelope Carnell, her pale hand draped over her stilled chest, reverently held a sprig of holly. Opposite, her husband Raif, who for once was lost for words, had curled the immaculately manicured fingers of his left hand into a claw to vainly pluck at his throat, his features manifesting an unbearable agony. The other hand posed a rigid finger pointing to two champagne goblets sitting elegantly upon the table between them, their contents drained...

Just as their lives had been.

THE WEDDING PLANNER

PRESENT DAY

*P*runella Pearce cupped her chin in her hand, carefully resting her elbow on the table. A marmalade-covered knife teetered on the edge of a plate which held what could only be described as an incinerated piece of wholemeal loaf. It sat side by side with a tepid mug of Yorkshire Tea. Binks, her black-as-midnight cat, took the opportunity to gracefully slink over the open pages of the local *Winterbottom News* and quickly poke his nose into the sticky substance. He recoiled, sneezed and shook his head.

'Disgusting, isn't it, Binks!' She gave his head a rub and ushered him down from the table. 'But not 'arf as disgusting as the bloody bird seed in *that!*' She prodded the piece of toast as an indicator and then jiggled the nail of her little finger between her teeth to prove her distaste of the allegedly healthy multigrain bread. 'Just look at this…' She jabbed a clean finger at the glossy magazine next to her.

Her intense green eyes scanned the double-page photoshoot that spread from corner to corner of *Chapperton Bliss Brides*. The model couldn't have been more perfect. Size 6, chestnut locks tumbling down her back with little diamantés peppered through her curls that sparkled in the studio lighting, and with a big dollop of youth on her side. 'Jeez, she hasn't even been around long enough to cultivate even one solitary wrinkle or a festering under eye bag.' Pru sighed loudly as she subconsciously rubbed under her own eyes, ignorant of the fact that Binks had sloped off to watch birds through the glass of the French doors, so she was now talking to herself. 'I can't even be bitchy about the rest of her either; she's gorgeous!' Taking in the vast expanse of white tulle and satin that cascaded around the model, Pru could only guess that she probably had slender, shapely legs that went on for ever. She tipped her head, held out her left hand and admired, probably for the umpteenth time that day, Andy's gift that now adorned her third finger. A stunning solitaire on a white gold band caught the light and sparkled back at her. It was a beautiful and very worthy replacement for the lime green and strawberry Haribo jelly ring with which he'd hastily proposed to her at the Montgomery Hall Hotel.

Her attention was drawn back to *Penelope Perfect* on the double-page spread. As a saving grace for her low mood, Pru was delighted to see that a couple of staples punched into the magazine had pierced the model's ravishing beauty right smack bang in the middle of her nose, stabbed her pert boobs on the second rigid sliver of metal and, with a bit of luck, judging by where the third staple had hit on the page, it had hopefully ravaged her other matrimonial bits as a bonus.

'How on earth can I compete with *that* on our wedding day?' she sighed.

'Compete with what?'

Pru startled, and quickly pushed the magazine underneath the pages of the *Winterbottom News*. 'Blimey, have you got a secret insurance policy out on me, Andy Barnes?' She patted her chest in order to quell the sudden pounding of her heart.

Andy, her Delectable Detective fiancé, kissed her tenderly on the nose whilst his hand sneaked around her and simultaneously pinched the half-eaten piece of toast from her plate. He bit into it and grimaced. 'Bird seed?' He made a show of wiping his mouth with the back of his hand. 'Go on, then. Compete with what?'

She proffered him a cheeky grin, grateful that her healthy option toast had been a temporary distraction, allowing her time to think. 'Oh nothing, just musing over the WI's cake competition for our next meeting. I don't think any of my offerings will raise a first, second or third!'

Prunella, better known to her friends as Pru, was the current president of the Winterbottom Women's Institute and part-time caretaker of the village library that was housed in a nice cosy shop, rather than a large, unwelcoming building like the one in the nearest city. She was also one half of *The Curious Curator & Co* Detective Agency. She was tickling the early years of her forties and should be planning her dream wedding – that's if she could stop getting distracted by an unusual and very unwelcome bout of self-loathing.

'Mmm, you'll always be a "first" to me...' Andy attempted to kiss her, but only succeeded in transferring a smattering of half-chewed pumpkin seeds onto her chin.

'Just as well, really, considering you two love birds are going to be married soon...' Bree Richards, Pru's right-hand mischief-maker, co-detective and best friend, with the added benefit of being a great gin-drinking buddy, flopped down on the chair next to Pru. She pressed her fingers against the pink spotty teapot. 'It's cold; why don't you brew a fresh one?' She tilted her head in expectation.

Pru playfully cuffed her across the head with a tea towel. 'And why don't you knock or ring the doorbell before you come sneaking in here, hey?'

'Because if you two know I'm here you'll start behaving yourselves, and then I might miss something worth gossiping about at the Twisted Currant Café on our Wednesday mornings with Ethel and Clarissa over a bath bun!' Bree's retort was followed up with a saucy wink at Andy.

Andy quickly took that opportunity to make his excuses. 'Right, girls; I'm off to work, we've got a shedload of follow ups to do on the recent spate of burglaries. I'd like to say I'll be home on time, but, well, you know…'

Pru did know. She had been with him long enough to realise that Andy being a police officer meant she frequently spent evenings alone, had dinner dates cancelled last minute, and that she had a duty to leave their bed warm in the morning for when he crawled into it after a night shift.

Bree grinned. 'That settles it then, girlfriend. We need to talk weddings whilst the man is out hunter-gathering.' She poured milk into her mug. 'So, wedding planner?'

It was now Pru's turn to tilt her head. 'Wedding planner?'

'Yep, you definitely need one, and I know just the person.'

Pru set her lips into a wry smile. 'And I know that that idea coming from you fills me with a feeling of complete and utter dread, Bryony Jayne Richards. It's a bit late now to get one; it's almost the big day – and I'm afraid it would be over my dead body.'

'Well, judging by Winterbottom's track record in that department with serial killers galore…' Bree took a slurp of her tea and gave her friend a knowing look. '…I'd be very careful what you wish for!'

THE CHRISTMAS MEETING

*L*adies, ladies, please take your seats as quickly as you can.' Kitty Hardcastle pitched her voice to just the right level. She smiled, watching the assembled ladies hunch their shoulders to their ears and scrunch their pink lips to their noses at the sound of her dulcet tones. Happy that her shrill command had produced the desired effect, she continued. 'In the absence of our president, Prunella, who is currently enjoying a wedding breakfast tasting session at Thornbury Manor, I have been asked to take this evening's meeting.'

A low murmur ran along each row of the pink velour chairs of Winterbottom parish hall that was currently hosting an eclectic mix of well-padded and slender bottoms belonging to the cheerful members of the Winterbottom Women's Institute. Kitty had been the previous president of their group and still took great satisfaction in being asked to take up the treasured mantle, ring the bell, and start the first line of 'Jerusalem' on occasions. She gave great gusto to the song, whilst simultaneously counting the heads of her ladies, and was pleased to see several new members and even more delighted to see they were, in the main, in a younger age group. Their WI relied heavily on stalwart members, but a little bit of advertising in the window of Betty's Village Store by way of a Post-it note seeking new blood, had clearly been successful. She had to hand it to Prunella Pearce that as much as she didn't hold with some of her slapdash approaches to WI business, attracting new members had been one of her better ideas.

'Right, ladies, first on the agenda. As you know our lovely Winnie is recovering well after her little fall outside The Dog & Gun...' Kitty paused to allow the muffled laughter to abate. '... No, no – she has assured me it had absolutely nothing to do with her love of a nice schooner of sherry!'

'Aye, but more to do with her greater love of a gin or two as a chaser, methinks.' Ethel Tytherington, her tongue and wit as sharp as ever, cheekily observed. She accompanied her aside with a jovial dig in the ribs of her friend Clarissa Montgomery who was sitting next to her. This led to more laughter from the gathered ladies, a spark of joviality that Ethel was more than confident Winnie would have approved of if she had been present.

Unperturbed, Kitty continued. 'Winnie has asked me to pass on her thanks for the lovely cards and flowers. She is now out of hospital and her hip is on the mend, but she has decided to take a room at the Rookery Grange Retreat in Chapperton Bliss for a few weeks to aid her recovery. She would be very amenable to see anyone who would wish to visit her.'

The ladies nodded their approval. Rookery Grange was well known to most, if not all, and had an excellent reputation for residential care. Some residents were permanent; others, like Winnie, would stay until they were capable and competent to return to independent living.

'I wouldn't stay in that place if you were to pay me a million pounds...' Brenda Mortinsen chuntered. She wrung her hands together, her plump fingers playing a dance across each other. 'It's haunted, you know, after that terrible murder. There's plenty of things that go bump in the night there – and it's not one of the residents falling out of bed, I can tell you! I heard all about it from Florrie Patterson at the Twisted Currant Café; her mum went there before the inevitable.' She puckered her lips and used her forearms to hoist her ample bosom upwards, delighted that she now had the rapt attention of the room.

Clarissa bristled. 'Oh please, give it a rest, Brenda. It's not bloody haunted. It had a tragedy years ago, was empty for God knows how long, and now it's a residential home. It's bricks and mortar, nothing more than that.'

It was now Brenda's turn to bristle. 'It *is* haunted! You're just too scared to admit it...'

Vera Williams, the new owner of Betty's Village Stores and the most recent member of the Winterbottom WI, took the opportunity to interrupt. 'Our Jack's mum is a resident there, and the only spirit that's taken residence in that place is the bottle of vodka I have to sneak in for the vindictive old bat every Wednesday!'

A ripple of laughter filled the parish hall.

'Ladies, ladies, please!' Kitty shouted as she banged order on the presidential table. Several ladies on the front row rolled their eyes and puckered their lips at Kitty's trademark statement, one that she often used to bring the ladies to order when they were engaged in anything she disapproved of. This action caused Brenda to turn heel and scurry off to the kitchen.

'Let's bring ourselves back to business: the only thing that's haunting anywhere is *this*...' Kitty held aloft a tapestry bag with a plethora of colours. The vivid orange and fluorescent green swirls accompanied by purple stars of the fabric glared back at the assembled women.

Ethel shielded her eyes and played to her assembled audience. 'Bloody hell, where's me sunglasses?'

'*This*...' Kitty sighed in barely suppressed disdain, '...was left in the hall around the time of our last meeting.' She held the offending bag, pinched between finger and thumb, at arm's length, and waved it in the air. 'Now I think I can safely say that this monstrosity would not belong to any of our WI members, regardless of what the caretaker might think.' She smirked, waiting for their agreement. 'It's pretty hideous, and one I certainly wouldn't entertain in my wardrobe, but I have to ask before returning it to him.'

Chelsea Blandish, all blonde hair, Lycra and leopard print, was the first to throw up her hand.

'Ah, Chelsea, I take it this is yours?' Kitty made a show of peering over her glasses at the younger and notoriously flighty member of the WI who was waving wildly at her.

Chelsea riled. 'Nah, it's yours, actually. I bought it for you in the Secret Santa last Christmas, you ungrateful old bat!'

Ethel smirked, licked her index finger and chalked an invisible '1' in the air as Kitty's eyes widened and her lips set in a Passionate Pink framed 'O'.

'I... I... oh dear, I...' Kitty stammered.

Relief washed over her as the barn door to the kitchen squealed open and banged against the wall, interrupting her uncomfortable moment. Brenda, having recovered from Clarissa's chastisement, bounced across the hall, a cake stand held aloft.

'Lemon drizzle, anyone?'

A collective groan rattled around the hall, one that was loud enough to notify Brenda that her tasty bake would once again go uneaten.

THE LETTER

...Taking into account how much of an asset this missive could be to you once in your possession, I think the sum of £10,000.00 is a fair price to pay. It would also buy my silence on another matter that could seriously damage your future.

I will be most heartened to hear of your positive response, upon which I will provide you with the bank details you will require to make the deposit. You have my honourable word that once payment has been made, you will never hear from me again.

Yours as always, my dark little angel,
Ouma

S he sat rigid, her breath stilled; the ability to move instantly torn away from her. Her heart, the only part of her that showed she was still alive, pounded painfully in her chest. The seconds passed slowly.

Tick tock...

Tick tock...

The ancient grandfather clock in the corner loudly marked the countdown as her life flashed before her, to seemingly spiral out of control. Every misdeed, every sin, every moment of cruelty, every single death – natural or otherwise – suddenly came back to haunt her, courtesy of the letter before her.

Her hand began to shake, the spell broken.

'A fair price!' she raged to the empty room. Her legs, finding the momentum she needed to stand up, propelled her from the armchair. She viciously kicked at the brass captain's floor lamp, sending it toppling over. It landed with a crash against the sideboard, scattering paperwork into the air. She watched the sheets of A4 undulate gently from side to side like a feather, before coming to rest on the blue-gold Isfahan rug.

'"Honourable word!" Pah, that woman wouldn't know an honourable bloody word if it jumped up and bit her on her bony ass...' She poured herself a large Scotch and stood in front of the log fire, nursing the glass close to her chest, willing her heart to slow down, to give her poor ribs a bit of relief. The glowing embers of the logs warmed the sudden chill that had enveloped her sitting room. She had always known the evidence she needed to prove her heritage was out there somewhere, but she had clearly been a fool to think the outcome would have been anything different than what she now held in her hand; a letter of extortion and blackmail from a woman she had thought long dead. She glanced at the screen of her laptop, the flashing 'jobs' alert pulsating in time with her heartbeat. In that split instant, her hand had been forced.

The plans she had tentatively made would now have to be more fluid, a bit like the amber liquid in her glass. She almost threw the last mouthful down her throat in haste, it burned beautifully and gave way to a cynical cackle.

'"Dark little angel". How woefully typical of her, always trying to balance evil with good...' She slammed the glass down and grabbed her jacket.

Actually, now she had said it out loud, she suddenly felt quite an affection for the moniker. Her fingers tightly gripped the vial in her pocket, its purpose now clear...

... and just like that, the Dark Angel was born.

THE REVEAL

'Keep your hands over your eyes, and don't look until I tell you to...' Pru's face appeared between the curtains in Without A Hitch Bridal Boutique. She pinched the two sides of the slubbed indigo curtain fabric together under her chin so Bree would not receive an accidental glimpse of her wedding dress until the time was right.

Bree happily obliged, although she felt like one of the three monkeys, perched on a purple velour pouffe with her hands obliterating the top half of her face. 'Aw, come on, hurry up! The excitement is killing me!'

Pru, as elegantly as she could amid the swathes of satin and tulle of the Justin Alexander gown, made her way into the centre of the room and stood on the small dais. 'Ta-da!' She held her breath in anticipation. Bree's opinion meant the world to her. 'You can uncover your eyes now, you dork,' she gently chided as the seconds ticked by and her friend had made no move to acknowledge her appearance.

It was now Bree's turn to hold her breath, hesitating before she removed her hands. *What if it looked awful, or it didn't suit her?*

Oh my God, or even worse! What if it made her best friend in the whole world look like an elaborately swirled meringue?

She'd sworn to be honest and tell the truth, never thinking the truth might not be what Pru wanted to hear. She opened one eye first and squinted before letting out a little gasp. She could feel the biggest lump imaginable beginning to form in her throat, whilst her eyes began to simultaneously prick with happy tears. 'Oh Pru...' She wiped the back of her hand across her cheek, pushing the unexpected trickle away. 'I'm lost for words!'

And she truly was. Pru was a vision of elegance and grace. The ivory chapel train fanned out around her, the little cap sleeves of the delicate lace and bead bodice sat perfectly on her shoulders. Lots of little satin-wrapped buttons worked their way from the nape of her neck to the waist, where they joined the smooth satin folds of the full skirt. Bree watched the seamstress busy herself around Pru, lifting the skirt high at the back, and just as quickly dropping it to allow it to billow out and find its own natural resting place.

'Do you like it?' Pru excitedly waited for a response.

'Like it? Like it? I bloody *love* it! It's perfect, it's so you. It will look amazing with the setting at Thornbury Manor; their decorations at Christmas are to die for. It will suit your theme beautifully.' Bree had been a little unsure of Andy and Pru's decision to hold a pre-Christmas wedding. She was very much a sun lover and had visions of a balmy summer's day wedding, clinking glasses on a perfectly tended lawn with bunting and marquees, but this was their special moment, and the more she shared Pru's vision of the perfect day, the more she fell in love with it.

Pru blew her fringe upwards in a show of relief. 'Thank goodness for that! I would have been mortified if you'd hated it. Look at this, too, talk about a bonus!' She twirled around, making a great show of the fact her hands had disappeared. 'It's got pockets – how cool is that?'

Bree couldn't help but laugh at her funny, quirky friend. 'Pockets! Please don't tell me that they were the selling point for you. What are you thinking of putting in them? Twenty quid for the taxi if you change your mind before you say, "I do", and a couple of sausage rolls swiped from the buffet on the way out?'

Pru's top lip curled up, Elvis style. 'Well, if I grab the sausage rolls, you can grab the egg 'n cress butties – I've got them to put pockets in your maid of honour's dress, too. I thought you'd like them so you'd have somewhere to put your lippy.'

Being typically Bree, her friend quickly voiced her own opinion of what her pockets would hold on the big day. 'Erm... don't think so. Mine will be rammed with as many little bottles of gin and vodka that I can snaffle out of the minibar in my room...'

'Ah, ladies, *there* you are!' A tall, spindly man gaily swept into the room, his gleaming white Turkey teeth lighting the way ahead of him, a beacon in the mood lighting of the boutique. 'Prunella, delighted to meet you at last. Fergus O'Brien at your service.' He fluttered his hand to his chest. 'A Christmas wedding at the one and only Thornbury Manor; this is all too much, I'm so honoured!' He held out a perfectly manicured hand.

Taken by surprise, Pru wondered if she was supposed to kiss or shake it. 'Oh... erm... What?' She quizzically looked at Bree for a clue before catching herself and quickly followed up with a greeting of her own so as not to appear rude. 'Erm... hello, nice to meet you too.' She thought she was probably expected to believe it actually *was* nice to meet this flamboyant looking man who closely resembled the guy with the double-barrelled surname from television – *Llewelyn-Botox* something or other – but not knowing who he was or why he should be at her dress fitting, made her hesitate. She side-eyed Bree, who to her surprise seemed completely at ease with his sudden appearance.

'Fergus, so glad you could make it. I thought here would be the best place to meet the blushing bride-to-be.' Bree gave Fergus a friendly hug, and as they parted they executed a double-air kiss, one on each cheek.

'Am I missing something here?' Pru was slightly irked by Bree's sudden indifference to her presence and the task at hand. 'Excuse me for interrupting, but we're supposed to be trying our dresses on together, and for you to see mine for the first time.'

'Darling, calm down...' Fergus delved into the designer satchel he was carrying and whipped out an iPad.

'Oh for goodness' sake – a manbag too!' Pru couldn't contain herself. 'Please don't tell me that you've gone ahead and employed a wedding planner after all we discussed?' She looked beseechingly at Bree, who didn't even have the decency to look embarrassed.

Fergus was not to be deterred by any little fallout between friends. He sat himself down, opened his iPad and began to elegantly scroll the screen upwards, ensuring his little finger remained skyward and prominent with every flick. 'Right, ladies, let's get down to business: ice sculptures at the reception? Are we having a *yay* or a *nay* for that one?'

Pru bounced down onto the chaise longue, an explosion of tulle and satin ballooned around her. 'Fergus, I need you to listen to me as I'll only say this once...' Her ladylike demeanour had now fully deserted her as her bride-to-be nerves clawed at her stomach. '...why don't you just fu–'

'Pru!' Bree was mortified.

'What? I was only going to say, *Why don't you just funnel your energy somewhere where it's needed...* Why? What did you think I was going to say?' Pru grinned mischievously. She threw her head back and inhaled deeply, trying to bring about a little calm. She couldn't believe that she'd almost uttered a Foxtrot Oscar at poor old Fergus.

Suddenly Andy's original suggestion of running away to Gretna Green to tie the knot was becoming quite an attractive proposition.

A MELANCHOLY MURDER

'*O*h, there you are!' Eleanor Parsons, manager of the Rookery Grange Retreat residential home for genteel ladies and gentlemanly gentlemen, elegantly swept across the black and white chequered entrance hall. The tailored grey jacket and skirt she was wearing complimented the cream chiffon blouse, providing her with an air of authority. She stopped midway on her travels to plump up a feather-filled cushion that had been left slightly squashed by the last well-rounded posterior to have graced the high-backed leather armchair. This action left her newly employed nurse to utilise the ticking seconds by counting the intricate folds of the curtain pelmet that draped the floor-to-ceiling window, waiting for Eleanor's next command.

Remembering she had a task to delegate; Eleanor finished her obsessive plumping. 'I need you to see to Mrs Clegg in Room 6, please.' She handed her employee a clipboard. 'It's all on there; don't forget to sign off on the medication column. It's just pain management after hip surgery.'

'Of course, Miss Parsons.' Nurse Alex Archer gave a willing smile before taking the stairs two steps at a time. '*Of course, Miss Parsons, anything you say, Miss Parsons, your wish is my command,*

Miss Parsons...' Alex whispered in a sarcastic whiny voice whilst taking care to ensure it didn't reach the ears of the said Miss Parsons. To be dismissed for insubordination before the first week was out would be a total disaster.

Eleanor watched Alex disappear up the next flight of steps to the east wing. 'Oh for goodness' sake, she's in the *west* wing...' she hollered up the staircase. She was in no doubt that her rebuke had fallen on deaf ears as Alex was nowhere to be seen. Tutting to herself, she made her way back to her office. A mountain of Care Quality Commission forms and paperwork was threatening to engulf her inlaid mahogany desk, and the last thing she needed was a CQC spot check visit and her files not to be up to date.

The soft click of the door behind her announced her safe space. Digging her hand into the cavernous colourful plant pot that held the lush areca palm she had lovingly nurtured over her many years at Rookery Grange, she pulled out a half-drunk bottle of Gordon's gin and a can of tonic water. She turned up her nose at the small can. Whoever had thought of putting decent tonic in a tin was a bloody heathen in her opinion, but needs must in desperate situations, and the lack of bottled tonic at the local late night store had definitely been a desperate situation. She eased herself into the green leather captain's chair and pulled open the bottom drawer of her desk.

The ensuing clink of crystal glass against the bottle meant her presence would not be gracing her staff for the rest of the day.

'Come on now, Miss Burnside, drink it up, all of it...'

Dorothy Burnside tried to turn her head away from the offending mixture. She pressed her cheek into her pillow and pinched her lips tightly together. Her aged eyes watched the dismal clouds scuttering past her bedroom window as she fought the urge to scream. She knew exactly what was about to happen to her; she had known since the very first day she had set eyes on her nemesis, but if she opened her mouth to scream, it would also open it for the method of what she believed would be her demise. The liquid failed to penetrate her lips and dripped along her cheek, pooling behind her neck before being absorbed into the pillow.

'Now don't misbehave, or I'll just have to break tradition and go with another method. We can't have you telling tales, can we?' Dorothy's tormentor worked effortlessly around Room 8 at Rookery Grange, opening and closing drawers, cupboards and, as a final act of control, Dorothy's handbag, throwing the contents on to the bed beside her. 'Where is it, Dorothy? It's got to be here somewhere.'

Dorothy shook her head; she could barely offer up a whimper, let alone a word.

'You've got less than a minute by my calculations. Do you really want to die and take that knowledge to your grave?'

Dorothy formed a steely defiant stare upon her face, the threat finally unlocking her ability to speak. 'No, no, never. I'll never give... you... anything...' she rasped.

'So be it, I'll just have to work that little bit harder myself then, won't I?'

The gloating face that loomed so close to her own held so much hatred, so much violence. Dorothy could barely catch the breath she needed to survive. 'Please don't...'

She could do no more than watch as her spare pillow, covered in a particularly nice brushed cotton case with pink roses and swirls, was pressed down hard upon her face, giving rise to a flurry of memories and hopes. She had been the mortar to the bricks of Rookery Grange for longer than she cared to remember, choosing to pass her waning years in the place she loved the most, hoping for a calm and peaceful end of days. How pitiful that her end should be neither peaceful nor natural, and at the hands of the nemesis she had dangerously awoken with her letter.

Her fingers plucked at her tormentor, scrabbling to get hold of flesh or fabric, as though that one action would stop the inevitable. Her lungs began to burn as she fought to breathe through the brushed cotton, the constriction of her throat pulsated with each spasm that racked her body. It matched her heart, beat for beat. She clawed at her tormentor's clothing, her bony fingers grasping at anything that might later provide evidence. What she was searching for came suddenly and silently away from the cloth; she could feel its hard coldness in the palm of her hand as she tightly closed her fingers around it.

Now she could let go.

As a strange peace began to wash over her, she half expected to hear angels sing, or at the very least, a tinkling of bells to herald her journey towards the afterlife, but to her disgust her one last sense picked up the fresh smell of Comfort Lavender Bloom fabric conditioner from the pillowcase. That was such a kick in the dentures as everyone at Rookery Grange knew she much preferred the more ironic but befitting, Comfort Heavenly Nectar.

How utterly, utterly disappointing that her last thought on this mortal coil should mirror a ruddy Tesco shopping list.

If the pillow had not been so heavy against her face, Dorothy would have elicited one last smile, but alas this was not to be. Her heart stilled and her final breath silently left her in a cloud of lavender scent.

As a flurry of wind whistled down the chimney of Room 8 and the door quietly clicked shut, poor Dorothy Burnside became the first murder victim that Rookery Grange had seen in a very long time.

A MEETING OF MINDS

*F*lorrie Patterson, proprietor of the Twisted Currant Café, carried out her regular morning duties around her cosy little tearoom. She mentally checked off her list.

Table flowers – *tick*.

Clean tablecloths – *tick*.

Sugar bowls filled (both brown and white) – *tick*.

She skipped around the counter and used her index finger to point to – but not touch – the fancies laid out in the glass case: scones, Bakewell tarts, brownies and muffins. She had already checked the stock in the kitchen for any lunches that would need to be prepared to order, so all was good in her happy world. She wiped her hands on her pink pinafore, straightened the bib and checked the bow was neatly tied behind her. No sooner had she finished that action than the little bell above the door tinkled, announcing her first customer of the day.

'Morning, Ethel.' Florrie picked up her little notepad and pencil. 'Are you ordering just for you, or have they sent you on ahead?'

It was common knowledge that when the Winterbottom ladies met for their regular tea, toast and cake mornings they would nominate one of the group to place a bulk order, so that when they eventually arrived en masse, their bottoms would have barely touched the gingham seat pads before their requirements would be served to them.

Ethel nodded as she plonked her navy handbag onto their regular table. Pulling out a notepad, she squinted as she huffed. 'Blimey, I can't even read my own handwriting these days! What does that say, Florrie?' She enthusiastically shoved the tattered booklet out in front of her, tapping the chosen word with an arthritic finger.

Florrie squinted. 'Erm... it looks like *chauffeurs*...' She tilted her head, first one way and then the other. '...chocolate *chauffeurs*. It says: "Two chocolate chauffeurs!"'

Ethel snorted loudly. '*That's* why I can't read it! I didn't write it – that's Hilda's handwriting. She means chocolate éclairs, the silly mare!' Her description of Hilda was not a cruel jibe but one born from a close friendship nurtured over many years. Hilda's forgetfulness had stabilised with the help of regular medication for Alzheimer's, but she was still prone to malapropisms, misheard words and ones she had simply made up herself because they sounded nice.

'Here they are...' Ethel gave a cheerful wave to her friends who, since their last adventure at the Montgomery Hall Hotel, were now better known as the 'Four Wrinkled Dears'. It was a little moniker they had given themselves to show their advancing years, coupled with an adventurous, daredevil spirit. Musketeers they might not be, but they had come a pretty close second with their mule slippers slapping and winceyette nighties flapping around the secret passages of the hotel looking for mischief.

They traipsed into the café, one after the other: Clarissa, Hilda and Millie. Clarissa, Ethel's closest friend, slipped off her coat and hooked it onto the coat stand before taking the chair next to her. 'Budge up a bit, fatty!' Clarissa grinned as she tried to carefully manoeuvre her own curvy posterior onto a seat. She nudged the edge of the table with her hip, making the vase and its little bunch of holly and artificial poinsettia wobble wildly.

'You can talk, 'Rissa! I've just bought your Christmas present. Did you know you've gone up three sizes in your M&S knickers since last year?' Ethel chortled and looked to the now gathered ladies for approval of her joke.

Millie Thomas was the first to speak. 'Ooh, we're not doing our Secret Santa now, are we? I haven't brought Hilda's with me.' She sat herself down opposite Clarissa and pondered her last comment. 'I shouldn't have said that, should I?'

Ethel took a bite from the scone that Florrie had just placed in front of her. 'Mmpf…' she spluttered. 'I really don't know why we call it a Secret Santa when Millie here can't hold her own water, let alone a surprise!' She quickly wiped her chin, flicking the crumbs onto Clarissa's skirt.

Florrie watched the ladies laughing and giggling amongst themselves as they gently teased each other, and then indulged in what they really held these coffee morning meetings for: juicy gossip.

'Noo, she never did! Please tell me you've made that up!' Millie was all ears as Clarissa regaled them with the latest exploits of their two younger WI members, Chelsea and Cassidy.

'I'm telling you, it's true; they've got a four-week ban from the Dog & Gun for… erm… now let me remember it exactly…' Clarissa made a great show of thinking. 'That's it, "Behaviour unbecoming for a customer". I think the manager of the pub was going to say "lady" but quickly changed his mind after what they'd been up to!' She took a sip of her tea and peered over the rim of the cup. 'I've got a feeling that Kitty will be making representations to Pru over their continued membership if they don't pull their socks up!'

Quick as ever, Ethel chipped in. 'It's knickers rather than socks that they need to pull up! That would be more appropriate, knowing those two and after hearing that story!' She waited for the laughter to die down before she continued. 'Just changing the subject for a minute; has anyone been to visit Winnie yet?' The gentle hum of Florrie's cold drinks refrigerator filled the silence in the cosy café. 'Don't all speak at once, will you!' Ethel snapped. 'Honestly, girls, it's the least we can do. How about we all club together, buy her some nice flowers, maybe take one or two of Florrie's fancies with us, and go and visit her this afternoon?'

Clarissa nodded in agreement. 'So that's you, me, Hilda and Millie. I don't think Brenda will be up for a visit, she's too scared of the dead that roam the corridors of Rookery Grange. She's terrified of anything supernatural.' She bit into the chocolate éclair that Hilda had ordered for her. 'I wouldn't mind researching the history of that place, though. It could be fun.'

This was now time for Millie to shine. She knew all about Rookery Grange. She timidly put her hand up as though she were at school, asking permission to speak. 'My mum worked in the kitchens there years ago for the people that owned it: the Carnells. They had two children, a boy and a girl, and there was a nanny, too. Dreadful story, I can tell you, absolutely dreadful. Mum was interviewed over it.'

This time the silence was created by rapt anticipation. Ethel, Hilda and Clarissa leant in expectantly, elbows on the table, chins resting in upturned hands. Millie took her cue and hunkered down to whisper her story conspiratorially. 'Well, they were both found dead, weren't they?' She sat back, triumphant.

Clarissa tutted loudly. 'I don't know, dear; were they? You're the one that's telling the story.'

Peeved, Millie pursed her lips before continuing. 'The parents were found poisoned. Honestly, it was awful. Christmas presents were still under the tree that was twinkling and shining as though it should be a happy occasion, but it was anything but happy for those two kids. Talk had it that the boy – now what was his name…?' she broke off to mumble the alphabet to herself.

'…S, T, U, V … yes, yes, that's it: "V" for Vincent, his name was

Vincent. There was talk that he'd done it because they found weedkiller scattered all over the nursery, the box it came in and his sister traumatised and unable to speak. He was a very strange child indeed, even the nanny was scared of him, but there was no real proof. In the end I think it was ruled murder by the father, who then took his own life.' She bit into her muffin, unperturbed as to the effect her story was having on her friends. 'Apparently the wife had been playing away so the motive was jealousy.' She gave a knowing look followed by a saucy wink.

Silence once again filled the cosy room, broken only by the rhythmic slurping of tea and rattling of cups on saucers.

'So what happened to the children?' Ethel was genuinely concerned.

Millie shrugged. 'Not sure. Talk had it they were removed immediately from Rookery Grange and went to live with a relative on the father's side and then sent to boarding school. Probate was completed and the place went to the brother. Then the next thing you know, it opens up as an old people's residential home. Apparently that's where there's money to be made these days.'

'There you go. Just because we get old doesn't mean we're not useful!' Clarissa quipped. 'I've just had a thought. Doesn't our Pru have something to do with Rookery Grange? I'm sure I've heard her mention it.' She tapped the pencil she'd pinched from Ethel on the side of her head to show that at some point her brain had engaged itself with that snippet of information. Florrie, who had been discreetly wiping tables nearby so she could overhear their conversation, quickly offered her knowledge. 'Yes, ladies, Pru does the mobile library there once a week. My old mum used to love a good book...' She became pensive before adding, '...God rest her soul.'

'Well, that's settled, then. Ethel, you go and sort out Albert. Millie, take Hilda to pick some flowers and we'll meet back here at...' She checked her watch. '...1pm. That should be perfect timing to get the bus over to Chapperton Bliss to grace Winnie with a little visit.' Clarissa stood to get her coat. 'Must dash; got things to do at home.'

Ethel harrumphed. 'What, like put your feet up with a nice cup of tea? You're lucky 'Rissa, you've only got yourself to think of. That's the one benefit of being single!'

'Ah, that's where you're wrong, my dear.' Clarissa grinned. 'There is definitely another benefit to being childless and a spinster – I've still got an unused and well-sprung pelvic floor!'

To the backdrop of laughter and with a tinkle of the doorbell to the Twisted Currant Café, the Winterbottom ladies' morning meeting came to a cheerful close.

SOMETHING IS AFOOT...

The old movie flickered its black-and-white colours of *Whatever Happened to Baby Jane* across the 32 inch flat screen television in Room 3 at the Rookery Grange Retreat.

Its sole occupant, an elegant woman, her face softly lined and powdered with a touch of cheek rouge, sat serenely in the old-fashioned leather-backed bath chair. A moss-green blanket draped across her knees complimented the tones of the vintage wallpaper that decorated the walls. Her rheumy blue eyes misted over, allowing a tear to trickle slowly down her cheek. She gently brushed it away with her fingers, not wanting her favourite line from Bette Davis to be missed.

Don't you think I know everything that goes on in this house? Bette's American drawl was music to Goldie's ears.

The Dolby speakers gave a wonderful depth to the soundtrack. It resonated around her room, making her feel as though she were part of the scene, that she could actually *be* Baby Jane Hudson for just a short while.

Miss Goldie Franklin, retired thespian, member of The Actors' Guild of Great Britain and long-term resident of Rookery Grange, absolutely loved that line. Since being confined to two wheels and a stabiliser rather than two legs after a very inconvenient stroke, she had made it her mission every waking morning to know exactly what was going on in and around what she fondly referred to as 'her home', just as Bette had. Well, she *had* been here long enough to become part of the furniture, so it wasn't too far off the mark calling it her home. She dramatically swept the curls of silver-white hair away from her forehead and, using a tortoiseshell comb, pinned them back to join the chignon she had created that very morning.

Her days were filled with nostalgia, prompted by the wonderful array of back-to-back films on the TCM channel, and the comfort and contentment of her room. The rich velvet curtains framed the floor-to-ceiling mullioned window, her green tapestry cushions sat regally on the burgundy leather suite; two on the parlour sofa and one on the winged back chair. Her ornaments and acting awards brought from her previous home, Cragstone Lodge, were dotted around the room, so that whatever direction she deigned to manoeuvre her wheelchair, she could admire them. They were her cues: her prompts to a previous life.

She watched Bette float across the screen, and for a fleeting moment she wondered why they were called black-and-white films when they were really more varying degrees of grey.

'I suppose a good old grey-and-white movie doesn't sound as romantic, does it, Errol?' Goldie pushed a millet spray through the bars of the budgie cage. Errol, a colourful yellow and green bird named after her favourite star from the golden screen era of Hollywood, leading man Errol Flynn, tipped his head in acknowledgement and hopped across to the nearest bar that would afford him access to the delicious treat. Goldie pushed herself over to the window to watch the rapidly evolving weather front coming through. The diagonal ticks of rain hitting the leaded glass formed a creative pattern, blurring the dull clouds as they scooted across the heavy sky, sweeping their shadows across the vast lawns of Rookery Grange each time the weak daylight broke through. Most days Goldie would yearn for her youth and her once shapely pins that could dance and skip across stage, grass or any other medium available. But not today. Today was a day when even a pair of working legs would not have encouraged her to brave the elements to venture outside minus her wheels.

The familiar *squeak, squeak, rumble* along the hallway outside her room interrupted her reverie and filled her with excited expectation. A gentle tap on her door followed, which heralded her visitor. 'Enter...' Goldie manoeuvred herself to a better position in front of the fireplace, ready to receive the caller. She patted the side of her hair and then pressed an imaginary crease from her blanket before striking a regal pose.

'Good morning, Miss Franklin, I hope today finds you well?' The door swung open and Pru entered the room, an old mahogany book trolley with round brass caster wheels trundling in behind her. She gave one of her warm smiles to the elderly woman she had become so fond of during her weekly visits to Rookery Grange. Pru carried a varied selection of books from the Winterbottom library that were designed to engage, entertain and enlighten the residents.

'Can't complain...' Goldie grabbed her reading glasses from the nearby drinks table and popped them onto the bridge of her nose. '...Well, I suppose I could, but who would be listening?' She gave Pru a knowing wink. 'What have you got this week, Pru?'

Pru pushed the trolley in front of Goldie so that she could have the opportunity to peruse the rigid colourful spines and titles of the books chosen for the visit at her leisure.

'That's the spirit, Miss Franklin, upbeat and positive makes the day seem worthwhile!'

'Is all that commotion still going on, Pru?' Goldie had been waiting for the opportunity to satisfy her curiosity. The rumpus from the main hall earlier in the morning had travelled along to her room, and no doubt had filled the staircase and landings of Rookery Grange too. She had also spotted the not unfamiliar sight of the black Ford Transit van used by Bellows & Burke, the local undertakers. With blacked out windows and a discreet signage that simply said *Private Ambulance* along the side in silver writing, it had parked in its usual place, awaiting whichever resident was requiring its services for their final journey.

Pru knew only too well that passing from this life to the next was to be expected in residential and care homes, mainly by virtue of old age, but it still made her feel sad. She had no idea – as yet – to who would be gracing the marble slab at Bellows & Burke's mortuary, but she had no doubt it would be common knowledge before teatime. 'It was a little busy when I arrived...' She tried to carefully measure her words. 'Now what genre do we fancy this week?' Pru quickly changed the subject and directed Goldie's attention to her books.

As Goldie's deft, but arthritic fingers swept across the books, Pru couldn't help but feel her spider senses tingling; when she had arrived, she had noticed a police car tucked away near the entrance to the kitchens. The Bellows & Burke's van was not alone either; a similar vehicle had joined it, and from experience she knew that this one was the property of the coroner's office. She also knew that if death had been sudden, unexpected and with even an inkling of suspicious circumstances, their services would have been called upon by the local constabulary.

'Oh for goodness' sake! Please, Pru, tell them to hush their mouths and keep their idle chitter chatter to themselves. I can't hear myself think...' Exasperated and annoyed, Goldie waved her arm towards her door where a collective murmur of voices was hard at work on the other side. Pru bit down on her bottom lip and instinctively went to open the door, but something made her pause, her fingers wrapped around the polished brass doorknob. She strained to hear the gist of the conversation taking place.

'They've said not to touch anything; police detectives are on their way as we speak...'

The voice of Eleanor Parsons, the manager of Rookery

Grange Retreat, sounded strained, almost fearful. Pru couldn't make out who the second voice belonged to, but whoever it was, they were more in control than Eleanor.

'*Say nothing. Keep your head down, and make sure all the records are in order...*'

Pru held her breath and squeezed her eyes shut as she tried to turn the doorknob without alerting them. She needed to see who was with Eleanor.

'Ooh, I think I'll have this one, Pru...' Goldie triumphantly held up her choice of book whilst inadvertently interrupting Pru's next move.

Her mind still fixed on the conversation she had just overheard, Pru turned back to Goldie and absentmindedly took the paperback edition from her outstretched fingers. Her gaze rested on the title for several seconds before it finally sank in. 'Gosh, Miss Franklin, I don't think this will be suitable for you!' She held the well-thumbed copy of *Fifty Shades of Grey* out in front of her, as though it were the proverbial hot potato.

Goldie took the opportunity to rearrange the tortoiseshell comb in her hair again. 'I don't see why not?' she said as she grinned. 'Charles, our hairdresser, comes in next week. If I have a good look at the pictures, I just might find a shade I like!' She gave a saucy wink and burst out laughing.

THE DELECTABLE DETECTIVE

'*R*ight, troops, listen up!' Detective Inspector Murdoch Holmes deliberately dropped the batch of case files onto his desk from a decent height. The ensuing thwump elicited the desired effect of immediate silence from his officers. He stood with his knuckles pressed firmly down onto the well-worn and tattered pink blotter in front of him and surveyed the room. 'We appear to have a prolific thief amongst us...'

Andy Barnes, the detective sergeant on the section, gave Detective Constable Lucy Harris, who was sitting next to him at the conference table, a furtive nudge to get her attention. His fingers plucked at the paperwork in front of him that was headed *Overnight Crime Report*; he knew what was coming. He gingerly turned the bottom corner to peep at the final figure on the page underneath. His eyes widened as he pointed to the number. Lucy pulled her mouth downwards and gave a barely perceptible shake of her head whilst rubbing her arm where his elbow had made contact.

Burglary x 4 between 0200 and 0500 hrs.

Tim   Forshaw,   their   trainee   investigator,   shifted uncomfortably in his chair, a smattering of perspiration that accompanied that action quickly adhering itself to his top lip. He failed to look to Andy for approval before his arm slowly snaked upwards, totally oblivious to the frantic shaking of his sergeant's head. 'Sir...'

Holmes closed his eyes and mentally recited his own personal mantra for patience, the one he had created for when Tim decided to grace him with a response. 'Yes, Forshaw...'

'It was me, but I promise I'll replace them.' Tim swallowed hard.

A collective groan rippled around the room, followed by an expectant silence as everyone waited for Holmes to respond. 'Replace *what*, Forshaw?' Homes bristled. He was in no mood for guessing games.

The lump in Tim's throat was now so big it threatened to rob him of any means of a coherent verbal reply, so he took to waving the crumpled biscuit packet in the air instead. Barely suppressed laughter from his colleagues came hot on the heels of that action. Holmes rounded his desk and targeted Tim like a rampant rhino, covering the floor space in a matter of seconds before snatching the offending empty digestive packet from Tim's outstretched fingers. 'Bloody biscuits, Forshaw! You're owning up to snaffling the office supplies when we're trying to locate and arrest Duncan "Drainpipe" Dobbins, our burglary target!'

Melv Hibbert, the team's crime scene investigator, discreetly propelled his chair towards Tim, narrowly missing the cavernous gaping wave of the one rogue carpet tile that threatened to sabotage anyone who didn't look down. 'Let it go, son...' he whispered out of the side of his mouth. '...Quit whilst you're ahead!' He sincerely hoped his words of wisdom would somehow drag Tim from the jaws of Murdoch Holmes and stop him from adding further narrative to his faux pas.

It didn't.

'You said there's a thief amongst us, I just didn't want you thinking it was anyone else...' Tim's voice tapered off as the penny dropped.

'*Amongst us* in the broadest sense, Forshaw. Amongst the good folk of Winterbottom and Chapperton Bliss, that is, us. Those that live and work here.' Holmes combed his fingers through his hair, patted down his quiff, and turned to face the projector screen on the wall behind his desk. It flickered momentarily before columns and figures appeared as if by magic. '*Four* overnight burglaries to add to the six that are already under investigation.' He tapped down hard on the laptop in front of him, making the image change. The faces of Winterbottom and surrounding areas' most prolific offenders stared back at them. 'That makes eleven unsolved crimes...'

Tim quickly utilised the fingers on both of his hands. 'That actually makes ten, sir...'

Holmes' head swivelled exorcist style. 'You just don't know when to shut up, do you, Forshaw!' he snapped.

Andy watched him turn a rather unattractive shade of purple, and fearing the potential for a heart attack, he quickly stepped in to calm the tense situation. 'Uniform have had a tip off they're checking out now, boss.' He made a show of looking at his watch. 'Word has it that Dobbins is lying low on the Brackenwood Estate. The MO is the same for all of them, which puts Dobbins clearly in the frame. We're just waiting to hear back on a print that was recovered from the Well Lane job.'

That news seemed to appease Holmes momentarily, and distract him from the target he had mentally painted on Tim's forehead. 'Okay, good. You and Harris liaise with uniform, if we get confirmation, I want doors going in until we locate him.' He closed down his laptop. 'Hibbert, you chase up the print results...'

The swing doors to the incident room were suddenly pushed forcefully open; one door hit the water cooler, making it wobble and glug loudly. Every head turned towards the culprit. Lyndsey

Shepherd, a probationer constable who had until five minutes earlier been staffing the general enquiry office, burst through the opening.

She paused, trying to get her breath. The two flights of stairs had challenged her thigh muscles and were currently making the tuna sandwich she had not long ago enjoyed, lurch around her stomach. 'Sorry to interrupt, sir, but there's a report coming in of a suspicious death at the Rookery Grange Retreat in Chapperton Bliss.' She waved the incident log in her hand.

The atmosphere in the room changed within seconds. Something other than burglaries, Dobbins, and digestive biscuits had immediately heightened the interest of each and every officer.

'They think it's murder, sir.'

THE VISIT

'*O*AP passes at the ready, girls...' Clarissa led the charge from the front as they piled onto the single-decker bus that had stopped just short of the quaint Winterbottom high street bus shelter. It had been built to resemble a small apex porch, the two sides of the shingled roof met where an aged carving of a rose, inlaid with the date '1923', held them together. Benches with the wood worn smooth from years of use were fixed either side, affording protection from the wind and rain for seasoned passengers. Each bench could easily accommodate two average-sized bottoms.

Hilda paused halfway up the steps. 'Who's got the mint imperials?' Exasperated, Ethel gripped her by the arm and almost hauled her up the rest of the steps. 'It's a twenty-minute journey not halfway around the ruddy world; you'll be asking for butties and a flask of tea next!' They were barely in their seats when the gentle hiss of the doors folding shut gave way to the bumping and swaying of the Winterbottom to Chapperton Bliss bus as it rumbled along the high street and out onto the country lanes.

Ethel plonked herself down next to Clarissa. 'Florrie bagged up an éclair for Winnie to have with her tea. Wasn't that kind of her?'

'Éclairs as in the plural, I believe,' Clarissa retorted as she side-eyed her friend whilst peering into the white paper bag. 'Where's the other one?'

Ethel feigned interest in the trees that were passing in a blur, whilst taking the opportunity to discreetly wipe away a smattering of cream that had stuck to her chin. 'I haven't got a clue what you're talking about...'

As the red bus rumbled its way along lanes and dual carriageways, the Four Wrinkled Dears chattered away ten to the dozen, covering subjects as diverse as when the next bin collection was due and what colour bin they needed to leave out, to the ever-hopeful possibility of finding someone who could once and for all advise Brenda Mortinsen that lemon drizzle cake was no longer appropriate at their WI meetings. Ever since poor Mabel Allinson had been found dead face first in the delicious delicacy with a 3.5mm crochet hook protruding from her neck, as the first victim of their WI serial killer Phyllis Watson, not one slice of drizzle had been devoured by the ladies – and yet Brenda still insisted on creating this tasty bake for every single meeting.

Clarissa checked her watch. 'Here we are, ladies. Gather up your stuff; we don't want to be leaving anything of value behind.' She popped her gloves into her bag and pulled the zipper closed. 'Hoods up too; it looks like rain...' Ethel grabbed the one thing that was of any value: the solitary chocolate éclair for Winnie.

The gates to the Rookery Grange Retreat glinted in the weak sunlight that broke through the heavy clouds. Vines and leaves intricately welded in metal wound their way through the large burnished bronze initials 'RG' that graced the top of each gate. Ethel peered through the heavy iron bars to marvel at the splendour of Rookery Grange. The gravel driveway edged by rhododendrons and trees devoid of leaves snaked its way towards the arched oak entrance doors. 'Blimey, I think we might need a taxi to the front door! It goes on forever!' Millie wasn't renowned for her distance walking skills, preferring short ambles to the Dog & Gun and Florrie's café.

Clarissa wasn't taking any slackers. She produced her umbrella and prodded it in the air. 'Right, ladies, onwards we go.' And with that she set about a steady pace, her lace-up brogues bouncing gravel in every direction, with Ethel, Millie and Hilda in her wake. She rounded the bend and came to a sudden and abrupt halt, utilising the umbrella to the side of her as a stopping barrier in front of her friends. 'We have visitors, girls...'

Hilda was perplexed. 'But aren't *we* the visitors, Clarissa?'

Pointing to a fully liveried police car, alongside what was undoubtedly an unmarked CID car, Clarissa singled out Andy Barnes for her attention. She had met him on many occasions when he had been with Pru. His presence confirmed for her that something must be afoot. He was busy talking to a woman who was animatedly waving her arms in the air.

'Something is definitely amiss, ladies. How exciting!'

Andy could feel his frustration rising rapidly; if he didn't hold himself in check he could see the situation escalating, a moment that would move him quickly from mild annoyance to downright anger. 'Miss Parsons, please! Whilst I can fully appreciate your situation, I also need you to appreciate mine. This is a potential crime scene, and you flapping your arms around like a rampant crow is not going to change anything.'

Eleanor Parsons quickly brought her arms down and fixed them firmly on her hips. 'Rampant? How *dare* you, I have never been rampant in my entire life!'

Andy felt he should regret his choice of description, but stubbornly jutted out his chin instead. He was quite sure that Eleanor had not indulged in anything remotely rampant, crow-like or otherwise, throughout her years, but he certainly suspected she had indulged in at least half a bottle of gin before lunchtime. The smell on her breath had been overpowering and the empty bottle in the wastepaper basket in her office had been a definite giveaway. He watched her stomp back inside Rookery Grange.

'Yoohoo, Andrew, oh Andrew…'

The sing-song voice carried across the lawns to reach Andy's ears. He inwardly cringed and rolled his eyes, letting out a deep sigh before turning round. 'Clarissa! What brings you here… and… oh dear, Ethel, Millie and Hilda too?' He could see his day going from bad to worse. He'd already given Pru not so much a cold shoulder but more a tepid one, when he'd arrived; there was never a time when police business could sit side by side with pleasure. He was lucky that she was so understanding. She had discreetly given her details to the uniformed constable and left Rookery Grange without so much as a petulant lip or a grumble.

Clarissa proudly puffed herself out. 'I have organised a Women's Institute welfare visit for one of our members. You may know her: Winnie Clegg?' She tilted her head expectantly as her three friends huddled around her nodding in agreement.

'Ah, I don't think so; the name doesn't ring a bell. Is she a resident here?' Andy fixed a smile which belied the little voice in his head that was saying: *This is all I need; three ruddy Miss Marples and a bloody Nancy Drew.*

'Yes, she broke her hip outside the Dog & Gun…' Ethel was the first to pipe up and then hastily added by way of explanation, 'She wasn't drunk though… Well, maybe she'd had a sherry or two, but no more than that. What are *you* doing here?'

Andy tapped the side of his nose knowingly. 'Ah, I'm afraid if I told you, I'd have to kill you!' He grinned. 'Shall we just say police business and leave it at that?' He was suddenly aware that neither Ethel nor the other ladies were paying him any attention. Their collective gazes were fixed on a point behind him.

The black zipped body bag on the coroner's gurney that held poor Dorothy Burnside was trundled out of the side entrance and placed in the back of the waiting van. Lucy, clipboard tucked under her arm, briskly walked towards the gathered group. 'Sarge, there's been a "find".' She emphasised the last word and nodded to the Winterbottom posse, not wishing to go into more detail than necessary in their presence.

'Thanks. Luce, I'll be back inside in a minute. Right, ladies, if you will excuse me, there's work to be done. I'm so sorry you've had a wasted journey, but visiting is suspended until further notice.' He offered his hand as a way of direction, showing the ladies their way back to the main gate.

Whilst Clarissa was bordering on a hissy fit, loudly tutting and mithering her disappointment, Ethel had hastily taken the opportunity to snaffle the paper bag containing Winnie's chocolate éclair. 'Oh dear what a shame; well, this won't keep, will it?' Not waiting for a response, she shoved the entire pastry into her mouth.

'Now that it's in your gob, Ethel, we'll never get the opportunity to know, will we?' Millie harrumphed and began the trek back along the driveway to the bus stop, just as the first drops of rain began to fall.

THE CURIOUS CURATOR & CO

*P*ru slumped down on the sofa and adjusted the faux fur cushion behind her head. Her long legs hung over the padded arm, a mule slipper dangling tantalisingly from one foot. 'There's definitely something going on there...' She waited for a response from Andy.

'Where?' He bent down to check the wine levels in the two glasses in front of him, and finding Pru's glass was lacking he poured a little more of the dark red liquid to even them up and offered it to her.

'Jeez, where do you think? Rookery Grange Retreat, of course!' Pru happily accepted the glass from him and took a sip. It had been a long day, one where she had spent half the afternoon worrying about Andy and what was happening at the residential home and the other half trying to come to terms with Bree's insistence that her maid of honour gift of a wedding planner in the form of Fergus O'Brien was a fabulous idea.

Andy moved her legs and sat down next to her. She adjusted her position and nestled into him. He loved how she gracefully moulded her body into his curves wherever and whenever they came together. 'If that's a precursor to get me to talk about the case, then think again, my Loony Librarian!'

'I'm not...' she insisted. 'I just overheard something, so if you're dealing with a possible murder, it could be valuable information.'

A comfortable silence swept between them as they enjoyed their drinks.

'Well?' Andy had waited long enough for Pru to expand on her comment.

'Well what?' she mischievously grinned.

'You know exactly what; don't make me beg!'

'Oh my, I do love it when you beg...' Giggling, she quickly added, 'Okay, okay, it was the owner, Eleanor. I couldn't see who she was talking to, but once she knew the police were on the way, I overheard her telling someone to say nothing, to keep their head down and that they needed to make sure all the records were in order. Now in my book, that has all the hallmarks of keeping something under wraps.'

Andy had to agree; it was definitely something that needed looking into. It might not necessarily have anything to do with the suspicious death at Rookery Grange, but if it was something the care commission authorities might be interested in, once he'd ruled it out from his own investigation, then he'd deal with it separately. 'When's your next library visit there?'

'Next Monday. Why? Would you like the Curious Curator & Co to go undercover and get the inside info for you?' She was now just a little bit excited.

'No. I most certainly wouldn't! I want you to keep out of it, Pru. You and trouble always seem to go hand in hand.' Andy made a point of making eye contact with her, just to ensure that she had heard him and understood. 'I've got enough on my plate without worrying about what you're getting up to with Bree. Just do your usual bookish stuff there, but of course if you should overhear anything that might be of interest, well, that's a different matter.' He was quite emphatic, and she was bitterly disappointed.

She sat quietly for a few minutes, her natural inquisitiveness for murder and mayhem giving way to the excitement – and dare she say it – trepidation of their forthcoming wedding. 'Andy...'

'Yes, my little turnip...'

'What do you think about having a wedding planner who wears Vivienne Westwood, carries a manbag and is called Fergus?' Her teeth nipped nervously at her bottom lip.

'I don't know. What should I think about a wedding planner called Fergus who carries a manbag and drapes himself in Vivienne Westwood?' He grinned, but seeing her look of concern, he quickly changed tack. 'Honestly, Pru, whatever you and Bree have cooked up is fine by me, I'll just turn up on the day and say "I do", once you've promised to love and obey ... definitely don't forget the "obey" bit though, will you?'

Pru grabbed the cushion from behind her and smacked him across the head with it. 'I'll promise to love you, but that's your lot, sunshine – I'll leave the obeying bit to your team at the nick. They don't have a choice if it's a lawful order!'

'I'll have you know...' But before he could finish his sentence, the jaunty beat of 'Another One Bites the Dust' rang out from his phone. 'I'll bloody kill them; they've changed it again!' he yelled as he scooped it up from the coffee table in front of him. 'Mind you, it'll teach me to leave it where they can get their mischievous mitts on it. Hello, DS Andy Barnes...'

Pru watched the muscles tighten around his jawline, the result of clenching his teeth together, while a barely perceptible twitch flickered at the corner of his right eye. She knew it wasn't good news.

'Thanks, Lucy. Yep, if you can get the ball rolling with the team, keep DI Holmes updated and I'll see you in the morning.' He jabbed at the 'end call' button and turned to Pru.

'Post-mortem has just confirmed our suspicions; it's now a murder investigation.'

THE CLUE

*E*thel Tytherington slipped her toes into her pink floral Easyfit fleece-lined slippers and pottered over to the bedroom window. Sweeping open the curtains, her eyes settled on the little cottage garden below. Crisp and white, and with an early morning show of frost, the trees, backlit by the winter sunrise, looked enchanting.

She loved this time of the year. Nippy mornings, ski boots and scarves with real fires and now, after much nagging, the added bonus of central heating. Albert, her husband, had lasted as long as he possibly could, firmly set in the era of the 1950s with his belief that germs don't breed in a cold atmosphere and therefore central heating was a health hazard.

We can just put another layer on, my dear, that will keep us warm... he had offered to support his pedantic stance on not having a boiler installed. Her quick retort that under no circumstances was she going to sit around with half her wardrobe on, resembling all twenty-six wobbly stones of Thelma Watkins from the next village, went some way to soften his stubborn facade. Albert had once inadvertently been thrown into Thelma's embrace at the Winterbottom Medical Centre when they had hurriedly converged from opposite directions in the narrow corridor. That meeting had left him seriously traumatised after being embedded in her matronly bosom for ten minutes, until Dr Robinson had found a way to extricate him. Neither Albert nor Thelma had suffered injury, but the stud wall of the corridor had been left with a large bottom-shaped indent on Thelma's side.

Ethel laughed to herself and then tutted loudly. 'Bloody cold atmosphere, my left cheek! It was tantamount to being like the ruddy North Pole in here.' She tentatively touched the warm radiator to reassure herself that all was still good and Albert hadn't turned the thermostat down. Christmas was only a matter of weeks away and as excited as she was for the celebrations, she still had so much left to do – food shopping, present wrapping, not to mention half a sleeve and a stitch up on the cardigan she was knitting for Albert. She checked her watch.

'Come on, Albie, time to get up.' She pulled back the duvet and gave him a tender kiss on the forehead, just as she did every morning. He snorted softly and pulled the feathered cover back up under his chin.

'Is that infernal money-guzzling piece of tin fired up again, Ethel?' he grumbled loudly as one foot peeped out to test the temperature.

'Morning to you too, Albie.' Ethel's lilting voice sang from the bottom of the bed. She pulled her fluffy housecoat around her and grinned mischievously. 'And yes, I've dared to switch it on, mainly because it's minus 5 this morning.'

She heard him grumble from under the depths of the featherdown duvet, but chose not to take heed of his words as she made her way downstairs, shouting behind her. 'Come on, up, up, we've got lots to do today – well, at least I have!' She knew that dig was a little childish of her, but it did seem that everything for the festive period was left to her each year. Albert was content to spend every day he could at the Winterbottom library shop on the high street that Pru ran for the community. Ethel was glad that Pru took such good care of him, furnishing him with biscuits and mugs of tea as he poured over the latest editions of the *Winterbottom News*. She was under no illusion that it was Albie's escape from her occasionally sharp tongue, but it did make her sad that they shared little in the way of the day-to-day things they used to enjoy earlier in their marriage.

She popped the kettle on and gazed out of the kitchen window. A robin was perched on one of the frosty branches of the hawthorn tree, its red breast vivid now it was winter. 'Did you know robins are supposed to be a sign that a lost loved one is visiting, Albie?' She heard the farmhouse chair scraping along the floor tiles, indicating that Albert had risen from his pit and had taken his place at the kitchen table to wait for his morning cup of tea.

'Yes, dear, I did.' He pulled the plaid dressing gown tighter around his neck. 'What's for breakfast this morning?'

'I'm saying we might have a heavenly visitor, and all you can think about is your stomach! Honestly, Albert Tytherington, is there no romance or magic left in you?'

Albert shrugged. 'As long as it's not your bloody mother! That's one heavenly visitor we could do without in this house. Even though she's dead and buried she'd still be complaining about the cold. It wouldn't be an extra shovel of coal on the fire anymore; it would be busting the North Sea pipelines. Our gas bill would be astronomical.' He gave Ethel a cheeky grin.

She couldn't help but smile back. 'Did I tell you about that death at Rookery Grange Retreat the other day – remember when we got turned away from visiting Winnie? Well, it's definitely a murder now. Florrie Patterson told me. We're going to try another visit today. She said they'd cleared the place and that it's all back to normal, so I'm meeting 'Rissa and the girls later.' Ethel poured the boiling water into the teapot and watched the corners of two teabags bob up and down before giving it a vigorous stir. The lid rattled back into place. 'Did you hear me, Albie?'

'Yes, dear.'

She flicked the tea towel at him, just catching his shoulder. 'I'll leave a sandwich and some fruit out for your lunch, but I'll be back in plenty of time for tea.'

'Yes, dear; no, dear…' he sighed, and then playfully added under his breath, '… three bags full, dear…'

The general hum of activity filled the Incident Room at Winterbridge police station. The constant gurgling from the water cooler as cups were filled and refilled partnered with the symphony of various mobile and landline ringtones. A murder investigation was now running alongside the 'Drainpipe' Dobbins burglary cases and the busy room had automatically split into two sections. Andy and his team had taken Area 2, which gave the bulk of the whiteboards and projector system to him, and although at times it could be a bad thing rather than a good thing, it had a direct door to the DI's office. He was under no illusion that Murdoch Holmes would poke his head out on a regular basis, just to keep himself in the loop whilst irritating the hell out of half of his team, but being at the top end of the room also had the added benefit of divider doors that could be pulled across if at any point in the investigation, complete confidentiality was required.

Andy pushed his fingers through his hair and looked at Lucy, who was hunkered down at her desk with several witness statement forms scattered in front of her. 'Anything?'

She shook her head. 'Nothing yet. Nobody saw or heard

anyone enter Room 8 at the crucial period. Dorothy was seen fit and well at 0930 when her meds were given.' She pushed an A4 sheet of paper towards Andy and pointed an entry with her pen. 'See here, all in order and all signed off. A cup of tea and some biscuits were taken to her at 1030 hours by the auxiliary staff on duty and she was fine; no issues reported.' She upended and tapped a file on her desk, pushing all the papers it contained into neat edges.

Andy studied the list. 'What about after that? What time was she found?'

'1202 hours exactly. Again, a member of auxiliary staff took her lunch in on a tray and found her as dead as a dodo. There was nothing to indicate a sudden illness, so they alerted Eleanor Parsons the owner-manager, who incidentally is also a registered nurse. She was the one that spotted there had been a struggle and recognised the signs of possible respiratory asphyxia, petechiae to the eyes, mild cyanosis and evidence of blood around the nostrils.' She gave the file to Andy. 'Here's the post-mortem report.'

He studied it carefully. 'So we're just waiting on the results of the fabric fibre aspiration extracted from the nasal cavities.' It wasn't really a question he wanted Lucy to answer; he was just thinking out loud. He had little doubt that it would be from the pillowcase. 'And the bagged and tagged pillows and bedding are already forensically preserved for cross-matching. That's good work, Luce.'

Lucy nodded. 'And there was this.' She handed him a sealed evidence bag, signed and dated. She checked the label against her list, noting the forensic pathologist's distinctive signature and qualifications.

Robert Limpett (MRCS, MB, BS, LRCIP) Exhibit No. RL/1

Andy lifted the clear plastic bag up to the light, studying its contents. He checked the written description with what his eyes were taking in.

1 x Matt black enamel 'angel wings' lapel pin.

'It was found during the PM, clutched in the victim's right hand, Sarge, almost embedded in the skin.' Lucy looked hopefully at him. 'All her belongings, including jewellery and trinkets, were noted when she moved into Rookery Grange; it's their protocol. I checked the book. As far as we can tell, it's not hers.'

BEST FRIENDS

$\mathcal{T}$he Dog & Gun was unusually quiet, considering it was the run up to the Christmas period, but that was really a blessing for Pru. She watched Bree at the bar chatting animatedly to Juicy Jason, the barman. She let out a resigned sigh. She had no doubt that Bree was regaling him with the finer details of the wedding and the benefits of having Fergus O'Brien and his manbag in their lives.

'Here we go, G&T for you and a V&T for me.' Bree carefully placed the gin balloon in front of her.

Pru watched the strawberry bob up and down, competing with the ice before it was surrounded by little fizzy bubbles. 'I still can't understand why you went ahead, Bree. I thought we'd agreed a wedding planner wasn't necessary.' She really hoped she didn't sound ungrateful.

Bree took a gulp of her drink, smacked her lips together and grinned. 'Ah, but you see he *is* necessary. Good old Fergus has already sorted out your little issue with the wedding photographer. How good is that?' She watched Pru soften a little.

'I know, and I'm really grateful, honestly I am.' Pru was very aware that a last-minute cancellation by the photographer she had booked; the much in demand 'Memories Through the Lens', had thrown her plans into disarray. She hadn't banked on the idiot abandoning his home, his business and his wife to run off with his eighteen-year-old secretary to live somewhere in the Seychelles. On second thoughts, maybe it was Anglesey; she couldn't remember, she just knew it was an island somewhere. 'It just seems a little over the top. It's a small-scale wedding, not a "smack-you-in-the-face" extravaganza.'

'Oh for goodness' sake! *Small scale*? You make it sound like you're building a plastic Airfix kit for one of those little toy planes, not hosting the wedding of the year!' Bree rummaged around in her bag for her notebook and pen.

Shaking her head, Pru realised she was on a hiding to nothing. Whatever she said about Fergus would fall on deaf ears. Bree had set her mind on helping to organise the wedding, and a planner was on her list. 'Anyway, how do you know him?'

Bree blushed. 'We were at university together, and sort of "did" the horizontal tango briefly…' She flicked her index fingers indicating air quotes.

'Shut the front door!' Pru nearly choked on the slug of gin she had just taken. Coughing, she grabbed a napkin from the rustic cutlery pot on the table and wiped her chin. 'No way!'

'Yep. Apparently I was his first and last before he decided he preferred Arthur to Martha.' She looked wistfully through the window, remembering times long past. 'I still can't believe a night with me put him off women for life.'

Jason, who had been busy polishing a glass, broke from his task on hearing the girls' collective laughter. 'Now, now, ladies, this level of joviality at lunchtime definitely needs a top up!' He grinned, pointing to the shelves behind him that housed colourful bottles of spirits.

Pru waved her glass in acknowledgement. 'Wish we could, Jase, but things to do this afternoon. We can't have Bree here hiccupping her way through a meeting, now can we?'

Bree looked puzzled. 'What meeting?'

'The Curious Curator & Co have a job. It's a historical one, nothing exciting – well actually that's a bit of an assumption. It could be; we've been tasked to trace a family tree.'

'Just for interest, or to benefit from?' Bree was all ears.

'Potentially the latter. Our client is in the process of making a will and wishes to ensure that no black sheep turn up after the fact to challenge it by laying claim to his hard-earned cash. If there are, he can be specific about cutting them out, which in turn will save any ambiguity in years to come.'

Pru's explanation was not greeted with enthusiasm by Bree. 'Huh, how very riveting – not! I was hoping for something to tickle our fancies and tantalise our senses.'

Laughing, Pru slugged back the remainder of her drink. 'Don't tell me you haven't had your fancy tantalised lately, Bree Richards! My goodness, girl, you seriously need some help!'

THE PLAN

The letter remained untouched on the coffee table. Every now and then her eyes would be drawn to it, but so far she had resisted the temptation to pick it up again. She knew what it contained, word for word.

Threats, demands and a promise of her ruination.

Her hand firmly glided along the back of her black and grey Maine Coon cat, who stretched out in pleasure, further elongating his already huge body. Frizzle gazed at her with his mesmerising gold eyes, burning into her soul, as though he could see her for what she truly was. She felt saddened by that knowledge.

'It doesn't matter what I do, you still love me, don't you, Frizzle?' The cat gave her no heed; he grew longer and thinner as he draped across her knees to eventually drop and melt onto the carpet before slinking away into the kitchen.

She checked her notebook for the umpteenth time in as many minutes. She had already resolved one issue that had now been marked as a task completed. It hadn't been as enjoyable as her other ones; usually assisting those that needed her intervention gave her an exhilarating high that lasted for days, but lately it was as though that pleasure was quickly waning. The time that lapsed between her undertakings was beginning to narrow.

Tick tock, tick tock...

The grandfather clock marked out the seconds in time to her own heartbeat. She felt it quicken slightly when she found the name she was looking for. 'Perfect, Frizzle, absolutely perfect. I think they are going to be happy with this one.' She closed the book and rested her head, waiting for the voices to be stilled. Satisfied with her choice, her eyes became heavy allowing slumber to take her to times once forgotten.

> *For the Angel of Death spread his wings on the blast,*
> *And breathed in the face of the foe as he passed.*
> *And the eyes of the sleepers waxed deadly and chill,*
> *And their hearts but once heaved, and for ever grew still.*

Lord Byron,
'The Destruction of Sennacherib'

Winifred Clegg, better known to her friends as Winnie, pulled the knitted throw over her knees. She tucked the edges around her, ensuring the slight draught that skimmed around Room 6 at Rookery Grange Retreat had no crevice to creep into her bones. Nurse Alex had just administered her pain relief and a nice cup of tea, and had informed her she would be having visitors.

'Would you mind passing me my hand mirror and that over there, please, dear?' She pointed to a tapestry wash bag on the dressing table. 'I'd like to make myself presentable before they arrive. Did they say who they were?'

Nurse Alex duly obliged, handing her the ornate silver-plated hand mirror and the bag. 'It's down as Clarissa Montgomery on the visiting slip, Winnie, and her friend Ethel, and two other ladies, so you've got quite the posse visiting you.'

Winnie gave a smug smile. 'They're my WI friends, I wonder if they've brought any cake...?' She carefully applied a pretty red lipstick to what was left of the Cupid's bow on her top lip. She angled a mirror to check she had kept within the lip lines. 'You know what, I could happily mourn my natural Bardot lips if I could be bothered, but these days my joints seem to take precedent.' She gave a slight moan as she shifted in the wheelchair as if to prove her point.

'Bardot lips?' Nurse Alex was intrigued.

'Ach, away with you! You're obviously too young to remember her. Brigitte Bardot, the French actress; she was a bit of a sex kitten, with no fake trout pouts like the youngsters have these days, I'll tell you!' Winnie examined her profile in the mirror. She pulled at the gentle folds of her face that evidenced her passing years. For a few seconds her skin, almost tucked behind her ears, brightened and smoothed before her jowls got the better of her actions and promptly slapped downwards to settle back into their natural position. She sighed loudly. 'Oh to be young again, not just in looks but to have bones that don't creak, ache and break. I sometimes wonder if you get to an age where death is a blessing...'

Alex gave a barely detectable smile, having heard that same wistful observation from patients and residents of care homes so many times over the years. It was now becoming more of a mantra than a passing aside. 'Right, Winnie, I'll leave you be. Just ring if you need anything. I think Eleanor has arranged for you to be brought down to the lounge to entertain your visitors. I've got to go and see to Goldie now, but I'll be back later with your bedtime meds.'

And with a soft click of the door, Winnie was left alone.

LUCKY FOR SOME...

'Oh for goodness' sake, Hilda, not there...' Clarissa huffed in annoyance. '...Over *there*!' She pointed wildly to the heavy carved mahogany coat stand in the hallway of Rookery Grange Retreat. Grabbing the beige camel-hair coat from the end of the staircase banister, she draped it over Hilda's arms. 'You're not at home now; you can't just chuck your coat anywhere.'

Hilda looked quite peeved. 'I hung it up, didn't I?'

'Yes, but not in its proper place!' Clarissa watched Hilda hang her coat up before she hooked her own on one of the scrolled arms of the coat stand. Then she happened to look down. 'Dear God, woman, where are your shoes?'

Hilda grinned and wiggled her stocking-clad toes against the black and white chequered tiles. 'I put them by the fire to dry out a bit.'

'May I ask who these belong to?' Eleanor Parsons crisply enunciated her question to the gathered ladies, a pair of Pavers Wilton Wellie ankle boots, one in each hand pinched between fingers and thumbs, her nose wrinkled in disgust. 'They were in my private quarters, and the aroma is not something I would encourage under any circumstances!'

Clarissa lifted her eyes to the heavens. 'I'm so sorry. Hilda here gets a little forgetful at times.' She gave a barely perceptible turn down of her mouth and a jerk of her head in the hope that Eleanor would take the hint and be sympathetic to the situation. It seemed to work. She dropped the offending boots in front of Hilda and muttered something inaudible under her breath.

'How rude!' Hilda noted as she slipped her feet back into the boots. 'Remind me not to shop here again in future. I can't abide cheeky sales assistants.' She turned her ankle to show her Wilton Wellies at their best angle. 'What do you think? They do suit me and they fit like a glove.' She paused to admire them a little more before finally answering her own question by making her decision. 'D'you know what? I think I will have these. I do so like them.' She rummaged around in her handbag and produced her purse. 'Don't bother wrapping them, I'll keep them on,' she gaily added to a backdrop of stifled laughter from her friends and a hand gesture of resignation from Eleanor.

The excitement that Winnie was feeling at having visitors, coupled with the prospect of biting into one of Brenda's delicious home bakes, gave her butterflies. She hoped that Clarissa had thought to bring the latest edition of the *Knitting Weekly* magazine with her too. A pair of number 8 needles, a couple of balls of 4 ply Sirdar and a decent pattern would help to while away the hours until her eventual release from Rookery Grange Retreat. Not that she was complaining; being waited on hand and foot did have its advantages.

As the minutes ticked by, impatience overtook excitement.

'Goodness me, how long does it take for someone to come and take me downstairs,' she chunnered to herself. 'Visiting will be over before I've even got to the lift, and I'll miss my friends.' Her fingers grasped at the wheels, pushing and pulling, backwards and forwards until the momentum took hold and she began to slowly propel herself towards the door. She hadn't driven a car for some years, but she still had the expertise to execute a three-point turn to enable her to open the door to her room. It took some effort, but after a further four-point turn she was out into the corridor.

As her wheelchair squeaked and rattled towards the lift that would deliver her to her friends, she paused momentarily at the top of the main staircase, looking down onto the black and white chequered tiles of the entrance hall. Welcome sounds of laughter drifted up to her as she watched Ethel ushering Millie and Hilda towards the lounge, whilst Clarissa was deep in animated conversation with Eleanor Parsons who appeared to be conducting an invisible orchestra with her arms waving and fluttering in the air.

'Cooee, Ethel,' Winnie hollered down the staircase whilst waving enthusiastically. Suddenly, and without warning, her wheelchair took on a life of its own, tilting violently forwards, bouncing and jiggling towards the top stair. Winnie thrust her hands out in front of her and grabbed the heavily carved oak newel post of the staircase, clinging on for dear life. A shadow with a flash of colour fleetingly swept passed her as the wheelchair continued with its momentum, the small front wheels teetering on the brink, before tipping sideways and spilling her out.

She landed heavily. The swooshing sound that assaulted her ears was accompanied by the 'thwump, bump, bang' of the wheelchair as it bounced on every stair, followed by the crash of aluminium on tiles and an ear-piercing scream…

Then there was silence.

SUSPICIOUS CIRCUMSTANCES

A new flurry of activity took over Rookery Grange and swept through the entrance hall, corridors and rooms. Where no information was available, the residents and staff took it upon themselves to create their own narrative.

'*She tried to wheel herself to the lift and misjudged the top step...*' Goldie Franklin in Room 3 loudly proclaimed at dinner.

'*I heard it was her heart; it gave her a bit of a turn and she fell...*' Resident of Room 4, Norma Appleton timidly whispered from behind her hand to her table of Scrabble friends.

'*It was definitely deliberate; she was pushed. This place ain't seen such a furore since those murders in the late 1980s...*' Not to be outdone, Rookery Grange's cook, Della Atkins, had pursed her lips and conspiratorially nodded her head to whoever would listen over the banging of pots and pans in the kitchen.

Lucy stood, notebook in hand, at the bottom of the Rookery Grange central staircase. Melvyn Hibbert, their team crime scene investigator, was busying himself with the battered wheelchair that still lay *in situ* on the highly polished chequered tiles. He swept a brush over the handles and carefully examined the result. His camera flash lit up the gloom that had crept in as the day wore on. He rolled out the clear lifting tape and tacked it across his finding before placing it on a latent lift card to preserve the print.

'Optimistic?' Lucy asked.

Melvyn snapped shut his forensic case. 'Debatable, to be honest. It's a communal wheelchair; they get switched around between rooms, residents, and anyone who pushes them. Unless it comes back as one that doesn't match staff or residents to make it unique, I'm not hopeful.'

'There's not really much to indicate it's anything more than an accident, Melv, but–'

Melvyn interrupted. 'Whilst I'm here for the other matter, I might as well cover all bases on this one, just in case.' He gave Lucy a warm, knowing smile.

'And *that's* why I love working with you, Mr Hibbert,' Lucy gaily added. 'I'll update Andy, and then I'm going to speak to some of the residents before we call it a day.' She paused long enough to take in the height the wheelchair had fallen from. 'Winnie has been one lucky lady, that's for sure.'

As Lucy left Melvyn to clear up, she quickly detoured to Eleanor's office. She gave a light tap on the door and went in. Andy was seated, taking notes whilst Eleanor paced up and down from behind her desk to the window and back again. She was distraught, not with concern for poor Winnie Clegg or sympathy for those that had witnessed the incident, but for herself.

'This could ruin me, do you understand? Ruin me, the business, everything I've ever worked for! I've got one murdered geriatric lying on a mortuary slab and another who is currently hyperventilating in my lounge, calming her nerves with my best sweet sherry after trying to score a perfect ten by diving headfirst into my entrance hall!' Eleanor slammed the Care Quality Commission incident form down on her desk. 'Health and Safety are going to have a field day with this one.'

Andy gave Lucy a raised eyebrow before turning his attention back to Eleanor. 'Miss Parsons, please calm down. This will help neither of us. Now, getting back to the exact moment you were aware that Mrs Clegg was at the top of the stairs…' He waited.

Eleanor made a show of thinking. After several seconds, she spoke. 'It was the wheelchair, the noise it made as it hit the first stair, I looked up and there was Winnie clinging to the banisters as the wheelchair somersaulted down.' She became pensive, staring through the window into the darkness beyond.

Andy gave her time to gather her thoughts. He watched her reflection in the leaded glass window. 'Can you remember anything else?'

She shook her head. 'No, nothing. I was just so frightened, thinking Winnie was going to fall headfirst… Oh dear… it just doesn't bear thinking about.' She nervously plucked at the neckerchief frill on her blouse. 'No, wait – yes, I *did* see something. There was someone else up there, only a shadow, but there was definitely someone else with Winnie. The wheelchair fell, Winnie was clinging on, and whoever was up there just vanished.'

Lucy could feel the change in the air; the room felt charged with electricity. 'Sarge, I'll arrange for a statement to be taken from Miss Parsons, preferably sooner rather than later, if I could just have a quick word.' She jerked her head towards the office door.

Eleanor sat down heavily behind her desk and waved her hand dismissively. 'I need a few moments to gather myself, so you just pop off and do whatever you people have to do.'

Andy duly obliged, leading first with Lucy in his wake. Once outside and away from anyone who could overhear, she briefed him. 'I've already spoken separately to Ethel, Millie and Clarissa; they all report seeing a shadow behind Winnie too. Hence the floor show we've just had with forensics as a precautionary measure.' She tried to pick her words. 'I didn't take them completely seriously; you know what those four are like when they get together. Blimey, I haven't even spoken to Hilda yet, but she'll probably report seeing Sandra Bullock swinging from the chandelier with a *Miss Congeniality* sash wrapped round her neck...'

Andy looked at her quizzically. Lucy rolled her eyes and sighed. 'She's having a bad day, Sarge. Apparently there were issues over her boots in the entrance hall when this happened; but if Eleanor, as lucid and level-headed as she is, also confirms their sighting, then there's a good chance this wasn't simply an accident.'

HOLLYWOOD OR BUST

*W*innie took another sip from the schooner glass that was wildly vibrating sweet sherry over her blouse. It matched in rhythm the nervous shake her hand had adopted since her near miss on the staircase of Rookery Grange.

The Four Wrinkled Dears sat in silence around the table watching their friend, not knowing which one of them should speak first. A spark from the large log that had been thrown on the fire crackled and hissed, breaking the spell. Ethel chose her words carefully.

'Well, Winnie dearest, I never had you down for a stunt double.' She took a sip of the dry sherry that Eleanor had reluctantly poured out for her. 'I didn't realise you were going for gold, silver *and* bronze at the same time!' The ladies released a mutual nervous giggle. 'How's the hip?'

Before Winnie could answer, Hilda, her sympathy having diminished greatly since the time of the incident, chose to speak up. 'I had an accident once, you know. The bloody cat tripped me up. Didn't half smack my Aunt Bessies on the wrought iron candlestick on the landing! I've worn a brassiere to bed ever since; it also stops them from dragging on the carpet on the way to the toilet.'

Clarissa was aghast. 'Hilda! What on earth have your bosoms got to do with poor Winnie's near miss?'

Hilda shrugged her shoulders and took another sip from her cup of tea. 'Dunno, just thought it might come in handy if there was a wrought iron candle holder on the landing here as well. My advice could save Winnie a lot of discomfort.'

Winnie looked horrified and chose to take Hilda's words on board with another large gulp of sherry. She coughed loudly, then genteelly wiped her nose with her hankie. 'I'll have you know, Hilda Mary Jones, my front bumpers have never ever dragged on a carpet, lino or any other style of flooring for that matter!'

'There, there, Winnie.' Ethel patted the back of Winnie's hand as a means of comfort. 'Are you sure you're not hurt anywhere?' Ethel had to admit to herself that she was bitterly disappointed with the absence of anything grisly; even a light smattering of blood would have upped the ante to make the day more exciting, and something she could regale the other WI members with in the Twisted Current Café.

Winnie smiled. 'No. I'm quite fine, thank you. I'll probably have a few bruises by tomorrow, but nothing a good night's sleep won't cure. I'm just so glad you came to visit. The days can get quite long in here.'

Once again the room fell silent as they each contemplated the afternoon's excitement, each wondering, but not daring to ask.

Ethel took another slug of sherry; a warm glow spiralled through her veins giving a flash of devil-may-care to the proceedings. 'Did you see who it was, Winnie, who pushed you?'

There. She'd said it.

Three concerned faces and one blank one stared back at her.

'Who?' Hilda was bemused. She'd been so busy admiring her new boots she must have missed something at the crucial point.

'No, erm… no… I don't know. I just remember feeling as though there was someone behind me.' Winnie was flustered, which in turn made Ethel feel rotten for bringing up the subject.

'Me, Millie and Ethel saw someone, Winnie. Even though the police don't think you're in danger, we certainly do, don't we, girls?' Clarissa, her face etched with concern watched the other three heads of the Wrinkled Dears nod in agreement. 'We need to speak to Pru. She'll know what to do; she's good at things like this.'

The ladies once again nodded in unison; their mutual agreement on their next step was set in stone. Silence once more reigned over the tableau of ladies with their sherries and tea, as their shadows cast upon the wall from the glow of the roaring fire in the hearth of Rookery Grange's spectacular fireplace. The mantel clock chimed the hour and then went back to marking time.

Tick, tock. Tick, tock…

The door to the lounge suddenly opened. 'Oh gosh, ladies, did I startle you? I'm so sorry, I think everyone is a bit jumpy at the moment.' Lucy smiled warmly. 'I just wondered if I could have a little chat with Hilda.'

Ethel held out her hand in welcome. 'Fill your boots, Lucy, she's all yours. Hilda?'

'Eh?'

'Lucy wants a word with you.' Ethel pulled out the chair next to her and indicated to Lucy to sit down. She duly obliged, setting out her notebook in front of her, pen at the ready.

'Hilda, I've already spoken to the others, I just wondered if you saw anything at the top of the stairs when Winnie had her little accident?' Lucy thought it prudent to keep her questioning gentle and not include anything that would alarm her.

Hilda looked intently at the detective constable and sagely nodded her head. 'She really needs to limit her fluid intake you know, that'll help with her little accidents.' She leant in closely to

Lucy to secretly impart the next bit of information. 'Our Winnie's a little bit too fond of the old cooking sherry!' she mouthed.

Lucy bit down on her bottom lip, trying to suppress her laughter. 'No, I mean when she nearly fell down the stairs, Hilda.'

Hilda suddenly seemed to remember the question that had been asked of her. 'Oh gosh, yes, I did. It took me a bit by surprise I can tell you when I recognised her.' Her facial expression changed to one of secretive smugness. Everyone leant forward, eagerly awaiting her revelation. The air stilled between them; not one of them daring to take a breath in case the sound broke Hilda's train of thought.

As the seconds ticked by, Lucy took the opportunity to gently prompt her. 'Take your time…'

Hilda puffed out her cheeks and grinned. 'It was that American actress off the telly, the Hollywood one, Sandra Bollocks… Yep, that's her, that's definitely who it was!'

AN ERROR OF JUDGEMENT

'Well, that didn't quite go according to plan, Frizzle.' She forked the flakes of tuna into the ceramic dish that had the word 'CAT' embossed on the side. It still puzzled her as to why pet bowls were labelled in such a way: 'DOG', 'CAT', 'HAMSTER', or whatever. It wasn't as though animals could read, and never once had she had the urge or the poor eyesight, to serve a spaghetti carbonara to one of her dinner guests in a bowl embossed with 'FERRET'.

She swilled the teapot with hot water and popped in two teabags. It probably wouldn't give her the enjoyment that a large Scotch and soda would, but she had to keep a clear head, so tea with a hint of lemon it had to be. The random thoughts of dog and cat bowls made her ponder how humans were pretty much labelled in the same way. There were the obvious descriptions such as gender or colour, hair type, weight and size, that sort of thing, but there was also another box that people liked to tick.

Behaviour.

She preferred to view them as personality traits rather than behaviour. Behaviour was what dogs were praised for. A treat for good behaviour, or a smack on the snout for being naughty. Not that she'd ever been smacked on the snout, although she'd had a fair few slaps on the back of her legs as a child. Mind you, if truth be told, her behaviour had been quite challenging at the best of times during her formative years.

'Did you know that would be classed as child abuse these days?' She watched Frizzle stretch in pleasure in front of the fire, followed by his two regular circles of the rug before settling down. She ran her fingers over the black hardback book that lay in front of her, the tips feeling the indents from the gold embossed lettering that sat deep into the leather. She carefully opened it to the right page and sighed; the entry she had made earlier in the day, now a jumble of failed words, mocked her. For all her meticulous planning she had made a complete and utter bollocks of what should have been a very simple despatch. She'd carried out lots more complicated ones that had required props and a fair bit of acting to boot; this should have been easy; a push and a shove and *voila* – job done!

'Never underestimate the steely grit of an old trout that's determined to wrap their geriatric knuckles around a stair post, Frizzle.' She chortled a little bit louder than she had meant to, setting off a coughing fit. 'How on earth can I be taken seriously as the Dark Angel when I can't relieve them of their last breath in a timely manner and in accordance with the Good Book?' She closed the tome and reverently carried it to her regimentally organised bookcase. Pushing aside several books in various stages of well-thumbed decline to reveal a small, inbuilt safe, she deftly twiddled the dial to the numbers she required. A barely audible click preceded the opening of the door. She placed her treasure inside, resting her hand on top of it for a few seconds, before feeling around for the small velvet pouch at the back. Carefully unravelling the cord, her fingers plucked out just one of its contents.

'I don't know where the other one went, Frizzle, but one is never dressed without it...' She carefully threaded the lapel pin through the cloth of her shirt and pressed the back stud into place. She didn't expect her cat companion to reply, but after years of solitude it was nice to have something to actually talk to that wasn't either a wall or a built-in kitchen cupboard. She arrogantly strutted to the mirror over the fireplace.

Her hand patted the new adornment before she admired the reflection of the black angel wings lapel pin that sat stark against the whiteness of its background.

'Just as well they come in a multi-pack isn't it, Frizzle?' She laughed and made air quotes with her fingers. 'A little bit like my "clients"!'

HELP!

*B*ree slammed the fridge door shut with her elbow as she juggled a bottle of Sauvignon Blanc in one hand and two wine glasses in the other. 'You're slipping, girl. It's half empty!' She jiggled the bottle in Pru's direction.

'I'm ever the optimist; in my world it's half-full.' Pru grabbed the tube of Pringles that Bree had brought with her, expertly flipped the lid, and popped one into her mouth. She crunched down. 'Eew! It's cheese and chive – how disgusting.' She made an exaggerated show of pretend retching.

'It's all Betty's Store had. Beggars can't be choosers, and besides which, if you don't like 'em, it'll help with your pre-wedding weight loss plan.' Bree tipped her wine glass and grinned.

'What pre-wedding weight loss plan?' Eyes wide, Pru paused with the freshly opened Cadbury's caramel chocolate bar mid-lips.

'Erm... the one that you're now embarking on in preparation for your big day.' Bree didn't look the least bit uncomfortable in blatantly bringing up the subject. 'Fergus thinks a few pounds would make all the difference.'

Pru took a slug of wine and savoured the burn as she swallowed. 'The difference in *what*? Are you two hinting that I'll look like a hippo in my wedding dress, waddling down the red carpet at Thornbury Manor to say "*I do*"? Honestly, Bree, I'm starting to believe that Fergus actually doesn't do much thinking – you have to have a brain between two ears to carry out that feat!'

Bree flopped down on the sofa, draping one arm around Pru's neck. 'Ooh, bitchy! The difference between squeezing or slipping into it nicely – come on, you said it yourself you wanted to lose a few pounds… or stones!'

'Only you could get away with a statement like that!' Pru laughed and punched her friend on the arm. 'I was just thinking…'

The comical ringtone strains of *I'm Getting Married in the Morning* from Pru's phone interrupted the gentle berating of her friend.

'Hello, Prunella Pearce speaking.' She listened intently. 'Ethel, Ethel, please calm down, I can't understand a word you're saying.' Bree tipped her head towards Pru, eager to overhear the conversation on the other end. 'Right, okay, not as the detective agency, but as a friend. Where are you all now?' A few *ums* and *ahs* followed before she continued. 'Right, stay there, don't do anything else – and by that I mean don't get involved in anything, and I mean *anything*, that could cause you, or me, problems. We'll be there shortly.'

Bree looked concerned. 'What's happened?'

Jumping up from the sofa, wine and Pringles forgotten, Pru grabbed her coat from the back of the dining chair. Huffing, she started to pull on her fur-lined boots.

'It's our Fearless Foursome… who are currently sitting in the Dog & Gun half scared to death. They've sent out an SOS!'

'What did she say?' Clarissa paused mid-sherry and cocked her head, waiting for a response, whilst at the same time keeping an eye on Hilda who, having finished her G&T, was now attempting to curl her fingers round the stem of Millie's brandy. She waved her index finger at her, school ma'am style. 'Tut tut, Hilda, not yours, my dear...'

A game of brandy-glass chess was artfully carried out on the worn mahogany pub table as Clarissa tried to salvage what was left of the brandy for Millie, whilst distracting Hilda with a top up of plain tonic water in her own glass.

'Pru and Bree are on their way now...' Ethel offered through a mouthful of smokey bacon crisps.

The Four Wrinkled Dears sat in quiet contemplation, the gentle hum of the teatime trade at the Dog & Gun providing normality to the scene. The booth they had chosen by the leaded-light bay window afforded them a view of the approach to the pub doors. It also gave a Christmas card backdrop to their gathering as large flakes of snow, caught in the light cast from the garland of amber bulbs strung across the beer garden, fell silently on the ground. Two figures suddenly broke through the darkness, huddled against the flurry of flakes. The door to the Dog & Gun momentarily swung open, throwing in a gust of freezing air before rattling back into its frame. Pru and Bree stamped their feet on the modular stone floor.

'There they are!' Bree pointed to the snug. 'Jeez, that came on quickly, didn't it?' She was quietly grateful that Pru had insisted on her borrowing a hat and a pair of gloves before they had left, as the sleet that had been intermittently falling for the last hour had rapidly turned to a full-bodied covering of snow. 'It's sticking; we could be in for a white Christmas at this rate,' she observed helpfully.

'Do me a favour whilst I go and start them off, and see what's up. Can you go to the bar? Mine's a G&T.' Pru slipped her gloves off and shoved them into her pocket, handing Bree a £20 note.

Pushing away a wisp of snowflake-laden hair, she gave Bree a wink. 'Make mine a double!'

'Would that be with a slimline tonic, my tubby friend?' Bree just managed to dodge Pru's playful punch for the second time that evening.

Some twenty minutes later, the six of them, still huddled together over a table of empty glasses and another fresh round of drinks that Juicy Jason had carried over, Pru and Bree had been brought up to date on the developments at Rookery Grange and their concern for Winnie's safety.

Pru was the first to speak after a short hiatus whilst they all sampled their respective alcoholic beverages. 'Did *any* of you, and that includes Winnie herself, see her being pushed?'

The Four Wrinkled Dears side-eyed each other before intently examining their hands. 'Well, not exactly...' Clarissa offered. '...But we all saw someone on the landing behind her.'

It was Bree's turn to intervene. 'Yes, we understand that, Clarissa, but did you *actually* see her being pushed. Could you make out if it was male or female, a member of staff, another resident, or even if it was a person at all?'

'It was a shadow, like someone was there but they were in the background so we couldn't see them.' Ethel was quite indignant that their collective observations were being questioned so vigorously. 'We're not senile, you know!'

Pru softened. 'I know, Ethel, we don't think that any of you are senile.' She paused momentarily and tried not to look at Hilda. 'It's just that this is something that should be left to the police. I mean have they even said that what happened to Winnie is linked to the murder at Rookery Grange, or are you all just jumping to conclusions because you're upset?'

Hilda harrumphed loudly. 'Well, they had their MFI man there...'

'MFI man?' Pru had heard Andy refer to many different roles

within the police by their acronyms, but she'd never heard of an MFI officer.

Clarissa almost choked on the sip of sherry she had just taken. 'Oh bloody hell, Hilda, MFI was a place that sold cheap crappy furniture that you had to put together yourself; it's been closed for years. It was a guy from their crime scene branch, you know, CSI.' Still giggling, she quickly wiped away droplets of Harvey's Bristol Cream from her paisley blouse. 'Just look what you've made me do! I've snorted most of it up my nose.'

Grateful for the clarification of a company that sold shoddy products, and smiling at Clarissa's inability to drink sherry and laugh at the same time, Pru pondered their position. First and foremost, she'd have a chat with Andy when she got home. She knew that he would be thrifty with any information from his side, but that didn't mean she had to be; after all she wasn't giving any secrets away or jeopardising an investigation. 'Look, ladies, let's put this into perspective. At the moment we don't have any evidence to suggest it was a deliberate act...' She paused, taking in the still concerned faces of Clarissa and Ethel. 'I know you still feel uneasy, but I'm sure that if there's anything in it, Andy and Lucy will investigate it thoroughly.'

Ethel pursed her lips. 'But what about Winnie?'

Bree took the opportunity to offer her a snippet of advice. 'I'm sure she'll be fine. The staff will be on high alert, and if it was just a simple accident, I'm sure Winnie has learnt her lesson not to go on a rampant "wheel-about" without waiting for assistance.'

'Have they spoken to Sandra Bollock yet?' Hilda eagerly asked. 'She must know something.'

Clarissa intervened, placing her hand over Hilda's, an action she found herself doing more frequently of late. 'I'm sure she's on their list; don't you worry about it.' She turned her mouth down as a way of apology to Pru and gave a slight shake of her head.

Pru could see that the advice they had given was more or less falling on deaf ears. Ethel's vacant expression and Clarissa's set jaw was giving her cause for concern. 'Look, I'll speak to Andy tonight and voice your worries, but please, please don't get up to mischief. Do you promise me?'

Clarissa spoke for the group. 'Why on earth would you think we would be up to mischief, Pru? Goodness me, it's not like we're The Famous Five minus one. Of course we won't.'

Pru really wished she could believe Clarissa's hasty assurance over a schooner of Harvey's, or Ethel's innocent face over a large G&T, but she knew these feisty women only too well. Their shared experiences at the Montgomery Hall Hotel told her the Four Wrinkled Dears were not about to give up on Winnie without a bit of madness and mayhem being thrown into the mix.

PILLOW TALK

*A*ndy snuggled into Pru, giving her a spoon's cuddle. He wrapped his arm around her middle and took the opportunity to gently kiss the nape of her neck. 'Are you very, *very* tired?' He tenderly stroked her hair that was fanned out on her pillow and waited. 'In fact, are you even awake?'

Pru continued to face away from him, a childish smile forming on her lips. 'I'm snoring, I'm fast asleep – in fact, I'm doing a rather delicious fandango with Morpheus – or at least I was until you poked me in the back!' She turned to face him, surprised to see both his hands in the air.

'It's a stick-up.' He laughed. Grabbing his pillow, he softly hit her across the head with it. 'Pillow fight!'

'Detective Sergeant Andrew Barnes, how old are you?' She swung her own pillow and didn't hold back; it hit him full force in the face.

'Oof...' He toppled backwards from the bed, landing with a thump on the floor. There was a hiatus of seconds before his head appeared, his hair springing in several directions from the static her pillow had created, with an indignant look on his face. 'That was brutal; mine was a love tap!'

'Love tap, my arse!' Pru giggled, before flopping back onto her repositioned pillow. She patted the duvet next to her, inviting him to safely return to their bed. 'Truce?'

He duly obliged, but not without caution. Years of pub fights and reluctant detainees as a uniform constable had taught him to never underestimate the 'enemy'. They lay together, Pru staring at the ceiling, taking the unexpected quiet moment after their light-hearted pillow duel to work out how she was going to bring up the subject of Winnie and the WI ladies. As sure as eggs were eggs, the twinkle in Ethel's eye had given the game away and she was in no doubt that as soon as her back was turned, they would be plotting something.

'Penny for them…' Andy knew from experience that when Pru was silent for more than two minutes, there was something troubling her. 'Go on, I know you've been dying to talk about something all night, I can read you like a book in your library!'

Pru took a deep breath, taking her time to pick the right opening line. She didn't want him to clam up on her before she'd even started. 'I saw Clarissa and Ethel tonight at the Dog & Gun…'

'Yesss…' Andy knew where this was going.

'Well, they're really worried about their friend Winnie, the one that almost fell down the stairs at Rookery Grange. So much so I think they're on the verge of doing something daft.'

'Yesss…'

'Do they have any need to be worried, Andy?' She turned to face him, waiting for a response other than a one-word *yes* that had a couple of extra 'ss' on the end.

It was now his turn to measure his words. The investigation into Dorothy Burnside had only just got off the ground. Every member of staff at Rookery Grange Retreat had been interviewed and their backgrounds checked, visitors to the retreat on the day of the murder were still being traced and spoken to by his team, and forensic recoveries were still being analysed. 'It was a precautionary measure with Winnie Clegg; it was deemed best practice whilst CSI were there. It's harder to go back after the fact if something flags up, so we utilised our attending resources, just in case. There's nothing to indicate at the moment that it was anything more than an accident.'

Pru pondered that reply for a few seconds. 'But what about the shadow that Clarissa, Ethel and Millie saw behind Winnie?'

'It could have been a false memory that they collectively created after chatting together about it; you know how witnesses can influence each other, particularly when they're suffering from shock.' He had early on decided not to mention the sighting by Eleanor Parsons. They hadn't yet had the chance to speak to Rookery Grange staff to plot their whereabouts at the time of Winnie's incident. It could just as easily have been one of the nurses making their way to another resident, and in the melee that followed their physical presence as a staff member rather than fleeting shadow had not been noted.

'Ah, okay. I thought that might have been the case. If anything changes though, you will tell me, won't you? I feel a sort of responsibility for the ladies.' Pru pulled the duvet up under her chin; a sudden chill had seeped into her bones.

'Okay, President Pearce, saviour of the Winterbottom Women's Institute Curiously Dangerous Ladies and Mischief Makers' group.' He laughed and kissed her gently on the lips before turning off the bedside light. 'Just don't be doing a Phyllis Watson or Montgomery Hall on me, please. Trouble with a capital T always follows you lot around, and I don't think my nerves can take it!'

THE GATHERING

The door to the Twisted Currant Café rattled in its frame as the wind pushed against the front of the building, bringing with it a swirling dervish of snow. The flakes whipped themselves into a frenzy, much like an excitedly shaken snow globe. Clarissa, huddled over a rather decadent hot chocolate that had a mountain of swirly cream and little marshmallows on top, intently watched the winter show through the window. A good three inches at least had fallen overnight, laying a blanket over pavements, trees, shop canopies and Winterbottom St Michael's Parish Church. If she craned her neck enough, she could just make out the large angel statue in the graveyard that rose up over the top of the sandstone wall; wings outstretched and majestic against the white. She shivered. There was something about the scene that made her feel uneasy, as though it was waiting for the next inhabitant of the hallowed ground to arrive. Her eyes scanned the High Street, which was currently deserted, waiting for any sign that she was going to be joined by the three remaining Four Wrinkled Dears.

'Can I get you anything else, 'Rissa?' Florrie, with savagely snapping cake tongs in hand, attentively offered, interrupting

Clarissa's train of thought. She acknowledged Clarissa's shake of the head before continuing. 'Do you think the others will make it today?'

Clarissa dabbed at her chin with a paper napkin. 'There's not much that keeps that lot away from your cakes, Florrie. I'm sure they'll be here shortly.' No sooner had the words left her crumb-laden lips than she spotted three dark figures slipping and sliding down the high street. 'Oh dear...' she muttered.

Ethel was the first to go down like a sack of spuds. Her legs raced beneath her as her new snow boots from Albert's latest edition of the *Chum's Catalogue* failed miserably to keep their grip. She slid first one way then the other, before finally succumbing to gravity. Clarissa watched in mild amusement mixed with concern, as Ethel grabbed hold of Millie's arm as she fell, pulling her off-balance. Millie frantically executed the same little dance that Ethel had only seconds before choreographed. They landed in a jumble of knitted lumberjack hats and dog-tooth trews on the snow-covered grass verge. Clarissa was just about to leave her seat and the warmth of the café to assist them, when she saw her two friends throw back their heads in laughter. Content they were not injured, she forked another chunk of coffee and walnut cake into her mouth and waited.

Florrie bit down on her bottom lip, trying not to laugh as she watched Hilda, totally oblivious to her friends taking a tumble, carry on picking her way through the snow, waving her hands and chatting away to herself on her way to the café door. She wondered when it would become evident to Hilda that she was actually talking to herself.

The little bell above the door jingled as it opened, letting in a blast of cold air. Hilda, still nattering away to herself, was first through, quickly followed by the still giggling Ethel and Millie.

'Nine out of ten for that display, ladies.' Clarissa, in the absence of score cards, held up two café menus. Her three friends took their respective seats and eagerly awaited their regular tea and cake that Florrie had started to prepare.

'I thought I was going to hit the afterlife full tilt for a minute, didn't you, Millie?' Ethel pulled the earflaps up on her hat and tied them together on the top of her head.

Millie giggled. 'Talk about "*If I'm going down I'm taking you with me!*" There was no loyalty there, was there?'

The Four Wrinkled Dears, huddled together over two pink-spotted teapots containing a good brew made from Yorkshire teabags and a selection of cakes and pastries on a three-tier cake stand, laughed and chatted animatedly. This was not one of their regular meetings but one called for out of necessity. They had all agreed upon leaving the Dog & Gun the previous night that although Pru's reassurances had been well received, it didn't necessarily follow that they were to be believed.

'So, ladies...' Ethel took it upon herself to take the lead. 'Do we all feel the same, even after Pru and Bree's little pep talk?' Three heads nodded back at her. 'In that case, we first need to formulate a plan...' she ticked off her index finger. 'Secondly, take a vote on it...' her middle finger was next to be accounted for. 'And thirdly, pick who does what. All agreed?' She waited for a response. Three heads vigorously nodded again, this time to show their approval of Ethel's timeline.

'We need to do something to protect Winnie; there's definitely something not right about that place and she's going to need all the help she can get.' Millie took a bite of her chocolate éclair. 'It's what they call a "safeguarding issue". I've heard them talk about it on that *true crime* series on the telly. Anyone got any ideas?'

They sat in silence around the table, contemplating Millie's question.

'Good grief, ladies! You lot look like you're conducting a séance!' Florrie busied herself on the next table, repositioning the placemats and napkins.

'Well if we don't do something to help Winnie, that might end up being the only way we can contact her,' Clarissa quipped. 'I know everyone is saying it was just an accident and that it's not linked to the murder, but I'd rather not take chances. Besides which, what I've got planned could be fun; I've been working on it all night.'

Ethel, Millie and Hilda were all ears. Cakes were left on plates and cups of tea were poised mid-mouth, waiting for Clarissa's plan. She made an obvious show of looking behind her to see if anyone was listening, which considering they were the only customers in the café was a wasted effort.

She pursed her lips and measured her words, aiming for tension and excitement in her revelation. 'It's quite simple really – we go undercover...'

THE INTERVIEW

'*C*offee?' From the far side of the incident room, Lucy jiggled the UK Cop Humour mug at Andy, who, like most people in the office, could spot the potential for a brew from a mile off. He grinned and gave her a thumbs up before focusing his attention back to the screen in front of him.

The rest of the room continued with its steady hum of activity, broken occasionally by a phone ringing. The 'Wanted' board still held the unattractive profile of Duncan 'Drainpipe' Dobbins. His weasel eyes stared out from under bushy eyebrows and a shaved head, the tell-tale gang tattoo of a teardrop visible under his left eye. A map of the Brackenwood Estate pinned next to the photograph was marked with several red Xs.

'New intel on Dobbins, hot off the press...' Tim Forshaw waved a sheet of A4 paper in the air. 'He's apparently holed up at his girlfriend's flat in Juniper Gardens; info is Grade 1 and good to go.' A flurry of activity quickly gave rise to new hope that their top target would be detained before the end of the shift.

Once upon a time, action like that would have attracted Andy's interest, but he was already on starter's orders from Murdoch Holmes to make progress with the Dorothy Burnside case. Apart from the angel lapel pin, nothing of any evidential value had come back from forensics. He closed the file and carried on scrolling through the control room incident log. Lucy, aware that his mind was otherwise engaged, placed his mug on the coaster and angled a digestive biscuit on the side for him.

'Thanks, Luce.' He took a bite of the biscuit and then checked around to see if anyone was looking before taking the opportunity to dunk it. He gave it a good soaking in the builder's-brew tea before lifting it out. The soggy biscuit drooped and, before he could save it, dropped onto his desk with a splat, leaving him with his mouth open and his tongue hanging out in anticipation of the tasty treat that never arrived. 'Damn... two seconds too long!'

Lucy smirked. 'Story of your life, Sarge?' She handed him a torn-off sheet of kitchen roll. 'The sister of Miss Burnside has arrived. She's downstairs in the interview room waiting for us.'

Andy shuffled the stack of papers and shoved them in a blue document wallet. 'Lead on then, Macduff.'

The witness interview room at Winterbridge police station had recently undergone a makeover of sorts. A soft lilac colour now adorned the previously greige walls that had been smeared with a plethora of undesirable bodily fluids over the years in its previous incarnation as a prisoner's holding room. A weeping fig, unceremoniously plonked in a chipped black pot in the dubious name of décor, sat in the corner next to a well-worn sofa and two chairs. Andy often thought 'weeping' was pretty apt for the poor thing as nobody ever thought to water it, judging by the confetti of curled-up leaves scattered on the dark grey carpet tiles. He cleared his throat.

'Good afternoon, Miss Burnside, I'm Detective Sergeant Andrew Barnes, and this is Detective Constable Lucy Harris.' He took the chair next to Beatrice Burnside. He was pleased to see that someone had already provided her with a cup of tea.

Beatrice Burnside sat with the bearing of the retired school mistress she was. Her back was ramrod straight with a handbag on her lap, and her hands folded neatly in front of her. A pair of navy gloves had been precisely matched together and placed on the coffee table. 'I'm really not sure what I can tell you, but if there is anything I can do to help find who did this…' her voice trailed off as she took a small cotton handkerchief from her bag, opened it out, and began to dab at her eyes.

'I appreciate this will be quite distressing for you, Miss Burnside, but anything you can tell us about your sister's life before she became a resident at Rookery Grange Retreat would help enormously.' Lucy gave her a sympathetic smile whilst still retaining her professionalism, pen poised in hand, notebook at the ready.

Beatrice took a sip of her tea and allowed the cup to rattle back on the saucer, giving herself time to think. 'Well, it's probably best if I go back right to the beginning.' Relaxing a little, she closed her eyes. 'Dorothy and I are sisters, as you know. We both had the same father, but different mothers. I am the younger by fourteen years. We had an unremarkable and happy childhood, and both went into careers that took us travelling around the world. I worked as a teacher and Dorothy cared for children, more often than not within their families. We kept in touch by letter and infrequent telephone calls, and would also see each other at occasional Christmas gatherings, but other than that I can't say we were particularly close.' She paused, her eyes misting over. 'She wouldn't even come and live with me when she became incapacitated, choosing instead to go into residential care. That's about it, really.'

Andy's heart sank. Dorothy Burnside had been on this earth for ninety-three years and her whole life had just been condensed into a concise and tart paragraph. He twiddled his pen, deep in thought. 'What about relationships, Miss Burnside? Did your sister ever have someone in her life, a gentleman friend, children of her own?' He was very aware that a lot of ladies of Dorothy's age had illegitimate babies, given up for adoption and never discussed again, but he couldn't lose the opportunity to ask; he had to explore every avenue, even though he half expected a show of indignation from Beatrice.

As expected, Beatrice bristled, but not for the reason he thought it would be. If it could have been possible, her back became straighter than it had been at the start of their conversation, her head wobbled slightly and she tightly pursed her lips. 'Men and babies didn't figure in my sister's life, sergeant...' She took another sip of tea before continuing. '...But women – now that's a completely different matter.'

Without missing a beat, Lucy, prompted by Beatrice's revelation, jumped in. 'Did she have a special lady; someone she was close to? It's so important that we speak to anyone that figured in Dorothy's life.'

Beatrice shook her head. 'She had a close lady friend in the 1960s when she lived with a family in Amsterdam; they were much more accepting over there in those days. All I know is that she died – a boating accident, I believe. Dottie left the family she was with, returned to the UK under a bit of a cloud, and eventually went to work with another family. She focused on her career, and as far as I'm aware, no one else was part of her life after that, not even me to some extent.'

Andy felt hopeful. 'What "cloud" would that have been, Beatrice?'

Beatrice stiffened and pursed her lips tightly together for the second time in as many minutes. 'You have to understand, it was not something I held with or condoned, but Dottie was always one for experimentation. She got caught with two bags of asparagus...'

Lucy and Andy exchanged discreet glances. 'Asparagus?' Lucy queried.

'Yes, asparagus.' Beatrice demonstrated a smoking action, bringing the two fingers of her right hand up to her mouth. 'It was for her own personal use; she wasn't going to sell it, but even though people were quite relaxed in Amsterdam, the family she was with… well, they weren't. She was sacked on the spot and then went back to England.'

The penny finally dropped for Andy. 'Cannabis? Do you mean cannabis as in drugs, Beatrice?'

She nodded. 'I most certainly do.'

Biting her bottom lip and trying to suppress a smile, Lucy pushed the evidence bag containing the black angel wings pin across the coffee table. 'We won't keep you much longer, but does this mean anything to you, Miss Burnside?'

Beatrice lifted the clear bag to the light, turning it slowly, examining the pin from every angle. 'No, I'm afraid it doesn't. Why? Should it?'

'It was found in your sister's hand. We believe it has some significance, and if we can rule out that it belonged to her, that is something we can investigate further. We have checked her property list when she came to Rookery Grange and it wasn't part of her personal belongings.'

Beatrice shook her head. 'Dottie would never have worn anything like this, or even had it in her possession. She had an inherent fear of ghosts, ghouls and dark doings.' She sniffed into her handkerchief; her eyes wide as she prodded her finger at the bag. 'That thing would have terrified her.'

THE REHEARSAL

For the umpteenth time, Pru checked her watch. 'He's not coming, is he?' She gave a mixed expression of annoyance and disappointment to Bree.

'Darling, darling, now don't be getting all uppity on me.' Fergus O'Brien flapped his way across the woodblock flooring of the Blenheim Suite at Thornbury Manor. 'Mr Detective is probably just running a little late; now let's get ourselves over to the red carpet bit where you, my girl,' he pointed his manicured finger at Bree, 'follow behind the bride. Chop, chop, ladies.' He clapped his hands together.

Pru rolled her eyes. This was exactly what she *didn't* want for her wedding. She wanted it to be fun, relaxed and shared with people that mattered to her. 'Fergus, I'm not getting uppity, but I just happen to think it's a good idea if the bloody groom is here to run through our nuptials too!'

Undeterred, Fergus waved away her concerns and began to move the burgundy velour chairs on one side of the room. 'I think we need to make the aisle a little wider, don't you?'

Pru was ready to explode. 'What for? To accommodate my large arse?' she snapped.

Suitably chastised, Fergus pinched his lips together and made a ridiculous show of bowing to her before turning to catch the attention of the hotel's events manager. 'Yoo-hoo, Miss Rusty,' he hollered in a sing-song lilt.

The attractive blonde, attired in a grey 'power' suit with clipboard in hand, gave Fergus a frosty glare. 'It's Rosti, Arabella Rosti.' She held out her hand in greeting. Fergus took the opportunity to kiss it rather than shake it.

Bree groaned. 'Oh blimey, I wish he'd stop fannying around. I'm really starting to regret interfering in your wedding by bringing *him* in. He's a bloody nightmare.'

'Only just starting!' Pru puffed out her cheeks, sending her fringe into a Mexican wave. 'Is there any way you can ship him off somewhere, like Outer Mongolia?' They both slumped down together on the gold damask chaise longue, neither of them caring one iota as to how many steps it would take to walk the red carpet to the front where the celebrant would be, or where the Winterbottom WI ladies would be sitting for the service.

'Are you inviting *all* the WI ladies?' Bree picked at one of her acrylic nails. She held her hand out in front of her, wriggling her fingers. 'I must get some infills done before the big day.'

Pru discreetly checked her own nails. At least five were broken and ragged from the shelf change she'd done in the library the day before. Nothing could destroy fingernails better than a heavy tome or two and a vigorous dusting. 'Most of them. Some obviously won't make it, but I think they're just happy to be invited, and I've promised to bring them some wedding cake after Christmas.'

'What about Chelsea and Cassidy?' Bree felt a sudden rush of panic mentioning their names. They were the youngest members of the WI and also the most trouble.

'We've been saved by a three-week holiday in Benidorm. They both jetted off last Saturday for a bit of winter sun, leaving their beloveds behind. Chelsea said, and I quote,' Pru wiggled the first two fingers of each hand in the air, "*I can't be arsed running around Primark looking for cheap skids and socks for an ungrateful twa...*" she stopped short of uttering Chelsea's unflattering descriptive of her better half. 'Well you get the gist, so she's left him underpants-and-sock-less and on his own for Christmas.'

Bree giggled. 'It's a nippy 12 degrees centigrade in Benidorm right now. Where are they tanning themselves: the Sandy Bums Solarium on the beachfront?'

'Do you really think those two would see a beach, even in the height of summer? They'll be on the pop all night, getting up to mischief and then sleeping all day! By the way, talking of WI ladies, has Ethel or Clarissa said anything to you?' Pru nervously chewed one of her nails.

'About what?'

'Oh, about Rookery Grange, dead bodies, wheelchairs with a mind of their own – that sort of thing.' Pru looked pensive. 'I don't trust those two. I think they're definitely up to something; they even asked me what days I go to Rookery Grange and what I do whilst I'm there. It was bad enough at the hotel when the four of them were sneaking around hidden passages. Can you imagine what they might get up to on familiar territory?'

Pru's concern for her WI ladies was suddenly interrupted by the double doors to the Blenheim Suite bursting open. 'Sorry, sorry...' Andy brushed his fingers through his hair and checked behind him to make sure the doors were still intact. 'It was work; I had to finish an interview and wrap a few things up.'

'Jeez, Andy, you're not on a drugs bust, you know. There's such a thing as pushing a door gently!' Pru wanted to be cross with him for being late, but seeing him standing there, forlorn and out of breath with his hair standing on end, she melted, just as she always did once she saw those mesmerising blue eyes, just as she had the first time she had met him. 'Come on, no time to waste. Let's get this over and done with and then we can battle the snow drifts up to the Dog & Gun!'

He grinned. 'And that's why I love you, Prunella Pearce, my Loony Librarian.'

'Oh purleese, can you two not get a room?' Bree pushed him towards the front. 'Right, you're here.' She positioned Andy just short of the steps to the dais and then grabbed Pru's arm. 'And you're with me.' Dragging her back along the red carpet towards the double doors, she spied Fergus, his radar locked in on them, skipping across the room. She quickly intercepted him.

'Where do you want me?' He grinned.

'Outer Mongolia…' Pru and Bree both chorused.

ELEANOR

ookery Grange Retreat's extensive gardens were Christmas-card perfect. The snow, draped across the estate's collection of cedar trees, offered canopies of cotton-wool white, flecked with the beautiful grey-green of their needles. Here and there, clusters of brown barrel-shaped cones poked through, providing a stark contrast. Eleanor stood in the window of her office nursing a single measure of brandy. She had often tried to estimate the height of some of the more mature cedars; they had been there for as long as she could remember. In fact, the groundsman reckoned they were older than Rookery Grange itself and were now probably thirty metres high or more.

On her quieter days, when a bottle of gin or a decanter of brandy hadn't yet dulled her senses, she had carried out a little research via the Woodland Trust's website, keen to know more about these stately and majestic trees. One little snippet she had discovered was their symbolism and why they had been so popular from the late 1740s and beyond.

Cedar represents purification and protection, incorruptibility and eternal life, the paragraph had informed her.

She had laughed out loud at that ridiculous observation.

'Protection and eternal life, my left buttock...' She turned away from the window, slumped down into the leather armchair and kicked off her shoes. Rookery Grange had come to her through a family tragedy, one of murder–suicide. It was one that she didn't much care to dwell on, which blew 'protection' and 'eternal life' right out of the proverbial window. She took another slug of her brandy and raised her glass to the portrait hanging over the carved oak fireplace.

'And you'd know a lot about incorruptibility – or should I say lack of it, wouldn't you, Daddy?' The irony in her voice was lost to anyone but herself. The portly man with silver hair and unkind eyes looked down on her. It never mattered where in the room she stood, those eyes followed her, judged her, and ultimately sentenced her, as much as the man himself had sentenced her so many years ago.

'Life imprisonment, wasn't it, Daddy?'

Eleanor's prison hadn't held bars; it didn't have a key and there was no prospect of parole. Her prison was like no other prison, and it held something more terrifying.

It held a terrible secret.

Eleanor grabbed the brandy decanter from the drinks table next to her and topped up her glass, slopping the overspill onto her skirt. Any other time she would have cared, but not today; today was a day to be indulgent with sorrow and alcohol, to bemoan the life she had inherited and mourn the one she had never achieved.

She tipped the glass to the portrait again. 'No travels, no love, and more importantly, no children, so what am I going to do with this place when I curl up my toes and shuffle off this mortal coil? I'll tell you what: nothing! Absolutely bloody nothing. It can rot for all I care, or burn to the ground.' Her eyes stung with the tears she refused to shed. She took another gulp of her drink, relishing the burn as it slid down her throat. Rookery Grange had been her casket for the living, so a full-blown cremation would be very apt.

She cursed herself for having highlighted her concerns over the death of Dorothy Burnside. She, and she alone, was to blame for the circus that followed. A murder of all things, one that could threaten her livelihood and her sanity. Her kindness and loyalty to Dottie had well and truly blown up in her face. If Rookery Grange Retreat was forced to close down, she would be left rattling around the rooms and corridors alone – and that was something she just couldn't bear to think about.

'Thanks for nothing, Daddy,' she whispered, as she slipped into a drunken slumber.

Pru stood outside the door to Eleanor's office at Rookery Grange, knuckles poised. Eleanor had fallen silent at last. She was unsure if she had been on the telephone or was just simply talking out loud to herself. Not quite being able to make out the words said, she had waited.

Now she tapped lightly on the door. 'Miss Parsons?' She gave a respectful few seconds before she tried knocking again. 'Eleanor, it's Pru.' The next few seconds were spent examining her nails, picking at imaginary fluff from her jumper and winding a lock of hair around her index finger. She felt like a naughty child waiting for the headmistress to call her in. Feeling a little embarrassed when her knocks went unanswered, she feigned interest in a large leather-bound book on the console table in the entrance hall. Her fingers traced the embossed lettering across the front.

BEYOND THE WALLS OF ROOKERY GRANGE

Ooh, interesting... She was just about to plunge into its pages when a commotion from the lounge drew her attention away.

'It's mine! Give it back right this minute!'

Pru didn't have to look to know who the voice belonged to. She lifted her eyes to the heavens and sighed before making her way back to where she had left the residents supposedly enjoying books of their choosing from her trolley. 'Goodness me, it's like a kindergarten in here. I've barely left you for five minutes,' she chastised.

Goldie Franklin had niftily utilised her wheelchair to pin Gertrude Postlethwaite from Room 5 up against the wood-panelled wall. A copy of Conan Doyle's *The Sign of The Four* lay on the floor between them. Gertrude, at a sprightly eighty years of age, wasn't going down without a fight. She was frantically pummelling Goldie's French chignon with a red velvet cushion she had grabbed from a nearby chair.

'Incoming...' Winnie shouted with a touch of comedy drama as Norma Appleton from Room 4 joined in the foray with a well-aimed haemorrhoid relief pillow. Heartily laughing as she watched the entertainment unfold before her, Winnie couldn't believe how much fun being in an old folks' home could be.

The pillow landed hard at the side of Goldie's head, sending her ornate hair comb flying through the air.

'Bitch...' hollered Goldie.

'Witch...' screamed Gertrude.

'Itch...' yelled Norma as she giggled and jiggled in her chair to show what the best use and subsequent relief had been of her just launched pillow.

As the whole room dissolved into a free for all, Pru's pleas for calm were drowned out by the banshee wailing and laughter of the residents of Rookery Grange. In sheer panic at losing control of her charges, she resorted to the next best thing. Grabbing the ornamental mallet from the brass display gong, she savagely attacked it.

Boing.

Boing.

Boing...

The room fell silent.

'Ooh fabulous! Lunchtime, everyone. I'm starving!' Goldie jammed her chair into reverse, allowing poor Gertrude the space to escape. The dog-eared edition of *The Sign of the Four*, the cause of all the commotion and geriatric violence, lay forgotten on the floor as she wheeled over it, the slight bump not fazing her in the slightest. Norma happily retrieved her haemorrhoid pillow and followed in Goldie's wake.

Winnie gave Pru a wry smile. 'Well, I can honestly say there's never a dull moment here at Rookery Grange Retreat, Prunella. You never know, I just might stay here a little bit longer...'

Pru gave Winnie a reassuring pat on the shoulder, but her heart sank. Winnie staying longer meant that she would have to ensure she kept tabs on the Four Wrinkled Dears for longer too, particularly as she'd failed to speak to Eleanor for added confirmation that what had happened to Winnie really had been an unfortunate accident. Winnie didn't seem the least bit concerned; in fact, she was positively enjoying her stay at Rookery Grange, an observation she would be sure to pass on to Clarissa and Ethel. She bent down and picked up Sir Arthur's work. Reverently wiping her hand across the cover, she checked it for damage before placing it back on the shelf of her trolley. She checked her watch.

'Looking forward to getting home, Pru?' Winnie's eyes twinkled. 'I know it's been a few years since I've had someone to rush home to, but I'd be skipping as fast as my arthritic knees would let me if I had someone like your gorgeous detective waiting for me.'

Pru gave a coy smile. 'He certainly has a huge influence on my getting home quickly, Winnie, but not tonight; he's working late.

It'll just be me and Mr Binks, a nice bottle of red wine and *Doc Martin* on TV.'

Winnie manoeuvred her wheelchair around Pru, the wheels emitting a mouse-like squeak, and fondly placed her hand on Pru's arm. 'Well, dear, you have a lovely night, you deserve it, but maybe slippers would be more comfortable than those clumpy Doc Marten things…' She pushed off, squeaking her way through the open door before gaily giving Pru another snippet of advice. 'They're buggers for making your feet sweaty too!' She laughed as she disappeared out into the corridor.

UNDER THE COVERS

'This is rather cosy, isn't it?' Ethel's hand delved into the large bag of Doritos that were sitting on the coffee table, alongside two bowls of popcorn, four schooners of sherry and a bag of Walkers cheese and onion crisps.

Clarissa busied herself around her little cottage, happily listening to the chattering of her best friends, Millie, Hilda and, of course, Ethel, the closest of them all, as they tucked into the nibbles she had purchased from Betty's Village Store and the several bottles of sweet sherry she had discreetly smuggled out of The Guilty Grape off-licence in her polyester shopping bag. She wasn't exactly ashamed to be purchasing liquor on a school night, but she did feel a little embarrassed at the quantity. The bottles had unfortunately given the game away when she had slipped in the snow outside Dylan's Dispensary. Desperate to protect her purchases, she had flung her shopper out in front of her, falling heavily on her well-padded rump. As luck would have it, Jason from the Dog & Gun was passing, and being the gentleman he was, he had carefully helped her to her feet before retrieving her bag from a small snow drift. The grin on his face said it all as she hurriedly made her way back home, the bottles clinking and rattling against her thigh as she went.

Millie placed her glass onto the rattan coaster. 'Nice bit of sherry, Clarissa, one can always tell it's Harveys. That's class for you.'

'Harvey who?' Hilda huffed. 'I certainly hope we're not having a man interfering with us this evening, Clarissa; it's supposed to be a girly night!' She paused long enough to cram a handful of popcorn into her mouth.

Ethel chortled loudly. 'Chance would be a fine thing! I've got my Albie at home, and I'll have you know he hasn't interfered with me since Wednesday 22 June 1983!' She slapped her own leg to evidence the quick delivery of her saucy punchline.

'Ooee, look at you getting a bit of "how's yer father" on a weekday, you wicked, wicked woman!' Clarissa toasted Ethel with her glass in admiration.

'Huh, says the woman who named her house "Cougar's Cottage". I mean honestly, I'm surprised you haven't had hordes of gentleman callers from the Winterbottom Crown Green Bowling club lining up outside your front door!' Ethel gave Hilda and Millie an overexaggerated wink.

'It was supposed to be "Coopers Cottage"! C – o – o – p – e – r – s.' Clarissa spelt out each individual letter. 'That idiot sign-maker in Chapperton Bliss couldn't read my writing. It was a nod to the history of my cottage; the village barrel-maker lived here in the early 1900s.'

'Yes, if you say so, dear.' Ethel sniggered as she tipped her glass at her three friends. 'Right, shall we get down to business? The Four Wrinkled Dears are going to be back in action, so I'll raise my glass to that!'

Huddled together, the log fire cracking and hissing as it cast a warm, comforting glow to the cosy room, the friends plotted and planned the protection of their good friend, Winnifred Clementine Clegg. Ideas were thrown onto the table, some agreed upon, some discounted, some put on the 'maybe' list, until finally they were happy with their plan.

'So, that's agreed. One of us will go undercover.' Ethel, her shoulders almost touching her ears in unadulterated glee, wildly waved an arm in the air, putting herself forward. 'I think it should be me; I'd be good at it.'

Clarissa poured a little more sherry into Ethel's glass, more as a consolation due to what she was about to suggest. 'No, Ethel, not you or Millie, and definitely not you, Hilda.' She saw the disappointed look on Hilda's face, and quickly offered an explanation. 'No offence, dear, but with your memory you'd forget why you were there within the first half hour. No, it is down to me to take the risk. I'm perfect for it. No husband, no children, no relatives to speak of. I'll be the best candidate to become a resident at the Rookery Grange Retreat to avail myself of their nursing care and services – and look, I've already got something to be recovering from.' She stood up, bent over and hoisted up her skirt.

'Bloody hell, Clarissa, the last time I saw a rear end like that it had a lion hanging off it!' Ethel dissolved into a fit of the giggles at her own joke.

Undeterred, Clarissa exuberantly pointed to her left butt cheek, the one that had taken most of the impact in her earlier fall. 'Look at that bruise! It's an absolute corker; it's a perfect guise for being at Rookery…'

Three of the Four Wrinkled Dears intently watched the reflection of the fire glow from Clarissa's bum, the vivid purple and green of the massive haematoma stark against pale skin and her white Marks & Spencer knickers.

After a few seconds had passed in stunned silence, Millie broke the impasse. 'Okay, Clarissa, you win. You're "it".'

AN IMPOSSIBLE TASK

JUNE 1990

*B*eryl Byrd shuffled along the east wing corridor of Rookery Grange, spreading dust motes into the stagnant air as she went. A shaft of sunlight from the stained-glass window illuminated them, just as a spotlight would an actor on the stage. They drifted and floated lazily in the haze. She checked her list, licked the end of her pencil, placed a tick beside 'Master Bedroom', and then returned it to the top pocket of her overall.

'Four rooms down, eight to go,' she mumbled to herself. Flinging open the door to the Florence guest room she stood on the threshold, hands on hips, and surveyed the room. It broke her heart to see the soul ripped out of her beloved Rookery Grange. She crept in quietly and waited, listening for anything out of the ordinary. She felt as though her very presence would disturb old ghosts.

Tap, tappety, tap...

Beryl smiled to herself. Anyone else could be forgiven for thinking a spectre from the 'other side' was asking to come in, but she was part of the fabric of this old manor house and knew better. She had been its live-in housekeeper for more years than she cared to remember, so every creak, groan and whisper the house could hauntingly produce, she was already familiar with. Her fingers caressed the turned brass knob of the bedhead before settling on the counterpane, the tapping of weathered ivy strands outside the window continuing their windy drumbeat on the glass as she began to fold the floral quilt from corner to corner. 'I shall miss you, Rookery Grange, no doubt about that,' she sighed.

Her task, given to her and handsomely paid for by Charter Willis & Company, Solicitors, was to put Rookery Grange to sleep. She was to close the house down, pending the outcome of probate proceedings after the passing of Mr and Mrs Carnell, and say goodbye to her job and her home. The new owner-to-be of Rookery Grange had made it very clear that he did not want her or any of the services that she could offer. In truth, she was virtually saying goodbye to her whole life as there was nothing waiting for her outside in the real world. She used the heel of her hand to savagely brush away a tear that had the temerity to escape from one eye. She swallowed hard, pushing down the tight pain as her throat constricted. 'Well I'll tell you now, I won't leave without taking a little something for myself, not with what I know...' She spoke to her own reflection in the tarnished vanity mirror of the dressing table.

Beryl had accidentally been privy to a very confidential conversation between old Jacobs, the Carnell family solicitor, and Raif Carnell's brother, Sebastian. Sebastian had been named as executor of the estate and he was to manage the interests of the two children, Violet and Vincent. Or at least that's what he was supposed to do.

'It's bloody dynamite, that's what it is. I just need to pick my time...' She flicked an imaginary dust speck from the top of the bedside cabinet as she left the room, confident that her future would be rosy and secure. She closed the door quietly behind her.

'Beryl... come here, will you? I need to speak to you.'

Beryl froze as the commanding voice travelled along the corridor to reach her ears. She didn't want to turn back, to come face to face with him just yet, but she had no choice. There was no escape ahead of her. She straightened her overall and tried to smile, the tic of her top lip producing more of a grimace than a sign of pleasantries to be passed. She forced herself to speak.

'Of course, Mr Carnell, just coming...'

∾

Rookery Grange had fallen silent.

His silhouette cast an eerie, elongated shadow along the corridor, backlit by the moon piercing the immense stained-glass window over the galleried landing. He bent over her, his face almost touching hers as he ensured there were no signs of life. He felt a little sad that he hadn't taken the time, as any good employer would do, to explain why she had been so brutally dismissed from her position at Rookery Grange. Maybe a few words now would alleviate any future guilt for him.

'You were such a nosy old biddy, Beryl; eavesdroppers rarely hear things that will benefit them.' He grinned. He made one final check to ensure that Beryl hadn't decided to fool him with an extra breath, a sudden heartbeat or a faint pulse.

Satisfied that he had carried out his own task to perfection, he set about the next part of the plan. He grabbed her by both ankles and began to pull.

Poor Beryl, her eyes bulbous and glazed, a look of abject terror on her face, suddenly became a makeshift carpet sweeper. Her body dragged along the same Axminster runner that she had only hours before hoovered and straightened as part of her final chores. Every few yards he had to stop to unravel the runner as it rumpled up beneath her, whilst cursing her corpulent figure and bemoaning the fact that he should have been more aware of what Beryl had been snaffling from the fridge and larders of Rookery Grange.

Swish.

He rounded the corner, moving towards the west wing.

Thwump…

He let out a muffled chuckle. That had been Beryl's head accidentally meeting the ornate console table. He paused, holding his breath as a very valuable collectable, the Lladró Allegory to Peace statue, wobbled precariously on the top. He was in two minds: to either drop Beryl's legs and make a grab for it, or just wait it out in the vain hope it would settle and remain safe on its own accord. As it was, his reactions were too slow, so the latter option was the only one available to him.

It teetered momentarily, but much to his relief found its original place.

As the seconds passed, he suddenly remembered to breathe again. That was all he needed. To pass out and be discovered lying slumped across his victim would be embarrassing at the least and a prison sentence at the most. He'd have a hell of a job explaining that one away. He continued in his quest, taking each corridor and turn in his stride. He was so focused on the task at hand he was totally oblivious to the soft click of the Mornington Suite door as it closed, hiding its occupant from view. He made his way around the next corner, leaving his unexpected witness behind.

Failing to take into account Beryl's weight, the damned Axminster carpeting all through Rookery Grange and the never-ending stairs, had made the job of removing her lifeless body to the cellar more difficult than he had anticipated. He hauled her over the top step of the servants' staircase and began his descent.

Bump.

Bump.

Bump.

He counted thirty-seven loud bumps as Beryl's head hit every stair. It amused him that they were almost rhythmic in their pattern. By the time he had reached halfway down the first flight he was singing MC Hammer's 'U Can't Touch This' as Beryl's body produced the near perfect beat to accompany his voice.

Ten minutes later he had finally reached his destination. Beryl lay crumpled on the cellar floor, her broken limbs angled and spread like a crab. The final flight down had done more damage to her than he had expected, not that she would be worrying about that now. He surveyed his tools.

Chisel, lump hammer, trowel and two bags of mortar.

He pulled on the hidden lever of the floor-to-ceiling wine shelves. Vintage bottles of 1970 Chateau Lafleur and Quinta do Noval rolled in *their hutches as the huge unit swung out across the floor. His fingers probed the aged brick of the wall behind, searching for the right place to start.*

Picking up the lump hammer, he found his spot and with much gusto and enthusiasm, he made his first strike.

TOTAL RECALL

'Here you go, Sarge.' Lucy jumped into the passenger seat and chucked a white paper bag at Andy. He gratefully accepted it and peeked inside as his stomach simultaneously grumbled.

'Bacon?'

'Yep, as you asked, together with brown sauce.' She took a bite of her own butty, quickly wiping the drip of ketchup from her chin. 'Where to now?'

Andy dropped a pink folder on her lap. 'Follow-ups on staff members from Rookery Grange; see if they've recollected anything different from their first account statements.' He nodded his head to the folder to clarify its contents. 'It'll be good to see them in their own home environment, and then back to Rookery to have a quick chat with Eleanor.'

They sat in silence as they hungrily devoured their sandwiches. It had been an early morning start with no chance for breakfast or even a cup of tea, as Lucy had testily grumbled. Duncan 'Drainpipe' was still on the loose, the early morning warrant at Juniper Gardens had produced nothing more than several bin bags full of festering food, a shattered door frame from the red painted enforcer, and several uniform bobbies wiping their boots on the grass verge on the way out. DI Holmes was apoplectic with frustration, and once the burglary team had been torn off a strip he had turned his attention to Andy and his murder team.

Andy wiped his fingers on the paper bag, scrunched it up and shoved it in the centre console. 'Remind me to stick that in the bin when we find one.' The last thing he needed was a bollocking for vehicle neglect on top of his failure to progress the Burnside case.

'I've gone over and over on what we've got so far for Dorothy, but there's nothing jumping out that would indicate a motive.' Lucy used her pen to scratch an itch over her left shoulder before utilising it as a pointer on one of the statements she'd taken out of the folder. Without a motive, any investigation was made so much more difficult. 'Means, opportunity and motive' was the mantra they all worked from. They had the means; the opportunity was simple, but it was the final part that was evading them. 'Apart from her sexuality, she was just a gentle soul who wouldn't harm a fly according to everyone I've spoken to. No other scandal, apart from her "asparagus" possession.' Lucy executed two air quotes with her fingers and smiled. 'No other love interests that we know of since the death of her long-term girlfriend in Amsterdam. It appears she just devoted her life to her charges wherever she was in the world, and that was her focus.' She returned the paperwork to the folder and sighed. 'Honestly, it's beyond me why anyone would want to harm an elderly, bed-bound lady who has really lived a pretty ordinary and simple life – apart from her foray into drug-taking.'

Andy turned on the ignition. 'That's our next line of investigation: her employment record. We need to trace everyone who employed her, and where she worked. Who's first on the list from the actual day of the murder?'

'Della Atkins. She's the cook, but she also does activities with the residents every other Saturday. Her statement is pretty straightforward: she was in the kitchen downstairs so didn't see anything significant at the time of the murder. All she did was plate up the lunch that was taken to Dorothy just after midday by another member of staff.' Lucy shuffled the papers, trying to find one potential witness that would make a further interview worthwhile. 'Here we go. We've got this one.' She held it aloft. 'She's one of the auxiliaries; in fact, she's the one who discovered Dorothy. She's got to be high priority, Andy.'

The terraced cottage in Chapperton Bliss sat opposite a small green that was now decked with snow. Snowballs were being hurled by young children dressed in knitted hats and scarves, with mittens to match. A lopsided snowman with a bent carrot nose had pride of place in the middle. A path of muddy green, where his body and head had been rolled and turned to pick up the snow, led to a young woman sitting on a nearby bench, her hands around a steaming mug; she intently watched the children play whilst warming herself with its contents.

Andy and Lucy stood on the doorstep of 6 Lilac Lane. It took a while before the door was answered by a waif-like young girl, her hair swept up in a high ponytail. As the door opened, a large cat sneakily inched around her legs and took the opportunity to disappear over the wall into the neighbour's garden.

'Jenny Smith?' Lucy produced her warrant card and identification. 'We're from Winterbridge CID investigating Dorothy Burnside's death. I wonder if we might have a quick chat, just to go over your statement?'

Jenny's eyes grew wide and her demeanour stiffened. 'Yes, that's me, I... oh... gosh, yes. Please come in.'

Her home was extraordinarily neat; nothing was out of place or gave the appearance of not being suitable for its surroundings.

Lucy was amazed that even the cushions on the small two-seater sofa didn't have a crease or a wrinkle in them, and the curtains were regimentally aligned, as though each fold had been measured to perfection to match. A large bookcase on the far wall was a vision to behold. Every book was placed with precision and they were all sectioned according to cover colour. Lucy had only ever seen such a display on an Instagram post. Her eye picked up several antique and well-used books that seemed out of place, but they had been positioned according to their size rather than colour.

Jenny noticed Lucy's interest in her home. Her fingers plucked nervously at the tie-cord to her hoodie jumper and her eyes darted around the room, as if she was seeing it through someone else's eyes for the first time. 'I have OCD,' she whispered, as though she was apologising for her condition. 'It can be such a pain sometimes. I mean, who on earth counts how many bricks there are on a fireplace before dividing them to find the middle so a Sainsbury's candle is dead centre, hey?' She gave an embarrassed giggle.

Lucy gave her a reassuring smile back. 'Then you'll be a perfect witness; your attention to detail will be amazing. If it helps, I'm a little bit the same too. I straighten pictures in people's houses.'

Jenny relaxed a little. 'Really? Gosh I'm so glad it's not just me. Would you like a cup of tea?'

Andy took a backseat; he could see how Lucy had made a connection with Jenny. He waited to be invited to sit, whilst hoping she would agree to the cuppa. The bacon butty had left him with a raging thirst.

Ten minutes later the three of them were deep in conversation, with Lucy taking notes.

'So, apart from Miss Burnside being deceased, was there anything else you noticed that was out of the ordinary? Did you see anyone entering or leaving her room during the lunchtime service?' Andy waited; his mental fingers crossed in the hope that something would come from this interview.

Jenny thought for a moment. 'No, not really. There was just me doing the lunches. Two of the nurses had been round doing the meds for those that have to take them with food. One was Susie Baines, but I can't remember the name of the other one. She doesn't often cross over on my shift. Like me, she's new to Rookery. In fact, we both started on the same day.'

Lucy made a note to cross reference with the statements already taken. 'Anything else, Jenny? I know you regularly looked after Dorothy; we got that from the residents list, so you would have been quite familiar with her room?'

Andy shifted uncomfortably in his chair. He hadn't dared lean back on the cushions; he'd noticed Jenny's look of despair when he first sat down. Now his back was aching; he hadn't sat this regimented since police training school.

Jenny glanced upwards and then looked to the left. A good sign of recall and honesty. Her eyes crinkled as she thought. 'Yes, there was one thing I thought was a bit odd…'

Andy and Lucy simultaneously leant forward, all ears.

'…She was always writing things down; she said it was going to be her life story. It was her journal, and it had roses on the front. She kept it on her bedside cabinet, so it was always within reach.'

'What about it?' Andy flicked through his exhibit notes, looking for any mention of it. He discreetly shook his head at Lucy. 'It's not listed on here.'

'That's just it…' Jenny interrupted. '…It was missing!'

THE INFILTRATION

*E*thel sat on the end of Clarissa's bed and watched as the latter held up a rather pleasant floral frock. 'What do you think of this? A yes or a no?'

'It's a very large and very old house, 'Rissa dear. Don't you think you should be packing things that are more suitable for this time of the year? I know they'll have central heating, but there's going to be times when a chilled gust or two will whistle up your hoop and tickle your fancy if you haven't got it well insulated.' Ethel chortled.

'I have these for just that occasion.' Clarissa held up a thick pair of thermal bloomers with a Homer Simpson motif on the front. 'I'm telling you: now't will get through these beauties!'

'Aye, I'm bloody sure they won't; no wonder you're a spinster, they're better than a cast-iron chastity belt. What on earth possessed you to buy them?'

Clarissa sniggered. 'I didn't – you did! Last Christmas, don't you remember?'

Ethel rolled her eyes at the vague memory. She grinned. 'It was a joke; you weren't supposed to keep them or wear them.

Dearie me, you'll get a sweaty gusset in those; they're fleece lined.'

Clarissa carried on with her packing whilst Ethel continued to witter away, talking all things WI and, of course, the dastardly goings-on at Rookery Grange. Clarissa was sure she was doing the right thing, being more able-bodied than Winnie meant she could keep a close eye on her until she was ready to come home. She didn't hold with the police line that there was no evidence to link it to the poor woman's murder. When her inner detective tingled, she always knew it was a sign to trust her instincts. She zipped up her toiletry bag and placed it on top of the folded clothes before closing her suitcase.

'Isn't this going to cost you a fortune, 'Rissa, not to mention how you managed to wangle your way in at short notice?' Ethel pushed an arm into the sleeve of her coat.

'Easy. Money talks. Eleanor Parsons couldn't wait to accommodate me when I told her I'd had a fall, and to be honest I'll just treat this as a little holiday. It's only for a week or so; Winnie will be ready to come home by then.' Clarissa very much hoped that would be the case as it was costing an arm and a leg just for the short period she was going to be there, even though Eleanor had allegedly given her a decent discount.

'What the hell is this?' Ethel held up a brown satchel bag that had the insignia of the 8th Chapperton Bliss Brownie pack stitched on the front. 'Please tell me you're not thinking of–'

Clarissa interrupted. 'Thinking of what? Thinking of snooping around at night, finding out more about Rookery Grange and that Dottie woman's murder?' She grabbed the bag from Ethel's outstretched hands. 'Too bloody right I am!' She checked the contents of the bag. Two torches, spare batteries, rope, camera, a pair of trainer shoes from Pavers, string, chalk, notebook, several pens and pencils, and a ten-pack of chocolate Penguins. Happy that everything she would need was there and that she was 'Brown Owl' prepared, she pulled on her coat and plonked her knitted aviator hat on her head.

'Right, I'm ready,' she puffed as she perfected an exaggerated limp. 'Rookery Grange, here I come!'

The taxi journey to Rookery Grange took longer than usual. The icy roads and the prospect of more snow had brought those who had dared to venture out on four wheels to a snail-crawling pace of twenty miles per hour. Every now and then, Clarissa detected a slight wobble of the wheels as they failed to find traction. The relief she felt when the taxi pulled up outside the main doors was palpable.

Eleanor Parsons was waiting to greet her in the entrance hall. 'So lovely to have you staying with us, Miss Montgomery,' she simpered, relieved that Dorothy carking it so suddenly and in such awful circumstances hadn't discouraged a new resident. 'Jenny here will show you to your room and help you settle in.' She flurried her hand to Clarissa's suitcase. 'Jenny, case please.'

Jenny duly obliged and bent down to pick it up. 'If you'd like to come this way, Miss Montgomery, you're in, oh...' She checked the brass key fob in her hand. '...Gosh, you're in Room 8.'

Clarissa was quick to note Jenny's obvious discomfort. 'Is there something wrong with Room 8, my dear?' she asked, fully aware from her little chat with Winnie last week that this was the room that had been the scene of the murder. How she felt about being placed in this room she wasn't quite sure; she just hoped it was pretty close to Winnie's room. She'd worry about spectral sightings of the recently deceased Dorothy later, that's if she decided to put in an appearance of course. Right now, though, regardless of Jenny's lack of confirmation on the history of the room, she just wanted to get herself settled.

'This way.' Jenny ushered Clarissa to the lift which took them slowly to the first floor. Stepping onto the landing, the whiteness of the snow outside forcing more light than usual through the stained-glass window, she took in the plush Axminster runner that ran the length of the long corridor ahead of her. She counted three doors on the left, the brass numbers indicating rooms 4, 6 and 8, and three doors on the right leading to rooms 5, 7 and 9.

Her heart skipped a beat. 'Wonderful, right next door...' She could have bitten off her tongue; her head thought had inadvertently popped out of her mouth and she'd almost given the game away.

Jenny didn't appear to take notice. She flung open the door to Room 8, revealing a larger than expected accommodation. The first thing that Clarissa noted was the heady scent of lavender that was trying to overpower the smell of bleach but was failing miserably. She wrinkled her nose and tried not to inhale too deeply. A large ornate double wardrobe and matching dressing table took up most of the side wall, a single bed with a dainty rose patterned quilt, matching pillow, two scatter cushions, a bedside cabinet and a chair filled the other wall. A good-sized bay window, draped with heavy brocade curtains, looked out onto the gardens of Rookery Grange, and an intricately carved fireplace took pride of place on the wall directly opposite the bed.

'Am I right in assuming that this is *the* room where it all happened?' Clarissa chose her words carefully.

Jenny sighed loudly. 'It's got a new bed and mattress.' She nervously tucked a wisp of hair behind her ear. 'Bedding too. It's just this is the only room that's available. I'm so sorry.'

Clarissa felt some sympathy for the poor girl. She was cross that Eleanor Parsons had left this important bit of information for one of her staff to face, rather than owning the situation herself and dealing with it. 'Don't you worry, dear, there's nothing that can frighten me,' she gently reassured Jenny. 'My old mum always used to say it's the living that you need to be scared of, not the dead.'

Jenny gave a knowing smile before she spoke. 'It's just that I was the one that found her, so it still makes me feel a little funny coming in here. Stupid really, as being a residential care facility, we often have our residents passing away; we're used to it. But this was different...' she tailed off and, clearly not wanting to continue, quickly changed the topic. 'I'll bring you up a cup of tea and biscuits shortly, Miss Montgomery.' Promising to pop back later to see how she had settled in, Jenny quietly closed the door behind her.

Clarissa padded over to the window to take in the view. 'Yes, absolutely perfect, and with Winnie as my next-door neighbour, what more could I possibly want?' she chuntered to herself as she unpacked her belongings. 'A place for everything and everything in its place.' She carefully positioned her notebook and pen on the bedside cabinet and then stuffed her Brownie survival satchel at the bottom of the wardrobe, draping the spare blanket that had been in there, over it.

She sat on the bed deep in thought. There could be so much more to this little jaunt than just looking out for Winnie. Being put in Room 8 had given her ideas. She took in every inch of the room, taking it to memory. She would definitely need that information on her nocturnal rovings around Rookery Grange. She clasped her hands together in unadulterated glee.

'Oh my, what excitement lies ahead.' She chuckled before keying in Ethel's number on her mobile phone. 'This is definitely one for the Four Wrinkled Dears!'

COUNTDOWN TO A WEDDING

*P*ru kicked off her wellies and left them in the hallway to create a puddle of epic proportions. Twisting her scarf around the coat peg, she made room to hang up her polar jacket. Her fingers brushed across the radiator underneath. Happy there was adequate heat not only to retain back-up to the cosy comfort of the log fire but also to dry her clothes, she padded into the kitchen, her thick fair-isle socks enabling her to execute a nifty slide on the ceramic floor tiles. She came to a halt, wrapping her arms around Andy's middle, being careful to avoid the large chopping knife he was currently using to decimate a red pepper.

'Whoa, way to go, Jayne Torvill!' He turned to face her, planting a gentle kiss on her lips. 'How was your day?'

Grabbing two glasses from the cupboard, Pru plucked the already open bottle of wine from the fridge and poured a good measure in each. 'Same old, apart from Albert Tytherington being missing in action again. It's funny, I do miss him when he doesn't pop in for his cuppa and a read of the paper.' She took a large gulp of the chilled Pinot Grigio blush. She wasn't the least bit surprised that Albert had failed to materialise at the library during this past week: the weather had continued to waver between being pretty as a Christmas card to being atrociously dangerous for anyone who was a candidate for a hip replacement. 'How was yours? Has Sherlock been giving you down the banks again?'

Andy stabbed the knife into two large Maris Piper potatoes. 'Blimey, don't ever call Holmes that to his face; he'd have you in handcuffs before you could shout "Moriarty".'

Pru grinned and pressed herself into him. 'Mmm, now don't you own a set of your own, my Delectable Detective?'

He playfully tweaked her nose. 'That's for *afters* not *starters*, my Loony Librarian. To be honest, we're not getting anywhere fast with the Rookery Grange job, which is as disappointing for the team as much as it is for Holmes. We've had a few leads, but it has just taken us full circle. I've never known a woman to keep such a low profile that nobody knows anything about her life prior to her being a resident there.'

Pru could feel his frustration, and the way he'd stabbed at the potato was a sure sign that someone or something at work had pissed him off. 'Is there anything I can do, not officially, but you know me and research, I'm pretty good at that sort of stuff.' She kept her fingers crossed behind her back; she'd love a bit of digging and delving as a distraction to the forthcoming wedding. She pinched a piece of pepper from the chopping board and popped it into her mouth.

'Haven't you got enough to do with the wedding? I thought all brides were committed and obsessed this close to the day.' He still secretly wished that she had taken him up on his offer of running off to Gretna Green together, all this fuss and rigmarole to say '*I do*' was just a little too much at times, but he'd gone along with anything she wanted simply because he loved her. He would have married her in the changing rooms at Primark for all he cared. He watched her flop down on the sofa, not spilling a drop from her glass, her damp hair sticking to her flushed cheeks. He really could not love her more than he already did.

Plumping up the cushion behind her, Pru reached for a pen and notebook. 'It's all in order, everything is signed and ready to be delivered on the big day and the rest… Well, Fergus might as well work for his money, so he's dealing with it. All I've got to do is turn up looking luscious on the day.' She pouted her lips and fluttered her eyelashes. 'I could do with the distraction, so fire away with any research you need doing – all very unofficial, of course, and my lips are sealed.'

Andy sat down next to her; he couldn't help but admire her enthusiasm, but he knew from experience that if she was left to her own devices she would turn out to be the proverbial loose cannon. She was an absolute nightmare when she started 'helping' without direction. Opting for the lesser of two evils, he'd already made the decision to give her a task to keep her occupied. He chewed on his bottom lip, concerned. Did that make him sound like some dinosaur that didn't believe women were capable, as though he was throwing her a treat to keep her happy like a performing seal? He gave her a side glance and was relieved to see that she hadn't sprouted whiskers or started clapping her hands in glee with a sardine dangling from her mouth. He started to laugh.

'What's so funny?' Pru was bemused.

'Nothing, I'm just happy. Look, if you want to help, can you use your expertise and research Rookery Grange? Go back as far as you can: all its history, who has lived there, what it's been used for – just anything that jumps out and waves at you might help the investigation.' He watched her contentedly making notes in her book and immediately felt guilty.

He didn't know why he'd just suggested a wild goose chase to her, their investigation team already knew a little about Rookery Grange, but only so far as was needed for the background for the file. Nothing had been discovered that would indicate Dorothy's murder was linked to the house rather than to her lifestyle. The murder–suicide in the late 1980s had already been looked into by the team; in fact, the report was probably sitting on his desk now; but it was the best he could come up with after being put on the spot by Pru. He just hoped it would keep her occupied enough to not get herself, or Bree – or anyone else for that matter – into trouble again.

Pru snuggled into him. 'Penny for them!' she whispered.

'I think they're worth a lot more than that.' He took her in his arms, his breath hot against her neck. 'But I'll gladly accept payment in kind, Mrs Barnes-to-be.'

THE DARK ANGEL RIDES AGAIN

*S*he sat nursing a mug of tea whilst simultaneously nursing the bitterness she felt for her lot in life and nurturing her hatred of humanity as a whole. It bubbled just below the surface every single day of her existence, contained only by the voice that kept her sane.

But was she sane?

As a child the voice had comforted her; it had become her best friend, but as soon as she became an adult it no longer gave her the solace or kindness she craved. It was content to rip her apart one day, rebuild her the next, and then begin the cycle all over again.

Day, after day, after day.

She used the heel of her hand to punch furiously at the side of her head, as though that one action would knock the voice into oblivion.

Whisper, whisper, whisper – silence – whisper, whisper, whisper...

And so on. It was endless.

She lived a double life, each life not knowing what the other was capable of individually, but when they collided, when they came together, that *was* the power. They were getting ready to meet now, she could feel it. She could feel her soul vibrating, a soft hum like a Buddhist chant, which would culminate in fierce energy as it grew.

She could do no more than ride the waves until they released her.

She reached for her book from the safe, caressing its cover, her fingers as always picking out the embossed lettering on the front. Closing her eyes, she felt each letter as though it were Braille. Falling into the vibrations, allowing them to dissolve her very being, she opened the book.

For this brief moment in time, she was now lost.

She swept each page over until the vibrations told her to stop, her palm sensing the heat of the page. Tracing her finger slowly down, the energy forced her to stop. With her finger rigid and unmoving, she opened her eyes to reveal the name.

Walter Henry Jenkins.

~

Walter Henry Jenkins, occupant of Room 10 at Rookery Grange Retreat, slowly made his way to the elevator. He refused point blank to call it a lift; that was the uncouth name for a marvellous product of machinery heaven. Being a retired engineer, he was very appreciative of gears, cogs, pulleys and motion. He checked his watch.

'Well, well, Walt my old boy, ten seconds faster today.' He congratulated himself loudly every morning when he could make it down to breakfast in record time. This morning he took a truly admirable fifteen minutes and twenty-two seconds from the door of Room 10 to outside the dining room. It didn't matter to him that everyone else produced a respectful four minutes eighteen seconds on average; apart from, of course, that awful faded actress Goldie something-or-other, in her bath chair. She was ground floor and on wheels, so she was always going to be faster than everyone else.

'Humph, talk of the devil.' He stopped in his tracks as Goldie whizzed past him across the entrance hall. 'You are a has-been and a bloody menace in that thing; you're not Stirling Moss, you know!' He managed to whack the back of her wheelchair with his stick as she motored through the double doors to the dining room, flicking him a very unladylike 'V' sign with her fingers as she went. She was now guaranteed first dibs on whatever was on offer for breakfast.

Walter followed in her wake. By the time he reached his regular table, he was the last one to sit down. Grumbling, he adjusted his chair, flicked out his napkin, tucked it into the top of his jumper, and waited, knife and fork at the ready.

Jenny breezed in with a tray held aloft. 'Morning, Mr Jenkins.' She placed a bowl of steaming porridge in front of him.

'What's this? Ruddy wallpaper paste? Where's the bacon and eggs?' he growled.

Taken aback by his rudeness, Jenny could feel her face flushing red and a panic starting to rise inside her. Now was not the time to lose it. She hated being spoken to in the way some of the residents here deemed it acceptable to do so. She swallowed hard and waited for the anger to abate. She exhaled deeply, back under control. 'You ticked the box for porridge on your menu sheet, Mr Jenkins.'

'Aye, lass, that's as maybe, but that was yesterday. I fancied porridge yesterday, but now I don't. I want bacon and eggs, with two rounds of toast and a–'

He was suddenly interrupted by Goldie's dulcet tones from the next table. 'Walter Henry, have some manners, you miserable excuse for a man! Your poor wife might have put up with your incessant moaning and bile before she popped her clogs to get away from you, but the staff here don't have to.' Goldie paused to spear a rasher of bacon with her fork. She held it aloft and jiggled it so it swung from the prongs. 'Yum yum, look what I've got, Walt. I've got bacon,' she sang tauntingly.

Walter's face ballooned purple with rage. Jenny could do no more than stand, mouth open, gawping in astonishment at the proceedings that followed. A never-before-seen spurt of speed empowered Walter to get up from his chair, porridge bowl in his hand, and like an experienced shot-putter he launched it at Goldie. It landed with an explosive thud on the table, right in front of her.

A collective gasp from the other residents filled the room before a shocked silence descended.

'Oh shit, that's done it,' murmured Gertrude Postlethwaite from Room 5.

Goldie sat stunned, porridge dripping from her nose and chin. Large globs had adhered themselves to her right eye, hair and her damson silk blouse. She remained regal and unnaturally calm. Scraping the glue-like gunge from her eye, she checked that her fork had evaded the onslaught. 'Good shot, you cantankerous old bastard,' she enunciated in a perfect impersonation of Zsa Zsa Gabor, whilst gloatingly shovelling the bacon rasher into her mouth. She mockingly jiggled her bent little finger at him. 'And remember, Walt, macho doesn't prove mucho.'

Clarissa couldn't believe that her first morning at Rookery Grange could be so entertaining. She was sharing a table with Winnie, who couldn't speak for trying to contain her laughter, opting instead to snort loudly into her serviette. She eventually found the words. 'Oh my goodness, this is like *Fawlty Towers*, isn't it, Clarissa? It's such fun here I'm actually thinking of making this permanent!'

Clarissa rolled her eyes. 'Please don't, Winnie. I don't think my bank balance could stand it!' She sat watching Jenny trying to bring order to the residents. Mr Jenkins had been unceremoniously carted off by Eleanor and a male nurse, and cook had been instructed to serve up more bacon to appease those who wanted seconds.

'He's not a very nice man, Clarissa. All he does is moan and shout at everyone. It must be awful to be like that. Most days he just sits and tells everyone he's used up all his allocated heartbeats, that he's on borrowed time and can't wait to die. I'd hate to have that outlook on life.' Winnie took a bite of her toast.

Clarissa had to agree. As far as she was concerned, she was going to use up every single one of her remaining heartbeats doing things that excited her – and some things that would scare the life out of her. In doing so, they would make her curvy posterior twitch just a little with delicious fright.

As the room returned to a more sedate breakfast sitting, the Dark Angel watched and listened. It was most satisfying to be able to assist the passing of those who had wished so dearly for it, and Walter Henry Jenkins had certainly done just that.

How very fortuitous that the Good Book had made a most perfect choice.

A LITTLE BIT OF HISTORY

*P*ru scrolled down on her laptop, watching the pages flicker and then slow when her keen eye caught a word that sparked her interest. A large lined notepad sat on the desk next to her, two pens, and what remained of a cold mug of coffee keeping it company. The tinkle of the library doorbell alerted her to a caller. Surprised that anyone would venture out in the current cold snap they were experiencing, her heart lifted. At last she had someone to browse her shelves and ask her for recommendations.

'Oh, it's you!' She felt awful as soon as the words had left her lips; she hadn't meant her greeting to sound so dismissive.

Bree stood in the doorway; blobs of snow adhered to the ridiculous multi-coloured bobble hat she was wearing. Her thick winter boots, topped around the edges with what Pru hoped wasn't a real dead animal, were carelessly pooling melting slush onto the woodblock flooring. Bree laughed. 'Nice to see you too, you old trout! I've brought you this, I thought it might give you a brain boost.' She dropped a paper bag on the desk. The old-fashioned lettering on the side announced it as something delicious from the Twisted Currant Café.

Pru peeked into the bag, and in a sign of appreciation, her tummy grumbled. She hadn't realised she was actually hungry until she had sniffed the aroma of one of Florrie's Cornish pasties. 'I'll put the kettle on; I could do with a fresh brew. Tea?' she jiggled her mug at Bree.

'Coffee would be lovely,' Bree peered at the stilled screen. 'How's it going?'

Pru sighed as she flicked the kettle on. 'Painfully slow, to be honest. I've got the basics on when Rookery Grange was built, and I'm just going over the press reports on the murder in the late 1980s now.' She heaped the coffee into a clean mug and threw a teabag into her already used one. 'If I didn't know better, I'd think Andy is just trying to keep me occupied and out of mischief!'

'Probably, but let's be honest: mischief and mayhem do seem to find you – and on that note what have you got so far?' Bree was as keen as Pru to get her teeth into something worth investigating, even if it was 'off the books' and more than likely only for their own interest, as Andy definitely wouldn't sanction any real involvement by them in his investigation.

Huddled over their drinks and pasties, the log burner belting out a cosy heat, the pair sat going over Pru's notes, a large screensaver style photo of Rookery Grange as it was in the 1930s dominating the laptop screen.

'Right, it was built in the late 1890s by the Carnell family, who were big landowners. Carnell Senior had several factories dotted around the northern part of England.' Pru took a bite of her pasty and hastily brushed the crumbs from the desk. 'It was handed down within the family in the years that followed, with the eldest son always inheriting it. Nothing to highlight, no scandals or transgressions that I can find – until Christmas Eve 1989.'

'The murder?' Bree was all ears.

'Yep. The family at the time were Raif and Penelope Carnell, with their two kids, Vincent and Violet, who were aged ten and eight, respectively, a live-in nanny and a housekeeper. Funnily enough the housekeeper is named but not the nanny.' Pru flicked through her notes. 'The housekeeper was a Beryl Byrd, forty-eight years of age. She's only mentioned because she did a runner with the family silver a few months after the murder, never to be seen again.'

'Makes a change from the "butler did it"!' quipped Bree. 'So what's the score on the murder, then?'

'Pretty straightforward from the report, but I'm sure Andy will have access to the crime records, which will provide more than the newspaper archives do. Two bodies were found: Raif and Penelope, both poisoned with weedkiller. Talk at the time was that the son did it; he was a bit of a psycho, apparently, but in the end the finger was pointed at Raif. He'd found out his wife was having an affair and was going to leave him, so in despair he killed her and topped himself.' Pru doodled a daisy in the margin of her notes.

'No witnesses?'

'Nope. The nanny was pissed as a fart in her bedroom after indulging in too much Christmas sherry. The kids were found in the nursery. Incidentally, there was weedkiller up there too, mixed in with fruit juice, so it was assumed Raif had tried to kill the kids, but for whatever reason, they didn't drink it.' Pru couldn't comprehend any parent wanting to take the lives of their own children; that smacked of psychotic revenge. 'Anyway, it was all neatly tied up and the case was closed.'

Bree cupped her hands around her mug, deep in thought. 'What happened to Rookery Grange afterwards? I suppose the kids must have inherited it?'

Pru shook her head. 'No, it was left to Raif's older brother, Sebastian Carnell. The will all but cut out Vincent and Violet. There was a small trust fund for them, but everything else went to Sebastian.'

'Blimey, that's a kick in the teeth for the kids. So there's nothing suspicious that links Rookery Grange with Dorothy Burnside's murder? That's a bit disappointing.'

'No mention of her anywhere, I'm afraid. However, would it surprise you to know that according to the land registry, the current owner of Rookery Grange is none other than the daughter of Sebastian Carnell...' she paused for effect.

'Bloody hell, Pru! Don't keep me hanging. Who?'

'The one and only – ta-da – Eleanor Parsons!'

GRAFTING

*D*uncan 'Drainpipe' Dobbins jiggled each finger into his favourite gloves, finishing off with a quick pull on the wrist cuffs to ensure not an inch of identifiable skin was visible. The plod might know it was him for all these jobs, but the less evidence he left at a scene, the better. These days experience and hunches didn't get convictions in court, only hard forensic evidence did, and he was not about to slip up again. He'd been quite careless lately.

He looked up at the imposing building, his eyes picking out the best and most stable route for his ascent. This was not his normal grafting ground; his forte was detached three- or four-bedroomed domestic houses, not something that was akin to a mansion. He very much hoped that Knuckles Kennedy was good with his info; if it panned out the way he hoped it would, he would be definitely onto a promise of some excellent pickings from a gaff like this.

He gripped the downpipe with both hands and pulled it towards him, testing that it was firmly anchored into the brickwork. Once satisfied it would take his weight, he began to scale it like a capuchin monkey. It took him seconds to reach one of the larger windows on the first floor. He paused, his warm breath visible in the cold air. For just a second it crossed his mind that a cosy bed and a few cans of Foster's lager would be preferable to him freezing his *cojones* off in sub-zero temperatures in the middle of nowhere. He could turn back right now, call it a day and start grafting again after Christmas, but his better half had bloody expensive tastes. He certainly didn't relish a black eye and six weeks of silence if he failed in his exploits and consequently didn't come up with the goods. Nothing less than a rose-gold Cartier Serpenti Tubogas watch; one of which he had been reliably informed was available at this location, would do on Christmas morning.

'*Oh darling, keep me in a manner I'm accustomed to...*' He mimicked in a high-pitched whisper before silently popping the window. His gloved fingers felt around the edges until they settled in the right place. A gentle pull and it was open.

Duncan 'Drainpipe' Dobbins quickly disappeared into the darkness.

∼

Clarissa woke with a start. Her light slumber had been broken by a dull thud outside her door. She sat bolt upright in bed, straining to listen, the pounding of her heart confusing her auditory senses. She could almost swear she could hear heavy breathing on the other side of her bedroom door. Her fingers plucked at her bedside clock, turning it towards her so she could read the red numbers.

03:48

She threw back the duvet and allowed her legs to drop to the side of her bed, her feet feeling for her slippers. Once they were safely ensconced in the warm fleece, she manoeuvred herself around the furniture by touch until her hand found her dressing gown. She quickly put it on and tied the belt tightly. The moonlight that streamed through her window picked out her reflection in the mirror. She cursed her head of curlers held in place with a pink net; she wouldn't have time to remove them now. She just hoped they wouldn't hinder her in her night-time recce. They couldn't be considered glamorous, but they were essential.

Her hand reached for the doorknob and slowly turned it. She held her breath.

Click ... creeek.

She squinted and pulled her mouth downwards, her shoulders scrunched up. She waited with bated breath, satisfied she hadn't disturbed anyone, before slowly opening the door. Out in the corridor all was as it should be. Dim wall lighting and exit lights cast an eerie glow across the doors to the other rooms. She checked, first to the left and then to the right, and that was when she saw the dark silhouette stealthily creeping across the landing, the stained-glass window acting as a backdrop. She watched and analysed their gait and presence.

Now what would an agile man be doing, sneaking around Rookery Grange dressed in dark clothing in the middle of the night?

Every fibre in her body told her to return to her room, to ring her alarm for assistance. But what if she did that and whoever came to her aid was ambushed? She'd be putting them in danger too. There was only one thing for it: she would do what the Four Wrinkled Dears were famous for.

She would follow him.

THE INTRUDER

*C*larissa reached the end of the corridor and tentatively peeked around the corner. She hadn't yet ventured to this side of Rookery Grange, so what stretched beyond was unknown territory. She paused, trying to get her bearings. There had been a fire escape plan on the back of her room door, one which she had only briefly glanced at upon her arrival. She closed her eyes, trying to conjure up a mental picture.

Four corridors in a large square, each with a sharp turn onto the next.

She edged her way along the next corridor.

Nothing.

In the gloom of the night lamps that barely radiated a glow more than a foot from the wall, she could just make out what lay ahead. Her eyes, now adjusting, picked out a console table, with two, maybe three, portraits, and a large mirror on the far wall, reflecting back her own image. That reflection had momentarily made her start, putting her on guard, until she realised that her intruder certainly hadn't been wearing a full set of pink sponge rollers and a hair net.

Her fingers curled around the small torch in the pocket of her dressing gown, tentatively stroking the 'on' button. She desperately wanted to bring it out with a flourish to light her way, to chase the shadows, but she knew that even the faintest beam of light would give her position away. She continued on in the darkness, her slipper-clad feet feeling the way as her left hand kept contact with the wood-panelled walls. It made her feel grounded. She reached the end of the corridor and peered around the next corner.

Nothing.

Three corridors down and one to go before reaching the staff wing and Eleanor's private quarters. It was at moments like this she wished she had her friends with her. She would be leading from the front, Ethel watching her back, with Hilda wedged in between them, and Millie wittering away bringing up the rear. But they weren't here. This time she was all alone.

That final thought made the decision for her. She would go back to her room and raise the alarm; it would be so much safer to let the night staff deal with it.

As her well-padded silhouette ambled along the corridor to Room 8, her fleecy dressing gown flowing behind her, Clarissa was completely unaware that she was being watched.

The figure came out of hiding from between the potted areca palm plant and the fire escape door. He inched closer to poor Clarissa, his intention firmly fixed. His hands reached out to grab his prey…

Duncan 'Drainpipe' Dobbins had never once in his dubious career as a burglar fecked up as badly as he had tonight. The promise of a trinket that was worth more than £13,000 had well and truly impacted on his ability to think straight and remain invisible when grafting on a job.

Getting inside had been the easy part, mooching around

trying to find the right room that Knuckles Kennedy had told him about had been another thing entirely. He'd never seen so many bedroom doors in his life. The first two had yielded nothing, forcing him to make his way to the other side of the house.

Maybe if he hadn't bunked school so often, had taken the time to learn to read and write, and know the difference between right and bloody left, he wouldn't be in this predicament now. He'd lost track of how many turns he'd taken and he was almost sure that where Knuckles had said go left, he'd actually gone right. He had stood there longer than he should, holding out each hand trying to figure out which one people usually held a pen in – and that had been the exact moment he had become aware that the old biddy had spotted him on the landing. The moon piercing the stained-glass window had lit him up like a bloody star turn on the stage of the local social club.

It was normally restless kids with nightmares that made him worry, but the golden oldies were just as bad with their weak bladders and night-time forays to the bathroom. He still couldn't believe she didn't have an en suite in a place like this. He quickly slid himself behind a large potted plant and waited. He watched her swish by him in her nightdress and slippers.

It's now or never...

And with added momentum, furnished by his fear of being arrested and banged up for Christmas, he went to make his move.

As Clarissa reached her bedroom door, she had barely time to place her hand on the doorknob when she was roughly grabbed from behind. She let out a surprised grunt, her heart missing not one but several beats. The intruder's arms were wrapped around her middle, squeezing tightly.

Her fingers plucked at the pocket of her dressing gown. Plunging her hand inside she felt the coolness from the metal of her torch. She had read all about the much-documented 'fight or flight' mode in a magazine, and her determined spirit and a stint in her teens in the Territorial Army quickly made her opt for fight.

Clarissa Ruby Montgomery wasn't going to go down without waging a battle to the death. Like every good Brownie or Scout, she was prepared.

Her hand curled around the torch, and in a split second she drew it out from her pocket, simultaneously twisting herself to face her attacker. Fist clutching it, she swung down and banged the base of the torch right in the middle of her attacker's forehead. A loud 'oof' rang out as he let go of her and stumbled backwards, falling against the door opposite.

Clarissa let out an ear-piercing scream to follow up on her defence move. She raised her torch, ready for another blow should it be needed, whilst simultaneously stamping her Marks & Sparks fluffy slippers onto the upturned buttocks of her attacker. With a brightness that hurt her eyes, the main overhead lights suddenly lit up the scene. Her assailant lay in a heap on the floor, his red satin pyjamas rumpled around him, with one navy slipper hanging from his foot, the other having been lost in the melee. He turned himself to face her.

'You!' she gasped.

'Of course it's me, my dear. Who did you expect? I got your secret signal at dinner. I must say, I do love a lady with a bit of feistiness.' Captain Oscar Burton from Room 7 leered at her whilst nursing his forehead. He propped himself up and rearranged his pyjamas. 'I've never had my affections rejected so fiercely and passionately before, I must say!'

'Affections!' squealed Clarissa. 'What's bloody affectionate about sneaking around in the dead of night, frightening the life out of people and assaulting them?' She was secretly relieved that it was the libido of a seventy-nine-year-old fellow resident rather than the real intruder that had caused the rumpus.

'What on earth is going on?' Eleanor suddenly appeared, flustered and still wrapping her housecoat around her. She took one look at Oscar. 'Dear God, I might have known it would be you!' she spat accusingly. 'And you too, Clarissa! Five minutes here and already you're trouble with a capital T.'

Oscar, not the least bit perturbed, even though the biggest egg of a lump was now sprouting from his head like a unicorn's horn, just grinned. 'I think I misread the signals, my dear lady. Oh well, I suppose you live and learn.'

Hauling him up from the floor, Eleanor continued to chide him like a naughty child. 'I've told you before, Captain Burton, if this behaviour continues I will personally drop bromide in your morning porridge!'

'Is that instead of syrup, or as an added healthy extra, my dear?' Oscar quipped.

Duncan had almost suffered a heart attack hearing the commotion rattling down the corridor. Seeing a figure jump out from behind another potted plant on the opposite side to his own bolt hole, he pulled back and returned to his hiding place. Part of him felt the urge to run and protect the old trout from her assailant, but the not-so-pleasant side of his personality reared its head and won the day. Racing to the rescue would reveal himself and bring his reason for being inside Rookery Grange at 4am into question. What could he say? He could hardly pass himself off as a visitor, neither could he pass for one of the inmates, even if he bent over, dragged one leg, and walked with a limp. No, it was best to wait it out.

Even though his heart was pounding and the sweat in the small of his back was threatening to flow like a river, he still felt the urge to laugh out loud on seeing the 'assailant'. As residents and staff alike milled around the corridor, the old boy in his satin pyjamas was totally oblivious to the chaos he had caused. Who would have thought there would be two of them mooching around the floors and corridors of Rookery Grange in the middle of the night, and what was even funnier, neither of them, for all the trouble they had gone to, had got what they wanted. He would have to rectify that, though. He had less than two weeks to get his mitts on that watch, so no doubt about it: there would have to be a return to Rookery Grange Retreat at some point.

Grateful for the distraction, Duncan took the opportunity to silently slip away, the same way he had arrived – by his trademark drainpipe. But not before he had secured the window behind him.

THE FOUR WRINKLED DEARS

A crisp winter morning had made way for a chilled but bright afternoon in Chapperton Bliss. Rookery Grange Retreat looked magnificent in all its splendour against the backdrop of the snow-laden cedar trees and rolling grounds blanketed in white.

The Swift Taxi, driven by a rather curmudgeonly man called Bert if his licence tag was anything to go by, had slowly made its way along the driveway before coming to a stop outside the main entrance. Bert jerked the handbrake on and turned to face his three fares occupying the rear seat.

'That'll be £7.50, if you please.' He held out his hand and waited.

Ethel made a great show of rummaging around in her purse. She counted out four one-pound coins. 'Actually I *don't* please, if you must know.' She prodded her finger on the company logo fixed on the back of the headrest, marking out a rhythmic tapping sound on the brass plate. 'Swift? Really? Aren't they supposed to be fleet of wing? You were hardly Speedy Gonzales getting us here, were you?' She made a show of checking her watch. 'It's Wednesday already; I think you picked us up on Tuesday!'

Millie blushed profusely and quickly grabbed the coins from Ethel's outstretched hand, adding a further three one-pound coins and two fifty pence pieces from her own purse. 'Honestly, Ethel, leave the poor boy alone. He can only go as fast as the weather allows.' She gave Bert a kindly smile as she dropped the money into his hand.

He gazed at the nine coins. 'You've given me too much, it was £7.50.' Bert held one of the fifty-pence coins aloft.

Before Millie could advise him it was a tip, Hilda had leant forward and snatched it from Bert's fingers. 'Well, now she hasn't.' She mischievously sniggered. Dropping the coin into her own handbag she snapped the gold clasp shut with gusto.

Ethel, Hilda and Millie stood on the steps of Rookery Grange and watched Bert reach snail-breaking speeds of ten miles per hour along the winding driveway as he made his way back to Winterbottom, probably to regale the lads in the office of Swift Taxis as to how he had to wrestle with a feisty old dear to retrieve his fifty-pence tip.

Ethel tipped her folded umbrella into the air, pointing the way. 'In we go, ladies. Clarissa will be so pleased to see us.'

Twenty minutes later, comfortably ensconced in the residents' lounge and when the initial idle chatter had been exhausted, the ladies sat in a brief hiatus of silence, broken only by Hilda's inability to drink her tea without making a slurping noise. They had got rid of their mutual pleasantries, moved on to Winterbottom gossip, and had finally finished on the general comings and goings at Rookery Grange.

Ethel was keen to hear more. 'So, does Winnie know you're here to keep an eye on her now?'

Clarissa looked aghast. 'Absolutely not! Not with her disposition. She'd be horrified if she thought that we thought she was in danger.' She gave Hilda a dig in the ribs. 'For goodness' sake, dear, do try and drink your tea without sounding like Millie's kitchen plughole!'

'It's a nice cup of tea; I'm just appreciating it.' Hilda took another slurp before allowing the cup to nestle back with a rattle into the saucer. 'It reminds me of when I used to visit our Freda. She used to wait until we'd gone, then she'd retrieve the teabags from the teapot.' She smiled wistfully as she reminisced. 'The wily old bugger would squeeze them within an inch of their lives and then peg them on the curtain wire in the kitchen to dry them out before popping them back in the tea caddy for the next visitor!'

Ethel grimaced. The idea of drinking tea made from dried out recycled teabags made her tummy flip. 'Was she your sister?'

'Who?' Hilda looked puzzled.

'Freda with the teabags! You know: Freda!' Ethel rolled her eyes in exasperation.

Hilda wobbled her head and huffed. 'Well, if you want to be leader that's up to you, but I thought Clarissa was our head honcho.'

'No. I said *Freda*... Oh, do you know what? Forget it!' Ethel had clearly had enough.

'I think she already has!' Clarissa laughed as she caught Hilda's vacant expression. She could see where this was going. Hilda was not having a good day, and at this rate they'd still be sitting there at teatime without a plan. It was time for her to regale them with her story. She'd been bursting to impart her nocturnal wanderings, but had chosen to bide her time, waiting for an appropriate moment to begin so that she could make the most impact. She leant forward, encouraging the others to lean in too, keeping their secret circle tight.

Hilda brightened; she could hardly contain herself; her legs were jiggling ten to the dozen under the table. 'Come on, 'Rissa. Don't keep us on tent hooks.'

'Tenterhooks,' Millie corrected.

Clarissa checked around her. Winnie was having her afternoon siesta by the fire; every second breath accompanied by a gentle snore. Frisky Oscar, sporting a large lump on his forehead from his night-time foray with Clarissa and a dollop of custard on his tie from lunch, lay slumped in the chair opposite her. He, too, was in the land of nod. Gertrude and two other ladies were having a game of gin rummy at the games table in the corner, and everyone else had retired to their rooms for the quiet hour. Happy that there would be no eavesdroppers, she lowered her voice until it was just barely audible.

'Last night there was a bit of excitement here. Old Randy Rupert over there…' she jerked her head behind her to indicate Oscar, '…ambushed me in the corridor at 4am, hence the massive swelling on his–'

'Oh God, really?' Millie interrupted. 'At his age too? I thought it got more difficult as they got older!' Millie was aghast as her eyes swept the slumped physique of Oscar Burton.

'…forehead! His forehead had a swelling, Millie dear.' Clarissa chuckled. 'I unfortunately had to reprimand him with the end of my torch when he grabbed me and tried to jiggle my pumpkins!'

Ethel tutted loudly. 'He got off lightly. I'd have chastised him with a foot in the family jewels if it had been me!'

'If it had been you, you'd have been grateful, dear,' Hilda quipped.

'Ladies! Enough now; I haven't finished. Old Oscar wasn't the only one mooching around Rookery Grange last night. There was an intruder too. I saw him as plain as you three sitting in front of me, but nobody believes me. There was no sign of a break-in; nothing was stolen, so they think I'm getting confused – which I'm most certainly not!' Clarissa paused for effect. 'There's only one thing for it. I'm going to need the assistance of the Four Wrinkled Dears to solve this mystery!'

DID YOU KNOW...?

*A*ndy swept his fingers through his hair and wiped his forehead with the tea towel he'd grabbed from the kitchen.

'Eew! That's gross. Whatever made you think a tea towel is for your sweaty bits?' Pru grabbed it off him and flung it at the wash basket; it missed. Rather than bend down and pick it up, she kicked it into the corner. 'Right, I think that's enough space, don't you?'

Andy stood with his arms crossed, feigning interest in the new temporary arrangement of the furniture. Pru had insisted on moving the sofa, coffee table and pouffe to give a clear space in the middle of the room. 'If you say so,' was the most enthusiasm he could muster.

Pru wasn't slow to pick up on it. 'Well, if you hadn't been late for the rehearsal, there would be no need to do this.' She gave him a flirty peck on the cheek. 'Right, you stand there, that's the front where you'll be waiting for me, and I'll...' Her voice tapered off as she disappeared into the hallway. '...Be back here waiting to walk up the red carpet bit to you.'

Andy stood facing the wall, his nose almost touching a framed picture of Winterbottom's town square, several ducks and a pigeon, due to the lack of available space for Pru's imaginary red carpet. He could hear Pru chunnering away to herself: 'Alexa, play Christina Perri's "A Thousand Years".'

The first few bars began, which strangely enough made Andy's heart flutter. He was flummoxed, his heart never fluttered. What on earth had this quirky, funny and adorable woman done to him? He had barely a second to answer his own question when Pru barked out her next instruction from the hallway.

'Don't turn round! You're not supposed to see me until I'm halfway down, then you can look, and if you can, try and show you're stunned and overwhelmed. If you can manage a bit of a teary-eyed expression, that would be fab too.' Her disembodied voice travelled into the room, just audible over the music.

He waited.

'You can look now.'

'Oh crikey.' He knew that was the politest exclamation he could come up with. Pru stood in the middle of the room, the sweat-covered tea towel she had kicked across the kitchen now adorning her head. She had utilised two cat blankets tied together as a train around her waist, and held lovingly in her hands in front of her was the plastic bog brush from the downstairs loo. He tried to look stunned and in love when in reality all he wanted to do was laugh.

She stood beside him and waited for him to fix an expression she felt was the most appropriate for the occasion. He caught himself fixing his lips tightly together so the laughter wouldn't escape. 'Stunning,' he mouthed.

She nodded in appreciation before adopting a thoughtful expression herself, as though she had just remembered something. 'Did you know Eleanor Parsons is actually the owner of Rookery Grange *and* the daughter of Sebastian Carnell? He was the brother of Raif, who murdered his wife, tried to kill his children, and then topped himself.'

'Jeez, Pru, you have such a romantic way with words – *and* you said all that without taking a breath! Where on earth did all that come from?' He was genuinely surprised.

'I couldn't tell you last night because you were late getting home, and I was already asleep. Then I forgot, but now I've just remembered.' She pulled the tea towel from her head and flopped down onto the sofa. Andy joined her. 'What do you think of that, then?'

Andy exhaled loudly, giving himself time to think. When he'd given her the 'safe' task of researching Rookery Grange to keep her out of mischief, he hadn't for one minute anticipated she would have done it so quickly. He had hoped for at least a week or two of respite from her well-meaning interference whilst engrossed in her research. 'Okay, we know about the Raif Carnell history; it's the first thing that got flagged up on a location search. We discovered Eleanor was related to the Carnells and that she was the owner. Parsons is her married name; she's a widow. Her husband died in a climbing accident years ago. Background checks on everyone working there or as residents have been carried out with nothing of note so far.'

Pru was disappointed. 'Oh, I thought maybe I'd brought you something worthwhile.'

He propped himself up on his elbow, and cupping her chin with his thumb and forefinger, he kissed her. 'You've confirmed what we know, which is a good thing. It's always best practice to get secondary corroboration from another source. Her relationship to the Carnells is an avenue we can look down. To be honest, anything is worth exploring at the moment.'

'Do you think it's someone who works there, Andy?' Pru nestled her head on his shoulder.

'I shouldn't be talking to you about this; apart from the fact we should be discussing our wedding, this is a confidential active investigation. But no, at the moment we aren't suspecting staff or residents. We're looking at a "walk-in" theory – and not someone that was booked in or registered in the visitors' book, which ultimately makes our job a lot harder.'

Pru could hear the frustration in the tone of his voice and opted to change the subject. This was something she could come back to. She'd agreed with Bree that they would do some more research into Rookery Grange when they had the time.

Andy shifted his position. 'Okay, I'll put the kettle on and then we can go over the order of the speeches and any other little bits that need tidying up.'

Pru laughed. 'Wine.' She held up a glass and jiggled it at him.

'You always do, my little sprout – constantly!' He winked.

SO LONG, FAREWELL...

Thomas Whittle, the occupant of Room 14 at Rookery Grange Retreat, eventually prised himself away from the window. His ninety-eight-year-old knee joints were in the process of complaining bitterly to him by way of an unexpected spasm. The pain twinged and radiated towards his shins. Holding on to the end of his bed, he shook first one leg and then the other to encourage blood flow. Passing his writing desk, he paused to pick up the silver-framed photo of his beloved Martha.

'I think you had the right idea, my love, shuffling off before Arthur Itis came calling.' He chuckled at his own joke. Tenderly placing a kiss on the glass, he set his treasure back in place. Behind him, the door to his room clicked open and then softly closed again. 'Ah, it's you, my dear. Please take a seat.' He indicated the rocking chair in the corner to his visitor. 'I'm just having a little chat with my Martha. I know I'm supposed to count each day as a blessing, but some days that blessing would be for me to join her. Is that too awful to think?'

His eyes misted over; the sadness they held was touchingly obvious to the visitor. 'I can help you with the pain, Mr Whittle, if that is what you would want. You only have to say.'

Thomas sat down on the edge of his bed and folded his hands into his lap. 'Would I wish for another Christmas?' He shook his head. 'Not another one without my Martha, no. I do think I'm ready now, I'm so very tired.' He sighed. He slid between the sheets and lay down, his head resting peacefully on the pillow.

'You sleep soundly, Mr Whittle. I will look after you.' The old-fashioned bedspread was pulled up and lovingly tucked under his chin.

'Thank you,' he whispered. 'Will I see you tomorrow?'

'Maybe,' replied the visitor.

'You're such an angel, bless you.' Thomas smiled as he closed his eyes.

She silently padded across the room and sat down in the old rocking chair in the corner and waited. Her fingers caressed the worn wood of the arms as she began a gentle rocking motion.

Backwards and forwards, backwards and forwards. The *thunk*, *thunk*, *thunk* of the wooden rockers beat out a rhythmic pattern on the floorboards.

She matched the rhythm with her own heartbeat. For as long as she could remember she had an unnatural ability to quicken or slow her own heart to whatever pattern she wished. Her eyes scanned the walls and vaulted ceiling. This was the last room in Rookery Grange, the highest one in the house. She pondered her list. It would now be out of its regimented order, which would be fortuitous for Walter Henry Jenkins for a short period of time, and an immediate blessed relief for Thomas Whittle. There were two very different motives, but both had the same result.

One would be in mercy and the other would be in malice.

The very masculine burgundy-striped wallpaper had started to fade and peel, and in some places, in the gentle amber light of the lamp, she could just make out the familiar old paper underneath. Leaning across she began to pick at a seam that had parted company with the wall. Her nails made a soft scraping sound as it unveiled a pattern of pink rosebuds. A childish wallpaper, one that would have been hand-picked for a nursery. Her imagination gave rise to games, laughter and fun in the very room that in a few hours she knew would be filled with sadness and grief. She checked her watch.

It was time.

Thomas stirred slightly as she stood over him, watching the gentle rise and fall of his chest. She held the syringe up to the light and pulled the plunger out, taking in air. She gently and reverently pulled back the quilt she had only moments earlier lovingly tucked in. Thomas sighed, but didn't wake, as she held his arm. The needle pressed against his skin, puckering until it found its mark. She slowly pressed the plunger and waited.

She dipped her hand into her pocket and pulled out her gift to Thomas. Turning his pyjama lapel, she quickly pushed the pin into the cotton material and popped the back clip into place. She admired the black angel wings before patting down his collar so that it was hidden underneath. Tucking the quilt under his chin once more, she stood back to admire her handiwork.

'Goodnight, Mr Tom…' she whispered, a reference to one of her favourite films. 'I do hope Martha will be waiting for you.'

She returned to the rocking chair and began the *thunk, thunk, thunk* rhythm again.

Waiting.

She watched the rise and fall of his chest.

She watched the morning break for a new day.

She watched as the snow danced and flurried past the window.

She watched and waited…

…until there was nothing left to see or hear.

And then as silently as she had entered, the Dark Angel left the room.

A FAIR COP

'You should think yourself lucky, Luce.' Andy banged the punch down on his file and carefully inspected the four holes. He picked at the one where it hadn't gone all the way through. 'You go home and that's it – you can leave all the shit we deal with in your locker until you come back on duty. But me? Oh no, not me – I have to contend with Pru wittering away in one ear about the Burnside case, and then I get bloody ambushed by Ethel Tytherington outside my own house!' The second file felt the full force of the punch as he savagely walloped it in a moment of frustration. 'What is it about people that make them want to be amateur sleuths?'

Lucy took the first file from Andy's outstretched hand. 'Probably because they watch crime films on TV, and they think doing a bit of detective work looks easy. What did Ethel want?' She didn't really want to ask about Pru's interest; she already knew that Andy was at odds with the Curious Curator & Co Agency. If Pru had been giving him grief because she was getting involved in their case, then Lucy knew she would be treading on volatile ground.

'Ethel wanted to know if we've had any burglaries around Chapperton Bliss over the last few days, or reports of an intruder. Now what makes whatever they call themselves...' He paused to think. '...The Four Wrinkled Dears, that's it! What makes one of the Four Wrinkled Dears suddenly start asking questions like that, hey?'

Before Lucy could reply, Andy began to answer his own question. 'I'll tell you why. Because at some point that quirky quartet are going to get involved and interfere!' The third file received the same treatment as the first one, only this time he caught the angle and missed, so only two holes were visible.

'I wouldn't be surprised if they've already started, Sarge. Pru told me that Clarissa is now a resident at Rookery Grange.' Lucy waited for his response. It came quicker than she expected.

'For what reason?' he spluttered. 'Jesus Christ! Can those bloody women not stay at home and behave themselves for once?'

The usual hum of the incident room fell silent. Lucy was shocked. Andy rarely had such a short fuse, and she'd never heard him shout or be so disparaging about the opposite sex. There was no doubt about it: the combination of the Wrath of Holmes for not progressing the case and the imminent wedding was getting to him.

As a diversionary tactic, Lucy held her mug up. 'Coffee?'

He gave her a curt nod before going back to the task at hand. Another file was promptly deposited on Lucy's desk as the room filled once again with chatter and the tapping of several keyboards in unison. 'As it is, "Drainpipe" Dobbins has gone quiet; maybe he's getting his head down for the festive period and nobody else is grafting on our patch, so I don't know why Ethel was so curious.' He made a mental note to pump Pru for more information.

Lucy returned to their desks with two mugs and a packet of biscuits. She gave Andy his mug and then wrapped her hands around her own, relishing the warmth. 'Right, employment history for Dorothy Burnside.' She opened her notebook. 'We've traced right back to when she first went into employment. She's been quite the seasoned traveller over the years, but after Amsterdam she dropped off the radar. That appears to have been her last term of employment, probably because of this...' She pushed a print-out towards Andy.

He studied it for a few seconds. 'An actual conviction?'

Lucy nodded. 'Yes, for possession with intent to supply. Amsterdam wasn't her last fall from grace. She was arrested at the Reading Rock Festival in August 1977, and it wasn't just her usual "asparagus" either.'

Andy's face lit up. 'Hawkwind and Ultravox appeared at that one; the woman sure had taste.'

'According to the file, she swore blind it wasn't hers, that she'd been set up, but the evidence was a slam dunk. She was searched and the gear was found in her rucksack, a lot more than personal use. It went to court.' She gave Andy the results paper. 'She still maintained her innocence right through the trial, but she was found guilty. I suppose being in her forties at the time didn't help; she could hardly claim to be naive because she was young and impressionable.'

Andy sat deep in thought. He shuffled the paperwork Lucy had given him, searching through each sheet. 'So, she gets sentenced, never works a day again, no trace of her making contributions or picking up unemployment benefits, and then turns up at Rookery Grange as a resident the first year it opened?'

Lucy nodded. 'That's about it.'

Andy ruffled his hair in frustration. Placing his elbow on his desk he massaged his forehead with his first two fingers and thumb. 'We need to speak to the sister again. Beatrice might be able to fill in the blanks.'

Lucy wasn't so sure. Beatrice had made it quite clear that they weren't particularly close. If they had been, surely she would have known about Dorothy's criminal conviction? Or, if she did, was she keeping it under wraps for a reason? If it were the latter, she didn't hold out much hope that Beatrice would be more forthcoming in a second interview.

GOOD MORNIN', GOOD MORNIN'

*E*leanor Parsons stood in the entrance hall of Rookery Grange and surveyed her domain. The hustle and bustle of breakfast always cheered her. As her team worked tirelessly to ensure every resident had their chosen start to the day, be it porridge, scrambled egg or a full English, she was content to know that the service she provided was akin to a five-star hotel.

'Jenny, when you've finished with replenishing, can you take care of...' she checked the loose sheet in her folder. '...Goldie and Thomas? According to cook, they are the only two not venturing down for breakfast this morning.'

Jenny, a plate in each hand, nodded her understanding. 'Of course, Miss Parsons. Has cook got their trays ready?'

'Of course I've got their ruddy trays ready, don't I always!' Della Atkins stood with her hands on her ample hips. Her face, flushed red from a combination of the heat from the kitchen and her indignation at her services being called into question, shone like a beacon from the doorway.

Not wanting to cause a rumpus, Jenny thanked her and quickly grabbed the first tray on the stainless-steel shelving. Checking the slip of paper, she disappeared up the main staircase. Happy her other charges would be taken care of, Eleanor made her way into the dining room.

'Morning, ladies and gentlemen, how are we all feeling on this bright but snowy morning?' Eleanor tipped her head at a jaunty angle to await their response.

A few grunts came from Table 1, which hosted Walter. He was dining on his own as usual, on account of his unsavoury habit first thing in the morning. Eleanor had received numerous complaints on his apparently uncontrollable flatulence. Whilst some of her residents were hard of hearing, and as a result received no prior warning of Walter's indiscretion, they were all still unfortunately gifted with a top-notch sense of smell.

'That looks tasty, Walter.' Eleanor admired his scrambled egg on toast, only as a way to induce conversation from him. 'I – oh my goodness!' She stopped short as she inhaled. Her nose crinkled and her eyes began to water.

Walter offered her a mischievous grin. 'Morning, Miss Parsons. That'll give you a run for yer money, I'm a bit proud of that one!'

Eleanor tutted in disgust before quickly turning heel to make her way to the table furthest away from Walter. She relished a gulp of fresh air before speaking. 'Morning, Clarissa. How have you settled in?'

Clarissa was just in the process of enjoying a nice rasher of well-done bacon. She quickly finished her mouthful before she spoke. 'Very well, thank you. I'm very comfortable and I've made some nice friends here too.' She dabbed the corner of her mouth with a napkin.

Eleanor smiled, satisfied that things were running smoothly. 'And how are we today, Norma?'

Norma Appleton didn't follow Clarissa's example of etiquette, preferring to speak with her mouth still full of scrambled egg. '*We* is pretty good, thank you,' she spluttered. Eleanor looked on in horror as a large dollop of gloopy egg sailed across the table from

Norma's mouth and landed on the sleeve of her navy-blue jacket. She grimaced, secretly wishing that Norma had simply been 'good' as the word 'pretty' had been the one to cause the unwanted missile.

'I'm a bit concerned about my bad teethies, though. I've felt a bit wobbly and grumpy lately. Is Nurse doing her rounds today?' Norma hungrily forked another dollop of scrambled egg into her mouth as she waited for a response.

Eleanor frowned. 'Bad teethies, Norma? Are your dentures giving you trouble? If so, it's the dentist we need, not the nurse.'

Norma shook her head. 'It's just my Glenn Close. If it goes a bit squiffy, I'll be in trouble.'

Clarissa, in the short time she had been at Rookery Grange had become quite proficient in decoding Norma. She smiled, remembering all the times she had corrected both Ethel and Hilda. Goodness knows what she would do if the dreaded malapropism curse descended upon herself. Who would translate for her? She offered what she hopefully thought was the correct malady for Norma. 'I think she means her diabetes, and she's worried about her glucose levels.'

'Ahh...!' Eleanor nodded, a discreet smile touching the corners of her lips. 'Leave it with me, Norma, I'll arrange Nurse to pop in and take a reading for you. We can't have Glenn Close taking a liberty now, can we?'

Shoving her napkin up to her lips, Clarissa made a feeble attempt to suffocate the giggle that had unexpectedly escaped. Eleanor Parsons having a sense of humour was quite a surprise.

Eleanor gave Clarissa a jaunty wink before moving on to the next table, but her progress was suddenly interrupted by a very flushed and excitable Jenny.

'Miss Parsons, may I have a word, please?' She pressed her fingers against her temple and rubbed, clearly perturbed about something. 'It's one of our residents.'

As Jenny and Eleanor made their way into the entrance hall,

Clarissa, her curiosity piqued, quickly followed them. She paused at the doorway, scouting the horizon. The large potted palm at the side of the central staircase was perfect. She nipped behind it, pressing her back against the wood panels, ensuring she was within earshot but not visible between the green fronds. She strained to listen.

'It's Mr Whittle in Room 14, Miss Parsons.' Jenny kept her voice low.

'What about him? Is he refusing to eat again?' The look on Eleanor's face was one of exasperation.

Jenny shook her head vehemently. 'He'd have a job to eat anything. He's dead, Miss Parsons.'

Clarissa felt a mixture of excitement and trepidation surge through her body. Another death at Rookery Grange Retreat!

Whatever next?

AN EXPECTED PASSING

*E*leanor plucked out the fresh bottle of gin from her desk drawer and kicked it shut with her foot. It racked along the runners before closing with a loud thud. She poured out the bottle's contents, breathing heavily in anticipation as the clear liquid splashed into the glass. She held it up to the light and sneered. Not content there was adequate in the glass to sate her current needs, she added more.

Another resident gone. She doodled on the open ledger, taking in not the sad loss of life but the loss her business would take. Two sets of fees less at the end of the month. She mentally totted up the figures, which in turn encouraged her to slop more gin into her glass. Slugging it back in one go, she cleared her throat before picking up the bottle again.

'Cheers, Rookery Grange, bane of my bloody life. I can see them taking me out feet first at this rate!' Most days she would relish a respite from this place, her mausoleum. It felt like her tomb already, claustrophobic and unyielding. She stood up, intending to return Thomas Whittle's file to the cabinet. She was at least grateful that old Doc Robbins had certified his passing;

the last thing she needed was another suspicious death overshadowing her domain again.

It was only natural and to be expected that old people in residential homes would die at some point, and Thomas had well and truly eked out his last years at Rookery Grange. Ninety-eight had been a grand age to reach. She was just grateful that it was in his sleep and appeared peaceful. She looked at the paperwork Dr Robbins had left for her. The medical certificate of cause of death listed *congestive heart failure, obstructive pulmonary disease, frailty of old age* and *high blood pressure.* She threw the file down on her desk.

The gin had graduated from the warm, facial glow it had initially given her to a limp-limbed feeling. She checked her watch; it was almost lunchtime. Not that she could face doing the tour around the dining room again that day; goodness knows what other vile accessory she might find adorning her designer jacket if she had to make polite conversation with the inmates. She staggered as she made her way over to the window, her hands flailed out in front of her as she grabbed the curtain and hung on for dear life, swaying like a human metronome. The embarrassing action, giving her the hallmark of a sozzled Miss Hannigan from *Annie*, was another reason why she would have to hide away in her office for the rest of the day. Her usual cast-iron constitution with alcohol was severely being tested this time, having imbibed on an empty stomach. She watched as the Bellows & Burke black Ford Transit van came to a respectful halt in its usual place. Terry Burke, attired in his black suit, white shirt and black tie, directed his young assistant to bring the gurney to the side door.

Eleanor wanted to stop watching, but the draw of seeing Thomas on his final journey from Rookery Grange was too great. Her hand felt behind her until her fingers rested upon the familiarity of the bottle. Grabbing its neck, she poured out another measure and waited.

Terry flung open the double doors of the van, ready to accept another of her residents. A lump formed in her throat as she desperately tried to hold back the tears. Who was she crying for? Herself? Thomas? Dottie? Or maybe for poor Beryl Byrd, the Carnell's shameful secret she had been forced to keep for all these years. As the first tear trickled down her cheek, Eleanor knew that Rookery Grange still had her in its fearsome grip.

One that it would never relinquish.

Ethel, with her slice of cake, paused mid-mouthful, looked up to see Hilda and Millie being blown into the Twisted Currant Café by an unexpected gust of wind. She placed the slice back onto her plate, content to wait until her friends had made themselves comfortable.

Millie, her feet encased in thick fisherman's socks and ankle boots, stamped down vigorously on the small coir mat, leaving a little pile of compacted snow. She hoped there wouldn't be too much of a puddle once the cosy warmth of Florrie's little haven melted it. Hilda followed suit, executing an Irish jig as her fleece-lined wellingtons pattered up and down on the tiles.

'Hurry up, ladies. I have news from Clarissa.' Ethel patted the chair next to her. All ears, Hilda and Millie sat down and waited in breathless anticipation. To make the most of the moment, Ethel pursed her lips together and produced one of her dramatic pauses until she felt she had reached just the right level of tension. 'We have another death,' she hissed from the corner of her mouth. Her friends' reactions were priceless. Millie gave a very ladylike gasp and would have clutched at her pearls had she been wearing them, whilst Hilda sagely nodded her understanding.

'Yes, I am a little out of breath, my dear, I think it's all this cold weather we're experiencing.' Hilda let out a small wheeze to show her condition.

Preferring to let it slide rather than have to explain the audible difference between 'death' and 'breath' before she could get to the next part of her story, Ethel continued. 'Word in the hood is it was natural causes, but Clarissa isn't convinced.' She felt quite proud that she had 'got down with the kids' and had picked up some of their lingo whilst she'd been earwigging their conversations in Betty's Store. 'She's sure it was suspicious, so she's called for a recce by The Four Wrinkled Dears, Sunday night, 2am at Rookery Grange.'

A silence stilled their table as they munched on their respective cakes and sipped their tea, pondering Clarissa's dramatic call to arms. No care was given or consideration that Clarissa could be wrong, or that by allowing themselves to become embroiled in another 'adventure', all four of them might be put in danger.

'So, who's in?'

If Millie and Hilda's excitable head nodding was any indication, Ethel knew she had a resounding 'Yes' from everyone. 'Excellent. I shall ensure all the necessary arrangements are in place. We have an idea about how we can infiltrate Rookery Grange without being seen.' She checked her watch. 'Make a note of the following for the mission, ladies.'

Millie, tongue pinched between her lips, sat with pencil poised over her notebook. 'Fire away, General.' She giggled. 'I'll make notes for both of us, Hilda.'

Ethel ticked off her fingers as she spoke.

'Dark clothing only, mobile phones on silent, comfortable shoes, and do make sure your hearing aid is charged, Hilda. Millie, no windy vegetables after 6pm on Friday night. We may or may not be in enclosed spaces, and please try and limit your fluid intake, girls; we don't want to be needing tinkles mid-mission.' Satisfied she had covered everything on her list, she closed her book, delighted that the Four Wrinkled Dears would ride again.

'Right, everyone happy? Yes? Let Operation Bloomers begin.'

FOOLED

Frizzle stretched lazily out in front of the roaring log fire. His mistress had twice in the last hour tried to turf him out into the dratted cold white stuff to do his business in the garden, but he had let her know in no uncertain terms that this wasn't an option for a cat like him. He watched her dabbing at the love scratches he had inflicted on her forearm.

'You're bloody lucky I love you,' she snapped as she examined the red welts, each one a perfectly uniformed distance from the other. Every time she removed the tissue, the blood would pinprick upwards along the lines until all the little dots joined together to make a thin river of red. She turned and loudly hissed at her cat, making him jump, which in turn made her laugh. She did feel a little mean, but as she rarely felt remorse, regret or concern, she wasn't sure if in doing so she was possibly losing her touch. And now was definitely not the time to suddenly develop a conscience.

'Right, a nice cup of tea and a little more research, I think.' She padded into the kitchen and checked the water level in the kettle before flicking the switch. Her notes were carefully documented and clipped into a ring binder that lay on the breakfast bar, along with her book. Everything she needed was perfectly catalogued in an ordered fashion. Pouring the boiling water over the raspberry and peach teabag in her Minnie Mouse mug, she took a moment to inhale the aroma. It had a strange, calming effect on her, reminiscent of happier times as a child. She sat down, carefully arranged her pen, pencil and highlighter, and opened her book.

'Right, Walter, you miserable old goat. Let's see what sort of demise I can create for you.' She tilted her head as her index finger ran down the list she had created over the years: it was her modus operandi for murder. 'Now what haven't I used for quite some time?' Her finger stopped at just the right place. It was a bit like divining for water, but instead she was divining for death. Her finger tapped a steady rhythm on the paper as the excitement built within her.

'Ah yes, how lovely and how very fitting for the festive period: the homicidal holly or the murderous mistletoe. I haven't used either of those for years.' She closed the book and took a sip of her tea, ensuring her pen was returned to the exact same spot.

All she had to do now was decide the when, the where and what with.

'I'm a little off track, aren't I?' She didn't expect the darned cat to reply to her, but sometimes it helped to think out loud, just so long as you weren't in the checkout queue at Tesco. Confessing to several murders whilst juggling a drumhead cabbage, two pots of Greek yogurt and a packet of cornflakes certainly wouldn't go down well with Netty on Till 4. She started to laugh, wondering how many Tesco Clubcard points one would get for a suffocation by memory foam pillow, and a hearty shove down the stairs in a wheelchair. She still couldn't believe that the old bat had managed to hang on to the banister. It had been such a wasted opportunity, but one that would no doubt come again.

She turned her attention back to what had really brought her to Rookery Grange. Dottie had been so uncooperative, and she now kicked herself for having jumped the gun. Maybe with a little more gentle persuasion, she might have given her what she wanted. Too late now; the deed was done. But it had left her with the unenviable task of having to search the place herself. She had found what she had been looking for, but it now led her to believe there was something else.

Her fingers caressed the rose print journal in front of her. She had read it cover to cover several times since relieving Dottie of it. Some parts were very informative, confirming what she had suspected for more years than she cared to remember, but the rest was indecipherable. Who would ever have imagined that in her youth Dottie had turned her hand to a pretty impressive system of cryptography.

Talk about having the last *code* word!

THE HEN NIGHT

The Dog & Gun was unusually busy for a Tuesday evening. Pru was grateful that she had got there a little earlier than they had planned to meet. Her premature arrival had ensured their favourite snug by the window and a double round, eagerly purchased in anticipation of the arrival of Bree and Lucy. The dream team were together for the first time in ages, and it was for a very special occasion. A few grumbles of complaint that she had chosen The Dog & Gun for her hen night had been forthcoming from her friends, and an even louder collective groan had met her ears when she had announced that it would be early in the week to avoid having a humdinger of a lingering hangover on the day itself. Undeterred, she had carried on with her plan of just a quiet evening and a few drinks with the people that meant the most to her.

Her fingers curled around the gin balloon as she held it in her cupped hand. She watched the lemon bob up and down, fighting with the ice for centre stage. It made her feel quite nostalgic, as it was a wobbly bar stool and a wedge of lemon in the beer tent that had thrown her into Andy's arms at the Chapperton Bliss County Crafts Festival. It had been lust at first sight and the rest, as they say, was history. She smiled to herself and undulated the fingers of her left hand, allowing the diamond to pick up the light. By the weekend there would be a wedding ring to adorn that finger too, just in time for their first Christmas together as a married couple. She scrunched her shoulders up as a shiver of excitement ran down her spine.

'Whoa, girlfriend, you've started before me.' Bree slumped down next to her, transferring a smattering of snow from her scarf onto Pru's shoulder.

Pru brushed away the offending flakes. 'Your drink's there, and a bag of crisps. Any sign of Lucy?'

Grabbing the glass that matched Pru's, albeit hers had a strawberry instead of a slice of lemon, Bree held it to the light in admiration whilst shaking her head. 'I've been looking forward to this all day.' She took a large gulp. 'Lucy sent me a text to say she would be a bit late – something to do with their boss wanting a tête-à-tête with her and Andy over the Dottie job – which I pointed out can't happen as a tête-à-tête is for two people not three.'

'Three's actually an orgy.' Pru laughed, and then just as quickly caught herself with an image of Murdoch Holmes cavorting naked around the incident room. 'Eew, scrap that thought!'

The door to the Dog & Gun blew open, sending a freezing cold draught across the worn stone flooring. It reached the window snug and morphed into a swirling eddy under their table. It made Pru shiver and briskly rub her chunky knit-clad thighs, her idea of a glamorous outfit for the evening having made way for a more practical and warm pair of leggings. 'I can't help wishing we could have had our honeymoon after the wedding rather than next year. A little bit of sun on my bones would be rather delicious.'

Bree offered her the bag of crisps she had been munching from and watched as Pru dipped her hand inside. 'I can think of something else that would warm your bones and be rather delicious at the same time, and you're marrying him! Look on the bright side; it'll be something to look forward to, and at least you've got the Bridal Suite at Thornbury Manor for the night.'

Pru's disappointment was evident, but a mixture of no available time off for Andy at work due to cover, and the all-inclusive luxury hotel they had set their hearts on in the Maldives not having dates to coincide with their wedding plans, had meant a later booking. She chewed her bottom lip, deep in thought. As a little girl she had planned the perfect wedding, from the dress she would wear to the man she would marry, with her dad giving her away and her mum fussing and fixing things, as she always did. Her feeling of disappointment had now made way for an overwhelming sadness.

'I wish Mum and Dad were still here to see how happy I am. They would have loved Andy,' she sighed.

Bree leaned into her friend and wrapped her arms around her, hugging her tight. 'I'm sure they'll be looking down on you – well, that's if you believe in that sort of thing–'

'Believe in what? Love at first sight?' Lucy's head appeared over the top of the wooden stall divider, grinning like a Cheshire cat as she burst into excited chatter. 'Sorry I'm late; I had to take a bollocking from Murdoch before he'd let us clock off, and then it took forever to get into this dratted thing.'

Pru and Bree looked at her in astonishment as she gaily bounced to their table, a plethora of vibrant colours dancing before their eyes. Bree spluttered her drink, trying not to laugh. 'Lucy, what on *earth* have you got on?'

Puzzled at her reaction, Lucy stopped dancing. 'Erm… a chicken costume, you know, hens, birds, aka a hen night. Just like you said – that we should take the opportunity to get dressed up.' She plonked a yellow hat on her head, making the red crest and beak that adorned the top comically wobble every time she moved. 'Actually, come to think of it, why are you two not in costume yet?'

Taking in her skinny legs encased in bright orange tights and the padded yellow bodysuit, Pru lost it completely, laughing until tears rolled down her cheeks. 'I said it would be nice to get dressed up, meaning something other than old jeans and leggings – not you coming as a stray broiler from Old MacDonald's Farm!'

Lucy shrugged. 'Whatever.' She giggled. 'At least my legs are warm. Do you know how hard it was to stay upright in the snow with these on, though?' She lifted one leg to show off a rubber chicken foot. Making herself comfortable on the small tapestry-covered stool, she plonked a carrier bag down on the table and proceeded to pull out a selection of goodies. 'Andy made me promise I'd look after you, but I had my fingers crossed. Here you go, this one is yours.'

A piece of white netting attached to an Alice band with a plastic tiara was flourished into the air before being vigorously pushed down onto Pru's head. Pru grimaced as the plastic teeth bit into her scalp behind her ears. Undeterred, Lucy threw a pink satin sash at Bree. 'And here's a little something for you. I had them specially printed.'

Bree held it up to read the words emblazoned along the satin material. '*Brie – maid of honour?*' she spluttered, 'B-r-i-e! Luce, that's a bloody smelly cheese! That's not how you spell my name.'

Lucy gave her an apologetic grin. 'If you think that's bad, wait until you see what mine and Pru's have on them.' She threaded her arm through hers, straightened out the fabric and waited for their reaction.

Pru held her gift out in front of her, mouthing the words, stark black against the pink background. '*Prune – Bride-to-Be…* You're having a laugh!'

'Nope, and mine says *Juicy – Bride's Security.*' Lucy shrugged. 'I think the woman in the shop had a hearing problem and I didn't notice until I got home; too late by then to do anything about them, but…' she delved into the bag again and whipped out an inflatable willy balloon. It exuberantly bobbed up in the air, almost touching the low ceiling. She pulled on the ribbon to keep it under control. 'I got one of these to make up for the mistake; everyone has a todger to wave around on a hen night, don't they?'

Pru could feel her cheeks flushing red. It was one thing to have a phallic symbol bobbing around a nightclub at a full-blown hen party, but to have one at what was supposed to be a sedate drink or two in a local pub was quite another matter.

The door to the Dog & Gun opened to allow another customer inside, and with it came a fierce gust of wind and a flurry of snow. The inflatable willy bounced up and down on the silver ribbon, caught in the thermal. It swirled and weaved before making contact with Pru's head.

Boing, boing… BANG!

The explosion as it caught on one of the tiara prongs caused every head in the pub to turn and stare at the trio. Lucy looked mortified, the silver ribbon hanging limply from her hand as she sat in stunned silence. A mass of deflated beige latex hung from Pru's head with a pair of wrinkled *cojones* partially obscuring her face. 'Oh dear, that brings a new meaning to having dropped a bollock or two, doesn't it?' She laughed. Peeling the remnants from her cheek, Pru gently chastised Lucy. 'Honestly, I really do appreciate the fun element, Luce, truly I do, but shall we just have what we planned: a nice, fairly well-behaved, girly night? We can have a couple of drinks here, and then we can hit that nice Italian in town for a bite to eat.'

Lucy looked like a naughty child, a mischievous grin playing on her lips. 'Oh, does that mean you don't want what's coming next?'

Bree gave Lucy a cheeky wink, which made Pru very uneasy. She loved her friends, but sometimes when they got their heads together this could only spell trouble. 'What else could possibly cause me more embarrassment than having an inflatable todger explode in my face in the middle of the Dog & Gun, apart from… oh I don't know, how about a stripper?' She suddenly caught herself as the penny dropped. 'Oh God, please tell me you haven't?'

Her friends sniggered in unison whilst Lucy pointed to the small podium at the side of the bar that was used for folk groups and acoustic sets on Saturday nights. 'Erm… this…'

Jason, temporarily leaving his post behind the bar, parted the crowd to give Pru a clear view, before projecting his voice to bring hush to the village pub. An excited murmur ran around the room before complete silence fell, giving Pru time to realise exactly why the pub was so unusually busy for a Tuesday night.

'Ladies, gents and the soon-to-be Mrs Prunella Barnes, I give you Winterbottom's very own "Magic Mick".'

As Pru slouched down in her seat, desperately trying to make herself smaller and less visible, Bree and Lucy had already taken to their feet, clapping, whooping and hollering to their hearts' content.

As Tom Jones' rich voice crooned that he was leaving his hat on, a very familiar villager gyrated his hips and strutted his stuff around the stage.

Covering her eyes, Pru seriously wished he would do just that, or at the very least, borrow a drip mat from behind the bar to cover the ridiculous red silk posing pouch that bounced and jiggled in time to the music.

THE MORNING AFTER THE NIGHT BEFORE...

*A*ndy crept quietly into the bedroom and stood at the end of the bed. A shaft of morning light prised its way through the gap in the curtains, lighting up Pru's very beautiful and very naked bum. One leg had sneaked out from under the duvet and was dangling over the edge of the bed.

Pru had arrived home just after 2am with her very sheepish but giggly friends, who had unceremoniously dumped her in the hallway whilst giving Andy profuse apologies for her condition. It had taken the three of them to haul her upstairs to bed, an action that had not been without incident. Poor Pru's head had hit several stair spindles on the way up, making her sound like a human glockenspiel. Bree and Lucy had not shown one ounce of sympathy; the resounding *thunk, thunk, thunk* had them both collapsing into a heap, guffawing like idiots. Pru had literally face-planted her pillow when they'd got her into the bedroom and had hardly moved since. He had even resorted to poking his finger up her nose when he woke this morning, to ensure she was still breathing. The resulting snort had been both reassuring and amusing.

'I always knew that first aid course would come in handy one day.' He bent over her and kissed her forehead.

Pru grumbled slightly and stretched her arms out above the duvet. 'Ugh...' She clacked her tongue to the roof of her mouth several times. 'Eew, I think something's died in there overnight!'

'Would that be your dignity, by any chance?' laughed Andy. He held out a mug of tea he'd just made for her. She sat up and gratefully accepted it, squinting as the sudden onset of a major hangover headache hit.

'Good night?'

She shrugged. 'Think so.' She took a sip of tea and relished the warmth. 'Oh dear, maybe not.' She groaned. 'I've just remembered: "Magic Mick"!' She fumbled on the bedside cabinet for her purse and mobile phone, grateful that Bree had taken care of her possessions. Her thumb quickly scrolled through her photographs. Finding what she was looking for, she held it out for Andy to see. 'This...'

It took a while for it to register, but when it did, Andy started to laugh. 'Please don't tell me that's our friendly neighbourhood postman Eric Potter in a fireman's outfit?'

Her hands cupped around her mug, Pru just nodded. Not capable of finding words to describe her experience of Eric's alter ego prancing around the Dog & Gun to the backdrop of 'You Can Leave Your Hat On', she shuddered.

'He's sixty if he's a day, and that's not a six pack; it's more of a wok, to be honest.' Andy pointed to Eric's rather portly frontage. 'What on earth possessed him to take that up as a sideline?'

'He hasn't; it was just a spoof for me. He was the only one in the village that was willing to do it after downing a couple of pints. Just wait until I get my hands on Bree and Lucy, though. They arranged it all.' She tried to suppress a smile. Even though being plonked on a bar stool in the middle of the little stage whilst Eric strutted his stuff around her had been embarrassing, it had also been such a good laugh and Lucy's drunken chicken dance had caused a riot of laughter – and an avalanche of fallen feathers scattered on the pub floor. Nobody, and that included Eric himself, had taken the night seriously, and Pru had been assured that his fireman's outfit would be returned discreetly to Winterbottom's very own fire station the next morning, before their first village shout on replacement smoke detectors.

'Right, I'm off. I've got a long day ahead, working on some of Dorothy's previous employers, and I need to have another word with Eleanor Parsons. Take it easy today, no driving either; you'll still be over the limit.' He pressed his lips on hers, which made him wish he could just jump back into bed to be with her.

'Rookery Grange…' she muttered before taking another swig of tea.

'Me?' Andy checked his jacket pocket to ensure his array of pens were still present.

'No, me.' Pru took a deep breath. 'I'm on library duty there today; don't worry, I'll get a taxi.' She grinned and blew a kiss to him as he disappeared onto the landing.

'Love you, Mrs Barnes-to-be.'

'Love you too, my Delectable Detective.'

SUSPICIOUS MINDS

*T*he atmosphere at Rookery Grange was teetering on an uncomfortable balance of festive high spirits from the residents and despondency from its staff. The cheerful tinsel and Christmas lights that were draped around the entrance hall belied the fraught undercurrent that seeped out from the open door of Eleanor's office.

Death has a nasty habit of sucking the joy from those who are privy to its presence, and its presence was definitely being felt this morning. Pru watched Jenny slowly making her way upstairs, crossing over with Alex the on-duty nurse, who was on her way down. Sometimes she quite enjoyed being a people-watcher; she was sure the authors of her beloved books were watchers themselves – how else could they develop their characters if not by observing real people? Maybe one day she too might write a book; that would be so much fun, particularly with her muses that consisted of the quirky and life-loving Winterbottom Women's Institute members, and plenty of grisly murders to boot. An unexpected shudder suddenly wormed its way down her back. Watching Jenny and Alex pass each other had brought a feeling of concern mixed with warmth, as though they were polar opposites, one good, one bad.

Why on earth she had suddenly had that thought was beyond her. She hardly knew either of them, but what was more confusing was that she couldn't attribute what vibe to which woman.

'Anything wrong, Pru?' Alex stood her ground in front of her, head tilted.

'Oh, uhm... what? No, no nothing.' The realisation that her facial expression had probably spoken a thousand words unnerved her. 'I was just feeling a little sad about Mr Whittle, that's all.' She hoped that would explain her behaviour.

Alex's eyes narrowed as her lips set into a thin line, which suddenly made her look hard. 'Yes, aren't we all, very sad indeed, but then again, these things are to be expected at that age.' She efficiently turned heel and disappeared into the meds room.

Pru was feeling a heat of epic proportions, and not yet being menopausal she touched the nearby radiator, quickly pulling her hand back as the heat tested her fingertips. She absentmindedly shrugged off her mohair jacket and hung it on the coat stand, still puzzled at her unsettling reaction to the two women. She pulled the new books from her bag and rearranged them on the shelves of the trolley, taking care to display them at their best angle. She hoped a good cover would encourage the residents to choose one, but was always prepared to offer her own recommendations based on how well she knew each individual.

Maybe her love of *Vera* and *Inspector Morse* was having an adverse effect on her, encouraging her to be suspicious, making her imagination run riot. Then again, wasn't that supposed to be a laudable attribute for a private detective?

Pru trundled the library trolley into the day room and stamped down hard on the brake pedal. She paused to watch as two members of the occupational therapy team sat with Gertrude Postlethwaite and Lillian Williams making paper chains. Gertrude's bony but nimble fingers were making short work of the colourful bands as she swiped the glued end over the damp sponge and pinned them together. Lillian, on the other hand, was content to be her usual cantankerous self.

'I'm not five years old, you know.' She swept the bands across the table, sending several of them fluttering over the side onto the carpet. 'This sort of thing is for children in kindergarten,' she snarled. She was certainly living up to the 'Lippy Lil' nickname the other residents had given her.

Gertrude smirked. Holding up her rainbow chain in glee with one hand, she playfully punched Lillian on the arm with the other. 'You can be such a miserable old cow sometimes, Lil; it's nearly Christmas. Now be a good girl, or Santa won't be paying you a visit.' She spotted Pru watching their exchange and offered her a light-hearted wink. 'We do the big Christmas tree on the 23rd, so you'd better find your festive fun before then, Lil. That's if you want to enjoy a sherry or two when they switch the lights on. If you're going to be a misery guts, they'll send you to bed with nothing!' Being a long-stay resident, Gertrude had spent many a Christmas at Rookery Grange enjoying its traditions, and the 'Sherry and Lights' night was one of her favourites.

'Pru, oh Pru, dear... Over here.'

Pru turned to see Clarissa alone at the table in the far corner. One hand was held high to attract her attention and the other was cosseting what looked like a very nice first edition of Agatha Christie's *Crooked House*, the aqua blue dust jacket being a perfect background for the bold yellow title. She gave Gertrude a gentle smile and a look of exasperation for Lillian before making her way over to Clarissa. 'Well, I must say, you're looking fit and rested, 'Rissa. Being waited on hand and foot must really suit you.' She sat down in the chair next to her. 'And before we go any further, I know what you're up to!'

Clarissa gave her a look of faux surprise. 'Who, *moi*?' She exaggeratedly pointed a finger at her own chest. 'What on earth would I be getting up to in a sedate and genteel residential home, Prunella?' She grinned and tilted her head as a challenge.

'Oh for goodness' sake! I've known you, Ethel, and the other two for long enough to know that you being here isn't just a simple coincidence. So come on: spill!'

Clarissa at least had the decency to look a little sheepish. She paused so that she could pick her words wisely. 'Look, it's really for Winnie. I'm not at all happy with the explanation that the incident on the stairs was an accident. It happened too soon after that poor Dorothy woman got murdered, so I think Winnie's life could be in danger. Ethel and the girls agree, so I'm here to keep an eye on her – and... erm... other things too.'

Pru shook her head in resignation. She knew it would be a pointless exercise to take Clarissa to task over her actions. As always, she would do whatever she wanted to do. It would be up to Pru to minimise the damage her interference might cause. 'But you could put yourself in danger, 'Rissa. Haven't you thought about that? There's no motive or reason for Winnie to be a target, and there is still a live investigation into Dottie's murder being carried out. All you've done is plonked yourself right in the mix. What if the murderer is actually someone inside Rookery Grange?'

Taking a sip of her tea to give herself time to think, Clarissa pondered Pru's observation; not that she hadn't already considered that point herself. 'Let's put it this way; if it was Bree and the wellington was on the other foot...?'

'Shoe,' Pru corrected.

Clarissa waved her hand dismissively. 'Whatever, shoe, wellie, slipper, it doesn't matter. What I'm trying to say is that you would do the same for Bree, and you can't tell me this isn't ideal for you too? You've now got someone on the inside for your detective agency thing. It's perfect: I can report back to you, and you can tell your delicious detective.' She sat back in triumph, before suddenly remembering her most important bit of news. 'And besides which, we've had another death. What do you think of that?'

Pru was already fully aware of the passing of Thomas Whittle and the reason for the melancholy mood amongst the staff, the story having been divulged to her by Eleanor that morning when she had arrived at Rookery Grange with her bag full of new books. 'It wasn't suspicious. 'Rissa, he died of... well, he just died of old age. We all will at some point, and not every death is full of drama and murderous intent.'

Clarissa was having none of it. 'I'm telling you, there's something not right. I saw Mr Whittle the evening before he died and he was fine – but the next morning he'd snuffed it.'

Pru's eyes were drawn to the Agatha Christie novel. 'I think reading *that...*' she tapped her finger on the book cover, '...is giving you an overactive imagination. Maybe something a little more sedate before bedtime would be more suitable. Now, let's change the subject. Saturday is my big day; you will be there, won't you? It wouldn't be the same without the four of you being together.' She secretly hoped the distraction of a celebration and being with Ethel, Hilda and Millie would keep her out of mischief.

Clarissa leant forward and gently patted the back of Pru's hand, just as a kindly grandmother might do. 'Of course I will be there, my dear; I wouldn't miss it for the world.' She scrunched her shoulders up to her ears and gave a devilish grin. 'Particularly if there are any nice available gentlemen on offer!'

Pru gave her a gentle hug. 'I think I'm going to do one round with the trolley and then call it a day. Is there anything you want? Maybe a nice cosy romance with no murder?'

'No thank you. I'm happy with my Agatha Christie. Anyway,

you've only just got here. Are you feeling a little delicate after your hen night?' Clarissa winked.

'Blimey, is there nothing you don't know? How has that news travelled from Winterbottom to Chapperton Bliss overnight?' Pru involuntarily shivered; the day room was considerably chillier than the hallway had been. 'Have a little look through; see if anything takes your fancy. I'm just going to get my jacket.' She left Clarissa perusing the shelf of new books.

'Ah there you are.' Eleanor bustled out of her office and waited while Pru donned her jacket and adjusted the sleeves. 'We're having our big switch on the 23rd. It's tradition that the last Christmas tree isn't decorated or lit until the day before Christmas Eve. It would be lovely if you could make it, Pru. I know the residents would be delighted if you could help out.' Eleanor paused. 'That's if you're not going away?'

Pru plunged her hands into the pockets of her jacket whilst she mulled over Eleanor's invitation. 'Thank you. That would be lovely, I'm sure I'll be able to jiggle a few things around.' She excused herself and made her way back to Clarissa.

In all honestly, what else was she doing on the 23rd? Andy was back at work, she would be three days wed, no honeymoon and on her own, so the prospect of tree-decorating in a festive atmosphere might be fun.

Her fingers plucked at a folded-up piece of paper in her pocket. Pulling it out she opened it. Her lips silently mouthed the words that were scrawled across the plain white background.

> *It doesn't always pay to be too inquisitive.*
> *Stick to flogging books, Prunella. It's so much safer for you.*

No signature, no niceties, just a stark warning.

Pru looked around, taking in the faces of those in the room, hoping that at least one would give the game away, or maybe start laughing at their inappropriate joke. It had to be a wind up, surely?

She balled her fist, scrunching the paper in her hand, a sharp edge nipping at the skin of her palm. Her chest constricted as a sudden wave of fear washed over her. She felt like a child again, teetering on the edge of a nightmare, willing the seconds to pass before waking. She closed her eyes and inhaled deeply to drown it.

In.

Out.

In.

Out...

Until finally it released its grip and she could breathe freely again.

DUNCAN

Duncan Dobbins stretched out his legs and wiggled his toes, trying to bring back some semblance of feeling to the lower extremities of his body. Over the years he'd been likened to a circus contortionist; capable of squeezing through the smallest of windows and limbo-dancing under padlocked gates, but one night on a battered old sofa had literally crucified him. He had aches and pains in places he didn't know existed, not to mention a glowing arse cheek courtesy of the previous night's grafting exploits.

One arm snaked out to grab his packet of cigarettes from the coffee table, accidentally knocking over several empty cans of Kestrel lager in the process. They clattered onto the cheap laminate floor, noisily rolling around until they found a natural settling place. He lit his first fag of the morning, inhaled deeply, and closed his eyes.

'Get yer bloody smelly feet off me sofa.' Holly Jacob's voice pierced through him, making him wince. 'And if you fink you can lie around here all day, you've got another fink comin', you lazy sod!'

Holly had been his better half for over ten years. Her classy good looks and her inability to pronounce any word that began with 'th' had been quite an attraction to him in their early days together. Now they both grated on him. Her good looks were more brassy than classy these days, and it had only recently dawned on him how many words in daily use began with the dreaded 'th'. He swung his legs out from under the grubby duvet she'd thrown at him the night before, and nonchalantly flicked his ash into the small opening of the one lager can that had escaped his game of skittles and had remained upright on the table. 'Thought you'd have calmed down by now,' he grunted at her.

'Calmed down? You've got a bloody nerve! I've had the plod almost putting me door in looking for you.' She flung the orange and brown cushion across the room. It missed him and landed on the floor. 'I've been in this place less than a week after doing a moonlight flit from me last gaff because of your shenanigans; do you know we've not managed to make six months in any one place?' He could tell she was on the verge of tears.

'Look, babe, I promise I've got a couple of good jobs lined up. I'll graft them and then I'll call it quits.' He hoped he sounded genuine and that she would be charmed by the idea he was considering giving up a lifetime of crime just for her, when in truth it was because he was starting to feel his age. Getting up drainpipes wasn't a problem; getting down them was starting to become more of a challenge and his deteriorating eyesight in the dark was going to be the death of him. He looked at the pile of soaking wet clothes in the corner and shuddered as Holly picked them up.

'Yeah, an' pigs might fly. What happened here?' She held up his trademark black jacket with a look of disgust as the dripping water puddled on the floor.

'Swimming pool.' He took a long drag on his cigarette and blew out an impressive smoke ring into the air. It floated up and circled the yellowing paper lampshade.

She looked at him incredulously. '*Swimmin'* pool? Yer having a laugh; six inches of feckin' snow and you go bloody *swimmin'* at night? Yer not right in the head, you.'

As Holly wittered away, picking fault with anything and everything, Duncan did his usual and switched off from her. She'd given him down the banks the night before when he'd turned up in the early hours from his grafting, freezing cold, dishevelled and without much to show for his troubles, apart from a cheap watch and a couple of dress rings. The icing on the cake had been the ruddy massive dog that had chased him across a garden, which had then been trumped by his inability to notice both the swimming pool and its cover under the heavy fall of snow. The vinyl tarp had folded as soon as his size ten feet had hit the middle of the pool. As the panic set in, it had wrapped him like a tortilla, pouring a mixture of snow and freezing water into the tunnel his flailing body had made.

By the time he'd managed to fight his way up and out to the side of the pool, the blasted dog had happily taken a chew from his left buttock. Dancing a clumsy fandango with the hell hound around the barren flowerbeds had been the lesser of two evils, as drowning alone and in the dark had definitely not been his number one choice. Biting his own hand to muffle his scream as forty-two pearly whites from a very angry Dobermann pierced his flesh, he'd stumbled and rolled across the vast lawn to throw himself over the boundary wall, landing with a squelch and a thud on the tarmac of St Stephen's Road, leaving the dog on the other side with the arse end of his black combat pants hanging from its drooling mouth.

Holly flounced into the small kitchen, still muttering to herself. He hoped her absence would offer him some respite from her sharp tongue, but he quickly realised he was out of luck when she came storming back, flinging a damp tea towel at him.

'And that's another fing – where's the money you get from fencing the stuff goin'? I ain't seen nuffink for months. I hope yer not playing away, Dunc, and some other tart is getting what should be mine.'

He felt the first flush of guilt. 'I do it all for you, babe, you know that.' He attempted to placate her with a kiss, but she swiftly repaid him with a swipe across his well-chewed arse with a rolled-up copy of the Argos magazine. His eyes pricked and stung with the effort of containing a squeal of pain. He knew the sensible course of action would be a quick visit to Winterbridge A&E for a tetanus jab at the very least, and more than likely a couple of stitches. He'd examined the puncture wounds with Holly's handheld mirror when he'd arrived home and could confirm it wasn't a pretty sight, but it was too much of a risk to go anywhere public, emergency or not. It would just be his luck to get his collar felt whilst bending over in Cubicle 2, mooning to anyone who cared to take a peek at his hairy buttocks.

He pulled Holly towards him, this time making sure she couldn't rattle his backside with another glossy magazine. 'You just wait until Christmas morning; I'll have the best present ever. Nothing is too good for my babe.'

He watched her demeanour soften as a tentative smile touched the corner of her lips. 'I could kill you sometimes, Duncan Dobbins.'

He ensured her ensuing silence by planting his lips on hers, whilst simultaneously wondering how the hell he was going to infiltrate Rookery Grange again to get that 'best present ever' in order to fulfil his hastily made promise. The prize was there, but if he'd been honest about his failed attempt several nights ago, for the first time in his criminal career, he'd had the living daylights scared out of him... not by the threat of the old bill catching him in the act, or another hell hound to chew what was left of his arse, but by a cuddly old trout in pink sponge curlers and a fleece dressing gown.

CLUELESS

*A*ndy sat back in his chair, fingers intertwined behind his head, giving him the best angle to view the evidence board on the wall. Centre stage was a photograph of Dorothy Burnside. She was a lot younger than the Dorothy he had seen at the initial scene, and, as expected, a lot happier too. Her enigmatic smile gave an air of mystery, as though she knew a secret that others were not privy to. She was surrounded by notes and arrows in a range of black, blue and red marker pens.

He took a deep intake of breath, aware that the wave of sadness he always felt for his victims was on the verge of overshadowing his analytical thoughts, the thoughts he needed to keep this investigation on track. He checked his own notes against those on the board. They had spoken to Dorothy's sister again and she had offered nothing more to the investigation. Beatrice had sworn blind that although she knew about the Amsterdam incident, she hadn't been aware of Dottie's drug conviction or subsequent spell in HMP Holloway. He subconsciously doodled on a scrap of paper in front of him.

Dorothy had dropped off the radar completely from 1979 through to 2004 when she had become a resident at Rookery

Grange. Every line of enquiry they had undertaken had drawn a blank.

'It's as though she stopped existing for those years, isn't it?' Lucy placed the mug of tea and a Penguin biscuit on his desk. He gratefully accepted it, tearing off the wrapper and hungrily taking the first bite. He nodded, always mindful that it was rude to speak with his mouth full.

Lucy sat down next to him and studied the board for a few seconds. She tapped the desk with her pen. 'In the absence of anything else to progress, that's where we need to concentrate. Those years are the ones that are going to give us a lead, I'm sure of it. I just can't believe how clean the scene was. There's usually a trace of *something* left behind, but there was absolutely nothing.'

'What if it's just a random, with no true motive that we can investigate? A thrill kill?' Andy didn't like to use terms that the media used to garner readers and extend its reach, but for want of a better word, he was aware that often the thrill was the only drive some psychopaths turned to. 'Anything back from forensics on the lapel pin?' He shuffled through the file until he found what he was looking for. The black angel wings pin lay on a stark white background, a ruler next to it to evidence its size for the photograph.

'Nope, it's clean. No prints, no skin trace or DNA from any other donor apart from Dorothy, as we expected.' Lucy looked as exasperated as he felt. 'We've run a search on it, and it's mass produced in China. To some it denotes the fallen angel, to others it's a way of showing their imperfections and their failings – like if you're a dork wear this as a badge so you can let everyone else know you're a dork.'

Andy smirked. 'In that case, shall we get one for our friend over there?' He jerked his head in the direction of Tim Forshaw, who had been affectionately referred to as the class clown at the police training centre. Everything he touched usually turned to shit, leaving his weary colleagues to pick up the pieces and put them back together again. In his defence, he was a hard worker and an all-round good egg – as long as he wasn't trusted with anything too taxing.

Andy studied the photograph. 'I know we've assumed it has something to do with the case because nobody can identify it as belonging to Dorothy, but we could be distracting ourselves with it.' He really wanted to believe that, but his spider senses were telling him otherwise, and if there was one thing he had learnt over the years, it was to trust his gut instinct. 'Anything on the secondary round of checks on the staff at Rookery?'

'They're all clear; there's nothing that's flagged up. All the staff have been subject to enhanced DBS checks prior to their appointments.' Lucy checked her watch. 'I've got Tim and a uniform to do the outstanding enquiries to trace Dorothy's employers in Amsterdam. We might hit lucky and get something from them to give us another route to work on. How did you get on with tracing the children, Vincent and Violet?'

'Vincent Carnell has lived in Australia for the last twenty years; he's not returned to the UK in all that time, and Violet was last heard of living in Scotland. I've got colleagues up there doing some digging on her, but apart from them both having lived at Rookery in the 1980s, there's nothing to indicate they're of any interest to us.'

The vibration from his phone as it hummed across his desk broke his concentration. He picked it up and checked the caller ID. 'It's Pru,' he mouthed, as he answered it. Lucy watched him produce a multitude of expressions to match whatever Pru was telling him. His eyebrows shot up in surprise, quickly followed by his mouth turning down at the corners; obviously it was something he was none too pleased about. He chewed the inside of his lip in thought as he nodded. 'Right, I'm not happy about this, but there's not much I can do. Clarissa hasn't broken any law, but she's on the verge of breaking me!' He gave a wry laugh. 'No, no, natural causes, it was signed off by his own GP. You can tell Clarissa that, and also advise her not to interfere – and that goes for you too!'

Listening to the one-sided conversation, Lucy knew exactly what was troubling her boss. A combination of a quartet of Miss Marples and a duo of Agatha Raisins. She stifled a giggle as Andy became more animated the more the conversation progressed. He eventually ended the call. 'Jeez, shoot me now, will you? I've got six bloody women in my life and none of the opportunities Henry VIII had to make them behave!'

Lucy patted him on the back. 'Oh, so you fancy a couple of beheadings to add to our workload, do you? Just look on the bright side; you've got two more shifts before you're off for a few days, and all this will fall on my shoulders. I'll be the one getting a roasting from Murdoch instead of you, and as a Brucie bonus, I promise I'll keep an eye on Bree and the others at the same time.'

As much as a few days away appealed to him, Andy hated handing over the reins on any investigation, particularly a murder case, but deep down on this occasion he was grateful. 'Thanks, Luce, I couldn't think of anyone better or more capable to take over the mantle.'

DADDY DEAREST

JUNE 1990

*E*leanor clung to the door, her palm flat against the aged wood as she pressed it quietly shut. A loud click from the antique lock filled the room, and in the pulsating silence of her bedroom, it seemed to bounce from the four walls.

She squeezed her eyes shut, bunched her hands tight against her chest, and held her breath. Counting.

'One potato,

Two potato,

Three potato,

Four...

– for he's a jolly good fellow and so say all of us'

She didn't know why that sing-song earworm had suddenly popped into her head, but she knew now he certainly wasn't a jolly good fellow. Fear rose in her throat as the vision of what she had just witnessed flashed onto the darkness of her eyelids. It played over and over again, stuttering like a videotape stuck on pause.

In the seconds she had allowed herself to peep out from the Mornington Suite into the corridor to investigate the noises that had awoken her, she had been horrified to see Beryl's bulbous and glazed eyes staring at her as she was unceremoniously hauled along the floor on her back. *Passing her room with a* swish, swish, swish, *Beryl had snaked and slithered from side to side in an uncoordinated dance. Frozen to the spot, she had watched Beryl being swept along the Axminster carpet, causing little rumples and ripples as she went.*

Beryl was dead.

Just like that. A simplistic eureka moment within her own horror story.

And she knew who was responsible.

Thump.

Thump.

Thump.

The muffled sounds came from the servants' stairs at the end of the corridor, and with sickening clarity she realised it was poor Beryl's body being dragged down to the depths of Rookery Grange. She had been rooted to the spot, reliving her worst nightmare, but suddenly an unexpected impetus gave her legs the momentum they needed.

Her bare feet slapped on the wooden flooring, becoming muffled as they found the large rug. Her cotton nightdress billowed in the draft her sprint had produced as she threw herself onto the four-poster bed. The blankets cosseted her as she pulled them around her; burying her face into her pillow to muffle her sobs, she began her mental count again.

One potato,

Two potato,

Three potato,

Four...

She sat bolt upright and listened.

Silence.

The moon pushed its way through the clouds, casting a stream of white light through the curtainless window. It acted as a searchlight across her face, picking out the darkness of her eyes as her lips murmured and muttered, allowing the lilt of a nursery rhyme to float in the air.

'Hush little baby, don't say a word, Daddy's getting rid of old Beryl Byrd...'

In all her sixteen years, Eleanor Carnell had never once been afraid of the dark or of Rookery Grange itself. But now, as the blackness enveloped her, she retreated to a safe place inside her head.

It was a place that welcomed ignorance over knowledge and obliteration over memory.

Turning the handle, she opened the bedroom door and made her way out into the corridor, her bare feet finding some comfort and warmth in the Axminster carpet. Her white nightgown shone luminously, picked out by the beam of moonlight that seeped through the large stained-glass window behind her.

She became smaller and smaller, the further she ventured down the corridor into the blackness, until she vanished from sight, leaving only the sound of her feet as they touched each wooden step of the servants' staircase.

Pitter,

Patter,

Pause.

TWO'S COMPANY, THREE'S A CROWD

Fergus O'Brien clapped his hands and skipped with glee around the thickly carpeted client room in Without A Hitch Bridal Boutique.

'Bloody hell! He's like one of those manic kids' toys. Remember them, the tin soldiers from the 1950s? My dad still had one from his own childhood when I was a kid – he used to wind it up tight and let it go. It scared the life out of me.' Pru let out a long sigh that caused her fringe to flutter. 'It's such a pity Fergie can't topple over and hit the deck when he meets a bump in the carpet, just like they did.' A vision of Fergus flat on his face, his legs still stepping wildly but going nowhere whilst his hands beat out a tempo, made her smile. 'And how on earth can you just sit there, calm as you like, stuffing your face with...' she picked up the wrapper, '...a giant Peperami?'

Bree grinned. 'I was hungry!'

The 'h' in the word 'hungry' gave Pru a blast in the face of seasoned pork with a trace of garlic. She wafted her hand in front of her nose. 'Thanks for sharing, matey!'

'What are friends for if not to share the ups and downs of life, the laughter and the tears, the heartache and the love, the arrows of despair – and my chewed up Peperami Firestick?' Bree giggled. 'And just for the record, you might remember stuff from the 1950s, but I sure as hell don't!'

'Girls, girls.' Fergus gave his manicured hands another flutter, not so much in applause but more in chastisement. 'This is your final fitting before the big day, so let's concentrate. The dresses are ready, so in you go. I'll wait here and you can surprise me.' He ushered them towards the curtains. 'Jayne, the owner, will help you dress, Pru, and Bree darling, I'm sure you can manage on your own.'

'Fergus, *daarling...*' Bree mimicked, '...it may surprise you to know that I've been dressing myself since I was four years' old. I think I've got this, don't you?'

Fergus held his hands up in resignation. 'If you say so.' He sat himself down on the circular velour chaise, plonked his manbag onto his knees, and almost disappeared into its depths as he rummaged around in the bottom of it.

He didn't have long to wait. Pru was the first to make an appearance, making him quite tearful. He let out a gasp of admiration. 'Beautiful, absolutely beautiful, Prunella; you are positively radiant.' He fussed around her, helping to rearrange the cascades of silk and tulle of the Justin Alexander gown, much to the chagrin of Jayne who came very close once or twice to slapping his hands away.

'Ta-da!' Bree burst through the curtains, the vibrant burgundy of her dress adding a richness to the ivory tableau of Pru's creation. She swayed around the chaise longue, finally coming to a halt on the second dais. She took a bow and promptly shoved her hands into the side pockets. 'Blimey, I'll get at least six miniatures per pocket.' She smacked her lips together. 'Gin in the left one, vodka in the right!'

Fergus stood back to take in the vision before him, making

notes in his book as he went. He flattened out hemlines, he checked stitching, he got Pru to hold a bunch of artificial flowers, coaching her as to the best level for them to be displayed so as to not obscure her gown, and he rearranged headdresses. Pru watched Jayne impatiently rolling her eyes, and could have sworn that she had mouthed *nob* as Fergus wafted past her. Then again, it could just as easily been *God*, as to be fair she had been gazing up to the heavens at the time.

Finally Fergus was satisfied. 'Perfect, absolutely perfect,' he gushed. He stood back, resting his right elbow in his left hand, fingers under his chin. 'Your intended is one very lucky man, Prunella.'

Pru grinned and then promptly burst into tears. Grabbing a nearby box of tissues, Jayne came to her rescue, with Bree hot on her heels to follow up with a hug. Fergus, his face contorted with confusion, was thrown completely by something that he could not organise, arrange, or fix. His role was purely based on practicalities; the emotional waterfalls and high tides of brides and their entourages were definitely not on his price list.

'I wish I'd gone to Gretna Green,' Pru wailed, dabbing at the corners of her eyes. 'We're not even getting a honeymoon; Andy can't get time off work, and I don't want to just sit at home two days later reading wedding cards and shuffling Marks & Sparks vouchers on my own as though it hasn't happened. It's supposed to be *special!*'

Fergus looked horrified and quickly decided to make himself scarce. 'Back shortly, luvvies,' he sang as he grabbed his coat, threw his bag over his shoulder, and headed for the door out on to the High Street. Bree watched him desperately trying to stay upright. He hit a patch of densely packed snow and ice in his Westwood booties that propelled him a little too quickly past the boutique window, causing a case of 'now you see him, now you don't' as he disappeared from view, landing on his back, legs akimbo.

'Ooh, that'll sting!' she helpfully observed before quickly turning her attention back to Pru. 'Jeez, Pru, where has all this come from? You *are* getting a honeymoon, it's just going to be later next year, and you won't be on your own; I'll be with you. We can drink wine and have take-outs, and we've got Christmas to look forward to. Andy's off for Christmas Day; you'll be together then.' She was shocked at Pru's reaction; there was definitely something underlying all this, and she didn't for one minute believe it was just to do with the wedding. Pru was always the sensible one, the one that coped with anything and always saw the positives.

'Come on, spill.'

Pru gave her nose a loud blow and dabbed at her eyes again. 'I got a note when I was at Rookery Grange, and it wasn't a nice one. It wouldn't normally bother me, but with all this...' She waved her hand to show her gown and the artificial flowers that lay where she had dropped them in favour of stifling a snort. '... It's all too much!' She lumbered over to her bag, heaving up the swathes of silk and tulle to stop them from hindering her progress. 'Here.' She handed Bree the note. 'What if something *is* wrong? Clarissa and Winnie could be in danger, not to mention the other residents. I can't believe that I told them it was all in their imagination. If they get hurt I'll never forgive myself.'

Bree studied the note. 'Have you told Andy?'

'Dear God, absolutely not, and nor will I. He'll never believe that I haven't been sticking my nose in, but honestly, Bree, this time I haven't; in fact, I've been the one trying to rein in Clarissa. She thinks there's someone at Rookery that's bumping people off.'

'You daft bat, of course there is! That's why poor Dottie is lying rather rigid in Bellows & Burke's chiller section, but she's the only victim and that's under investigation. It certainly doesn't make for a serial killer, and I mean how unlucky could

Winterbottom and Chapperton Bliss be to have not one, not two, but three psychopathic killers in their midst in as many years?'

Pru's eyes widened. 'Phyllis, Montgomery Hall and now Rookery Grange.' She counted them off on her fingers. 'I think we might be very, very unlucky indeed.'

BELLOWS & BURKE

erry Burke slid the stainless-steel tray back into place and rammed the handle sideways to the lock position. He checked his clipboard and deftly penned the occupant's name on a small white card with a black Sharpie pen, which he then slipped into the slot on the door. 'Ada Denman is completed, Joe, she's in No. 2. I'll sign off on it, and then we can get on with the guy from Rookery Grange.'

Joe Gascoigne barely acknowledged his boss. He managed to emit a guttural grunt through a mouthful of doughnut before heaving his bulk up from the office chair. Admiring the remnants of sugar on his fingers, he watched the crystals catch in the overhead mortuary lights before stuffing them in his mouth to lick them clean. He kicked down on the gurney's brake lever and pulled it to the centre of the room, ensuring the black body bag that lay upon it could be easily transferred to the prep table. He checked the label.

Thomas Whittle dob 18/01/1925.
Removed from Rookery Grange Retreat 14/12

Terry popped the rubber apron over his head and studded the straps behind his back. He unzipped the bag and, as he always did, he took a few seconds to afford dignity and respect to his charge. 'Right, pass me the tray. I'll start with his clothes. Have the family indicated if they want any of this back, or any preference to what he'll be dressed in?'

Joe flicked through the paperwork. 'They've signed for what he's wearing now to be disposed of, and they'll drop off a suit for him tomorrow. I'll grab a gown for the interim.'

'Okay, old chap, let's get you sorted and settled.' Terry began the task of discreetly removing the navy-blue striped pyjamas from Thomas. He slid his hand along the shirt buttons. 'Ouch!' He quickly pulled his hand away and examined the tip of his middle finger. The latex rubber of his glove was torn and a small globule of blood rose and swelled underneath. 'Damn! What the hell was that?'

'What?' Joe moved around the gurney and watched as Terry turned back the cotton fabric on the collar of the shirt.

'This!' Terry tentatively revealed a lapel pin, the black wings spread out from the sharp post that had been pushed through the material. He stood for what seemed like an eternity as his brain kicked into gear. He knew this trinket meant something, but it was just a wisp of a conversation he'd recently had, and one that he couldn't quite recall. Suddenly it came to him. 'Got it! Can you get Detective Sergeant Barnes on the phone for me, Joe – and don't go any further with Mr Whittle. Don't touch him or move anything.' He unwrapped a sterile paper sheet and covered the body.

He could do no more now except wait.

'DS Andy Barnes.' Andy held the phone close to his ear, trying to drown out the hum of not only his own team, but also that of the burglary lads and lasses who were animatedly working on the Duncan Dobbins case on the other side of the incident room. News had just come in of a sighting, so there was quite a bit of excited anticipation that an arrest could be imminent.

He listened intently. 'Absolutely, yes. Yes, you've done the right thing. Don't touch anything else; keep anything you've removed from the body sterile and away from anything else. I'll be right there.' He hung up and rapidly propelled his chair across the room towards the CSI desk. 'Melv, sorry, mate, got to call you in for this, so grab your special bag. Where's Lucy?' He scanned the room and finally spotting her, he waved her over before he returned to his own desk.

'Right, we might have a lead. Terry Burke from the undertakers has just phoned in. He's found something of interest on a body that was brought in from Rookery Grange a few days ago. The death was signed off as natural causes by the local GP, but when he came to prepare the body, he found something pinned to the clothing – it had been hidden under the collar.' Andy grabbed his jacket and shrugged one arm in whilst holding a sheet of A4 paper between his teeth.

Lucy cottoned on quickly. 'Would it be a black angel lapel pin by any chance? Well, that's a bit of a coincidence! Two people dead, both with an angel pin on them, and both from Rookery Grange.'

Andy nodded. Folding the piece of paper, he popped it into his pocket. 'I'll speak to Murdoch, but I think we should call this as a possible sus death and request a post-mortem. Better to be safe than sorry.' He knocked on the DI's office door and waited. 'Coincidences are the one thing I don't believe in on murder investigations, Lucy.'

A LITTLE DISASTER

$\mathcal{T}$he spare bedroom at Bree's house had been converted into a makeshift bridal boutique. Pru's gown hung from a satin-padded coat hanger, her headdress had been carefully placed on the dressing table, and her shoes sat side by side next to her overnight case. On the other wall Bree's burgundy creation cascaded down the dated cream Anaglypta wallpaper that she had been promising herself to rip from the walls for more years than she cared to remember.

The two of them stood next to each other, taking in the moment, their arms linked together and their heads tipped to one side, touching. Bree gave Pru an excited squeeze.

'Well, this time tomorrow you'll be getting ready; Andy will be checking the soles of his shoes to make sure they don't read "help", and "me", and I'll just be simply stunning and available for the best man.' Bree giggled. 'Actually, sack that. I'll probably give that one a swerve, to be honest. Billy Bunter's not really my type.'

Pru looked mortified. 'Aw bless him, he's not Billy Bunter; he's just a little bit cuddly, that's all – and his name is Philly Hunter! Don't get that mixed up tomorrow, will you?' She smiled and squeezed her shoulders up to her ears in glee, hardly daring to believe that the big day was finally here. 'Philly and Andy have been best mates since they joined police training together. I believe they got each other out of quite a few scrapes in the early days, so they're pretty much tied to each other because of what they know.' She laughed, imagining Philly spilling the beans during his best man speech; she might even get to learn something new about her Delectable Detective.

'Changing the subject just a little bit, I've been thinking about your note and how much stress it's giving you, worrying about Clarissa and Winnie.' Bree gave Pru another hug, this time conveying a mutual understanding. 'Let's get the wedding out of the way, and whilst Andy's back at work we can both do a bit of snooping around Rookery Grange, speak to the ladies again, and see what we come up with, even if it's just to reassure you. We can do that in your role as librarian: you'll have an "access all areas" pass, won't you?'

As tempting as it sounded, with her natural curiosity and need to investigate nipping at her heels, Pru was a little hesitant. What if Andy found out and was angry with her, like he had been the last time she'd poked her nose into one of his investigations? She'd almost got herself killed in the Phyllis saga, and even if he didn't find out she would have to lie to him about where she was going and what she was getting up to. It would definitely not be a good start to married life. 'Mmm... I don't know. Maybe we should wait and see how the land lies in a day or two?'

'Yep, you're right, but–'

Before Bree could finish her sentence, a loud and frantic knocking on the cottage door startled her. 'Oh dear! That sounds urgent.' She half skidded in her socks down the staircase, jumping the last two steps before landing with a dull thud on the rug. Through the frosted glass she could make out a squished nose and a pair of nostrils adhered to the window.

'Blimey, have a nosey in, why don't you?' She jerked the door open to see a bedraggled and snow-laden Fergus falling over the threshold. This time his ever-present manbag was dramatically clutched to his chest, probably in lieu of the proverbial string of pearls. He pushed past her and came to a grinding halt when he looked up at the staircase to see Pru on her way down.

'Oh dearie me, I just don't know how to tell you, I really don't.' He wiped his brow vigorously with the end of his scarf. 'This is such a disaster – we're *doomed*,' he wailed.

Pru looked horrified, tentatively taking a further two steps down the stairs so that she was level with him. 'Tell me *what*? What on earth has happened?' She felt physically sick. 'Fergus, what the hell's wrong?' She had shouted louder than she had intended, but panic was gnawing at the pit of her stomach.

He threw back his head and fluttered his eyes. Dramatically dropping down his bottom lip, he flung his hands into the air. 'It's Thornbury Manor; oh darling, I'm so sorry… the roof has caved in!'

The three of them sat in silence, their respective fingers curled around mugs of hot chocolate as they watched the dancing flames spit and rise above the stacked logs in the fireplace.

'Chocolate in some form or another always makes things seem a little better.' Bree looked more hopeful than she actually felt. Fergus looked as though his little world had dropped on his big toe; he was alternating between sipping his drink and frantically texting. Who to, she had no idea, but from his expression he wasn't getting the replies he had hoped for. She leant forward and tenderly touched Pru's arm. 'Daft question, I know, but are you okay?'

Pru nodded as another tear slowly slipped down her cheek. She quickly wiped it away with the back of her hand, angry that it had sneaked out to betray how she was feeling. She was trying so hard to put on a brave face. 'I'm okay. I just can't believe it's happened. Oh God, what will I tell Andy? It's just my luck that the one and only bloody avalanche that Chapperton Bliss has ever experienced could happen to fall on our wedding venue!'

Fergus looked uncomfortable. He had tried to explain the current state of Thornbury Manor without being overly dramatic, but if he was honest, he didn't do understatement. He knew that everything he usually said would come out as either flamboyant or worthy of an Oscar nomination. He didn't disappoint in his news to Pru. Yes, the snow had played its part in the mini disaster, so had a huge quartet of barley twist chimney stacks that had lost their footing, along with a roof that had seen better days, but it was hardly on a par with an Everest avalanche. 'It's been deemed too dangerous for it to remain open, so the entire place has been evacuated. There won't be anything happening there for months at the very least.'

Pru blew her nose into what was left of the tattered piece of toilet paper scrunched in her hand. 'That's it, then, the wedding is off. I won't be wearing my dream dress and I won't be marrying my Delectable Detective!' She began to sob again.

'Right, where's our old girl's indomitable spirit? This moping around will never do; we're made of stronger stuff. You *will* get married, particularly if I've got anything to do with it!' Bree jumped up from the sofa and grabbed her phone from the coffee table. 'Fergus, now is the time for you to do your wedding planning thing, so look after the bride-to-be. I'll be back in a minute.' Before he could acknowledge her instruction, she had left the room, the door slamming shut behind her. She quickly made her way into the kitchen and keyed in the number she knew in her heart would save the day. It was answered on the third ring.

'Hi, Kitty, it's Bree. We have a bit of a disaster on our hands. We need to rally the troops – your president needs you!'

MANY HANDS

The landlines and 4G phone masts of Winterbottom sizzled with an unexpected surge of activity. All around the little village the ladies of the Winterbottom Women's Institute were being called to arms.

'Parish hall, 2pm sharp. Can you get in touch with the Reverend Baggott? Get him to meet us there too?' Kitty Hardcastle's familiar and well enunciated voice was crisp and to the point on the other end of the telephone, Brenda virtually squealed with excitement. 'Oh my days, this is wonderful, what fun we shall have! We can make it perfect.'

Kitty wasn't sure how perfect they could make a wedding that was to be organised in less than twenty-four hours, particularly one that needed to match up to the sumptuous event that had been planned at Thornbury Manor, but, as the saying goes, beggars can't be choosers. She checked her notebook and ticked Brenda's name before moving on to the next on her list. So far she had promises of sandwiches and salads, a finger buffet from Florrie at the Twisted Currant Café and, of course, from the WI ladies themselves: cake. A special event wouldn't be special without cake. She made a mental note to remind her ladies that this time they should definitely swerve the lemon drizzle. She had already despatched Frank to collect the three-tier wedding cake that had been delivered to Thornbury the previous day. It was by sheer good luck that it had been temporarily housed in Arabella Rosti's office and had remained unscathed in the ensuing chaos of the roof collapse.

'Booze!' She chuckled as she caught herself. 'Dearie me, when had Kitty Hardcastle ever referred to alcoholic beverages using that term?' she chided. She actually rather liked the idea that she had suddenly become one of them – airs and graces could be so limiting at times. She quickly keyed in the number for The Dog & Gun, hoping that even at short notice she might be able to call upon their mobile bar for the wedding breakfast. Though popular in the summer months, she knew Jason and his team had very few bookings in the winter months, so fingers crossed he'd have tomorrow free.

'Good morning, Jason, Kitty here.' There was a silence on the other end of the line. She tried again. 'It's Kitty, Kitty Hardcastle from the Women's Institute!' She felt quite indignant that Jason had taken such a long pause to think who she was. Mind you, she wasn't what you would call a regular at the Dog & Gun; she much preferred Pimkins Wine Bar in town. 'I just wondered, have you heard the news? Yes, yes, it's terrible for them, isn't it? We're all rallying together to try and give them a lovely day. Now, down to business, Jason. Are you and your little booze cart available to set up in the parish hall?'

As Kitty wittered on making arrangements with Jason, her WI entourage traipsed into the kitchen of her cottage, stamping the snow from their boots on the stone floor. She waved them through to the sitting room, but not before she had indicated by way of a pretty nifty show at charades that they should remove their foot coverings first to protect her expensive carpets. 'Super-duper, thank you, Jason. We're going there now to decorate the room, but I'll open the hall at 8am prompt tomorrow for you. Thank you again; we do appreciate it.' She quickly hung up.

Ethel was barely visible amongst the swathes of chiffon ribboning and bunting that was piled high on the floor, Hilda was busying herself folding the white linen tablecloths, her nose twitching in delight, which gave her the appearance of Mrs Tiggy-Winkle on a wash day. Millie was counting the gold and burgundy balloons that had fortunately not made it to Thornbury Manor. She popped a red one between her lips and began to blow vigorously.

'*Phwee...*' She paused for breath, her face alternating between a flush of pink and vibrant purple. 'Oh my goodness, whatever do they make these out of nowadays?' She tried again. '*Phwee... oops!*' She juggled the top set of her dentures as her exuberant blowing had dislodged them, dropping them onto the table. They scuttered across the polished mahogany and thudded to a halt against Kitty's Christmas centrepiece. She quickly picked them up and inspected them to ensure they were the right way round before ramming them back into her mouth.

'They need one of those big gas cannister things that blows them up, Millie. Frank got one and has already dropped it off at the hall. Just make sure all the balloons are together in the box with plenty of ribbon to go with them. We can do them at the hall later. The gas actually makes them float in the air.' Kitty helpfully imparted before disappearing into the kitchen.

'Helium,' Ethel offered. 'It's called helium, and it can make your voice go funny if you inhale it. That should be good for a giggle later after a few sherries.'

The room was alive with the happy chattering of the Winterbottom WI ladies doing what they always did best: caring, supporting and helping each other. Kitty reappeared and breezed back into the room, a tray laden with coffee and biscuits held high. 'Ladies, ladies, please...'

The room fell silent, Kitty's familiar words ringing in their ears, only this time they were not to precede chastisement or despair for someone's shortcomings or behaviour. For once, they were to herald praise.

'I can't tell you how proud I am of you all. Thank you just doesn't seem adequate,' she gushed. 'This might not be the day that Prunella and Andrew had planned, but I'm sure we will give them a very special memory nonetheless.' She clapped her hands together with glee.

A low murmur of agreement ran between the ladies, each one delighted to be able to play a part in what was going to be the biggest surprise Winterbottom, and Pru herself for that matter, had ever seen. Ethel continued to tease out the tangles of ribbon carefully whilst she spoke. 'I don't think I'd try to find another hubby if anything were to happen to my Albie,' she wistfully acknowledged. 'I'd be too busy whooping and hollering with joy that the toilet seat was permanently down and I'd got the TV remote all to myself!' She puckered her lips and crinkled her eyes in mischief.

Millie shifted in her chair, propping up the cushion behind her. 'Men usually do marry again; it's more common for them to have second wives than wives to have second husbands. Henry the Eighth had a lot of wives, because he clearly didn't like his own company!'

Hilda was keen to join in the conversation and showcase her knowledge. 'They had a lot of Henrys in those days,' she wisely offered. 'At least three or four of them before him, you know.'

Millie chuckled. 'I think you'll find there were seven, Hilda. That's why he was called Henry the Eighth.'

'Really? Oh my days, now who would have thought that?' Hilda laughed as she gave a cheeky wink to Ethel.

As the snow continued to gently fall outside Holly Cottage, the cosy gathering, framed by the Georgian bullseye window and the backdrop of an inglenook fireside glow, continued in their quest borne out of deep affection for Prunella Pearce, their president and Loony Librarian.

WALTER

*W*alter Henry Jenkins, at the grand age of eighty-seven years and three months, admired himself in the mirror. He used his comb to carefully tease the white hairs that adorned his upper lip, paying particular attention to the ones that curled slightly at the corners of his mouth. Tipping back his head, he checked his nostrils for rogue hairs. Finding one that seemed to have sprouted overnight, he plucked it savagely with a pair of tweezers from his pocket manicure set. Momentarily suffering the agonising sting and watery eyes of a job well done, he held his breath and waited for the pain to subside.

'Not bad, old chap, not bad at all – even if I do say so myself!' He patted down and smoothed his thinning grey hair with a small blob of Brylcreem and inhaled deeply, taking in the over-enthusiastic splash of Old Spice aftershave he had earlier treated himself too. 'No wonder the ladies can't keep their hands off me,' he preened to himself.

A muffled click from the lock of the toilet cubicle in the washroom heralded the sudden appearance of Chester Minnet from Room 9. He ambled over to the wash basin and stood next to Walter, fixing him with his steel-grey eyes that were reflected in the wall mirror. He gave a curt nod. 'Don't flatter yourself, old boy, the only time they can't keep their hands off you is to give you a much needed and well-deserved punch on the nose,' he grunted.

Indignant, Walter rose to the bait. 'Better to be acknowledged than ignored, eh, Chester? You've got to admit that Mr Riveting Personality you ain't!' He straightened his burgundy dickie bow and cocked a salute. 'See you later, alligator.'

Chester sighed loudly as he shook the excess water from his hands. 'Not if I see you first.'

Leaving his fellow resident to complete his ablutions, Walter made his way to the residents' lounge. 'Ladies, I'm here.' He flung his arms up in a display of attraction, much like a peacock would fan out its tail, only to be met with complete indifference from the small gathering present. Goldie, parked in her bath chair by the fire, barely acknowledged him; she momentarily glanced his way before returning to her book, the sneer on her lips speaking volumes. He turned his attention to Geraldine, who was with Winnie and the new woman, Clarissa. They had a table full of holly and mistletoe in front of them. Geraldine was expertly winding florists' wire around the stems, whilst Winnie was carefully tying a bow with a length of red ribbon. 'Afternoon, my dears, how are we this snowy, festive day?'

Clarissa, not yet being completely au fait with Walter and his habits, conceded a curt but polite response. 'We're good thank you, Walter.' She immediately returned her attention to the holly garland she was piecing together, hoping he would take the hint and move on.

Walter sidled up to Geraldine and picked up a sprig of mistletoe from the table. He examined its deliciously creamy berries before holding it above her head. 'My oh my, this could be my first Christmas kiss; what do you say, Geraldine dear?' He shook the sprig at her and puckered his lips.

Geraldine looked horrified as he began to bear down on her,

forcing Clarissa to intervene. She swiftly manoeuvred herself so that she leant awkwardly between Walter, the shivering piece of greenery, and Geraldine. 'Only with a "Y" in the day, Walter!' Clarissa chided him, and just as quickly realised she had inadvertently misquoted the saying, which had somewhat altered the meaning of what was meant to be a clever retort.

Her gaffe was not lost on Wily Walter. 'In that case, ladies, I shall have my fill every single day of the week!' He shook the mistletoe eagerly. 'Anyway, she should be bloody grateful for my attention; it's not like men are queuing up to give her any, is it?'

'Walter Henry Jenkins!' Eleanor's voice rang out loudly, causing the room to fall silent. 'That is quite enough. How many times have you been warned about harassing other residents? Now put that down and go and find something useful to do; there are plenty of Christmas decorations left to put up. Why don't you go and see Jenny? She'll sort something for you.'

Not to be deterred, Walter ambled over to Eleanor, still waving the mistletoe. She was quick enough to see the twinkle in his eye and the puckered lips, along with a sudden turn of unusual speed that saw him cross the room in less than two seconds flat. She quickly sidestepped him as he came in for the kill, sending him hurtling through the doorway into the entrance hall. Unable to stop his momentum, he crashed into Della as she was trundling the afternoon tea trolley across the chequered tiles. The trolley teetered on two wheels before dropping back down onto all four, the cups and saucers rattling loudly.

Della wasn't impressed. 'Watch where you're going, you old buffoon … and would you please extricate your nose from my cleavage?' She savagely pushed him away. 'As much as I frequently dream of suffocating you, it would be with my bare hands and not my Elmer Fudds!'

Still waving his sprig of mistletoe, Walter took the opportunity to test the water with Della. 'Surely a man can't be rebuffed three times in one day?' He chortled as he puckered his lips for the third time whilst brandishing his now limp mistletoe like a wet fish.

The resulting smack across the face with Della's damp tea towel soon gave him the answer he had been seeking, but definitely not in the way he had wished. The commotion had attracted the attention of both Alex and Jenny, who rushed to Della's aid – not that her formidable presence really needed rescuing. She had always been quite capable of looking after herself.

'Come on, Mr Jenkins, enough is enough. Let's get you back to your room. I think a little afternoon siesta is needed, don't you?' Jenny ushered him towards the elevator. 'Alex, I'll take him up and get him settled. Do you think someone could arrange a cup of tea?'

Reluctantly Walter shuffled into the elevator, still clutching his mistletoe in one hand and shaking his fist with the other. 'I'll tell you now, you bunch of harridans, you don't know what you're missing; there's still life in the old dog.'

Clarissa couldn't resist. She looked him up and down and shook her head. 'I still don't think Mae West would have jumped at the chance to take you for a run in the fields with a ball, Walter. From what we can see, your gigolo qualities are all up top and not down below.' She tapped the side of her head to clarify that his perceived prowess was all in his imagination.

Laughter rippled through those that had gathered, drawn by the commotion Walter had caused. They watched the elevator doors close, taking Walter back to his room, with a palpable relief that they would now be able to continue to enjoy their afternoon without further interruption.

'What are Elmer Fudds, 'Rissa?' Curiosity had got the better of Winnie.

Clarissa coughed loudly. 'Bosoms, Winnie; they're bosoms.'

Accompanying the ensuing joviality, a haunting air of gentle humming filled the entrance hall and followed them back to the lounge. The words to the melody would not grace them to fall upon their ears, so they would all remain in blissful ignorance, unaware of its content, oblivious to its creator… although if they had, maybe the subsequent outcome would have been different.

Wily Walter isn't nice
He's been told not once but twice
To rein it in, to curb his lust,
Now Wily Walter will soon be dust…

BAD NEWS DAY

The driveway and parking bays of Bellows & Burke Undertakers were a hive of activity. Limousines, their own ambulance van and staff parking occupied the main section, leaving the overflow car park free for Andy's car. He parked next to the coroner's vehicle and made his way to the entrance of the mortuary prep room.

'Lucy...' Andy beckoned her to join him inside. She was quick to take him up on his instruction as it had been at least ten minutes since she'd last felt her toes. Standing in slush and snow working on the continuity of evidence just wearing shoes hadn't been her brightest idea. Several times she dreamily cosseted the idea of her fleece-lined boots that were currently sitting in the locker room back at the station.

'Sarge, coroner's officer is here now to take the body.' She handed him the clipboard. Since police arrival and confirmation that the lapel pin was identical to the one they had recovered from Dorothy Burnside, Lucy had begun the process. Thomas Whittle's body would be transferred once Melvyn had finished up with any immediate forensic preservation and recovery, and a full post-mortem had been arranged for Monday.

'We'll need the body bag you collected him in, Terry. It won't leave you short, will it?' Andy marked a tick against the evidence request box. 'Fingers crossed, if this does turn out to be a suspicious death, something worthwhile might have been transferred inside.'

'It's not been touched since we took it off; it's literally just as we left it.' Terry was keen to assist. He had more body bags than he had clients at the moment, so he wouldn't miss this one.

Andy indicated the bag's location to Melvyn. He chewed the end of his pen, deep in thought. 'I appreciate you being so on the ball with this; how did you know?'

Terry looked quite sheepish. 'Erm... I was dropping paperwork off at the coroner's office and I sort of overheard a conversation about the recent murder at Rookery Grange. They said there was a black angel wings lapel pin that everyone had been interested in, so I thought it was best I let you know when I found this one.'

'I'm glad you did; this could be quite significant.' If truth be known, it was only the second real bit of physical evidence they had received in the investigation on Dorothy. If it transpired that Thomas had also been a victim, Andy and his team would have another murder on their hands and potential for more links to a motive. His mobile sent out a jolt of vibration in his pocket seconds before the ringtone burst into life. He checked the caller ID. 'Sorry, I'll have to take this. Luce, can you finish up here? Make sure we have some elimination prints and a DNA swab from Terry. Also from anyone else who has had contact with the body, and in particular the lapel pin.'

He knew Pru would never call him at work unless it was urgent; his heart sank and his stomach lurched as he answered his mobile. 'Pru, is everything okay?' The door to the mortuary hissed shut behind him as he made his way out into the corridor. 'Is Bree still with you? I'll just finish up here and I'll pop home, okay? Please don't cry; I promise we'll sort something... Can you put Bree on?'

Lucy, sensing something was amiss, had boxed up the documentation and followed him outside. She waited, watching him. His expressions ranged from despair, to resignation, to what looked like hopeful expectation.

'Bree, you're a lifesaver! It'll be even more special; I know it will, and so will Pru too. Just give her the bare minimum and we'll take her over there later tonight. I know, I know, but these things happen. I've been that wrapped up with this murder investigation, I hadn't got round to checking our incident sheets today.' He carried on thanking Bree profusely before hanging up and returning to Lucy. 'You hitching a lift back to the nick with me?' He dangled his car keys as an invitation. 'I could do with your calm and sensible outlook.'

'What's happened?' Lucy hoped she sounded concerned rather than nosey.

'Thornbury Manor is what happened! Its ruddy roof has caved in – we won't be having our wedding there, that's for sure!' He twiddled a finger in his right ear, a habit that he'd always had, right from when he had been a child whenever something out of his control happened.

'Jeez! How's Pru taking it?'

'Badly, very badly. But, and it's a big but, we do have some wonderful friends, and it looks like Bree and Kitty from the Women's Institute have pulled out all the stops. It's not going to be the spectacular event we had planned...' He thought about that for a few seconds. 'Well, what Pru had planned, really. I'd have been happy with Gretna Green, but I have a feeling it's all going to work out so much better in the end.'

Lucy loved his optimism. 'Please don't tell me it's going to be at the Dog & Gun.' She still hadn't quite got over the misunderstanding about dressing up for the hen night; her appearance as a 5'8' yellow chicken had done nothing to enhance her dating cred with Juicy Jason. She'd had her eye on him for some time now, but knowing her luck he'd probably turn out to be a vegetarian.

'Being married to Pru is all that matters. It looks like the Reverend Baggott at Winterbottom St Michael's has agreed to do the job. A church wedding wasn't what we expected, but finding somewhere that's licenced for marriages at such short notice is impossible.' He shook his head and smiled. 'And the ladies of the Winterbottom WI have come to the rescue with the parish hall and a buffet with cake. What more could we want?' He slid behind the steering wheel of his car and turned the ignition on.

Lucy eagerly joined him and twisted the heater thermostat to what Andy always called the 'burning cheeks of hell' temperature. She stamped her feet on the mat, trying to bring some feeling back into her toes. 'Oh, I don't know – how about the perfect wedding? The one she's just spent the last twelve months meticulously planning?'

Andy looked crestfallen. 'Thanks, matey. You sure know how to make a guy feel an abject failure!'

WHAT'S IT ALL ABOUT, FERGUS?

Winterbottom St. Michael's parish hall had suddenly come alive. This was unusual for a late Friday afternoon, but all hands were now on deck. Kitty waved her arms, directing the WI ladies in the same manner as a conductor would direct an orchestra.

'Bella, dear, not there – over here.' She stood stoic, hands rigid and pointing in front of her. 'The cake goes here; it has to be placed so everyone can see it from their respective tables when Andrew and Prunella are cutting it.'

Bella Morgenstern reluctantly complied, dragging the table to the spot indicated. The legs squealed and grated against the floorboards, making Kitty wince. 'Here?' Bella stood her ground, hands on hips. She had already made up her mind that she wouldn't be dragging it another inch, regardless of Kitty's wants or needs. Kitty, completely unphased by Bella's lack of cooperation, made her way to the centre of the hall. She clapped her hands loudly to gain everyone's attention and total silence.

'Bloody hell, throw that woman a fish,' Ethel sniped, causing a ripple of laughter amongst the gathered ladies. 'We usually have to pay to see that trick at the zoo, Kitty!'

As expected, Kitty was not amused. She pursed her lips together and tutted. 'Ladies, ladies, please.'

'Here we go again.' Millie giggled behind her hand.

Kitty gave her a withering look and continued. 'We have until 7.30pm tonight to get this place into shipshape fashion for a wedding. Now, you all know what each of you has to do, but remember we are not in competition with each other; we are complementing each other's talents.' She paused, waiting for heads to nod in agreement. A solitary hand rose into the air. Kitty peered over the gathered heads to see who it belonged to. 'Yes, Hilda?'

'I was just wondering, are we going to have prizes for the winner, or maybe even a medal? That would make it so much more fun.'

Kitty looked baffled. 'What on earth are you on about, dear?'

Hilda rolled her eyes and shook her head. 'The sledding competition, you just said we'd be competing against each other. Mind you, I haven't got a sled so I'll have to borrow someone else's.'

'*Wedding*, it's a wedding, Hilda.' Ethel gently took her hand. 'It's Andy and Pru's, remember? We're going to help them have a wonderful day.' Any other time she would have thought of a quick retort or a quip at Hilda's expense, but taking in her obvious confusion, she decided the time wasn't right for frivolities on dementia. 'Tell you what, why don't you help me with the bunting?'

Hilda gleefully nodded. 'Ooh, yes please! I'm good at hanging things, I even do my own washing sometimes.'

Millie grabbed the swathes of chiffon whilst Ethel unravelled the bunting she had carefully rolled up at Kitty's house. Keeping her voice low, she elicited the undivided attention of Hilda and Millie out of earshot of anyone else. 'I've spoken to Clarissa and explained what's happened with Pru and the wedding. We've discussed putting off Operation Bloomers until Monday night and she's agreed.'

Millie hunkered down, getting as close to Ethel as she could. 'Roger that.' She saluted.

Hilda hissed loudly. 'No, no; I'm sorry but it's supposed to be women only. The Four Wrinkled Dears are all women, there's not a todger amongst us; we shouldn't allow men to intrude into our adventures.'

Millie's face said it all. 'It's just a saying, Hilda. We don't really–'

The swing doors to the hall suddenly banged open, cutting Millie off in her prime. Spilling through them was what Ethel thought was a vision akin to *Nanook of the North*. They just as quickly rattled back to pendulate slowly several times until they met once more, providing a seal to keep the heat within the four walls. Ethel continued to stare in amusement at the vision that had taken root, one that was dropping lumps of slush and snow from their Eskimo boots onto the floor she had only just mopped.

'Voila, my dears, Fergus O'Brien at your service.' Fergus adopted a model style pose, the fur-trimmed hood of his coat obscuring most of his face. Seeing the perturbed expressions on his audience, he quickly removed the offending article. 'It's me, wedding planner to the stars… oh, and Prunella too.' If he had been expecting acknowledgement of who he was and his talents, coupled with a warm welcome, he was very much mistaken. 'Ooh it's chillier in here than it is outside.' He laughed. 'Right, what does one want me to do?'

Ethel was quick to assist him. 'Mop and bucket in the kitchen; you can give the floor a once over, and when you've finished that, the toilets need cleaning.'

Fergus stood like a deer caught in the headlights, his mouth opening and closing like a goldfish whilst he struggled to find the right words. 'I *beg* your pardon! A mop? Toilets? I'm an organiser, not a cleaner!'

'Well organise these, then.' Bella threw a packet of 3-ply toilet rolls at him. 'Organise them whatever way you want, two in each cubicle, under or over. We're not fussy.'

Fergus took the hint and flounced over to the kitchen, where he was warmly welcomed by Brenda who promptly shoved a slice of lemon drizzle cake in his hand. 'Nice to meet you, Fergus, and welcome to the Winterbottom Women's Institute,' she trilled. 'We are a friendly lot, really we are; it's just a little fraught at the moment.' She took a bite from the slice she had been hiding behind her back. Licking her fingers, she gave a sheepish grin. 'Slimming World Failure of the Week again, I'm afraid.' She chuckled.

'Well I think there's a lot more to life than being skinny, Brenda.' Fergus grinned as he bit into the cake. 'And do you know what? This really is to die for!' He ran his tongue over his top lip, relishing the sugar crystals.

Brenda chuckled again. 'Aye, you're not far wrong there, son, there's a story behind that. I'll tell you about it one day!'

As the ladies happily carried on with their respective tasks, Fergus stood at the open door enjoying every crumb of Brenda's cake. He watched the flurry of activity within the hall, he listened to the laughter, became engrossed with the chatter, and felt at home with their warmth and kindness... and suddenly planning a wedding, wherever it was, took on a whole new meaning for him.

It wasn't about expensive venues; it wasn't about ice sculptures or flamboyant flower displays, white doves and five-course menus, and expecting everything to be just perfect. It was about the things he was being privy to right here...

Love, loyalty, friendship and fun.

A CHANGE OF PLAN

'Walter, I won't tell you again; this type of behaviour is not acceptable – on any level. I don't care how old you are; age doesn't stop you from being a gentleman with manners.' Eleanor bristled, trying to curtail her annoyance with him. 'If this continues, I will have no choice but to give you notice, and you will have to find another residential home that will take you.'

Walter harrumphed loudly and took a slurp of his tea. He made sure he didn't give the old cow his undivided attention as that would then give credence to her presence. He continued to stare out of the window, taking his time before he finally spoke. 'I don't seem to remember you giving old Oscar an ultimatum when he gripped that Margaret Rutherford lookalike the other night?'

Eleanor rolled her eyes and sighed. She'd certainly hoped that Walter would keep that observation to himself; she was pretty sure that Clarissa would have something to say if he didn't. 'How I dealt with Captain Burton has nothing to do with you, Walter. Don't you think I have enough to contend with having *two* men in residence here that give me nothing but grief?' She rearranged the tea tray she had brought in with her, bringing the cup and saucer to the front. 'I think you should remain in your room for the rest of the day, I will get someone to bring up your meals and drinks. You need the time to reflect on your actions and what the consequences will be for you if you don't mend your ways.' She quickly turned heel, not waiting for his response, and closed his room door behind her.

Walter sat for some time pondering his choices, listening to the general background noise of the comings and goings within Rookery Grange Retreat. He really didn't want to be thrown out on his ear; he was actually quite fond of the place. He loved his room, he enjoyed the food and, best of all, relished being waited on hand and foot. Ever since Doris had inconveniently left him, Walter had been left to fend for himself, something he definitely wasn't used to.

He rose from his chair and pottered over to the bookshelf, picking up the framed photograph of her in her younger days. 'Oh Doris…' He sighed wistfully as his finger traced the outline of her face, her chestnut curls devoid of any colour within the frame. The old black-and-white photograph was all he had, apart from his memories of her. The colour of her hair would always be an abiding one. 'I do miss you, Doris. I know I didn't always appreciate you…' Deep down, he knew that he was being frugal with the truth. He hadn't appreciated her at all, not once in all their years of marriage. It was funny how everyone at Rookery Grange had assumed he was a widower, a grieving one at that. He hadn't gone to any great lengths to put them straight. The truth would probably surprise them.

'I'm an abandoned husband, aren't I, my dear.' He quietly chuckled to himself, remembering the day Doris had upped and left him for another man. 'How bloody predictable: the ruddy milkman!' He remembered the day as though it was yesterday. She had stood in the kitchen, a battered old suitcase at her feet and a box of Friskies cat biscuits tucked under her arm. He'd laughed fit to burst at her quirky ways; they didn't have a cat, and as far he was aware, Pervy Pete, the disparaging name he'd given to their milkman, didn't have one either. He had checked the suitcase to ensure she wasn't absconding with any household possessions, and once satisfied that she would leave the way she had arrived all those years ago – penniless and without assets – he'd opened the front door for her. As Doris had made her way down the path and along the street, he hadn't turned an eye. He hadn't called out to her. He hadn't made promises to be a better man if she came back. He hadn't felt guilt, sadness or despair. Banging the front door shut, he had simply counted his blessings that at least she'd had the decency to clean the house before she left.

It was two days before grief and sadness finally hit him. Not at the loss of Doris, not with loneliness, and not from despair, but from the missing £20,000 he had stashed under the floorboards in the bathroom. Money hard won on illegal gambling, purloined from customer accounts and from Doris's very own savings, ensuring she had to come to him for every penny she needed throughout their marriage to retain his control over her.

Standing looking down at the vacant space between water pipes and insulation and the note that simply said *Screw you*, it had suddenly dawned on him what the box of Friskies had actually held as she'd skipped down the street, suitcase banging on the pebbledash of the suburban garden walls, never to be seen or heard of again. Doris had finally had the last laugh. He had been well and truly screwed – but not in the same enjoyable manner that Doris had so obviously been by Pete.

'Every single bloody penny,' he grumbled to the photograph. And there hadn't been a thing he could do about it; ill-gotten gains were never legal. He sipped at his cup of tea and bemoaned the fact Eleanor hadn't included the usual plate of biscuits. It was probably her mode of punishment for his apparent misbehaviour.

His eye was suddenly caught by the battered piece of mistletoe on his bedside table, the root cause of his current predicament. It lay somewhat droopy and tired, a little bit similar to himself. It was a feeling he was only too familiar with these days; his prowess having deserted him sometime in 1998. He knew he was now all blather and pretence, but he had an image he needed to maintain.

'Oh, it's you.' He gave very little in the way of a welcome to his visitor as his bedroom door pushed quietly open. 'Have you brought me some biscuits? That woman forgot to put them on my tray,' he grumbled.

'A little change of plan, Mr Jenkins. I've got something so much better than a couple of old digestive biscuits. What I've got for you are to die for.' Her voice was calm and measured with a hypnotic lilt.

Walter's eyes glistened with anticipation, like a child's would at Christmas. He held out his hand to receive her offering. 'Ooh, Ferrero Rochers! My favourite.'

'I know. Enjoy, Walter.' She smiled and silently left his room, closing the door with a gentle click.

'My, oh my...' he murmured to himself as he admired the gift. Tearing the cellophane from the chocolate delights, he made himself comfortable in his chair, taking great pleasure in unwrapping the gold foil. Opening his current read at the page marked by his bus pass, he popped the first chocolate into his mouth. 'Delicious and what a treat.'

The second and third chocolates went exactly the same way, devoured and relished in a matter of minutes. Walter, satisfied and content to spend the afternoon reading, settled himself down to enjoy the peace and quiet of Room 10, his home at Rookery Grange Retreat.

Tick.

Tock.

Tick.

Tock...

The clock on the wall tapped out the passing seconds that quickly became minutes. Walter was beginning to feel unwell; a wave of nausea washed over him, making him shake. The book slipped from his hands and landed with a muffled thud onto the carpet. He wiped the perspiration from his forehead and brought his hands out in front of him, intrigued by the slight tremor they had suddenly begun to produce. 'Oh dear,' he mumbled to himself as he tried to stand up. His legs were like jelly and vigorously disobeyed his instructions, forcing him back into the chair in a crumpled heap. 'Help me,' he wailed.

His voice was reedy and weak, not the voice of a man who had been used to barking orders throughout his life. A spasm of unbearable pain suddenly racked his body; he jerked and stiffened, his head arched backwards to bang against the upholstered wing of the chair. As his legs transitioned to become rigid and unyielding, his breath was simultaneously ripped from his lungs. 'Nooo...' he gasped as his throat suddenly and violently constricted, forcing him to choke.

It was akin to having an epiphany, an awakening, but one that was at the end of his life and too late to make any difference to the man he had been. Death was upon him, its tentacles spreading throughout his body, slowly, painfully and savagely. His arm jerked out and knocked the table lamp over. It teetered momentarily before falling to the floor with a minimum of sound. His eyes frantically searched for anything else that was within reach to highlight the horror he was enduring and to bring help.

The tray. If he could only reach the tray.

His muscles weighed heavy and his arm slumped back onto his lap, his fingers having barely touched the china cup. The futility of his attempts was now obvious to him. He was going to die, and there was absolutely nothing he could do to change that fact.

In resignation, he let go.

With one final, fierce spasm, Walter Henry Jenkins gurgled loudly and went to meet his maker.

'Regrets are idle; yet history is one long regret…'

Charles Dudley Warner (1829–1900)

SURPRISE, SURPRISE

*A*ndy trudged along Winterbottom High Street, his collar turned up and scarf wrapped snuggly around his neck and knotted at the front. He hunkered down and plunged his hands into his jacket pocket for added warmth. A fresh fall of snow fluttered onto bare branches, glistening in the streetlamps and the Christmas lights that were artistically strung from shop to shop.

He loved Christmas, and he loved snow, but not in the persistent frequency and quantities that the county had been experiencing over the last two weeks. Snowmen, built on the village green in the early days by the local children, had morphed into misshapen lumps of ice, an odd blackened carrot protruding from what would have been a face, or a fallen branch that had days ago waved enthusiastically as an arm, were all that were left of a once-festive tableau. He ploughed on towards Bree's house, desperate to see Pru. He looked over to Winterbottom St Michael's parish hall. It was ablaze with lights that cast orange-yellow hues across the white that blanketed the pavement and road outside. A faint strain of music came from the partially open main doors. He checked his watch: 7.30pm; he was running late.

'Andy, over here...'

He looked up to see two figures slipping and sliding towards him. As they got closer, he could see it was Pru and Bree, arms linked to keep themselves from falling over. 'I was just on my way to yours,' he shouted. He quickened his pace to reach them, an anxious feeling still gnawing at the pit of his stomach when he saw Pru's face.

He grabbed her in a bear hug, pulling her into him. 'It'll be okay; everything will work out fine, I promise,' he soothed. She pulled away from him, her eyes puffy from crying, searched his, looking for reassurance that he too believed it. Her knitted bobble hat was pulled awkwardly over her forehead, leaving a curl of hair to escape. Flakes of snow adorned it, stark white against the rich chestnut, whilst her vivid green eyes held a teary pinkness. He tenderly wiped his thumb across her cheek and held her face in his hands. Her quiet vulnerability with an inner strength he knew she possessed would always melt his heart.

'You are perfect in every way, Prunella Pearce, and tomorrow *will* be our perfect day.' He grabbed her mittened hand and gently ushered her towards the parish hall. Bree took the opportunity to nip ahead of them. He watched as she disappeared through the doors waving one hand with five fingers.

'Give me five,' she mouthed. He nodded.

'It's all such a mess, isn't it?' Pru's voice wobbled.

'Well, I suppose that's a bit of an understatement, particularly for Thornbury Manor.' he sighed.

She hugged him and nestled into his chest. 'Bree said we shouldn't cancel; she said everything was under control, but it can't be, can it?' A single tear streaked down her cheek. She angrily brushed it away as though it had no right to expose her. 'She also said a brisk walk would do me good too, to get some fresh air, but it hasn't. I feel worse than I did before.' Another wave of tears threatened to fall, welling up and just barely tipping over her lower lashes.

'Well, a mess it might be, but what we have that Thornbury Manor doesn't have is good people in our lives – and this…'

He pushed open the doors to Winterbottom St Michael's parish hall and stood back, allowing Pru to go first.

'Surprise!'

A chorus of voices rang out, filling the hall. The sound lifted up to the beamed rafters and swooped back down again, enveloping Pru like the biggest hug she had ever experienced.

Aghast with shock, her eyes swept the room. Bunting and chiffon swathes covered the walls; twinkling fairy lights hung from the beams, festooned across the hall from one side to the other, and then back again. Round tables, draped with white linen cloths hosted Christmas candle centrepieces, surrounded by sprinkled red heart confetti. She spun around, trying to take everything in, her heart pounding. Trestle tables laden with hot plates, platters and cake stands set out ready to accept food, lined the far wall. A makeshift dance floor in one corner with a DJ deck that announced *Vinyl Richie Disco Sounds* had been adorned with helium-filled balloons.

Bree and Kitty stood with Ethel, Millie, Hilda, Brenda and the other ladies of Winterbottom WI. Their eager and expectant faces beamed back at her, each one feeling immense pride in what they had achieved in such a short time.

'How? Oh my goodness, I… I can't believe you've done this for us…' Pru blubbed, but this time with happy tears.

Bree stepped forward. 'The church is getting warmed up as we speak; it'll be lovely and toasty for tomorrow. Reverend Baggott will conduct the ceremony and the ladies of the Fellowship group are going to do the flowers.' She paused, catching her breath. 'Ethel is going to play the organ.' A ripple of laughter followed that revelation. 'We've let all your guests know about the change of venue – and…' Bree couldn't contain her excitement as she moved to one side to reveal the creation that

Frank had safely transported from Thornbury Manor, '…we've got your cake!'

It was then Kitty's turn to step forward, eager to add her bit. 'Brenda and the ladies have taken care of the food. Now it won't be a sit-down wedding breakfast; it's a buffet, but we've got Jason with his erm… oh dear, what's it called again? Oh yes, that's it, his "Booze Bar", right through until midnight.'

An eager but nervous silence filled the hall as they waited for Pru's reaction: an intake of breath that had been collectively held threatened to choke each and every one of them. Bree half expected to see bundles of tumbleweed blowing across the floorboards as the seconds ticked by.

Pru finally found the words she needed. 'I don't care if it's not a sit down, I don't care if it's not Thornbury Manor.' She squealed as she jumped up and down in unbridled excitement. 'It's perfect!' Her eyes shone in the reflected fairy lights. 'This is going to be so much better, I… I mean *we* – we want you all to come; you're *all* invited!' She turned to Andy and whispered, 'That's okay, isn't it? You don't mind if we share it with everyone who has made this possible, do you?'

Andy took her in his arms and kissed her tenderly. 'I'd share you and our special day with the entire world if needed, as long as I get to call you Mrs Barnes by this time tomorrow night.'

A rousing round of applause filled the parish hall, drifting up to reach the rafters and bouncing back to smother them all in a warmth that was borne out of true friendship and community spirit.

THE BOX

The door to Room 10 silently swung open and closed again with a gentle click.

The Dark Angel stood for a while, reverently admiring her latest production, content that her presence would not be felt nor suspected by anyone else at Rookery Grange Retreat. Mr Walter Henry Jenkins lay slumped in his chair, his eyes glassy and unfocused, with his mouth open. It did amuse her that for a man who could not usually control his verbal bile, it should now be left wide in potential oration, but with no words to spit forth. His book lay on the floor, open at the page he had no doubt been reading prior to his last breath, along with three gold foil wrappers and the table lamp.

This was her tableau of death, one in which she felt immense pride.

There was just one small detail that was lacking, one which would spoil the overall effect if it were not included in her work. Her fingers danced in her pocket, searching for the last piece. Finding it, she carefully popped the back plate from the pin and approached her subject. Pulling forward the knitted welt of Walter's V-neck jumper, she carefully placed the lapel pin into the cotton pocket of his shirt and pressed the stud into place before finally patting his jumper back into place. She picked up the lamp and returned it to the table and then scooped up the foil wrappers and cellophane, secreting them in her now empty pocket. She stood back and gave him a final once over.

'Perfect...' she murmured to herself. 'Now, let's get down to business.'

As Walter sat gazing at her with eyes that could no longer see, she began her fingertip search of Room 10, the very room that had once belonged to the live-in nanny of the Carnell family, the very same one that was documented in the rose print journal. More than thirty years had passed since that woman had graced the floorboards, but time had stood still in some parts of the room. The built-in cupboard was an original, as was the fireplace.

She peeled back the carpet in the corner and located a loose floorboard. Using a pair of scissors, she prised open the edges. It popped up surprisingly easily. She tentatively plunged her hand into the void, her fingers probing the darkness until it touched what she had been searching for. The old tin document box had stood the test of time well. Although slightly rusted at the edges and with a layer of dust, crumbled plaster and cobwebs, it was still secure enough to protect its treasures within. She sat back cross-legged to admire the prize and test its lock. To her surprise, it was unlocked.

'Well, would you credit it...?' This was not what she had expected; this was all too easy. Her heart pounded against her ribs. She paused, her thumb just touching the edge of the lid. 'This is my proof...' she whispered.

The box opened awkwardly, straining against the rusty hinges until it was wide enough to reveal what it had kept hidden for three decades. She still had her eyes closed, a mixture of excitement and trepidation. She counted softly.

One,

Two,

Three...

She opened them.

The pupils of her eyes became darker, they dilated to such a size she appeared almost demonic. 'No, no, it can't be... this can't be happening...' She allowed a muffled feral wail to escape from her lips.

The box was empty.

I DO

*E*thel repositioned the spotted cushion underneath her, stretched her legs out and pumped her feet to ensure they would reach the pedals. She intertwined her fingers and pushed out, making the knuckles crack. It had been a while since she had bashed out a song or two on Big Bertha, the Winterbottom St Michael's church organ, and a case of the jitters was just starting to take hold.

Brenda skipped across the metal grating in the aisle and leant over the choir stall. 'Ethel, oh Ethel,' she excitedly squealed. 'Clarissa said to remind you not to play "Beside the Seaside" like you did at Betty's funeral.'

'One ruddy mistake years ago, and I'm still reminded of it! Of course I won't, I'm not daft, you know.' Ethel adjusted the sheet music in front of her and twiddled with a few of the knobs.

Despite the weather, the pews were filling up nicely, the promise of the old under-floor heating wafting upwards to toast toes, knees and nether regions was as much a draw as the bride and groom were. The Winterbottom WI ladies Fellowship group had provided a stunning display of poinsettias, holly, jasmine and roses for the altar stands, and the end of each pew held bunches of mistletoe, ivy and pine cones.

'Budge up, Hilda, there's room enough for a little one to squeeze in.' Brenda wiggled her purple polyester-clad bottom to clear a space, shoving Hilda at least two feet down the polished wood, which in turn pushed everyone else along the row. She settled herself down, handbag comfortably nestled on her knee, happy that she had an aisle seat.

'Room for one more?' Millie suddenly appeared beside her, looking anything but cheerful.

'Not really,' Brenda huffed. 'Can't you go and sit somewhere else?'

Millie quickly snapped back. 'I was actually on this row until your fat backside forced everyone along and shoved me off the other end!'

'Ladies, ladies, please,' Kitty warbled. 'Andy has just arrived. Don't let him hear us squabbling.' Excited, they strained their heads in unison to get their first look at the groom.

Andy stood at the front, animatedly talking to the Reverend Baggott, his best man Philly Hunter by his side. The ladies watched as pockets were patted and rings were checked and double-checked.

'Aw, look at him! He's so nervous, poor man. Tell you what, he is a bit of a hunk though, isn't he? I definitely wouldn't kick him out of my bed.' Avaline Prendergast lecherously sighed.

'Neither would I,' Fergus laughingly chipped in. He had been demoted from his role of wedding planner to that of usher and guest – not that he was complaining. He clapped his hands to bring everyone to attention. He flung his right arm out towards Ethel, conducting the proceedings from the aisle. 'One, two, three... Ethel love, you're on!'

With great gusto Ethel pumped her feet, pulled out stops and danced her fingers across the keys of Big Bertha...

～

A fresh flurry of snow blew into the vestibule of Winterbottom St Michael's church. It swirled under the brown stone arch like the casting of a magic spell, before billowing upwards to frame Pru in a fluttering of nature's confetti.

'Nervous?' Bree squeezed her hand.

'Absolutely shitting myself...' was the less than ladylike reply from Pru, which in turn made Bree snort with laughter. She dug deep into the famous pockets of her bridesmaid's gown and pulled out a tissue. Blowing her nose with gusto, she followed up with a slick of lipstick to replenish what she had inadvertently wiped off and popped both back into the pocket. 'Bloody godsend, these are!'

'Bree...'

'What?'

'Thank you for being my friend.' Pru's voice, choked with emotion, seemed mouse-like and small.

Bree smiled. The last twenty-four hours had been a nightmare of hastily put together plans, ideas, laughter and mayhem. And it had all been possible because of the friendship and kindness of Winterbottom and its residents. Today was going to be a good day.

'Well, what would I do without a Pru in my life, hey?'

Pru laughed. 'Stay sane, probably!' The first chords of Ethel's organ music drifted through the aged and worn doors that led to the nave where Andy would be waiting for her. Pru adjusted her bouquet and took a deep breath.

'Right, Miss Pearce, are we ready?' Albert Tytherington stepped forward and held out his arm for Pru to take. She linked into the crook of his elbow. His rheumy blue eyes, set underneath a veritable hedge of white eyebrows, twinkled and crinkled with delight. 'I can't tell you how proud this has made me, Prunella.'

'It's me that's proud and so very grateful, Albert. With not having a dad to give me away, this means the world to me.'

'You're the daughter I would have loved to have had if my Ethel and I had been blessed.' He pushed back his shoulders and jutted out his chin. 'Shall we?'

The doors to Winterbottom St Michael's church opened wide to reveal the flickering orange glow of candles, the scent of jasmine, the warmth of good friends, and the joy of a much-anticipated happy union.

LET'S PARTY

*D*ancing lights pulsated from the windows of Winterbottom parish hall; the dull *thump, thump, thump* of the music barely broke the silence that hovered over the snow-covered high street. It was deserted. The residents of Winterbottom were either in the hall dancing and making merry, or were snuggled up under blankets at home in front of roaring fires. The doors would burst open to spill out a drunken merrymaker or two in desperate need of some fresh air, before the chill would encourage them back inside to top up from Juicy Jason's Booze Bar.

Inside, Brenda was frantically waving across the room whilst shouting loudly to be heard above the music. 'Millie dear, can you make mine a double whilst you're there?'

'Is that a drink or a double gateau, Bren? I told you before: a moment on the lips is a lifetime on the hips,' joked Millie.

The wedding had been perfect. Even Hilda's misheard wording and her inability to hold her peace, which resulted in her dramatic objection to the perceived discrimination of the vicar for calling it an *awful impediment,* had caused more laughter than consternation. Clarissa, Ethel, Hilda and Millie sat huddled together at a table, all slightly the worse for wear from champagne bubbles and sweet sherry.

'What time have you got to be back at Rookery?' said Ethel as she slugged back the remnants of Millie's gin, then topped it up with tonic before pushing it back into place, hoping her friend would be none the wiser.

Clarissa gave her a look of disgust for minesweeping the drinks. 'Open door policy for tonight; it's a special occasion. They have night staff on, so they'll make sure I'm okay.'

'I still don't agree with you being there, 'Rissa. If one resident has been murdered and you still think Winnie was a failed target, what's to say they won't pick on you?' Concerned, Ethel waited for a reply.

Clarissa raised her glass as both a toast and a very swift change of subject. 'I know what I'm doing; come on, this is a party. We don't need to be talking about death; we should be talking about the happy couple!'

'In that case, if Pru plays her cards right, she'll be having an origami or two tonight, I shouldn't wonder.' Hilda slapped the table hard, almost snorting the sip of sherry she had just quaffed, down her nose. She quickly grabbed a serviette and gave a vigorous wipe. 'I almost remember having one of them myself!'

'Hilda!' Their disbelief was in unison, making Hilda laugh even more.

'I very much doubt they'll be working towards a Blue Peter badge in paper folding on their wedding night, I think the word you're looking for is orga–'

'That's quite enough, Ethel!' Kitty, nearby and beside herself with embarrassment, chipped in.

'Right, come on, who's up for "The Time Warp"?' Ethel tucked her knees in tight and gave a jump to the right, whilst grabbing Clarissa by the arm, pulling her from her chair. 'Oof, blimey, me hip; I don't think I'm as young as I used to be. You'll be all right, Millie, you've had a new one fitted, haven't you?'

As the Four Wrinkled Dears made it to the dance floor, gyrating hips old and new, their mutual laughter rose to the rafters and bounced back like a warm hug.

Winterbottom was in the midst of a celebration, which was in stark contrast to the dark undercurrent that Chapperton Bliss was currently experiencing.

'At last, I've got you all to myself.' He held her gently by the waist as he spun her around on the makeshift dance floor. He had waited all night, watching her dance and skip from table to table, a Cinderella in plumes of ivory silk and tulle, laughing and hugging those that had made their day so special.

Now it was his turn.

Pru coyly nestled herself into him. 'Well, Mr Barnes, how is married life suiting you so far?' She brushed her lips against his as her fingers danced across his chest, relieved to see that his tie had been discarded and the top two buttons of his shirt were open.

'The first thousand miles are just a try out; ask me again in two weeks.' He grinned, gently returning her kiss. 'Yeow…' His hand quickly covered his chest.

Laughing, Pru pulled away from him and picked up the pace as the music changed to something a bit more upbeat. She held out her finger and thumb. 'Got it!'

'My one and only chest hair, how could you? I am now totally bereft of manly accoutrements,' he wailed.

Grabbing the folds of material on her dress, Pru hitched it up and let rip with her own version of 'The Time Warp'. 'I certainly hope not, Mr Barnes. You've got a one-night honeymoon to cater for later – and then *I'll* let *you* know if the test drive was successful!'

OPERATION BLOOMERS

'Have you got everything?' Ethel checked her own Operation Bloomers' recce pack: torch, mobile phone, pen, paper and a packet of chewing gum. She'd even gone as far as borrowing a special little something from Albert's garden shed. She checked it was in working order and pushed it to the bottom of her bag.

Hilda grumbled loudly. 'I still don't know what we're supposed to be looking for at this place, and I hate wearing black; it's like I'm going to a funeral.' She paused for a few seconds before adding, 'I'm not, am I? Has somebody died and I've forgotten?'

Millie put a comforting arm around her. 'No, you haven't forgotten, dear; nobody has died, we're all well. We're just going to help Clarissa. She's worried there's some mischief afoot at Rookery Grange. It's just an adventure.' She didn't think they would discover anything that would assist the police in their investigation into Dorothy's murder, but what else did they have to do with their evenings other than watch *Heartbeat* on repeat on ITV3? She checked her own little bag and, content that all was there, zipped up the holdall.

Three of the Four Wrinkled Dears stood side by side in Ethel's lounge. Dressed in black from head to foot, they toasted each other with a small sherry each. 'A little bit of Dutch courage never did anyone any harm.' Ethel observed, whilst eyeing up the bottle and wondering if her constitution could cope with another large slug before the taxi came to pick them up.

Hilda drained her glass, and not having the sensibility that Ethel possessed, held her glass out for a refill. 'Might as well go in for a penny as a pound, and besides I've heard a good sherry is excellent for the skin.' She giggled.

'I don't know about that, Hilda; your wrinkles are getting a bit out of hand lately, if you don't mind me saying so,' Ethel quipped.

Indignant, Hilda rose to the bait. 'I *do* mind you saying so – and you can talk! I don't have wrinkles – they're actually called laughter lines!'

'If you say so, dear. I just hadn't realised you'd had that much to laugh at!' Ethel slapped her thigh and sniggered, setting Millie off. Seeing their jollity, Hilda joined in. They giggled like schoolgirls, refilling their glasses and offering up several cheers and chin-chins until the bottle was drained.

'Oops… *hic…*' Ethel held up the bottle. 'I think it's empty. Not to worry, I've got another one here.' She glanced at the clock on the wall. 'Plenty of time before the taxi arrives, and it'll ensure we're all lovely and warm from inside out by the time we have to brave the cold and face our enemies. Remember, nothing can stop us! We are brave WI ladies with the constitution of warriors, we are resolute, we are strong – and we've got this.'

The wall clock ticked away the seconds in the pensive silence that followed.

'Erm… hands up if anyone needs the toilet first…'

~

Duncan Dobbins ensured his grafting kit was well stocked and that he had everything he needed for the night's foray. He was not a happy bunny at all, knowing he would have to brave Chapperton Bliss's version of a lunatic asylum again, and in particular the old bat with the pink sponge hair rollers, but needs must. He had less than two days before Christmas and if he didn't produce the gift of all gifts for her indoors, then as well as the imprint of thirty-two canine teeth from his last job, his arse would suffer several more puncture wounds from Holly's six-inch stiletto heels, courtesy of a good kicking from her before she withdrew his conjugal rights until at least the middle of next year.

He groaned. Never had his life been so feckin' complicated. His dad had warned him that there were three rings to marriage: the engagement ring, the wedding ring and the suffering. What he couldn't figure out was how he'd managed to avoid the first two, but had well and truly been hit across the back of the head with the third. Holly sure knew how to make him suffer.

He had a few hours before he needed to start making tracks, so he poured himself a beer and took the time to familiarise himself with the MO for the job. Same way in as before and straight to where the prize was, grab it and go, then leave by the same route.

'Don't get side-tracked, buddy, keep it simple. In, out, and gone.' He took a slurp of the chilled drink whilst dreaming of a Christmas without strife – and, with a bit of luck, maybe a horizontal tango or two with Holly thrown in for good measure.

He just had to find a way of remembering which was left and which was right to assist him with his poor navigational skills; the last thing he needed was to be wandering around like a lost soul leaving himself wide open to discovery. He tipped the almost empty can in cheer to the sorry-looking Christmas tree in the corner of the room.

The twinkling lights bounced from the aluminium can clutched in his hand, and that was when he saw it…

His eureka moment – a most brilliant idea and the best head thought he'd ever had!

THE TIPSY TRIO

*C*larissa stood with her hand on her hips and tutted loudly. She had adopted a school ma'am stance in response to the appearance of her three friends, who were currently holding each other up in the middle of her bedroom, giggling like silly schoolgirls.

'What bit of our recce instructions didn't you understand?' She jutted out her chin in an attempt to not laugh herself. 'Discretion? The need to be alert and ready for anything?'

Ethel, Millie and Hilda had the decency to look a little embarrassed. Millie swayed slightly, grabbing hold of Hilda's arm to stop herself from staggering forward, while Ethel nonchalantly examined her fur-topped boots. The taxi had literally spilled them out at the gates of Rookery Grange some ten minutes previously, whereupon a great deal of effort and uncoordinated bodily movements had followed to enable them to reach the staff entrance to the manor house as arranged.

'What I didn't expect was to open the door to three lushes who couldn't moderate a tipple of sweet sherry between them!' Clarissa shook her head in exasperation as Ethel released a loud burp. Trying to get the three of them discreetly up the back staircase and into her room without being seen had been a nightmare. 'Right, this is what's on the cards for tonight...'

Clarissa lectured whilst her three friends listened intently. 'So, we keep in pairs and basically patrol the corridors without being seen. I have my suspicions that Eleanor is the one behind Dorothy's murder. There is definitely something about this place that keeps her here, and I think it's kept in that office of hers, so that's our target.' She waited for the *oohs* and *ahs* from her co-conspirators to overwhelm her, impressed by her train of thought. Instead she was met with deafening silence followed by sniggering.

'The only thing that woman has hidden in her office is two bottles of gin and half a litre of vodka!' spat Ethel. 'I've seen her staggering across those chequered tiles in the entrance hall, and it ain't chess she's playing.'

Wanting to add her two penn'orth, Millie had a question to ask. She sat down on Clarissa's bed, tested the springs, and ran her hand over the counterpane. 'I still don't understand, 'Rissa. Why do you think it's Eleanor, and what could she possibly have in that office that would make her kill one of her own residents?' Ethel and Hilda nodded in unison, also keen to understand what Clarissa was thinking.

Stumped, Clarissa stumbled over her words. 'I... well, what I mean is... erm...' she waved her hands in exasperation, '...I can feel it in my water, that's all. Call it intuition, there's something fishy about her. Winnie told me that every time a resident causes problems, they end up dead a few days later. There was another one the other day; you remember him? That Walter from upstairs? He caused a commotion, and Eleanor had to banish him to his room and now he's dead.'

'Rookery Grange is just one of God's waiting rooms for old people, granted a bit more up-market than most, but what do you expect?' Ethel quipped. 'You come here, throw your dentures in a plastic glass, crayon things in and make Easter bonnets, and then you die, it's as simple as that.'

Clarissa threw her hand up in a staying motion. 'Well, whatever... Let's just go with my theory to start with. We consider Eleanor first, and if nothing comes from that, then we re-group and reconsider our options.' She tapped the face of her watch with her finger. 'Right, let's get going, Operation Bloomers is underway.'

The door to Room 8 slowly creaked open, spilling out four figures of various shapes and sizes, all dressed in black. The soft amber safety lighting cast eerie shadows on the walls that elongated and receded as they rounded the corner. Hilda's humming rendition of *The Pink Panther* theme tune accompanied them as they skipped and stumbled along the silent corridors of Rookery Grange Retreat to embark on their exciting adventure.

Duncan Dobbins angled his gloved fingers into the window frame and found the right spot. It popped first time, just as it had done on his previous visit to Rookery Grange, and with catlike agility he quietly slipped inside, momentarily pausing to listen for any sounds that would alert him.

Happy that Rookery Grange and its occupants were safely ensconced in their respective rooms, and it was to be hoped in the land of nod, he kept his back tight to the wall and crept along the corridor, confident that this time he would be able to successfully navigate his way around. He grinned to himself, his clever idea to differentiate between left and right had come to him in a eureka moment whilst finishing off the last can of Foster's lager and toasting his Christmas tree. He bunched his hand into a fist and pressed, feeling the light pressure in his palm. He might not have achieved much at school, or been successful in getting and keeping employment, but when the going got tough,

Duncan knew, just like the song promised, he would always get going. His brainwave to superglue the ring pull from that last can onto his palm had been genius. He only had to squeeze his hand and he'd know which way was… He stopped in his tracks.

Had he glued it to the hand that was left or the hand that was right? He couldn't remember.

'Bugger!' he muttered under his breath. As usual, Duncan's lack of anything up top had once again scuppered his plans. There was nothing for it, he would just have to resort to guessing where he was going and hope for the best. This time he'd take the opposite route to the one he had taken previously. He edged along the corridor and disappeared through the fire door.

NOW YOU SEE ME...

*E*thel's face appeared between the fronds of the areca plant in the entrance hall of Rookery Grange. Behind her Millie was clinging on to the coat stand, with Hilda bringing up the rear whilst muttering to herself. Clarissa had boldly gone where they had feared to tread; she was already halfway across the chequered floor, her rubber-soled house shoes squeaking on the tiles.

'Shh,' Ethel hissed. 'And will you stop chuntering to yourself, Hilda. You'll wake someone up; we have to stay silent.'

Hilda exhaled loudly, but did as she was told. They watched Clarissa's hand caress the large brass handle and tentatively turn it. She pushed against the solid wood, and with a soft click it opened. She turned and beckoned her co-conspirators inside. Ethel was the first to flit across the tiles, the moonlight through the large windows casting her shadow. Millie was next, throwing two shadows across the floor as she went.

Once inside, Clarissa closed the door behind them. She kept her voice low. 'Right, what we're looking for is anything to do with Rookery Grange and Eleanor, its history and hers, a diary maybe.'

'I'm a bit scared. I don't like this. What if we're found out?' Millie whispered.

Ethel tittered. 'Look, if we get caught, Hilda's daft, your deaf, and I don't speak English!' She plunged her hand into her pocket and pulled out Albert's head torch. Stretching the elastic band, she pulled it firmly over her head and adjusted the lamp to the middle of her forehead before scanning the room with it.

'Jesus, Ethel, you nearly burnt my retinas out!' Clarissa scrunched her eyes up and opened them again, a white light burning her vision. 'Great! I can't see anything now.'

'It's okay, I've found something.' Millie held up a leather-bound book and read out the title: '*Beyond The Walls of Rookery Grange...*' she murmured to herself. 'This could be it! How exciting.'

Clarissa had to agree, it was an interesting find, if nothing else. She rattled each desk drawer in turn, none yielding to her indelicate touch. 'Bugger, they're locked!' she grumbled. 'Right, back to my room. We can have a little read through and see where it takes us before we recce out again later.' Completely unaware that until recently, the book had been freely available on the console table in the hallway, she excitedly clutched it to her chest and opened the office door.

'Hold on a minute...' She counted heads. 'Where's Hilda?'

The assisted passing of Walter had not satisfied her as much as she had anticipated. The desire to kill again gnawed at the pit of her stomach. The discovery had been depressingly ordinary, and one that had caused little, if any, reaction from the staff or residents. No weeping or wailing or downcast mouths had accompanied the news he was gone. He had been so universally disliked that the consensus of opinion had been 'good riddance'.

Strangely, she had felt as though she had done more of a

service to others than to Walter himself. If she could have taken a bow and accepted their accolades of gratitude, then she would have done. But now was not the time to dwell.

She had work to do.

Pushing open the door to Room 6, she slipped inside. Allowing her eyes to adjust to the amber nightlight, she stood and watched Winnie Clegg. She was tucked under her duvet with just the tips of her blue rollers making an appearance above the floral material. A little snore, followed by a click and a sigh allowed her to reach the conclusion that Winnie was in a deep and restful sleep, although not half as deep and restful as what it would be in the minutes that followed.

'I sometimes wonder if you get to an age where death is a blessing...' Winnie had pondered in the Dark Angel's presence.

If she had twenty quid for every time she'd heard that little nugget of wisdom, she would truly be a wealthy woman. Instead it had become her calling. Rather than snuff out a life just because she could, she now had a vocation. She was providing a service whilst still satisfying her own needs.

She quite liked Winnie so she had decided upon a straightforward overdose of Pentobarbital. She held the syringe up, checked the barrel and popped off the safety cap. Winnie stirred in her sleep, throwing her arm over the top of the duvet. She was grateful for this action, as the less she had to touch or move, the better. Holding the syringe to the light, she stepped towards the sleeping Winnie.

'Hush, hush, dear Winnie. Death will be such a sweet release for you, one which I will take such pleasure in providing,' she whispered.

Suddenly a movement in the corner stilled her. She stood rooted to the spot, desperately trying to see through the darkness. The door opened behind her, allowing a faint shaft of light from the corridor to pattern through and light up the floor in front of her. Her heart thudded and then missed a beat as her breath caught in her throat. She turned; syringe still held high in her hand to see a figure disappear through the gap.

Winnie stirred again, releasing a soft sigh. The Dark Angel, momentarily frozen, willed her legs to move. Whoever had just escaped the room had been lurking in the darkness and would have heard and seen everything. She bit down hard on her bottom lip, drawing blood. The metallic taste alerted her senses and gave her the momentum she needed.

The unexpected reprieve for Winnie had just become a death sentence for someone else.

BANG TO RIGHTS

*D*uncan had never been so scared in all his life. He'd been caught red-handed a few times in his grafting career, but his arse had never twitched as savagely as it had just done in that old trout's bedroom.

He'd almost had his fingers on the prize when that bloody psycho had come swanning in, talking to herself. He'd been left under no illusion that she was giving out cocoa and biscuits at bedtime. He'd remained hidden at the side of the wardrobe, holding his breath for as long as he could, only fearing discovery at that stage. But once she'd started waving a syringe around like a light sabre whilst mumbling about death, he had quickly decided it was time to make himself scarce, and if bolting out of the room like Red Rum in the Grand National meant the old dear lived another day, then that was like being the bookies' favourite with decent odds for a win.

His feet automatically carried him at a great rate of knots along the corridor. He came to the end and stopped, his breath coming in sharp, rasping gasps.

Right or left? Left or right?

'Feck me,' he grunted. He chose right, glancing behind him as he went. She was on his tail, bearing down on him, her eyes wild and her white plimsolls making no sound on the carpeted corridor. He was sure he could almost feel her breath on his neck.

He turned left into familiar territory.

This was it. This was where he needed to be, the moon shone through the window at the far end of the corridor, a beacon in the darkness. His saving grace.

Closer.

He kept running.

Closer still.

He ducked through the open window, one leg dangling over the sill as his hands flailed out, looking for the drainpipe. As he grabbed it, a searing pain burst through the palm of his right hand.

The bloody ring pull!

Unfortunately for Duncan 'Drainpipe' Dobbins, the fleeting second it took for him to register the agony of an aluminium ring pull through skin and the epiphany that he had, for the first time in his life, recognised right from left, was time enough for her to reach him.

Her hands, palms towards him, hit his chest with such force that every millilitre of breath was expelled from his lungs. He scrabbled furiously to find purchase on the window frame, to hold on to anything that would save him, without success. He grabbed at the drainpipe, his fingers burning until they too lost their grip. He toppled backwards with his arms flailing out and flapping like a fledgling bird that had been kicked out of the nest.

The wind silently rushed past his ears as he plummeted down, his eyes wide with fear as his stomach lurched heavily. Before he could count to three, he had landed with a dull, sickening thud on the thick snow below.

He lay silent, staring at the sky.

He wondered if he might see Father Christmas and his

reindeer on an early flight as they swished across the inky blackness, weaving through the twinkling stars. He wondered how much the thick snow had broken his fall, maybe he'd been lucky and suffered just a few broken bones. He couldn't feel any pain, so surely that was a good sign. He wondered what Holly would say when she realised he had once again failed in his quest to find her the most perfect present. He wondered, if he willed himself to move, would he be able to stand up and just walk away, promising to turn his life around and never graft again?

So many questions; so much wondering.

He watched the cotton-like flakes of snow, so very white against the Stygian sky as they drifted down on him. He wanted to stick out his tongue and let them settle, just as he had as a child, but instead they silently danced to rest upon his lashes, blurring his vision.

His eyes drifted from the sky and finally came to rest upon his chest, to the source of his rapidly growing discomfort. A section of broken drainpipe protruded upwards, just below his ribs. Even in the moonlight he could make out the flaking black paint and a lump of moss clinging to the edge. 'Feck me, I'm a human kebab,' he gurgled as a pink bloody foam spluttered and poured from his lips.

His right hand spasmed as his last breath, weakly expelled, clouded upwards into the freezing air like ghostly ectoplasm. His body shuddered, stiffened and then fell still.

Duncan 'Drainpipe' Dobbins was dead, ironically killed by a tool of his trade.

ONE OF US IS MISSING...

'*B*ut she was right behind me,' Millie wailed as she flounced down onto Clarissa's bed.

'Well she isn't now, is she?' Clarissa grunted. 'I knew we should have left her at home, I'll never forgive myself if something has happened to her.'

Clarissa's response only served to compound Millie's distress. 'She'll be so confused and frightened; you know what she's like, she'll never cope on her own. I bet she's cowering in a corner somewhere, scared to death.'

Ethel squeezed Millie's hand as a show of support. 'She'll be here somewhere. We just need to be methodical in searching for her. She'll have just wandered off; you know what she's like.'

The book, now forgotten, was left discarded on the bedside cabinet as they frantically discussed their next move. Millie contributed very little, apart from wringing her hands together in anguish, whilst Clarissa, always the more practical and bossy of the group, went into full Brown Owl mode. 'Right. She can't be far; we need to split up. Ethel, you take the second floor. Millie, you do this floor, and I'll do downstairs.'

'I'm not wandering around this place on my own.' Millie

folded her arms to show her stance on the matter. 'It's stupid to split up; we could get picked off one by one.'

Ethel snorted. 'Oh for goodness' sake! It's not like we've got a serial killer in our midst. We coped with Phyllis when she actually *was* picking us off one by one. This is just a little adventure – and, as I've said before, Millie; the fatty in the group never gets kidnapped; it's too much like hard work!'

The three of them stood in the middle of the room, with Clarissa and Millie eyeing each other up and clearly wondering which one was the fatty Ethel was referring to. The look that Ethel gave Millie left her under no illusion that her curvaceous derriere and ample bosom were all the evidence needed to single her out as the one.

'Okay, we stick together. Have we got everything? Right, let's go.' Clarissa opened the bedroom door and peered out into the corridor. Satisfied it was safe, she beckoned the others to follow her.

Hilda shivered and scrunched her shoulders up to her ears. She listened intently whilst scanning the room with her torch. How she had ended up in this cold, dank place, she had no idea. One minute Ethel had been berating her for talking; the next – well, she wasn't quite sure.

She shuffled her way across the uneven flooring, her feet feeling for any dips or holes that could ambush her progress. She had her eyes on something special. She had spotted them when she had hit the last two stone steps on her downward descent into the bowels of Rookery Grange. On the wall furthest away from her, her torch had illuminated hundreds of bottles all neatly stored inside hutches on aged shelving. She didn't need to be a genius to know she had fallen upon a wine cellar, and as her earlier indulgence of half a bottle of sweet sherry was now starting to wear off, she gleefully anticipated topping herself up. She might even take a bottle or two back to their room for later once she'd sampled a few of them herself.

Her fingers traced across the bottles nearest to her, leaving tell-tale tracks in the dust that covered them. She pulled one out and blew vigorously on it before resorting to using the sleeve of her jumper to wipe it.

'Ooh, I like the sound of this one,' she muttered to herself. She shone her torch on the label. 'Chateau Lafite Rothschild 1985 – my goodness, it's nearly as old as me.' She chuckled. She gave the cellar another sweep with her torch and found the light switch. Flicking it on, she felt a sense of relief. It bathed the room in an eerie, dusty light, illuminating a small table and chair in the far corner, and, as luck would have it, a rather pretty wooden box that contained a cutter and a corkscrew. She didn't need any encouragement to take up the utensils and open the wine, and, in the absence of a glass, she gaily resorted to swigging it straight from the bottle. She would bide her time drinking red wine until the others came to find her. She took another swig, scrunched up her nose and checked the label again.

'Yuck, I certainly hope Mr Rothschild didn't pay more than a tenner for this one!' Not to be beaten, she took another gulp. It was odd that the more she drank, the more she began to like it. Maybe she'd finish this bottle and try another, and if the girls hadn't found her by then, she'd grab a few more bottles and go and look for them herself. She replaced the cutter in the wooden box and absentmindedly picked at a corner of the plush navy velvet that covered the base. It unexpectedly lifted away, revealing a compartment underneath. She removed the tray and allowed her fingers to probe its depths. She plucked out and deposited her finds on the table in front of her.

An engraved silver fountain pen.

A faded photograph.

Two hospital birth bands, the names on them barely legible.

A vellum envelope with a red seal that had previously been broken.

She held the aged and yellowing envelope in her hand, curious to know what it contained. She carefully slipped out the contents and smoothed down the creases.

The Last Will and Testament
of
Raif Victor Carnell

'I'm a little bottle short and stout, pop my cork and pour me out…' she trilled as the wine began to take effect. Slumping back in the chair, she swung her feet up onto the table and toasted the cellar wall of Rookery Grange Retreat before continuing her riveting read.

IN THE NIGHT, IN THE DARK

A new flurry of snow blew in sideways, whipping the Dark Angel's hair into a frenzy as she hung out of the window looking down on the lifeless body below. In those last moments before she had summoned the strength she had needed to push him, there had been a spark of recognition that ran both ways.

Dozy Duncan had been the son of Rookery Grange's gardener many, many moons ago. He had come to work with his dad on numerous occasions. He had very little in the intelligence department, but he would make up for it with his enthusiasm for flora and fauna. He was a village kid who would admire the trappings of a wealthier lifestyle, and maybe even harbour a little jealousy too. She was in no doubt that he had recognised her, which gave her some solace for her actions. Her fingers gently traced the scar on the side of her forehead, the scar that Dozy Duncan had given her all those years ago. It was one thing to change the colour of your hair, to have little tweaks here and there to facial features and a new bomb-proof identity that would withstand any checks, but a scar, particularly one as unusual as hers, was inevitably going to be the giveaway.

The brief sojourn into her memories had allowed her to become complacent and momentarily unaware of her surroundings. She heard them before she saw them. The one she knew as Clarissa Montgomery was the first to speak.

'She's not here, we've searched everywhere, something has happened to her...'

She pressed herself flat against the wall, hoping the large linen closet next to her would offer her decent cover whilst she continued to listen to them.

'We need to tell the police...' The tubby one at the back muttered.

'No, absolutely not. Phone Pru. She'll know what to do.'

She had heard this one being called Ethel by Winnie. What on earth a bunch of geriatrics dressed like 007 on a mission were doing, skulking around Rookery Grange in the middle of the night, was anyone's guess. They stopped suddenly, right by her hiding place, forcing her to hold her breath. She actually wanted to laugh at the one called Ethel who with every shake of her head, sent the ridiculous torch on elastic stuck to her forehead into overdrive. A staccato searchlight pierced the darkness, bounced off the walls and blinded her friends every time she agreed or disagreed with the other two.

'We haven't looked in all the bedrooms, only the vacant ones. Oh dear, this just gets worse. We're going to be found out, I know we are...'

The tubby one was close to having a meltdown.

The Dark Angel briefly considered a triple killing spree. She dreamily ran through possible scenarios in her mind, but just as quickly dismissed them. She couldn't take on all three at the same time; she would have to separate them. No sooner had that thought crossed her mind than she realised that Clarissa and Ethel had disappeared around the corner, leaving the tubby one pondering her choices. Her fingers felt for the unused syringe in her pocket. Placing the barrel between her fingers and her thumb on the plunger, she waited for the perfect moment.

Millie, oblivious to her would-be assassin, suddenly took the opportunity to check inside the linen closet for Hilda at exactly the same moment the Dark Angel made her move. Flinging the door open with torch poised, Millie was shocked to hear a loud bang as the door found some resistance and bounced back.

'For goodness' sake, Millie, hush.' Ethel had returned. Grabbing Millie by the arm, she half dragged and half pushed her around the corner.

The Dark Angel's head had snapped backwards on impact, the door having found its target with some force. Stunned, she ran the back of her hand under her nose and felt a wetness slither across the skin.

'What on earth is going on?' Eleanor's voice echoed down the corridor. She quickly tied the belt on her dressing gown and flicked the master lights on. The mellow safety lighting was instantly replaced with a stark, bright whiteness that flooded every nook and cranny.

The Dark Angel pressed herself against the wall, taking advantage of the cover provided by the linen cupboard. She waited for Eleanor to turn her back before slipping out to make good her escape down the servants' old staircase.

Bloodied, but still unseen.

Eleanor made her way along the corridor, tentatively peering around corners as she went, unsure of what would confront her. She pulled her mobile phone from her pocket and keyed in the number for the night office downstairs. If a resident was up and wandering, she had staff to deal with that sort of thing.

'Alex? Yes, first floor, I think we have a resident that's on a wander. Yes, bring Jenny with you. Quick as you can.' She hung up. Her eye fleetingly caught sight of a floating floral dressing gown and one slippered foot disappearing around the corner to the corridor that led to Rooms 4 to 9. She swiftly followed and picking up pace she made an abrupt right turn.

Empty.

'Mrs Parsons, do we know who it is?' Alex, the night duty nurse panted, the exertion of taking the stairs two at a time had taken its toll. Eleanor pointed to the doors either side. 'I was quick, but not quick enough; they've got to be from one of these rooms. If you do the odd numbers, I'll do the evens.'

Methodically, they both checked on the residents. Eleanor reached Room 8 and quietly opened the door. Clarissa was lying on her back in bed, sheets up to her chin, mouth open and gently snoring. She discreetly closed the door.

Alex shook her head. 'All present and correct and sleeping on this side.'

'Same here.' Eleanor was not convinced that all was as it seemed; one of them had been floating around and unless either Oscar in Room 7 or Chester in Room 9 had taken to wearing floral dressing gowns in their dotage, it had to be either Norma, Gertrude, Winnie or Clarissa. If her memory served her right, all four women possessed flowery nightwear and slippers.

'I'll take a check on the second floor, just to be sure, and I'll mark the night call sheets to show we've had a possible incident.' Alex looked at the nursing watch pinned to her uniform. 'I have a round at 5am with Jenny, so I'll mark that up too.'

Happy that her night staff would ensure all would be well, Eleanor returned to her room to continue her routinely troubled sleep.

EUREKA!

*C*larissa lay in bed staring into the darkness, waiting for Eleanor to go back to her room. A muffled thump from her wardrobe indicated that Millie was starting to get a little anxious and claustrophobic in the enclosed space. She leant over her bed and pulled up the counterpane cover to check on Ethel, who had hastily found the only other available hiding space in the bedroom and was now tightly squeezed under the bed.

'Bloody hell, 'Rissa, stop bouncing on the mattress, one of the springs under here has just nearly given me a nipple piercing!' Ethel shuffled out from underneath, turning on all fours to push herself up onto the bed.

Clarissa laughed. 'Don't flatter yourself, Eth; yours are more droopy than mine. Are you sure it wasn't your knees getting stapled?'

A disembodied voice came from the wardrobe, interrupting their joviality. 'Please can someone let me out, there's something furry and smelly touching me,' bleated Millie. 'I think it's alive!'

Clarissa turned on the bedside lamp and opened the mirrored door. 'It's just my coat, you silly woman. Well, that was close; I wonder if Winnie made it back to her room okay?'

Winnie had woken to the sound of hushed voices outside her room, and with her curiosity pricked she had donned her dressing gown and gone in search of the culprits. She had bumped into Clarissa, Ethel and Millie only seconds before Eleanor had come charging out of her room. They had all scattered like naughty school children.

Suddenly the door handle began to turn. Ethel shot down the side of the bed and Millie lunged for the wardrobe. The door opened and Winnie in her floral dressing gown, slipped inside. 'Sorry, girls, I didn't mean to startle you.' She limped over to the end of the bed and stood with her hands on her hips. 'Come on, spill the beans! I know you lot are up to something.'

For the third time in as many minutes, the door handle rattled and turned. Millie shot inside the wardrobe, Ethel jumped into bed with Clarissa, top to tail so her toes were almost poking up Clarissa's nostrils, leaving poor Winnie to limp over to the corner and hide behind the curtain.

The door creaked open, and just as quickly closed again.

The chink of bottles banging together made Clarissa question who her visitor might be. Hoping against hope it wasn't Oscar again with a rum tonic nightcap clutched in frisky hands, one eye peered over the blankets to see.

'Hilda!' Clarissa gave an audible gasp of relief as she jumped out of bed and flung her arms around her. 'Thank goodness you're okay. Where on earth have you been and how did you find your way back?' Getting a whiff of the alcohol on Hilda's breath, she recoiled. 'Blimey, did you fall in a vat of claret or just have a bath in it!?'

Hilda opened her mouth to speak, but could only contribute a very loud burp to the proceedings. She hiccupped as she offered out three bottles of wine. 'I found these; they were going free.' She swayed slightly, forcing Ethel to help her to sit down on the bed. 'It was easy to find you. I left a little trail earlier on, just in case any of you lot forgot where 'Rissa's room was.' She held out a large handful of mint imperials, smug in the mistaken belief that at least one of her friends could have a worse memory than her own. 'They've been in me pocket since last Christmas. I only suck them a few times and then I save 'em. Always knew they'd come in handy one day. I just had to follow them.' She popped one into her mouth, rolled it around for a few seconds, and then just as quickly spat it out and returned it to the scrunched-up paper bag. 'Oh, *and* I found these…'

She dropped the wooden box onto the counterpane, opened it and took out the tray. Spreading out the will, she arranged the photograph and the two baby wrist bands next to it. Clarissa picked up the will and began to study it, but it was Winnie's reaction to the photograph that attracted Ethel's attention. 'What is it, Winnie?'

Winnie studied it closely, taking it over to the bedside lamp so she could be sure. 'That's Dorothy Burnside, a lot younger, granted, but there's no mistaking her.' Her finger tapped decisively on the print.

The Four Wrinkled Dears gathered around Winnie and the photograph. It depicted a handsome couple with two young children, perfectly poised, alongside another man with a young girl. A decorative wrought iron table held a high tea, a three-tier cake stand hosting fancies and scones took pride of place in the middle. Ethel was struck by the downturned mouth and frown of the little girl and the forced smile from the boy, it made her involuntarily shiver. The adults looked happy enough, though. Behind them was an older lady, her carefully arranged brunette hair had paint brush strokes of grey at the sides. It flicked and curled at the collar of her lemon polka-dot dress.

Clarissa turned the photograph over. It had been marked and dated:

9th June 1988 — Rookery Grange

Raif and Penelope Carnell with their children,
Violet and Vincent,
  Sebastian Carnell, his daughter Ellie, and Nancy
Lawrence

'It can't be her, Winnie; it says "Nancy Lawrence".' She flicked the photograph over and carefully studied it again.

Millie was eager to help. 'I told you that my mum worked for them. Well I can tell you *that* is definitely the family nanny.' She stabbed a finger at her. 'I couldn't recall her name when I told you the story in Florrie's that day, but she looked after Violet and Vincent, and I remember now. Her name was Nancy, although the kids used to call her "Ouma", which I think came from the time they were living in South Africa with Raif's job. It's like a term of endearment or respect.'

Ethel was impressed with Millie's input, but it still intrigued her as to why Winnie thought it was Dorothy Burnside. 'What makes you think it's Dottie, Winnie?'

Winnie smiled. 'Besides her looking exactly like Dottie – see the nose and mouth? – I saw her secret tattoo, she showed it to me, she had it done at a rock festival in the 1970s. Upper left arm, a double daisy chain, if you look carefully here...' she pointed to the short sleeve of the lemon dress, '...you can just see it. And the Ellie Carnell that you see there...' again her finger snaked out to point at the young girl, '...she's our very own Eleanor Parsons. I'm exceptionally good on faces, and it's just a shortened version of her name, ladies.'

The five of them sat hunched over the photograph and the will, the bed taking as much of the strain as it could. Ethel had decanted the wine into any available receptacle: a toothbrush glass, the lid from Clarissa's hairspray, a vase, once she had disposed of the dried flowers, and finally an ornamental potpourri holder, and Hilda had once more happily offered to drink from the bottle.

Between them they polished off Hilda's purloined gift whilst making notes and questioning the evidence before them. The book they had taken from Eleanor's office yielded very little. Its pages contained the history of the house itself and the surrounding park land, which was a bitter disappointment to them. Finally Clarissa spoke.

'Okay, there are two things we need to do tomorrow. First, we must let Pru know what we've found out. She'll know what's useful to the police and where we can go to do a bit more research, and secondly we need to speak to Eleanor herself; she must have known that Dottie was Nancy Lawrence.'

They all nodded in unison. The discovery that Dottie had used an alias during her employment at Rookery Grange would surely be of interest to the police. The fact that it might even have something to do with her murder caused them to bristle with excitement, which was further fuelled by copious amounts of wine.

Their concern that any one of them might be in danger had been forgotten. They had stupidly let their guard down.

FIVE EMPTY BOTTLES

*A*ndy chewed the end of his pen whilst studying the board. A second photograph now kept Dorothy Burnside company. He carefully wrote *Thomas Whittle* underneath it with a black marker pen. The post-mortem result had contradicted the GP's original cause of death, and they now had another murder on their hands.

He read the report again. 'So, this drug Midazolam that was found in the tissue samples is what caused the respiratory arrest, and it was nothing to do with his pre-existing conditions.'

Lucy joined him at the board. 'Well, not quite. His pre-existing conditions were what made the implementation of the drug successful, particularly in the quantity that was administered.' She counted off on her fingers. 'First, he was very elderly, secondly he had a lung condition and Midazolam is a risk to the respiratory system of people who have obstructive pulmonary disease, which Mr Whittle had. It makes me wonder if the murderer knew his medical history.'

Andy sighed and nodded in agreement. 'Apparently it's one of the drugs used in end-of-life palliative care. Did you know that?' He involuntarily shuddered, remembering his father's last days.

'Right, so now we've got two confirmed murders at Rookery Grange. Luce, I need you to task one of the team to see if there's a connection with Thomas Whittle and Dorothy Burnside, anything that would indicate why they have been the targets as opposed to any of the other residents.' He gathered up Rookery's blue file marked RGR/1 from his desk, 'I'm going to speak to Murdoch to see if he'll sanction a PM on the latest one.' He checked the notebook by the phone, searching for the name he had taken that morning. 'Here it is: Walter Jenkins. He died four days ago – another one signed off by the GP, this time as a heart attack. In view of Whittle's PM results, we'd be remiss not to go with it. We'll give Rookery Grange a visit this afternoon to break the news to Eleanor.'

Lucy gulped down the remainder of her tea and took a bite from the piece of half-eaten toast. 'Where's the burglary team? It's like the Marie Celeste in their section.'

'Out looking for Drainpipe; his other half reported him missing this morning when the troops went round to her new place. Apparently he didn't come home last night, or so she says. She's probably covering for him, trying to keep him out for Christmas!'

Lucy grabbed her bag and car keys and followed in Andy's wake. A sheet of A4 paper featuring the face of Duncan Dobbins caught in the momentum of their haste. It wafted up into the air before lazily drifting from side to side as it settled on the carpet tiles.

The door to the incident room hissed shut behind them, leaving the images of Dorothy and Thomas to stare out from the board onto an empty office.

'We were having a girlie sleepover; it's not against the rules, is it?' Clarissa feigned ignorance coupled with innocence.

The Four Wrinkled Dears and Winnie stood in a regimented line in the office at Rookery Grange. Eleanor was holding court behind her desk, Her anger at their night-time frolics was strangely coupled with a hint of admiration at their quirky bravado and, more importantly, her concern that one of them had been in the cellar, the very place where her father's secret still lay. His deathbed confession had ensured she would never set foot down there, not even to retrieve the valuable assets it held, but she was versed well enough to know that their little soiree had cost her a small fortune. Five empty wine bottles stood to attention on top of the green leather inlay of her desk.

'Out of lemonade, were we, ladies?' Eleanor tapped each bottle in turn with her pen.

Tink, tink-a-tink, tink, tink...

'Name that tune in five.' Hilda giggled.

Millie kept her eyes firmly on her shoes; she didn't dare look up in case she caught Ethel's eye. She could see her shoulders jerking up and down as she too tried to suppress her laughter.

'You might find it funny, ladies, but what you did was a safety issue. If anything had happened, like a fire, there would have been no record of you being here.' Eleanor shuffled the paperwork on her desk. 'What I do not expect is my staff to find you lot bunked in with each other like a bloody Girl Guide's Jamboree when they do their rounds. How on earth did you get into Rookery Grange?'

They all stood in silence.

'Well, I'm waiting!'

'Through the staff door and then up the back staircase,' Clarissa sheepishly offered.

Eleanor made notes. 'I see, and what explanation do you have for these? Do you know that one of those bottles, the 1985 Chateau Lafite Rothschild, was valued at over £800? No? And these ones here add up to another £700. That's over £1,500 in total for those of you who didn't get an O level in mathematics.'

Hilda looked outraged. 'I drank that one and I wouldn't give you eighty pence for it; it was bloody disgusting. You really need to sort your cupboards out and get rid of stuff that's out of date, I mean 1985, for goodness' sake! I could be full of Cinderella!'

Eleanor looked confused, which prompted Ethel to step in. 'Salmonella; she means Salmonella.'

'It's a ruddy pity you weren't Cinderellas – then you would have been at home tucked up in your beds before midnight, and not wandering around my residential home like a flock of lost sheep,' snorted Eleanor. 'How are you going to pay for these? Out of your pensions?' She tapped the empty bottles again before returning to the paperwork in front of her.

A lull in the proceedings whilst Eleanor finished her notes gave the Winterbottom ladies the opportunity to elbow each other in turn, a hint for one of them to take the lead. 'You ask her,' Ethel hissed to Clarissa. 'You're our spokeswoman.'

Clarissa placed the photograph on the desk, pushed it towards Eleanor, and waited for a reaction. Eleanor ran through a gamut of facial expressions as she gazed upon the image, but it was the one where her eyes widened and her jaw set solid that gave the game away. 'Recognise anyone, Eleanor?'

Eleanor slumped back in her chair, her heart pounding in her chest. Was she defeated? Frightened? Weary? Probably all three, but she did recognise one thing: her house of lies was now dangerously close to tumbling down around her.

'I was quiet, but I was not blind…'

Jane Austen, *Mansfield Park* (1814).

DON'T POKE THE BEAR

*S*he carefully placed the unused lapel pin on the table next to the *Good Book* and gave Frizzle a tickle under his chin. He stretched up to reach her hand before flopping back down onto his side, inviting her to waste more time on him.

'Not now, Frizzle. Things to do, plans to make and deeds to carry out,' she sang. She sipped from her mug and took a bite of toast, using the uneaten end as a pointer. 'See her...' the corner of the toast brushed against the handwritten name in the book. 'She got a reprieve last night. Such a pity, but I did get a wonderful adrenalin rush with an unexpected kill.' She relived the moment the palms of her hands had thudded into the chest of Duncan Dobbins pushing him backwards. The look of terror on his face was a joy to behold. Her pleasure had always been achieved with relatively peaceful deaths, with the occasional butt-clencher thrown in to add perspective and an added frisson of excitement. Duncan's had begun as a necessity; he had been a dangerous witness; but had ended as an act of revenge. Her fingers automatically traced the scar that Duncan had given her all those years ago after months of bullying. She smiled, remembering his filthy face, streaked with tears and snot, his body rigid with shock, the spade still in his hand.

She had touched her head that day too, pulling her fingers away, mesmerised by the copious amount of blood that flowed down her face. It had taken longer than she had expected, but at last he had snapped, broken by her constant cruelties. He had seen her dark soul and was now a danger to her; he needed to be gone.

'I'm going to tell. They will sack your daddy and you'll be even more poor...' she had threatened whilst relishing his distress.

'You're a psycho. You're crazy!' he had screamed back.

'And don't I know it!'

Her grin had become wider and with her lips pulled back over her teeth, she threw her head back and laughed long and hard, barely drawing breath. Her one regret? That she hadn't been the one to wield the spade across his head first.

Frizzle let out a low yowl and buffed her hand with his head, knocking her out of her historic reverie. 'Okay, little man, breakfast it is.'

In the main she saw herself as an assistant to the Grim Reaper and a saviour to her victims, helping those that had outlived their uses to cross over. She adored the feeling of control, of being the one who decreed who would live and who would die. Her early kills had been influenced by rage, but not now. These days they were influenced by simple choice and circumstance and her maturity. Some asked to be released, others were selected by her own fear, the fear of being incapable, of being reliant on others with no free will.

That would never be living, it would be merely existing.

It would be worse than death itself.

'Here you go.' She dropped the small ceramic dish onto the floor. 'Right, it's nearly time for mummy to go; you be a good boy whilst I'm out.' She checked the cat flap was unlocked and grabbed her coat. Suddenly remembering her *Good Book,* she picked it up and carefully placed it back in the safe. The lapel pin was just about to join it when she hesitated, deep in thought. Changing her mind, she popped the pin into her pocket.

Her recent kills were just a delicious sideline and had rather distracted her from the real reason she was at Rookery Grange. Her plan had been clear cut at the beginning, muddied only by the letter and Dorothy Burnside. She hadn't really thought it through properly; she had committed a typical knee-jerk reaction that she was now paying dearly for.

'Are you sure you want to come with me?' Pru slugged back the rest of her coffee, kicked her slippers off and hooked her leg up, fluffy sock at the ready.

Bree shrugged her shoulders and sighed. 'What else have I got to do with my spare time two days before Christmas? I can't have my newly married friend alone whilst her husband gallivants around Winterbottom and Chapperton Bliss playing detective!'

Pru was still miffed that Andy had only managed two days leave from work after their wedding, but had resigned herself to the fact that it was going to be par for the course being married to a police officer. She couldn't quite imagine telling *him* that *she* wouldn't be available for a honeymoon because she was busy cataloguing Stephen King and Val McDermid whilst stuffing old editions of the *Winterbottom News* into box files. 'It's Rookery Grange's Sherry & Lights, tonight. They put up the main Christmas tree and finish off decorating the dining room before the switch on, so an extra pair of hands will be grand.'

'If you say so.' Bree pulled her boots on and wrapped a warm tartan scarf around her neck. 'Am I on spit, lick and stick duties then?'

'Bleurgh! You make that sound like something naughty.' Pru laughed. 'Probably. They do cosset their colourful paper chains, and they're pretty easy for even the most arthritic of fingers.' Before she could finish her observations on occupational therapy, the vibrating buzz of her mobile phone on the breakfast bar interrupted her. She held up a finger to Bree, indicating she would only be a minute. 'Hello…' She frowned as she listened. 'Clarissa, calm down. Take deep breaths, right… and now start again…'

Bree, alerted to hearing Clarissa's name, moved closer to Pru. 'What's the matter?' she mouthed.

Pru waved her hand whilst still listening intently. 'Hilda, Millie *and* Ethel – all of you? Okay, we're on our way. Just keep together, don't antagonise anyone or poke your noses into anything else. I know it a hard ask, but for goodness' sake just try and act normal!' Pru abruptly ended the call.

'Act *normal*? You're having a laugh – with those four?' Bree already had her coat on and her bag slung over her shoulder. 'What's happened?'

Pru shoved her feet into her boots and patted the pockets of her jacket to ensure she had everything. 'That's what we're going to find out.'

THE FOUR LIABILITIES

*G*oldie Franklin applied a final slick of lipstick and feathered the edges of the eyeliner she had just applied. It was quite stark in contrast to the muted lilac eyeshadow she had chosen that morning. 'Oh drat and damnation,' she grumbled. Her signature winged eyeliner was becoming a bit of a devil to apply the older she got. She inspected the end of the brush and then checked her reflection in the mirror again. The flicked wing had almost disappeared in one of the folds of her crow's feet. 'It's like painting a bloody Shar Pei these days – there's no positives in getting old, is there, Alex?'

Nurse Alex tucked Goldie's favourite blanket around her legs, ensuring no corners were dangerously draped that could inadvertently become caught in the wheels. 'Oh I don't know, surely there is always something positive to greet the day, Ms Franklin. It's Christmas Decoration Day today. The tree is going up, and we've got the lady from the library coming in to do crafts with you. That'll be fun, won't it?'

It was on the tip of Goldie's tongue to snap back with a withering comment, but she bit down on the jibe and instead opted for a more acceptable phrase. 'I suppose so, but it's a bit like going back to school. They get you with their sticky glue pots and glitter when you're five, and then the buggers come back for you when you're eighty-five.'

Alex laughed. 'I would go with that, but you're only eighty-three!'

Goldie thought for a while. 'Am I?'

'Yes, so there you go. *There's* a positive: you're two years younger than you thought you were.'

'Maybe I am, but that's just as bad…' Goldie harrumphed. 'I thought I looked good for eighty-five, but can you imagine what another two years' worth of ruddy wrinkles and decadent living will do to my face?'

Their mutual laughter caught the attention of Goldie's next-door neighbour, Lillian from Room 2. She stood in the doorway of Goldie's room, her flower-decorated walking stick propping her on an uneven tilt. 'Can't nobody get a wink of sleep around here for you lot giggling like a… well… like whatever does giggle, a zebra or something? You've ruined my siesta!' Clearly having forgotten the comparison she wanted seemed to annoy her more. She offered up a few expletives as she tucked the half-bottle of vodka provided by her daughter-in-law into her handbag. 'Are you coming down to the lounge, Goldie? I don't want to be stuck on me own on a table with that Winnie woman from the village. She'll drive me bloody nuts!'

They all sat in silence. The only sound that filled Eleanor's office was the ticking of the grandfather clock in the corner.

'I just don't believe it! The four of you are an absolute liability!' Pru shook her head in exasperation. 'You're all grown women; what on earth made you carry out a ridiculous stunt like that?'

Eleanor sat quietly behind her desk, Bree was propping up the fireplace, Pru sat on the edge of the desk and Clarissa, Ethel, Hilda and Millie sat rigid in four high-back chairs that had been brought in for them, their facial expressions giving nothing away. It was more an impassivity scene than a nativity one.

Ethel plucked up the courage to speak first. 'It was just a bit of fun. Nobody got hurt and we did find out something that Andy will be interested in – didn't we, Eleanor?'

Eleanor squirmed in her chair. 'That is something I will discuss with Detective Barnes when he gets here. It still doesn't explain you lot thinking you were on a Butlin's holiday trip with a wine-tasting session thrown in.'

Bree stifled a giggle; she was actually quite impressed with their quaffing prowess. 'Maybe a couple of bottles of cheap vino from Aldi would have sufficed, ladies, rather than raiding the speciality wine cellar here. I think that's been the problem.'

'No, the problem is that they could have put themselves in danger. We don't know why Dottie was murdered, and…' Pru suddenly remembered that although she had been privy to inside information on the investigation, it wasn't her place to inadvertently let slip that Thomas Whittle had also been a victim. 'Well, I think we should leave this now until Andy and Lucy arrive. Eleanor, I think it would be advisable to tell the police everything you know about Dottie and her links to Rookery Grange; keeping back that information may have had implications for the investigation.'

Hilda wriggled in her chair. 'I've got a special piece of paper, too. I found it in the cellar, it was hidden in the box. Clarissa says it could be important.' She waved the envelope with the broken red seal at Pru.

Pru took it from her. 'Thank you, Hilda. I'll have a look at it, and if it's important I'll give it to Andy. Eleanor has said you can all stay for lunch, so if Andy or Lucy need to speak to you, they can do so here. You're lucky she's being so magnanimous under the circumstances. You can join me and Bree to do the Christmas decorations later; it'll keep you out of further mischief.'

The way Eleanor was feeling she was grateful that Pru had taken the lead. Keeping the feisty foursome together in one place gave her at least some control, but she knew she was going to have to confess and face her demons; she just didn't know if she was strong enough to do battle with them.

PRELUDE TO A MURDER

Pru patiently waited for the ladies and gentlemen of Rookery Grange Retreat to pick their tables, find the comfiest chairs, and choose which fellow resident they wished to sit with. The earlier peace and quiet, coupled with an empty room, had given her the opportunity to lay out the brightly coloured cardboard, glitter, felt pens and glue pots ready for the craft class. Each table had their equal share. She still wasn't quite sure what she was doing. A quick YouTube tutorial the night before had given her the basics for Christmas garlands and make-your-own Christmas cards, but she hadn't realised how much effort and planning it would take when she'd agreed to help out.

She inhaled deeply, trying to bring some calm to the knot in her stomach. She had briefly looked at the papers Hilda had given her earlier. Along with the impact of Eleanor's confession of knowing about Dottie and her previous employment at Rookery Grange, the potential implications that would come from the Last Will and Testament of Raif Carnell, would be absolute dynamite if it hadn't been superseded by another one. The sooner Andy would arrive, the better.

'Here you go, Miss Franklin. If you sit here, there's more room for your wheelchair.' She helped to manoeuvre Goldie into position next to Winnie, who was now happily ensconced on a chair with a memory foam cushion.

Lillian, who had been ambling behind the rest of the group, stopped dead in her tracks and without warning, raised her walking stick. Prodding the air, she voiced her feelings loudly. 'I've already told you, cats will fly before I sit next to that old bugger!' She gave Winnie a well-rehearsed look of disdain.

'It's pigs,' Winnie helpfully offered and then just as quickly went back to folding her yellow cardboard into a star-shape, totally nonplussed that Lippy Lil wasn't her biggest fan.

'Don't you dare!' Lillian was almost spitting fire. 'That corpulent trout has just called me a pig!'

'Ladies, ladies, please!' Pru gently coaxed Lillian's stick down to a more acceptable level. 'I tell you what, why don't you sit here with Mr Burton? You don't mind, do you, Oscar?' She gave him her warmest smile and in return he gave his usual frisky wink.

'I don't mind if I do, Prunella. I'd be delighted to warm to the charms of dear Lillian.' He patted the seat next to him. A retired army captain, Oscar had never been known to turn down any request that, in his humble opinion, meant he would enjoy the charms of someone of the opposite sex. Pru was totally oblivious to his frisky and inappropriate behaviour, the source of amusement and angst in equal measure to the female residents of Rookery Grange, and the very reason why Clarissa actively avoided him.

Lillian sat down next to him, shuffled her chair forwards and grinned, all whilst ensuring the leg of her chair settled nicely on the top of Oscar's foot. She mischievously wobbled from side to side, watching his face turn a different shade of red with each movement she made. 'Just a little warning, Oscar. Don't be trying any of your shenanigans with me, or the pain you're feeling now will be nothing to the pain you'll feel later!'

Oscar, his breath momentarily taken away, frantically nodded his understanding, a look of relief washing over him as Lillian released his foot. 'Ah my dear, you are a little tiger, aren't you?' He grinned.

Watching the exchange, Pru quickly realised her mistake in partnering them up. Fearing an all-out war between them, she intervened. 'I've got a better idea: some of the team have set out the boxes of Christmas decorations in the quiet room. They could do with a hand in sorting them out before they go on the tree, so how about you, Lillian?'

Lillian grunted. 'If it'll get me away from Captain Octopus here, I'll volunteer for anything.' She eased herself up from the chair. 'And as an added bonus, I won't have to sit with you lot either.' Her floral stick hit the horizon and scanned the room in sniper fashion.

As Lil made her way to the quiet room, grunting away to herself, Pru was privy to a few whispered asides from the rest of the residents, clearly showing their relief that Lillian had left the room. Such was their mutual joy she wouldn't have been at all surprised if they had burst into a round of spontaneous applause.

The Four Wrinkled Dears who had created so much consternation the night before ambled along the corridor towards the lounge. Millie once again brought up the rear, dragging a multi-coloured paper chain behind her. Clarissa led from the front with Ethel and Hilda holding the middle with balloons and tinsel.

'Just look as though we're decorating, girls, at least until we can shut ourselves away in there.' Clarissa pointed ahead of her, utilising a plastic red-and-white striped candy cane for direction. She stopped at the end of the corridor, flattened her back against the wall, and ushered her friends ahead of her. Satisfied they hadn't been followed, she slipped in behind them and shut the door.

'Right: seats, ladies, and let's recap.' She waited whilst they shuffled themselves around, pushing chairs into a small circle. 'Okay, I'll begin with what Eleanor has so far imparted. We have the murder of Dorothy Burnside, who we now know was the Carnell's family nanny to their two kids, but under an assumed name because of a drugs conviction. She then disappeared shortly after the murders of Raif and Penelope.'

Hilda scanned her notes and pointed her pen at Clarissa. 'Was that when her girlfriend fell off a gorgonzola in Venice and drowned?'

'It's called a gondola and no, it was a boat in Amsterdam, not Venice, Hilda,' chuckled Millie.

Indignant, Hilda poked her pen into the spiral spine of her book. 'Same bloody thing; it's got water, hasn't it? I went to Amsterdam once. They were years ahead of us, you know. Instead of having tailors' dummies in the shop windows to show off the fashions, they actually had real live women in them.'

Millie wriggled in embarrassment whilst Ethel guffawed loudly. 'I think you'll find the price tag wasn't just for their underwear, Hilda; they were selling a lot more than that!'

Clarissa clapped her hands. 'We're digressing here, girls; let's get back on track. So, feeling a sense of family duty, Eleanor gives Dottie a place for life at Rookery Grange Retreat when she turns up here in 2004, fourteen years after the Carnell tragedy, and confesses her drugs history and reveals her real name. Then we've got the will of Raif Carnell, which left everything to their kids, Violet and Vincent…'

Ethel jumped in to add her observation. 'Including Rookery Grange. So why is Eleanor the owner and not them?'

Clarissa looked pensive. 'That's the million-dollar question.

Eleanor said she inherited from her father Sebastian, who was Raif's brother, but the will says otherwise. Dottie's murder has got to be linked to the Carnell's somehow, as well as to Rookery Grange. It's all too much of a coincidence, but what we don't know is why.'

THE BIG SWITCH ON

'*M*iserable bloody shower of has-beens and old farts…' Lil grumbled to herself as she simultaneously slugged vodka neat from a bottle and chucked a sparkly gold bauble into the box marked 'Glitter Decs'. Several other boxes were laid out in front of the sofa she was sitting on, each marked with either colour or finish, according to where in Rookery Grange they would be adorning. A 1,000-light string of Christmas tree lights coiled themselves around the coffee table and draped onto the floor. Lil couldn't comprehend why anyone would put lights away in such a higgledy-piggledy manner, it was odds on that some poor sod would have to untangle them the following year. She took another swig from her bottle and held it aloft to measure how much was remaining. Seeing the line wavering near the bottom, she reluctantly realised that she could either kiss goodbye to the rest of the day and finish the whole bottle or take it easy and save some for tomorrow. She couldn't remember if today was Monday or Tuesday. That was the thing about being in a place like Rookery Grange: every day became the same as the last, and you lost track of time. She took another swig and licked her lips. 'Tuesday, it's definitely Tuesday.'

She felt content once she had made that decision. Her Jack's miserable excuse of a wife would be calling tomorrow with her weekly top-up. 'Dear God, son, you could have done so much better than that old cow,' she muttered as she aimed a red satin bauble at the box marked 'Red Decs'. Vera, her daughter-in-law, had never been top of her Christmas card list, but she had suffered her in the hope she would have offered Lil a place to live at their house when she reached her dotage. What she hadn't envisaged was for them to have a late life bloody crisis, up sticks from a five-bed house with granny-annexe in the country, to a village convenience store in the back of beyond and a two-bed flat above it. In a flurry of activity to move and start a new life, Lil had been consigned to two suitcases, a new mohair coat and a tumbler with her name on for her dentures. That was quickly followed by being unceremoniously dumped in the entrance hall of Rookery Grange Retreat for the rest of her miserable life.

She knew deep down that it hadn't really been like that, but that was how it had felt to her. She had cleverly used her mental anguish and her son and daughter-in-law's guilt to blackmail Vera into a bottle of vodka every week. This time she took a smaller sip and quickly replaced the screw top. 'Think I might have to up the anguish and get the old boot to make it a litre bottle in future.' She chuckled to herself.

'What are you doing in here all on your own, Lillian?'

Startled, Lil quickly shoved the vodka bottle under the nearest velour cushion. She opened her mouth to speak, but instead a most unladylike burp escaped. 'Oops, pardon me. Mind you, better out than in though … *hic* …' If she could have been bothered, she might have looked a little embarrassed, but seeing it was only one of the staff she preferred to save most of her emotions for people that mattered. However, even they were few and far between these days. 'I'd rather be on me own than with that shower of miserable feckers,' she spat. 'We're all sitting here waiting for God like that TV programme, and some of us are lingering a lot longer than they should be allowed to!' Throwing another bauble into the correctly labelled box, she didn't even bother to look up. If she had, then maybe one more Christmas for Lillian 'Lippy Lil' Williams would have been on the menu.

Lil's uninvited companion stood behind the sofa, mimicking Lillian's *yatter, yatter, yatter* with her thumb and fingers, much like you would control the opening and closing of a sock puppet's mouth.

She tilted her head and watched Lil chuck bauble after bauble into the various size boxes, whilst all the time chunnering and spitting spite to herself. She had come in today to assist the next name on her list from the *Good Book,* but Lillian with her cantankerous ways had inadvertently put herself forward for that honour. She tenderly stroked the lapel pin that was tucked under the collar of her blouse, and feeling a charge of electricity from her talisman, she grabbed the coil of Christmas lights from the coffee table. 'These could do with a little bit of TLC, Lillian; they're in such a mess, all knotted and jumbled in the middle.' She bent down and plugged them in, and they immediately flashed into life. Reds, greens, blues and amber hues produced a rainbow of colours that immediately lit up the quiet room.

Lillian wasn't impressed. 'I'm busy. Do it yerself, I don't get paid to do your job!'

'Oh dear, Lillian, that's not what I wanted to hear at all...' She quickly moved behind the sofa again, the lead wire from the socket stretched taut between both hands. '...But I do get paid to do mine, and tidying up and putting things where they belong is such fun!'

Before Lillian had chance to react, the Christmas tree lights were wrapped tightly around her neck.

'I want to be a happy Christmas tree,
With bright twinkling lights draped over me,
Over my body and around my neck,

One last breath, oh blinking heck…'

Her sing-song voice was meant for Lillian's ears only and belied the fear that her client was currently feeling. 'Oh no, wait – they're not twinkling or blinking are they, Lil?' Her laugh brought a sudden chill to the room.

As Lil fought with her assailant, her hands grabbing at the wire and lights, she clawed at her throat, desperately trying to find space to curl her fingers underneath the wire to relieve the pressure. Her legs became rigid and unyielding as her back arched violently.

'Here we go, soon solved.' The Dark Angel kept the wire taut around Lil's neck with one hand and pressed the mode button with the other so the lights went through a flurry of spectacular phases, each phase accompanying Lil's last throes of life.

Steady.

Lil's feet spasmed and stamped against the rug.

Sequential.

Lil's nails tore at the delicate skin on her neck.

Slo-Go.

Lil's eyes bulged bloodshot and glassy.

Chasing.

Lil's rictus grin gave no indication of humour.

Fade.

Lil's waning heartbeat throbbed in her ears.

Combination.

Lil's body gave one last heave to accompany her last breath.

Flash / twinkle.

And Lil was gone… just like that.

IT'S YOU...

*C*ontent that everyone was engrossed with their crafting tasks, Pru beckoned Bree over. 'Do me a favour, I can't find Eleanor anywhere, so can you keep an eye on this lot, particularly Captain Tentacles over there?' She pointed to Oscar. 'I just need to check on Lillian.' She rolled her eyes to evidence her reluctance to be crossing paths with the cantankerous old witch she had banished to the quiet room almost an hour ago.

Bree grinned. 'Rather you than me! I'll give you a shout as soon as Andy arrives. Have you still got it?'

Pru patted the pocket of her jacket. 'Yep, safe and sound, although what it means, I don't know. It could have been superseded by another will, but he definitely needs to know about Dottie's connection to this place.'

Leaving Bree to mind the flock, Pru took the opportunity to discreetly check out the ground floor of Rookery Grange, find her missing WI ladies who hadn't been seen since before lunch and, if she was lucky, locate the cellar where Hilda had found the 'treasures' she had handed over to her. She would then make her way to ensure Lillian hadn't ambushed another resident or set fire to the place, such was her reputation. Della from the kitchen gave her a cheery wave as she breezed along the corridor, a hastily grabbed pile of books under her arm to provide a reasonable excuse for wandering the chequered tiles of Rookery Grange. There was no harm in doing a bit of snooping at the same time; you never knew what you might find or overhear. Each door that she passed bore either a number or a description of its use: laundry room, stores, pharmacy, and so on. Then she came to a door that had neither a number nor a name. She checked to ensure she wasn't being watched before she allowed her hand to rest on the brass handle. She slowly turned it until it clicked. A cold draught seeped through a small gap, bringing with it a sweet, musty smell.

'Can I help you?'

She almost jumped out of her skin. Her heart pounded and a slick of sweat along her back suddenly appeared from nowhere. She turned to see Della standing behind her in the corridor. 'Oh gosh, I... erm... I was just looking for the ladies' room, I need to powder my nose.'

Phew, talk about thinking on my feet, the little voice that often chattered away in her brain, exclaimed.

Della stood firm, her hands on her hips. 'You've come the wrong way. If you go back to the entrance hall, turn right by the staircase; it's there.' She gave Pru a knowing smile. 'If you get lost again, Jenny and Alex are on duty, they'll help you.'

'Thank you.' Pru instinctively patted the pocket that held the will before making her way back the way she had come, aware that Della was watching her every move.

After a short detour to the toilet – not that she really needed to go, but she had made a show of flushing the loo and washing her hands just in case her actions were being monitored – she arrived at the quiet room. She opened the door and slipped inside.

'It's only me. Just checking you're okay, Lillian, and to see if there is anything you...' Pru's heart jolted for the second time in as many minutes. She stood rooted to the spot, barely able to breathe as a wave of terror washed over her. Not one muscle, sinew or nerve obeyed the order that her brain had rapidly given out.

Run, Prunella, run.

Lillian, her protruding eyes and lolling tongue, lay sprawled on the sofa, a set of twinkling Christmas tree lights wrapped so tightly around her neck they had forced a purple blush to mottle her face. Pru's eyes were drawn to an empty bottle of vodka as it rolled across the rug, and then to something she wished with all her pounding heart she had not had the misfortune to see. 'You!' Her voice croaked, strained with fear. 'It's been *you* all along...'

The Dark Angel smiled at Pru as she completed her task. 'You should have stuck to flogging books, Prunella. I did warn you.' Ensuring the lapel pin was in place, she began to sing as she bore down on her next target.

'Look at me, I'm a Christmas tree,
With bright twinkling lights wrapped over me...'

A sudden rush of synapses to Pru's brain successfully kickstarted her muscles into action. She felt as though they would explode with the power that burned through them as she turned and began to run for the door.

Out into the corridor, across the chequered tiles, her eyes darting from side to side looking for somewhere to hide, all whilst her conscience told her others would be in danger too. 'Bree, Bree get help!' she screamed as she turned the corner of the staircase, her hand rolled across the smooth oak pillar ball, anchoring her so she wouldn't collide with the display case. Instead her leg kicked the plant pot, it teetered momentarily before crashing to the floor.

Oh my God, Ethel and Clarissa – where are they, where's Bree – why isn't Andy here yet?

Don't think, just keep running...

She was back in the long corridor. 'The Pharmacy' wall sign told her she was not far from the unmarked door that she knew was unlocked. Reaching what she hoped was going to be her sanctuary, she grabbed the handle and turned, pushing open the door that led to an inky blackness. She hesitated, until the momentum of being viciously thumped in the middle of her back had her tumbling forward into an uncontrolled fall.

Pru splayed her arms out to save herself. She had no idea what was ahead of her, her body carrying her forward with no means to stop. The side of her head hit what she assumed was the wall; it pivoted her sideways, forcing her left shoulder to collide with the other wall. The momentum continued as she lurched ahead and down, her knees hitting what she now realised were steps, as she rolled and bounced into the depths of Rookery Grange Retreat.

The pain coursed through her body and burst into a million stars against the blackness behind her eyes. She let out an involuntary grunt as her body hit the stone floor below.

A true darkness then descended and enveloped her, leaving her silent, broken and alone.

A CONFESSION

$\mathcal{B}$ ree moved between the tables, paying compliments to various tatty-looking paper chains and sticky Christmas cards that had been created by the residents. She had wanted to say 'lovingly created', but that would have been a great big fat lie. She smiled. 'Loathingly created' would have been a better description, judging by their faces and constant grumbles.

In all honesty, she couldn't really blame them; it certainly wouldn't be her idea of fun in her dotage. When she got to that age she had already decided that she would spend her twilight years outrageously, just like Ethel, Clarissa, Millie and Hilda. They were frequently a pain in the arse, but they did have so much sass and a thirst for adventure. She quite admired them for last night's shenanigans: the vision of them creeping around and then getting hammered on expensive vintage wine before bunking in together was comedy gold. Talking of which, they had been absent for quite some time. She groaned. That could only mean one thing: they were probably up to mischief again.

'Talk of the Devil...' She laughed as the Fearsome Foursome wandered into the room. 'Where on earth have you lot been?'

Ethel looked to Clarissa for a reason, but just as quickly created her own. 'We've been practising carol singing,' she lied.

'Have we?' Hilda harrumphed. 'I don't remember singing for anyone called Carol.'

Millie quickly jumped in. 'It's "Silent Night", Hilda, come on, you know the words.' She gave her an exaggerated wink as she began a particularly awful rendition of the well-known carol. 'Round yon virgin mother and child...' she warbled.

Hilda cupped her ear with her hand. 'Eh? Honestly, I don't know what these women get up to these days, what's she verging on?'

Bree put her arm around Hilda and ushered her to a vacant table. 'Tell you what, why don't we have a go at making a Christmas card and then we can all go and decorate the tree. I think Lillian will have finished her bauble-sorting by then.'

An ear-piercing scream, followed by frantic shouting and a loud crash, suddenly echoed along the corridors, to be amplified once it reached the entrance hall. Bree paused in her task with Hilda, momentarily stunned, trying to process what she had just heard. She threw down the glue brush. 'That was Pru, something's wrong...'

A ripple of panic ran through the residents as their anxious, chaotic chatter filled the room. Bree swung into action. 'Hilda and Millie, please can you stay with everyone in here, keep the ladies calm. Captain Burton, once we leave the room I need you and Chester to push that bookcase in front of this door. Lock yourselves in and don't come out until I tell you to. Have you got that?'

Oscar Burton rose to the challenge; he puffed out his chest, full of self-importance and threw a salute. 'Yes, ma'am. Leave it with me.'

As much as Bree regularly moaned about Clarissa and Ethel being a nuisance, she wanted them with her, there was a real need for safety in numbers. 'Ladies, can you come with me?' She tentatively opened the door and checked that the coast was clear before beckoning them to follow her out into the corridor. The heavy oak door slowly closed shut behind them, allowing her to wait briefly until she heard the bookcase being dragged along the floor on the other side.

'*This way,*' she whispered.

Pru blinked her eyes rapidly, trying to adjust to the dim lighting around her. Her head felt as though it was about to explode. Shards of pain flashed across her temple, accompanied by a thick wetness that trickled down her cheek. Her instinct was to test it with her hand, but her wrists were tied tightly together, the same as her ankles. She took stock of her situation. She was still on the floor, but her back was propped against a damp brick wall.

Ahead of her were hundreds of bottles picking up a muted reflection in their dust. Row upon row of them were lined up on a custom-made wine rack. To her left she could see the last three or four steps of a staircase, and then a blackness that reached up into a void. A table and chair occupied one corner. A large metal ceiling lamp cast its muted lighting across the floor, as regimented lines of dim wall lights complimented its weak reach. In the other corner was an industrial scale generator housed in a floor-to-ceiling cage. She inhaled deeply, trying to wash away the nausea that had suddenly swept over her.

'Pru, are you okay?'

The voice came out from the darkness, close to the wine storage. It made her startle. 'Who's that?' She didn't recognise her own voice as it croaked out from her throat, the dryness giving it a rasping quality.

'It's me, Eleanor. Oh God, Pru, I'm so sorry you've got dragged into this. It's all my fault.'

A soft sobbing filled the cellar, accompanied by intermittent low moaning. As much as Pru wanted to be angry, and to concentrate solely on her own predicament, there was something heartbreakingly sad in Eleanor's tears. They seemed to be of regret, grief and fear more than self-pity. 'Are you tied up too?'

'Yes, and she's gone back upstairs, I didn't get chance to warn anyone; it all happened so quickly. I think I was hit on the head with something, and then I woke up here.' Eleanor whimpered as she pulled and writhed, trying to free her hands. 'Ouch…' Her skin burnt as it twisted in unison with the rope. She shuffled forwards on her bottom to be closer to Pru.

'The police are on their way, my husband is a detective… it'll be okay; we'll get out of this, we just need to stay calm,' Pru promised. She tried to sound positive as she pushed back the memory of her last near-death experience in the cellar of Magdalen House when serial killer Phyllis Watson had gone on a murderous rampage. At any other time she would have thought it amusing that only she could inadvertently find herself in a similar predicament. 'What on earth is going on, Eleanor?' Dead air filled the room, broken only by the sound of their respective shallow breathing. Pru waited. 'I need to know; anything you can tell me might help us.' She winced as a sharp pain dug into her ribs, making her gasp.

'It's Rookery Grange; it's all to do with this place.' Eleanor was clearly measuring her words. 'There are too many secrets; this place has housed evil for far too long.' She began to cry again, forcing Pru to offer words of solace. Not because she wanted to be empathetic, but because she had no choice; she had to keep Eleanor calm and on track.

'The basics, Eleanor, just give me the basics, and then I can think through what we need to do.'

Eleanor sighed loudly. 'There's a dead body holed up in that wall over there.' She jerked her head towards the wine bottles. 'My father murdered Beryl our housekeeper and bricked her up behind that. It was years ago.' She felt a sudden sense of relief that she had actually spoken this out loud, but why the age of Beryl's death should lessen the impact of her confession and excuse the deed was beyond her reasoning.

Pru almost choked. 'Bloody hell, break it to me gently, why don't you!'

Eleanor snorted. 'You told me to give you the basics.'

'Yep, but you could have said something like *"Once upon a time my dad lost his rag and had a dispute with the cleaner..."* sort of build up to it; you don't just blurt it out.' Pru gave out a nervous giggle, she wasn't best pleased to now be privy to a murder confession, and neither was she ecstatic to know she was sharing a cellar with a decomposing Mrs Mop.

'I think what's happening might have something to do with Beryl's death and the fact I should never have inherited Rookery Grange in the first place. I know I should know who is doing this. She seems familiar, but I don't know why.' Eleanor sobbed.

Pru closed her eyes. The image of Lillian slumped on the sofa lit up like a budget Christmas tree played back to her like a vintage movie reel. 'She's murdered at least two people, Eleanor, and goodness knows what she's doing upstairs. Come on, think!'

'I am, truly I am, but I just don't know…'

'Bloody hell, she's been working for you for goodness knows how long! You must have interviewed her. What about her references? Where did she work before here? Why would she target Rookery Grange, and why do you think it's got anything to do with your psycho dad and the housekeeper? That's like putting two and two together and making five!' Pru was exasperated as well as frightened.

Eleanor shook her head in resignation. 'Because she told me.' She wept. And then her comfort counting began in earnest.

One potato,
Two potato,
Three potato...

A MUTUAL UNDERSTANDING

*T*he Dark Angel sat quietly in the rocking chair of Room 14. The late afternoon sun that had earlier broken through the clouds to make the snow-covered landscape sparkle was now quickly fading to reluctantly release its hold on the day and offer itself up to dusk.

Thunk, thunk, thunk.

She rocked backwards and forwards, a steady rhythmical music to her troubled soul. Her hand caressed the aged envelope, her fingers tracing the broken seal. She was finally holding what she had spent so long looking for, and quite by chance. All she had to do now was clear up the two little problems she had left in the cellar and make good her escape. Given time, she would reinvent herself and come back to claim what was rightfully hers.

Thunk, thunk, thunk.

She paused her hypnotic rocking to turn on the table lamp; the amber light provided a warmth to the room as it chased away the chill she had brought with her. It lit up the face of Martha Whittle who was still sitting poised on the dresser. She briefly wondered if Martha and Tom had been reunited; if they had, then she was content to know she had done her part to facilitate that reunion.

Thunk, thunk, thunk.

She encouraged her fingers to pluck out the parchment inside and as her eyes, wide in wonderment, scanned the print, she silently mouthed the words.

The Last Will and Testament
of
Raif Victor Carnell

'I knew it,' she whispered, as a single tear cleared a path along her cheek.

～

Late afternoon was beginning to cast a shadow of darkness over Rookery Grange. The timer for the Christmas lights suddenly blinked into life. Their merry twinkling, draped down the staircase and festooned along the panelling, belied the threatening atmosphere that had suddenly enveloped the rooms and corridors.

Bree pressed herself against the wood panelling, holding her arm out behind her to stay Ethel and Clarissa, not wanting them to advance until she was satisfied ahead was clear and safe. She peered around the corner. 'Okay, girls, this way.'

Ethel followed first with Clarissa behind her. Clarissa was mentally bemoaning the fact that she was now the fatty at the back, and as such would be in danger of being the first one to be picked off should whatever caused Pru to scream creep up on them. Bree felt as though her heart was in her throat. She wanted to shout out to Pru, but her ignorance of whatever was going on made caution her default position. She pointed to the back staircase and mouthed, 'Up there!' Clarissa nodded.

They turned the staircase, rising up to the first floor, oblivious to the fact they were being watched. The cheap hessian carpet of the stairs made way for the plush thickness of Axminster as they crept out onto the corridor.

'Can I help you, ladies?'

'Feck me!' Clarissa let out the most unladylike scream, which in turn made Ethel jump into a ninja stance, both hands flattened out in front of her, giving her the appearance of Kato Fong in the *Pink Panther* films. Bree turned too quickly and knocked a small vase from the console table. It wobbled and fell, bouncing across the carpet. 'Jenny, good grief! You scared the living daylights out of us! Thank goodness. Are you okay?'

Jenny looked on with some amusement. 'And why shouldn't I be?'

Ethel dropped her hands and shrugged the tension from her shoulders. 'We think something has happened to Pru. We heard her scream, and now we can't find her. It sounded like it came from upstairs, and with everything else going on around here we're naturally worried.'

'Ah well, what I can tell you is that in Rookery Grange, sound travels up as well as down. As there is nothing up here, maybe we should try downstairs? What do you think?' Jenny smiled.

Nurse Alex suddenly appeared from behind Jenny. 'Dearie me, ladies, look at us all bumping into each other; shouldn't you be downstairs with the others finishing off the decorations? Come on, down we go.'

'But something has happened to Pru; we need to find her,' Ethel pleaded.

Alex stiffly stood to attention. 'I'm sure we will. Come on, chop, chop.' She clapped her hands together and beckoned them to follow her down the main staircase.

Reluctantly, Bree followed, pushing Ethel and Clarissa ahead of her. Jenny hung back to pick up and reposition the vase. They cut a sorry sight as they descended down to the entrance hall. Bree was beside herself with worry for Pru, and Clarissa was concerned about Hilda and Millie being left in charge of a group of geriatrics, completely missing the point that none of the Four Wrinkled Dears were spring chickens themselves.

Ethel abruptly stopped on the bottom stair, forcing Clarissa to collide with her. 'I'm not happy about this,' she grumbled. 'We need to call…' she hesitated, tipping her head, a frown forcing her lids to crinkle over the bright blue of her eyes that suddenly became hawk-like. An unexpected flash of an envelope sent a chill down her spine. 'Where did you get that from?' She pointed accusingly and then just as quickly realised the implications and recovered herself.

'What?' Alex looked puzzled.

Ethel feigned innocence. 'That painting over there. It's nice, isn't it?'

Stumped, Alex shrugged her shoulders. 'I don't know; Jenny, do you?' But Jenny's response was as negative as Alex's had been.

'Not to mind. Silly me, just having a brain fart. I do that sometimes, I go off track.' Ethel grabbed Bree's arm to stop her from following Alex and Jenny. 'We'll catch up with you in a minute, just going to check on Millie and the others.' She dragged Bree to the side of the staircase and used the areca fern to camouflage them.

Bree looked at her and shook her head. 'We're supposed to be looking for Pru. The others are fine. Millie is quite capable of looking after a bunch of geriatrics. What on earth has got into you?' she snapped.

Ethel leant conspiratorially towards her and whispered, '*She's got the will, the one that Hilda found. I saw the envelope with the red seal poking out of the pocket of her cardigan. The last person to have that was Pru, and no way would she hand that to anyone other than Andy.*'

A slow methodical handclap followed Ethel's revelation. It echoed around the entrance hall and bounced back like a standing ovation for a great performance. Bree took a sharp intake of breath, whilst Clarissa and Ethel frantically searched behind them to see from whose hands the applause had originated.

'Well done, ladies, I salute you. Clever, interfering little buggers, aren't you?' the Dark Angel enthused. 'You should have just done as you were told and gone back to join the others. Now you've put me in a very awkward position.'

Bree could hardly breathe as her heart thudded in her chest. Still half hidden by the fronds from the large fern, she fumbled in her pocket for her mobile phone whilst utilising Clarissa's cuddly frame to mask her further. She quickly pressed number 4, her speed dial for Andy, and popped it back into her pocket.

'If you don't come with me now, then Pru will suffer the consequences.' The Dark Angel tipped her head and smiled. 'I do hope we have a mutual understanding, ladies.'

RIGHTING WRONGS

*H*e had always experienced a form of second sight when it came to her. Over thirty years apart, and it was as though they were still connected in some way. He rattled the ice in his glass and emptied it in one gulp. The phone call he had earlier felt compelled to make had endorsed his darkest fears. He poured himself another Scotch, but weakened this one down with a good measure of dry ginger. He needed to be on top of his game; he had work to do.

He had been a fool to have been so complicit in those early days, and now the day had come to right those wrongs. His guilt would always be how many more had suffered at her hands because of him. He wrapped the thick scarf around his neck and tucked the ends into his ski jacket before zipping up the front. A decent pair of gloves and snow boots completed his ensemble, along with a woollen hat. It would be safer to walk to Rookery Grange through the woods and use the back entrance rather than make a grand, if somewhat shocking, appearance through the main doors.

He paused in front of the family portrait that hung over the fireplace in the estate cottage, the warmth from the dying embers of the fire glowing across his legs. Had there ever been happier times? He truly couldn't remember. He had kept the portrait as a lesson, as an example. It showered him with neither love, security, nor loyalty, just a deep, dark sadness that he had carried within him every single day of his life.

But tonight it would end.

He just prayed he would be in time.

~

Lucy dropped down a gear to approach the bend. The snow plough and gritters had done a pretty good job on the main roads, but she wasn't taking any chances. 'So Murdoch has agreed to the post-mortem on Jenkins?'

Andy jiggled in his seat, trying to reach his pocket through his seat belt. 'Yep, and if that comes back as a suspicious death, then he's already instructed the team to look back at all deaths at Rookery Grange over the last five years.'

'Blimey, that'll be a lot, considering it's a residential home!' She pulled a face. 'They pop their clogs with monotonous regularity.'

Andy checked his watch. His meeting with Murdoch Holmes had overrun, then there had been the furore from Drainpipe Dobbins' family, who were convinced he'd been abducted by either aliens or Winterbottom CID. They had arrived en masse at the enquiry office, Drainpipe's mam wearing her best Primark pyjamas and fluffy mule slippers, with a half-eaten bag of Doritos poking out of the plastic bag that was slapping against her thigh with each stride she took. She had demanded to see the chief super to voice her concerns, and the ensuing chaos had all hands to the deck, including him. It had ended with at least two members of the Dobbins clan currently in custody for public order offences. Everything today had been designed to make him late. He'd promised Pru a nice romantic evening together with a bottle of wine to make up for their lack of a honeymoon, but the way things were going, he'd be getting a bollocking from her rather than a frolicking.

The theme tune from *Z Cars* buzzed from Andy's phone, making Lucy laugh. 'Jeez, haven't you changed that yet? You need to get down with the kids; nobody remembers *Z Cars* anymore.'

Indignant, Andy sniffed. 'My dad loved watching it.' He swiped the button. 'Hello… hello… hello…' He pulled the phone away from his ear and looked at the caller ID. 'It's Bree; penny to a pound she's butt-cheek dialled me again.' He chortled and popped it on speaker.

'No wait, just listen…' Lucy slowed down to concentrate, it was faint and slightly muffled but she could still hear the voices.

'I warned her … interfering, suffer … consequences … *crackle* … should have stuck to books … *crackle* … we need … *hiss* … help … Grange … *crackle* … now!'

'Bloody hell! What's she got herself involved in now? That woman will be the death of me, Luce. Put your foot down, I'll radio it in.'

Whilst Andy called on his troops to make to Rookery Grange, Lucy put her police driver training into practice. It had been a while since she'd driven a marked police vehicle to blue light jobs, but her skills were still there and this time the adrenalin was fuelled by personal fear for her friends.

WEIGHING UP THE ODDS

*B*ree was the first to take a tumble down the cellar steps, the darkness had thrown her and she missed at least two, the momentum plunging her forwards. She landed heavily with a thump on the stone floor, her knees and left elbow taking the brunt of the force. She heard Clarissa's slippers slapping on the steps, followed by Ethel's leather soled house shoe tapping out a Morse code as she tottered down to join her.

'I think I've broken my bloody arm,' she wailed.

'Bree, Bree over here, help me...'

She could hear Pru's voice, but her eyes hadn't adjusted enough to be able to see into the gloom. 'Pru, are you okay? I've got Clarissa and Ethel with me and...' she hesitated and looked up at the figure that loomed over her.

'Ladies, ladies, please allow me to introduce myself. I'm more than capable; in fact, I'm capable of a lot of things, but first you three come with me.' She led them to the generator cage and opened the door. 'Inside!' she barked.

The glances that Ethel, Bree and Clarissa shared spoke volumes.

'Don't even think about it. I know you're weighing up the

odds of three against one, but I promise you, they're not good odds, are they, Pru?'

It was only then that Bree became aware of the contraption that had been rigged up. She blinked rapidly, wondering if her poor eyesight was giving her false images. She followed the rope that was looped around the generator wheel. It ran under the chair that Pru was tied to, across the floor and finished in a clove hitch knot over the decorative wooden pole of the wine rack. Wedged between two bottles, a long-bladed stiletto knife pointed directly at Pru's neck.

'Ah, I can see those little cogs whirling, Bree. Are you impressed? One flick of this...' her finger hovered over an old toggle switch, '...and the generator will start up, tighten the rope and pull that rack out across the floor on its little wheels with much gusto and, bingo, we have an almost instantaneous death for your nosey friend. So, may I suggest you simply do as you are told?'

Reluctantly, the three of them slipped silently into the cage. The door rattled shut behind them and the lock clicked firmly into place.

'*Inky, pinky, ponky,*' she hummed as her index finger pointed to each of them in turn. She stopped at Eleanor and grinned.

'Right, I think you should be first, but before I send you on your way, I have a gift for you, as well as an explanation.' Her fingers plucked out the lapel pin from her pocket, and with her hands trembling with excitement and anticipation she pushed it through the silk collar of Eleanor's shirt. She popped the back plate into place and patted the collar down. 'There, now, doesn't that look nice?' She picked up the chef's knife, allowing Eleanor to gaze upon its blade.

She held it to Eleanor's neck, relishing the puckering of her skin as the sharp edge played its part. 'I've saved this one for you. You will bleed out ever so slowly, and whilst you do, I will tell you a little story which will explain all. At least you won't die wondering, dear.' The laugh she gave to Eleanor filled the cellar; it cackled and howled until she began to choke with the effort. She caught herself, wiping the spittle from her lips with the back of her hand. 'So, on that note, I'll begin...

'Once upon a time there was a naughty little girl who had a bear called Tattlington Ted. She lived in a great big house with her mummy and daddy and her horrible brother...'

GOODNIGHT, SLEEP TIGHT

*H*e slipped quietly out of the shadows and made his way along the building line. It had been such a long time since he had graced Rookery Grange with his presence. Not much had changed, but certain parts had become overgrown. Pushing his way through the snow had been hard enough, but tackling brambles and dense winter shrubbery was something he hadn't anticipated.

Finding the staff entrance, he tried the door handle. As expected, it was locked. Eleanor had not picked up his second flurry of calls, so he was heightened to danger, particularly in light of what she had revealed to him. He counted his strides along the wall until he came to a brick-built shelter that housed two large wooden doors, angled at forty-five degrees. It was the entrance to the old coal hole. He tested the wrought iron handles. Pulling them towards him; they gave slightly, opening up a small gap between their edges. Allowing one door to drop back and the other to open wide, he quickly and silently slipped down into the darkness.

Inching his way through familiar territory, his foot feeling the way for any unknown obstacles, his eyes adjusted to a faint glow of light ahead of him coming from the wine cellar. He cocked his head and listened.

'*... you will bleed out ever so slowly, and whilst you do, I will tell you a little story...*'

The chilling voice drifted from one basement room to another, the brick corridor between them acting as a conduit to reach him. He grabbed the ribbed edge of his hat and rolled it down over his face, ensuring the slits of the balaclava sat precisely over each eye before snapping the head torch into place.

He had never had the guts to be a hero before, but maybe tonight that would change.

The Dark Angel had finished her narration. She took a dramatic bow to her captive audience and giggled. 'I bet you didn't see that coming, did you?' She pulled out a wine bottle and examined the label. 'Not a bad year, even if I say so myself. 1989 was just the beginning...'

Pru shifted in the chair, trying to bring back some feeling to her legs. 'Please, you don't have to do this. We can't hurt you; just leave us here to be found; it'll give you plenty of time to get away, I know you really don't want to hurt anyone else.'

Knife in one hand and bottle in the other, the Dark Angel dramatically threw back her head. 'Oh gosh, why didn't I think of that? Just be a good girl, Alex. Put down the knife, Alex, toddle off, Alex... Yeah, of course I will.' She quickly snapped round to face Pru. 'You don't get it, do you? I enjoy it – in fact I *bloody love* it... I always have.'

A low moan came from Eleanor, distracting Alex. She whipped back to confront her. 'It started with Mummy and Daddy, didn't it, Ellie?' Her eyes blazed with anger. 'You still haven't recognised me; you still don't know who I am, do you?'

Eleanor's eyes held such terror they darted from side to side.

'Please, I don't know why you're doing this. What have I done to you? I don't know you.' Fat, hot tears poured down her face.

Alex dropped her head down so her mouth was by Eleanor's ear. 'Oh but you do,' she hissed, bringing the knife back to her neck.

'Stop it, stop it, Alex. Enough is enough. Please, I'm begging you; don't hurt anyone else.' The desperation in Pru's voice was palpable. She glanced over to the cage. Bree, Ethel and Clarissa, their fingers hooked through the metal honeycomb, rattled the doors in frustration and fear.

Eleanor gasped as Alex, her hair in disarray, falling in wisps from her usual formal ponytail, pushed back her fringe. 'I see my little story was not enough. Do you remember me now, cousin?' The crescent-shaped scar, clearly visible, was a chilling invitation to the past. An invitation that offered no joy, only a nightmare filled with fear.

'No, no – it can't be!' cried Eleanor.

'At last the penny drops! What does it feel like to be helpless, Ellie, to have everything taken away from you?' The blade pierced Eleanor's neck, forcing a peppered line of blood to suddenly appear. 'It's payback time, and this is just for starters,' she crowed.

Click, thunk...

The sudden noise echoed around the cellar as the lights went out. A brief silence followed – before giving way to chaos. A scream pierced the air, accompanied by several expletives from Ethel and Clarissa. The darkness had brought a blanket of added fear and confusion.

A small white light darted across the room like a dancing star, its reach lighting in staccato bursts the faces of Alex and Eleanor.

Pru held her breath, mesmerised as the light flickered and spun mid-air. Straining her eyes, she could just make out the shadowy silhouette of a man hurtling across the room. Before Alex could react, he was on her, bringing her to the ground. The sound of the bottle smashing on the floor was followed by a loud, guttural scream. The white light hit the floor, then, just as quickly, arched up to illuminate the wall behind Pru. With every turn of his head, the light continued to dance and bob as he fought with Alex.

'Oh my God, what's happening?' screamed Bree. 'Is it Andy?'

A low choking and gurgling sound filled the room, to accompany the pandemonium that was already being absorbed into the walls of Rookery Grange.

He hadn't anticipated his task to be so simple. His unhindered and unnoticed entrance into the wine cellar had been to his advantage. He had momentarily watched her from his dark place, his heart pounding with fear, whilst also breaking with the knowledge of what he was about to do.

He waited.

He listened.

He saw the blade draw its first cut and he knew he couldn't wait any longer. He flicked the cellar lights off and slid the switch on his head torch to on, whilst simultaneously pushing the adrenalin into the muscles that needed it most.

He used every ounce of his bodyweight to bring her down, slamming into her with such force, the chance for her to do more harm to Eleanor was taken away from her. She hit the floor, the knife skittered across the tiles and the bottle smashed on impact. He could feel a wetness underneath him as he struggled with her. She fought and bucked him, letting out a low gurgle as his arm tightened around her neck. With his forearm on her carotid artery, he brought his other arm up to support the pressure. Her feet kicked and scraped the floor, desperately trying to find a hold to push back against him, her fingers clawing at his arms, but he held firm.

Finally she stopped struggling, and with one final violent spasm, her body went limp. 'Sleep well,' he whispered, as he relinquished his hold. Drawing her to him in a loving embrace, he tenderly stroked her face as he sang to her.

'Hush little baby, don't you cry…'

His time with her done, he laid her gently down and disappeared the way he had come, back into the darkness.

THE AFTERMATH

*R*ookery Grange Retreat was a veritable hive of activity. Bright lights on stands lit up the nooks and crannies of the wine cellar which had been divided into areas for forensic preservation. Officers in white suits paraded backwards and forwards carrying evidence bags to be collated in the main office, and in the vast grounds police dogs sniffed and barked their approval as blue lights from a mass of vehicles strobed the night and bounced from the whiteness of the snow.

The Four Wrinkled Dears sat in silence on the large sofa in the day room. Each was wrapped in a blanket and cosseting a hot cup of sweet tea provided by Jenny, listening to the clattering and banging that echoed through the corridors beyond the door. Ethel was the first to speak. 'Well, that didn't quite go according to plan, did it? I think our Operation Bloomers got a bit frayed around the edges and lost its elastic somewhere!' She shook her head in resignation. 'Can you imagine breathing your last lit up like bloody Electra from Gypsy Rose Lee, but without the bikini? What a way to go. Did you know Lil was still on combination mode flashing blue, red and green from her nellies when the police got here?'

Hilda took a bite from her biscuit. 'I find a good dose of prunes is pretty good for constipation.'

'Good grief, Ethel, have some respect!' Millie huffed. 'And it's *combination*, Hilda, you really do need to get another hearing aid, or I'm going to end up with an "ology" in translation tactics!'

Ethel curled her top lip. 'I'm just saying, that's all. I didn't like the woman when she was alive, and I'm not going to give her a glowing eulogy now she's dead. You know what they say, life's a bitch and then you die, and to give Lil credit where it's due, she's managed both!' She laughed and gave Clarissa a conspiratorial wink.

Clarissa let out a resigned sigh. 'All right, Ethel, calm down. Andy said once they've finished down there with that Alex or whatever her name is, they're bringing in a team to unbrick poor Beryl. I can't help feeling guilty. We all gossiped about her legging it with the family silver when all along she was innocent.'

'Aye, and just a tad dead too,' Ethel offered by way of an explanation for Beryl's ensuing absence from the village of Chapperton Bliss.

They all fell silent again, their dark humour lost in a sudden, overwhelming sadness that had swept over them. It had been an adventure, and at times it had been exciting, but the ending to their story had not been one they had envisaged.

'I wonder how Pru and Bree are?' Millie's concern had her visually checking the door every few minutes, waiting for someone to return to offer them an update.

Ethel shrugged. 'Bree has definitely broken her arm and, fingers crossed, Pru will be okay with a couple of stitches. Not sure about Eleanor. Andy seemed to think the cut on her neck was superficial, but I think it'll be the psychological effects that will be more troublesome. Anyway, they've taken her away to be interviewed.'

The room became quiet again, broken only by the chorus of cups rattling in their saucers and dentures crunching on ginger biscuits. The backdrop of twinkling Christmas lights on the small tree in the corner, and the snow-laden cedars outside the mullioned windows lit up by blue flashes, belied the heaviness that had cloaked Rookery Grange Retreat.

The door suddenly creaked open, causing the Four Wrinkled Dears to collectively hold their breath in anticipation of more news. Millie clutched her chest and patted it rapidly, as though that action would afford her some calmness.

'Oh, there you are, ladies.' Captain Oscar Burton stood regimentally proud in his striped pyjamas and navy silk dressing gown, framed by the doorway. 'I was just wondering, seeing as Eleanor hasn't started me yet on that fluoride stuff to dampen my enthusiasm, would any of you lovely young ladies fancy sharing my memory foam mattress tonight?' He gave an exaggerated wink.

Millie was so horrified by his suggestion that the gentle patting of her chest became an absolute frenzy. Ethel quickly stepped in. 'Sir, I really think that at our age the only thing that would be capable of remembering what it's all about *would* be the bloody memory foam mattress!'

Oscar threw a salute, causing his dressing gown to part in the middle.

'Dear God!' Clarissa shrieked. 'For goodness' sake, man, you're flying low!' She frantically pointed to his pyjama bottoms.

Nonplussed, Oscar adjusted his dressing gown. 'Madam, I'm a Navy man; the RAF wasn't for me, I've never flown high or low in my life… although I have bobbed up and down on a few waves in my youth!'

Their laughter filled the room, giving new hope that the Rookery Grange Retreat could once more, given time, be filled with much happiness and joviality.

～

Pru, wrapped in her dressing gown, sat at the window looking out onto the garden of what was now their marital home. Even though it had been Andy's home too since their engagement, he would often still refer to it as 'Pru's place'. She smiled as she pulled her dressing gown tighter to ward of the sudden chill. Now it would always be home to them both. The snow had begun to fall again, filling in the footprints that she and Andy had left on the path less than an hour ago. Her fingers tentatively touched her head, making her wince. Fortunately she had only needed four stitches and a tetanus jab; she had been very lucky. The bruising around her eye would no doubt make itself known just in time for Christmas morning, but other than a banging headache and some nausea, she was okay.

Andy brought her a mug of coffee and two paracetamol. 'I won't ask "When will you ever learn?" because somehow I just don't think you ever will.' He put his arms around her and pulled her close to him, inhaling her scent of baby powder and soap. 'I love you, Mrs Prunella Barnes, even though I'm still cross with you, and will probably remain so well into the New Year.' He gently kissed her forehead.

She gave him a weak smile. 'Honestly, Andy, it wasn't me this time. I was just there in my "Valerie from *Blue Peter*" capacity to make Christmas stuff with them.' She made air quotes with her fingers. 'Like crappy paper chains and angels from bog rolls; it was Clarissa and Ethel that started it all, and it just went tits up from there.' She took a sip of coffee and relished the bitter tang of caffeine as it slid down her throat. 'So what're the scores on the doors?'

Andy pulled back from her as though seeing something in her for the first time. '"Scores on the doors"? You mean how many bodies so far? Blimey, Pru, where's your compassionate side disappeared to?'

Pru shrugged her shoulders and wistfully gazed out of the window again. 'I must be getting hardened to death. I mean how can a quaint collection of villages like these attract so many bloody serial killers.' It was more a statement than a question.

Andy hesitated, unsure if he should be totally honest with her, but he knew she would find out eventually. 'Six in total. Dorothy Burnside, Thomas Whittle and Lillian Williams are confirmed suspicious deaths and are now being investigated as murder.'

'Ha, I can vouch for Lillian being suspicious. Somehow I don't think she was joining in our activities by presenting herself as a budget Christmas decoration with a three-amp fuse!' She closed her eyes, remembering the scene that had greeted her. 'I know about them, and that Walter is having a post-mortem, but even with Beryl, that only makes five.'

'Well we got a bit of a Brucie bonus when the grounds were searched. Tim had a bit of an accident and trod in a pile of Rover's leftovers from one of the police dogs. He found what he thought was a mound of snow-covered grass to wipe his boot on, only it wasn't – it was another body.'

Pru's eyes widened. 'Was it the intruder from the cellar?'

'Nope. It was one of our regular miscreants, Duncan "Drainpipe" Dobbins, a well-known burglar of this parish. Looks like he took a tumble from one of the windows. It was ironic, really, as he was impaled on the tool of his trade: an old piece of drainpipe.' Andy knew it would be no loss to the people of Winterbottom and Chapperton Bliss, but he did feel a twinge of sadness for Duncan's family. 'Anyway, there's nothing more you need to worry about; everything is in hand and I'm confident we'll wrap this up neatly.'

'But what about Alex and the intruder?' Her throat tightened as she fought back tears. She refused to cry again; what was done was done. 'He saved us and then just disappeared.'

'We're searching for him. We're still not sure if it was intentional or sheer luck that Alex survived. I'll know more once we get a confirmed ID on her, but there's quite some background for us to go over. We know some of her kills have been purely for her psychopathic pleasure, but there is also a more personal motive linked to that will Hilda found. We're doing a softly softly approach with Eleanor, in the hope she can shed more light on it.' Now was the time for him to change the subject. 'Come on, time for you to get some rest and if you don't get to sleep soon, Father Christmas will not be coming down our chimney.' He grinned as he led her towards their bed.

'Can you leave the curtains open?' Her voice was soft and small, almost childlike.

Snuggling down together, she watched the Christmas lights of Winterbottom, reflected by the whiteness of the snow, bounce a spectrum of blues, greens and reds through the bedroom window and onto the wall. A single star shone brightly from the inky blackness of the sky. She imagined a couple of shepherds trudging through the snowdrifts in their best sandals trying to reach their destination. Come to think of it, did they actually have snow in Bethlehem? She'd have to check that out, but in the meantime a pilgrimage to a ramshackle stable wouldn't encourage her to brave this weather, although a trudge in her flip-flops to the Dog & Gun or The Guilty Grape might, particularly if there was a decent bottle of wine on offer. The bedside clock flashed red, the numbers changing.

00:01.

'Andy…'

'Yep, my little mischief maker…'

'Happy Christmas.'

'If that's a hint to get your presents early, think again!' He laughed.

'I love you.'

'Then it's just as well I love you too.'

ONE POTATO...

ȝ

*B*eep.
'This interview is being conducted in an interview room at Winterbridge police station. The time by my watch is 11:16 hours. I am Detective Constable Lucy Harris of Winterbridge CID. Please state your full name.'

'Oh, erm... I'm Eleanor Victoria Parsons.'

'Eleanor, as you know we attended Rookery Grange Retreat, which is your home and business premises. Would you like to tell me, in your own words, what led to us being there?'

Eleanor sat like a startled rabbit in the small room. She watched the recording light pulsate as it waited for her response. She counted the sound proofing tiles on the wall and listened to the intermittent tap of Lucy's pen on the notepad in front of her. She balled her fists until her nails dug painfully into the palms of her hands.

Taking a deep breath, she closed her eyes.

In 1989, Rookery Grange was owned by my uncle, Raif Carnell, and his wife Penelope. They had two children, Vincent and Violet. On Christmas Eve that year, Raif and Penelope were found dead. They had been poisoned. As a family, we believed Vincent had been responsible as he was quite an odd little boy, but it was ruled a murder–suicide by police and the coroner's office, in that Raif murdered Stephanie and then took his own life. My father, Sebastian Carnell, was the executor of their will. Under the instructions of the will, he inherited Rookery Grange and the money, with a small trust for Vincent and Violet. They had a live-in nanny who was given her marching orders and the children were sent with immediate effect to boarding school.

My father ensconced himself into Rookery Grange as though he was to the manor born, bringing me with him.

Eleanor felt perplexed. Had she spoken out loud or had that narration just been a head thought? She couldn't remember opening her mouth for words to come out. She looked at Lucy who was still expectant in her demeanour towards her. Maybe she should continue.

Raif and Penelope had a housekeeper called Beryl Byrd. Beryl knew that Raif's will had left everything to the children, and that the only part my father had was as executor. Somehow he had forged a new will and Beryl knew that. I saw my father murder her and hide her body in the cellar, I wasn't supposed to be in the bedroom I was in; I had switched rooms. I was just sixteen years old...

'Eleanor, are you okay?' Concerned, Lucy tried to prompt Eleanor to speak; she had just sat in silence staring at the wall since the interview began.

'Hush little baby, don't say a word, Daddy's getting rid of old Beryl Byrd,' Eleanor sang in a hushed, childlike voice. She abruptly stopped and tilted her head. 'Did I tell you that Dorothy Burnside was the children's nanny? She had an assumed name, calling herself Nancy Lawrence so her drugs conviction wouldn't ruin her chances of getting the job.'

Lucy was relieved to hear her speak and took the opportunity to encourage her further. 'No you didn't, but that's very interesting. Is that why you offered her a place at Rookery Grange?'

'Yes, she looked after me too when we were little. You have to look after the elderly, you know. It was the least I could do; my father treated her appallingly.'

'Why do you think she was murdered, Eleanor?'

'Because she wouldn't hand over the letter.'

'What letter?'

'Dorothy knew everything. She had a letter from Vincent. She knew there was another will, the one that Hilda found in the cellar, and she knew who had really murdered Raif and Penelope.' Her breath caught in her throat as a loud sob made the red sound level on the machine peak and drop. 'It was Violet. Vile Violet did it!' Eleanor slumped back into her chair as tears brimmed and trickled down her cheeks.

Lucy broke from her note-taking. 'Violet did *what*, Eleanor? I need to hear it in your own words.'

'She murdered Raif and Penelope, and then they covered it up. Father said if I ever told about Violet or Beryl I would be arrested, and I would go to prison because I knew. So I didn't tell anyone. She was evil; even as a child; Dorothy called her a dark little angel.'

The pieces had fallen into place for Eleanor in the seconds it had taken for Alex to press the knife across her neck in the basement at Rookery Grange. The scar had been the giveaway.

'One potato, two potato, three potato, four...' she quietly whispered as she melted further and further into herself.

EPILOGUE

WINTERBRIDGE COMMUNITY HOSPITAL

One year later...

*T*he occupant of Room 127B rarely had visitors these days. The name plate on the door had been replaced with a new one. It no longer announced that Alexandra Archer was in residence.

He stood outside, taking in the moment. A sense of sadness, mixed with a strange kind of justice, filled his heart as his fingers touched the new name it now bore. That one action elicited a memory he had tried so many times to forget, its tendrils of terror plucked at him now as chillingly as it had on that fateful night.

The clock in the hall had struck 8pm.

Ding-dong, ding-dong...

He had stood in the centre of the entrance hall, one small foot on a white square, the other on a black one, counting them until the clock had fallen silent. The chequered tiles stretched out ahead of him, leading to the door of the drawing room. He felt like Alice from the book that Nanny had read to them and, just like Alice, he was getting smaller and smaller.

He wondered if he would disappear altogether if he remained where he was, and would it be preferable to what he would find behind that door? He knew it wouldn't be Alice's Wonderland; it was more likely to be Seymour's Little Shop of Horrors.

His legs suddenly found the strength to move.

One step.

Two steps.

Three steps...

And before he could stop himself, he was there, standing in front of the huge oak door. His hand clutched the ornate brass handle; it turned as if by magic, opening out to reveal a world he knew he did not want to be part of.

The Christmas tree, lights twinkling, stood festive against the mullioned windows, the fire had spluttered its last flame, giving way to orange embers that gave a faint glow to the room, its reach not quite making the darkest corners. His parents, their soulless eyes focused on the nothingness, sat slumped in their chairs. Dead.

And then she was there, standing behind him, clutching Tattlington Ted.

'This is all your fault, Vincent,' she had growled. 'I'm going to cry lots and tell them it was you...'

He pulled his hand away quickly from the new name plate on the door, as though his fingers had been burnt. She had tried and failed to put the blame on him, and in the process had sullied the Carnell name forever. He wiped away a tear with the heel of his hand. He had been forced to lay his eyes on Violet's handiwork that night, and had lived every single day since with guilt, fear and loathing...

...Now it was time for him to see his own handiwork.

He pushed open the door to 127B and slipped inside.

He was here.

She stared at the ceiling, just as she did every single day.

Hello, Vincent, long time no see.

He loomed over her and gently kissed her cheek.

Fancy seeing you here! I suppose you've come to wish me Happy Christmas and to gloat.

He moved the chair to her bedside, sat down and tenderly held her hand. She could still see him from her peripheral vision. He began to cry.

'I'm so sorry, sis. I had to stop you.' He wept.

I know, but this... to do this to me – how could you?

'You would never have stopped; you enjoyed the killing. So many innocent victims, so many broken families. I had no choice; I had to come back and stop you.' He held her hand against his own cheek, feeling the warmth from her skin. 'As soon as Eleanor told me she had an "Archer" on her staff, I knew it was you; such a clever use of the meaning behind our family name. Carnell – The Bowman, the defender, but you didn't defend anyone, did you?'

Ha, on the ball as ever, Vincent. Come on, to kill for pleasure, to kill for release, to kill as a mercy, what's the difference? Some begged me for it; did you know that?

He reached into his pocket, bringing out his handkerchief. He reverently laid it on the bed and unfurled it, plucking out what it held. He placed it on the pillow next to her. 'You gifted Mum and Dad a sprig of holly, remember?' He sneered at his own stupidity. 'Of course you remember, they were your first kill.' He admired the dark glossy green spikes and the red berries, stark against the whiteness of the cotton pillowcase.

Oh gosh yes, of course I remember, but I moved on, we all did. I grew up, Vincent, I became the Dark Angel to help more pitiful souls cross

331

over, I gave them lapel pins to mark the occasion, black angel wings. They were lovely. I think my clients really appreciated them too.

'Poor Eleanor, she never recovered from it, she had a complete breakdown. All those years living with Sebastian's secret and then your little performance just sent her over the edge.' He rearranged the bedsheet, tucking it in around her whilst smoothing out the creases. 'Another one of your victims.'

Pah, she deserved it, she was always a snivelling little creep. She got what should have been ours, Vincent. Doesn't that make you angry? I would have got Rookery back – I had a plan.

'But there is good news.' He stood up to ensure he was within her full vision. 'Let me introduce you to the new owner of Rookery Grange Retreat.' He took a bow. 'Vincent Carnell at your service, madam, with a ready-made business, several lovely OAPs to care for, and an adopted cat called Frizzle, lying in front of my fireplace. I managed to get that dreadful mess with Father's will sorted. Sadly, you're in no fit state to enjoy your share, so I've made reparation to the families of all your victims.' He carefully placed the enamel black angel wings pin onto her gown, pushed it through the material and popped the back into place. 'Oh, and a rather nice leather-bound book from your safe, which I handed to the police. It was marvellously helpful of you, they were delighted with your meticulous notes, but all those poor souls...' His eyes misted in sadness as his fingers tenderly stroked her hair. 'You deserve what you have now become, you have to understand that. Nobody should ever go without punishment.'

No, no, no – this is wrong. You can't do this. I'm the one in charge; things are always done my way. I'll kill you before you get your hands on Rookery.

He kissed her again on the cheek to bid his farewell to her. 'I know you're lying there probably wanting to kill me, but that won't be today, or any other day for that matter.' He smiled as he gazed at the tubes, wires and beeping monitors that sustained her, quietly proud of what he had achieved in that one small moment in the cellar of Rookery Grange. Unlike her, he was incapable of murder; that was true, but he had been quite adept at executing a manoeuvre called 'The Everlasting Sleep'. 'Well I must go. Until next Christmas, sis.' He gently placed the battered old teddy bear next to her. It settled against her arm, with its one good eye that he had painstakingly stitched back into place, staring at the ceiling to mirror her eyes.

'*Grrr...*' Tattlington Ted loudly objected before slumping to one side.

He left the room as discreetly as he had entered it, pausing only to tap the name plate on the door once again.

VIOLET CARNELL
ROOM 127B

'Goodbye, Violet,' he softly whispered.

You come back here right now, Vincent Carnell! Don't you dare leave me! I'm talking to you; why can't you hear me? Vincent, I'm talking to you. Vincent, come back here, now...

But thoughts cannot be heard, can they? Thoughts are privy only to the person who creates them. Violet's whole life was now a theatre of a thousand seats in her mind, and she was the only one in the audience. The plush red chairs, stretching ahead, behind and to the left and right of her, remained empty. The stage was her eyes, but its pulleys, ropes and sound system were irreversibly broken, and the spotlight had been turned off.

She was locked into a strange new world. A world from where she could only look out and one where others would never reach. She now had the life she had always feared; one that would be sustained and maintained, but never truly lived.

It was no longer just a dream.

It was her worst nightmare.

Beep...

Beep...

Beep...

THE END

'There had stood a great house in the centre of the gardens,
where now was left only that fragment of ruin.'

William Hope Hodgson, *The House on the Borderland* (1908)

ALSO BY GINA KIRKHAM

ACKNOWLEDGEMENTS

I usually start with *'I never quite know where to start with acknowledgements,'* and then rattle on for an eternity – and to be honest, after five previous attempts on my other books, there's sadly still no sign of improvement!

I am always so very grateful for the smallest of things as much as the biggest of things in my life.

To the wonderful ladies of The Women's Institute. Without you there would be no Kitty, Ethel or Clarissa, and no tales to tell. Your kindness, generosity and fabulous sense of humour became the inspiration for my characters. I loved your excitement and enthusiasm to be included, and hopefully I have created them just as you asked, like you, full of mischief and so much larger than life.

Thank you for inviting me to speak at your meetings and thank you for all you selflessly do for others.

To Loulou Brown. It has been a pleasure to work with you again and to get another chapter of *Murders* into shape. You made the whole process so simple, straightforward and stress free and, best of all, you 'get' me, my humour and my style of writing. Here's to being together again in the future.

This is a special thank you to Tara Lyons from Bloodhound. Tara you are an absolute dream to work with, not only did I gain a fabulous Editorial & Production Manager when I signed with Bloodhound, I also gained a beautiful friend. Thank you just doesn't seem enough.

To Abbie Rutherford, who had the unenviable task of proofreading *Rookery.* Thank you so much, and whilst I'm here, any bloopers you found were definitely down to predictive text and not me – honest! Massive thanks also go to Betsy and Fred for once again taking a chance on this quirky old trout!

I was honoured to be asked to participate in the **Children in Read** charity book auction again last year. Paddy and his team from CiR do an amazing job and work so hard, they have raised a staggering £91,222.00 from their auctions. The winning bid for a dedicated, signed copy of *Murders at the Winterbottom Women's Institute* and to have a character named in book three of the series, *Murders at The Rookery Grange Retreat,* was Tyler Shepherd. Tyler asked that his sister Lyndsey be included, rather than himself. Lyndsey sadly passed away in 2021 from sarcoma. Tyler tells me she was a writer, loved travelling, cupcakes, the Golden Girls and had a passion for rescuing animals. More about Lyndsey can be found here:

https://pinkcrush.net/lyndsey

Thank you for allowing me to create a character in her name Tyler, it was a privilege.

On 22nd October 2022, the world became a little darker with the loss of my dear friend Drew, a beautiful soul who this book is dedicated to. I am heartbroken that you could not stay longer on this earth, you will always be so greatly missed, but know that you had such an impact on this life, and on so many people. Your legacy lives on with *Owen Drew England* and your wonderful friend and soulmate, Mike. My love always.

A huge thank you to Linda at the stunningly beautiful *Beck Hall* in Malham. Hubby and I, along with our doggie, enjoyed two fabulous nights here relishing the peace, tranquility and your delicious food, so that I could finish the edits for *Rookery Grange.* Room 9 overlooking the river from one window and the sunrise from the other was just perfect for creativity and a clear mind. Linda's hospitality and sense of fun was second to none and their pink gin is to die for... ooh, now that's an idea for my next book –

death by copious amounts of gin, I can easily research that one myself!

To Vanda, thank you for reading through my ideas and drafts of *Rookery* giving me valuable feedback and support. You've been a superstar.

I very quickly discovered how amazing readers and book bloggers are. There are too many to mention individually, and I would hate to miss someone out, so this is a collective thank you. A bit like a group hug. As writers, where would we be without them? Our words wouldn't be heard, our stories wouldn't be told. They would lie dormant on paper or screen, meaningless. They only come to life because people read them, enjoy them and spread their love of our books.

To the lovely Emma Franklin, who filled me with warmth when she messaged me on Facebook to describe her love of books by saying, *'I can never leave my seat but travel a million miles, and live a thousand lives...'*

She has a gorgeous little girl named Aurelia, who is fondly known as Goldie. I was over the moon when Emma happily allowed me to use her name – so say 'hello' to Miss Goldie Franklin, fading star of stage and screen and feisty resident of *Rookery Grange!*

Once again (I have to mention him as I truly am the doting elder sister), to my very handsome, debonair brother, Andy Dawson – for no other reason than him being handsome, debonair and of course, my brother, and to his gorgeously funny wife, my new sister-in-law, Anne-Marie (aka Mrs Dawson). What a fabulous addition she is to our madcap family.

To my sister Claire, so far away but you will always be in my heart.

To my beautiful daughter, Emma and my gorgeous grandchildren, Olivia, Annie and Arthur. You are my sunshine, you make me smile every day, I'm so very blessed to have you in my life.

And last but definitely not least, to my handsome and very funny hubby, John. The love of my life, my bodyguard, chauffeur and human SatNav. The man who makes me laugh every single day (and frequently think of murder too). He has endured hours of torment as my muse and 'go to' for ideas for this book and my previous ones. He rolls his eyes and groans but still continues to reluctantly participate in the most bizarre acts all in the name of research – well, at least that's what I tell him it's for! Without his love and support there would be no stories to tell – and I'd still be driving around various parts of the UK, panic struck and lost.

I hope I haven't missed anyone out, but knowing me and my scatterbrained head-thoughts, I probably have. I'm so sorry if you haven't appeared here because of my forgetfulness, but please know there's a humongous 'thank you' in my heart for you. You will always be so very much appreciated.

Gina x

A NOTE FROM THE PUBLISHER

Thank you for reading this book. If you enjoyed it please do consider leaving a review on Amazon to help others find it too.

We hate typos. All of our books have been rigorously edited and proofread, but sometimes mistakes do slip through. If you have spotted a typo, please do let us know and we can get it amended within hours.

info@bloodhoundbooks.com

Printed in Great Britain
by Amazon